ERIC SAT BOLT UPRIGHT IN BED....

The sound of laughter still rang out of his dream, and he could still see that face as he had in so many other nightmares.

"Shandal Karg!" The name exploded from him like a curse. *The Heart of Darkness*. She ruled the Dark Lands, and in his first hour on Palenoc, he had earned her enmity. Now she wanted to punish him for that deed.

A cold dread seized him. He had never had a premonition before, but Shandal Karg had just appeared to him in Katy's form. She knew about Katy! He leaped from bed and ran from his room, racing through the corridors to find Katy's room.

"Katy!" he cried, throwing his weight against the wooden door. It didn't budge. With an iron fury, he backed up and kicked the door. The door smashed inward.

Katy lay upon her narrow bed, heaving and gasping, unable to awaken. Over her hovered a black amorphous shape with eyes that shone with a cold malevolence. A semblance of a hand reached down to cover Katy's mouth and nose. It began to suffocate her!

FLAMES
OF THE
DRAGON

by

Robin Wayne Bailey

A ROC BOOK

ROC
Published by the Penguin Group
Penguin Books USA Inc., 375 Hudson Street,
New York, New York 10014, U.S.A.
Penguin Books Ltd, 27 Wrights Lane,
London W8 5TZ, England
Penguin Books Australia Ltd, Ringwood,
Victoria, Australia
Penguin Books Canada Ltd, 10 Alcorn Avenue,
Toronto, Ontario, Canada M4V 3B2
Penguin Books (N.Z.) Ltd, 182–190 Wairau Road,
Auckland 10, New Zealand

Penguin Books Ltd, Registered Offices:
Harmondsworth, Middlesex, England

First published by Roc,
an imprint of Dutton Signet,
a division of Penguin Books USA Inc.

First Printing, April, 1994
10 9 8 7 6 5 4 3 2 1

Copyright © Byron Preiss Visual Publications Inc., 1994
Illustrations by Louis Harrison
Cover art by Cirulo

All rights reserved

Printed in the United States of America

For Mike VanZandt and Vince Eshnaur,
who put their money where their hearts are;
For Kate Graf, who used to be "wilde";
And for Diana,
the lady who plays with stingrays.

Chapter One

THE smell of burned timber wafted in the air. Plumes and wisps of gray smoke curled up from the fire-ravaged ruins of homes and shops. Smouldering posts and planks jutted at awkward angles, some yet flickering with tongues of blue flame.

A dog wandered up and down the only street sniffing the ground and whining forlornly, its eyes round and empty and full of tears, its tail between its legs. In a blackened front yard, a pair of fat chickens pecked at the scorched grass. A red-crowned rooster perched imperiously on the shoulder of a dead girl-child.

Bodies lay everywhere.

"What could have done this?" Alanna spoke softly, her eyes full of horror and anger. Her fingers curled tightly around her blowpipe, the knuckles straining at the fabric of her leather gloves. "The fire alone couldn't be responsible."

Shaking his head, Eric stopped as they reached the center of the town. Alanna continued to the end of the road until she stood by the charred ruins of a pier that had once reached out into the wide river. The afternoon sun glinted on her smooth leather garments as she gazed down into the water. The wind stirred her black hair.

Evander and Doe stopped beside Eric. Tall and

slender, the two men could have passed for brothers. They leaned on the staves they carried, adopting the same grim expressions and nearly identical postures as they looked about. Neither seemed inclined to speak. Doe had been the first to spot the cloud of smoke from the air and suggest they delay their mission to Wystoweem and investigate, but none of them had expected to find such destruction.

A young girl lay beside the road in the shadow of a crude picket fence that the flames had not touched. Eric bent down beside her, rolled her gently onto her back, and pushed the strands of black hair away from her face. Wide brown eyes stared blankly up at him. He eased them closed with his left thumb and forefinger. *Maybe twelve years old*, he thought. *Quite pretty, too.*

A shadow fell over him, and he glanced up as Evander bent nearer.

"Not a mark on her," Eric said in a muted voice.

"Maybe she inhaled too much smoke before she managed to get outside," Evander suggested.

Eric frowned. "No," he answered, tight-lipped. "Look how she's lying here." He pointed from the fence's gate to a pair of smoking doorposts and the collapsed structure of which they were a part. "Her head is toward the house, not away from it. And from the look on her face, she was scared. Terrified. I think she was trying to run inside."

"From something she saw in the street?" Evander suggested.

Doe walked over to join them. "The fire must have started later," he said. In his right hand, he held a child's doll. He set it down in the crook of the dead girl's arm. "If there was a panic, somebody could have bumped a lantern or dropped a candle. That's all it would take to destroy a village like this one."

Eric moved through the gate into the yard. The rooster squawked and ran behind the ruins, wings aflutter. The hens scuttled the other way. The sudden movement startled him. He paused and glanced around again. The dog had crept a few paces nearer. It emitted a low whimper, crept a few inches forward, and stopped again, afraid to come closer.

In the yard, he found another body. From the look of her, she might have been an older sister, or perhaps a young mother, to the girl in the street. Her plain, homespun dress was ripped where she had tripped on the hem as she ran. One outstretched fist clenched a handful of grass that she had torn from the earth in her last painful moment of life.

Like the girl in the street, there was no visible mark on her. Eric bent down and began to loosen her clothes.

"What are you doing?" Alanna called over the fence as she hurried back up the road and pressed between Evander and Doe to get through the gate.

Eric tore open the neck of the woman's frock. "Looking for wounds," he answered matter-of-factly. "Maybe darts."

Alanna put on a disdainful look as she leaned over him. "Are you suggesting these people were murdered?" She shook her head, glancing to Evander and Doe for support. It was plain enough the idea appalled her. "Not a whole village! Who would dare?"

Out-and-out murder was rare on Palenoc, and for reasons Eric knew well. In this world so different from his own Earth, ghosts were real, and the victim's spirit almost always sought revenge on the murderer. That didn't mean Palenoc was free from killing, though. Subtle men found subtle means. Nevertheless, something or someone had ended these villagers' lives.

"The fire didn't kill this little one," Doe said stonily from the street as he regarded the dead child.

"Nor this one here," Eric said as he continued his examination of the woman's body.

"If it was only a fire, there would be survivors," Evander added as he leaned on his staff and let go a soft sigh. His watchful gaze swept the village and the edge of the thick forest that surrounded it.

Alanna bit her lip as she knelt down by Eric. "Let me do it," she insisted. With gentler hands, she began to remove the dead woman's clothes, shifting position as she worked so that she blocked the men's view.

Eric rose and walked back into the street. He rubbed one hand over the crown of his head as he glanced around, perplexed. He hated puzzles, particularly in Palenoc where the answers so often were deadly.

Finally, he headed for the river—the Kultari, he remembered from the maps he had studied before beginning this journey. In his own world, it would have been the Missouri. The village's pier had burned to the waterline. Some of the boats had escaped the flames, yet the villagers hadn't used them. Whatever struck them down had done so swiftly.

The dog gave another low whine and brushed against his leg. It had followed him. It looked up with moist, begging eyes, and Eric reached down to pat its head. A tail lifted a bit, and after that the poor animal stayed right by his side.

Evander came up behind him. "Alanna didn't find any marks."

Eric hadn't thought she would. One man with a blowpipe couldn't have taken out the entire village. He scratched his head as he tried to puzzle out an answer. Bands of marauders were known to roam the Gray Kingdoms, but such a force would have left some evidence. A Dark Land army, maybe? Again, some evidence would remain.

"That's Markmor, isn't it?" Eric said as he pointed to the land across the river. Markmor was one of the largest nations in the Dark Lands, an alliance of kingdoms under the sway of the mysterious Shandal Karg.

Evander nodded. "The Kultari forms the border between Markmor and Sybo."

Eric pursed his lips. Sybo was one of the Gray Kingdoms, a group of ostensibly independent buffer states positioned uncomfortably between the warring Dark Lands and the Domains of Light. Their allegiances were ever-shifting as they sought to steer clear of the conflict.

Evander laid a gloved hand lightly on Eric's arm. "I know that look, my friend," he said in a near whisper. He, too, turned his gaze across the water toward Markmor. "Do you still dream of her?"

The moisture suddenly left Eric's throat, and his tongue felt too thick in his mouth. For a moment the world seemed to vanish, and an ivory face floated before him, framed by the night and by a swirl of shimmering black hair. He had never tasted those ruby lips, though he knew their honeyed flavor. He had never met those coldly laughing eyes, though they threatened to draw the soul from his body.

She was Shandal Karg, though few dared to speak her name aloud. Most called her the Heart of Darkness.

Eric had never been this close to the Dark Lands before. Suddenly every tree and bush on the other side of the Kultari seemed to hide a pair of spying eyes.

"They're only dreams," Evander reminded him as he sought to draw him away from the river.

Eric knew his friend was wrong. They were more

than dreams. There was no point in arguing it though. He had a mission to think about, and now he also had a mystery.

By his knee, the dog suddenly stiffened and gave a low growl. Eric became instantly alert. "What is it, pooch?" he said, peering around. "Hmmm? You smell something?"

The dog gave a sharp bark and shied away from Eric. It barked again and bared its teeth, dancing back and forth, tearing up dust from the road with its front paws. Then it let go a howl and fled across one of the yards and behind the still-smouldering wreckage of a barn.

Alanna and Doe ran down the street toward them. "Magoths!" Alanna cried. She waved a hand in the direction from which they had come. "At least three. Probably more!"

Eric shook his head. "May-goths?"

Before she could explain, a huge shaggy beast lumbered on two powerful legs around the remains of a smoking wall. Arms thick as tree trunks hung down past its knees. Bits of leaves and twigs tangled and matted its dull brown fur. The magoth was not a man, but neither was it an ape. It stood too easily erect and moved with a startling grace for a monster its size.

It hesitated, sniffing the air, as a second magoth moved around the corner. Small dark eyes peered intensely at the four humans. The beast snarled, showing teeth and four-inch fangs. The first magoth bent over the body of the child by the fence, picked up the doll Doe had placed in her arms, and regarded it curiously before casting it aside with a disinterested flip of its wrist. It crouched, arms between its legs, and leaned forward to sniff the body.

Eric heard a loud, nauseating crunch. "My God!"

he gasped as the beast looked up and chewed its first bloody mouthful.

"Magoths are scavengers," Alanna whispered.

Eric's breath caught in his throat as a third monster stepped into the street. It was larger than the other two, quite clearly male, and its maw was already a crimson mess. As it spied the humans, it raised its arms threateningly and screeched a warning.

Alanna caught Eric's arm in a firm grip. "Stay absolutely still," she said. She swallowed, then went on in her soft, tense whisper. "They can smell death the way we smell dinner."

Eric frowned at her choice of words. "My brother's rubbing off on you," he commented dryly.

Evander dared to shuffle a bit closer and spoke from the corner of his mouth. His knuckles strained at the fabric of his gloves as he clutched his staff. "They roam the wilds of the Gray Kingdoms in herds of twenty or thirty," he said, his gaze riveted on the beasts. "There's bound to be more close by. Normally, though, magoths are cowards. Chances are good they won't attack us if we don't provoke them."

Another crunch caused Eric to wince. The first magoth lifted the dead child in its hairy arms and held her as it ripped her throat out. The second beast spied the corpse of the woman lying in the yard while the huge male sniffed and shambled toward the burned-out shop across the street.

"I can't stand here and watch this," Eric said as a fourth and fifth magoth appeared around a corner at the far end of the street.

Face pale, Alanna nodded. She opened a small pocket on the back of her gauntlet and withdrew a single dart for her blowpipe. "Go slowly toward the river," she told him, "and make no move that would startle the creatures. Remember, there are probably more that we haven't seen yet."

Doe and Evander led the way down the grassy bank to the water's edge, skirting the remains of the pier. The Kultari flowed swift and deep with a gurgling rush on their left as they headed north. Safely out of sight of the magoths, they mounted the bank again and prepared to circle around the village. Their dragons were in a clearing several miles through the woods on the far side.

"Behind that tree," Evander said in a sudden whisper, pointing.

Eric peered ahead through the thick foliage. At first he saw nothing to cause alarm. Then, twenty yards to their right, a long tuft of brown fur rippled in a soft breeze. A magoth stood perfectly still, nearly camouflaged, watching with suspicious eyes from under a low limb. Eric gave his comrade a questioning look.

"I smelled it," Evander answered as they steered a course around the beast.

"Smelled it?" Eric scoffed. "How could you smell it?"

Evander allowed a patient grin. "Your senses are too dull, Son of Paradane," he replied.

Eric raised one eyebrow as he shrugged. "Yeah, well you live in a world with tons of garbage in the air you breathe. You'll be glad when your nose goes a little dead."

"Robert would call it *survival adaptation,*" Alanna deadpanned.

"You can learn a lot from my brother," Eric told her with mock disgust, "but please, not his sense of humor."

They pushed on through the woods, moving eastward now away from the Kultari. Eric wondered if in ancient times Iowa had been this lush and forested.

The ruined village might have been Ida Grove in his world. They sat at about the same points on similar rivers.

Over and over for long days and nights he had studied the maps in the library back in Guran, half a continent away, preparing for this mission to Wystoweem. He couldn't put out of his mind the similarities between North America and Sinnagar. The rivers were the same, the mountain ranges, the great lakes—never precisely identical, just close enough to be startling.

"Stop." Alanna's tense whisper snapped him out of his reverie, and he cursed himself for letting his concentration lapse. They all froze as her gaze swept around. Even Eric suddenly noted the smell of filth in the air. From off to their left came a sharp, now-familiar snarl.

"As I believe you would say, Eric," Doe muttered nervously, *"shit."*

"You're rubbing off on him," Alanna said to Eric with a chiding shake of her head.

They stood absolutely still. A pair of magoths glared down at them from the thick branches of the maple that spread above the path. Three more shambled out of the trees directly in front of them. Another, the largest Eric had seen yet, almost twice his own six-foot-plus height, emerged from behind a tree not twenty feet away. In the deeper shadows of the woods, still more of the great shaggy creatures stirred.

One of the magoths above them gave a scream and jumped down. With a back-handed stroke, it sent Evander toppling. Eric started to move, but Alanna caught his arm in a firm grip as she pulled Doe back a step, effectively putting herself between the creature and her two comrades.

The magoth glared at her almost nose to nose. Alanna glared right back.

On the ground, Evander rose up stiffly on one elbow, his eyes not quite focused, as he groped one-handed for his staff.

"Be still!" Doe hissed to his friend.

A bead of sweat trickled down Eric's temple. The other magoths all looked their way now, attracted by the commotion. The giant fellow eyed them menacingly, and the remaining monster in the trees above gave another blood-chilling shriek.

Then an immense winged shadow passed over the forest, momentarily eclipsing the sun, leaving a wake of wind that rippled the leaves and filled the air with a susurration. The magoths looked up as the shadow wheeled about and skimmed the treetops again. With a quiet speed that belied their size, the creatures melted away into the woods. No angry screams, no challenges. The magoths simply departed.

"Shadowfire," Eric said softly as he watched the dragon make another pass and turn back toward the clearing where the other *sekoye* waited.

"Almost as if he knew you were in trouble," Alanna said. She and Doe helped Evander to his feet. "It's a strange bond you two are forming."

Eric felt the harmonica he carried in a special pocket on his belt. "He's just grown fond of the blues," he answered. "Why'd the magoths run away like that?"

Evander brushed himself off and accepted the staff Doe pressed into his hands. "They fear the *sekoye*," he answered.

"That's probably why the one who attacked Evander hesitated," Alanna added. She grabbed the neck of her tunic. "It got a whiff of our leather. Must have been pretty confusing."

Their garments, like all *sekournen* clothing, were made from the molted skins of growing dragons. The dragonriders felt it heightened the bonds they formed with the great winged beasts.

"Let's make a report at Sheren Hiawa when we pass over Imansirit," Eric suggested as they started through the woods again. "There's a mystery here that bears closer watch. I'm sure those villagers were murdered."

Alanna nodded. "After that, we'd better get on to Wystoweem. Councillor Salyt will be waiting for us, and she isn't known for her patience."

"I think," Doe added, giving a short chuckle, "a steak had better be waiting for Evander's eye." He pointed to the bruise that was already darkening the side of his friend's face.

They marched on through the woods, but Eric grew quiet as his thoughts turned back to the village. Those people had been dead for nearly a day. The fires had burned down, leaving the ruins to smoulder and smoke. He kept seeing the woman's face, the little girl's, the doll Evander had found. Murder wasn't supposed to happen in Palenoc. Yet nothing else could explain what they'd found.

A small stream cut suddenly across the path. They followed it to a long, narrow valley where the grass grew as high as their waists, where their *sekoye* waited. Alanna's dragon, Mirrormist, lifted its sinuous neck and trumpeted a shrill greeting. Heartsong and Sunrunner, Evander's and Doe's mounts, fanned their wings enthusiastically. Overhead, Shadowfire gyred in lazy circles, preferring to stretch his wings in the open sky.

Before they reached the dragons, however, Doe stopped. His expression went blank for an instant. Then he turned his head as if he were seeing something Eric couldn't see.

"What now?" Alanna snapped impatiently. "We're overdue in Wystoweem."

Doe didn't answer. He reached out and took Evander's hand. The two *sekournen* closed their eyes. Each dropped his staff and extended his empty hand, as if to join with yet a third person.

The air took on an abrupt chill. Evander and Doe inclined their heads subtly backward, their faces sublimely relaxed.

Then they were indeed three: two men and a vague, opaque *presence* barely perceptible in the light of day, all holding hands to make a small circle in the tall grass.

Eric felt the goose bumps rise on his arms. The *ghosts* of Palenoc still frightened him, and it made him no less nervous that this one had chosen to appear in broad daylight—something such creatures abhorred. Though it had a shape and after a fashion a face, he could make out no features. It was naked and hairless, stooped and gnarly with pale, translucent limbs. A very old soul, Eric decided as he watched this strange communion.

The visitation lasted less than a moment, then the ghost faded away.

"That was a messenger sent by Phlogis," Evander explained as he rubbed the chill from his fingers. "The mission to Wystoweem is delayed. We're going back home."

"What?" Alanna cried in disbelief.

Eric was equally startled by the news. He knew too well the importance of their mission. The entire outcome of the Millenias War was at stake. Councillor Salyt would not be pleased.

"A woman has just arrived in Rasoul," Doe continued, his voice filled with concern. He bent to retrieve his staff. "She says Robert Podlowsky is in great trouble."

Eric stiffened. "What woman?" he asked. "Where'd she come from?" His brother had gone back home to earth over a month ago in hopes of finding a new clue to the disappearance of his friend, Scott Silver.

"From Paradane," Doe answered. "The spirit said a name, but it was difficult to understand. The sunlight was causing it considerable pain. I think the name was Cat-a-dowd."

Fear struck Eric like a bolt, and he put aside any thought of Wystoweem and his mission. "My God," he muttered, all he could think of to say, though his friends stared expectantly awaiting some explanation. He shot one hand toward the pocket on his belt, drew out the silver harmonica, and blew a sharp desperate riff to summon Shadowfire.

Two days flight to Rasoul, he thought, shivering inside. *Two days.*

Chapter Two

KATY Dowd stared at the sheer stone walls that rose around her, and listened to the hiss of the wind as it ripped through the narrow, canyon-like clove. The pines and tall maples shivered. A full moon and a few bright stars burned in the sky directly overhead. Wildly spiraling leaves swept across the moon's refulgence like strange birds. She could feel, but not quite see the mountains that loomed beyond the rim of the secret clove to which she had come.

Standing on a shelf of flat slate, which formed the bank of one side of a small pool, she picked up her shoulder pack from where it had rested all afternoon, slipped into the straps, and listened to the rush of the waterfall. A fine, chill mist brushed her face and throat. She clicked on her flashlight and shined the beam on the thin, glimmering curtain of water. It was more than seventy feet, she guessed, to the top. She switched the light off again, her eyes adjusting quickly. Kneeling, she stuck one hand into the pool. Icy cold. She cupped her palm and took a quick drink while her gaze wandered to the other side of the pool and after the narrow silver stream that cut its way toward the mouth of the hidden gorge that disappeared in the darkness.

A sudden rustle made her jump up, thumbing on the flashlight switch. A small, dry bush trembled in the white beam. She forced a sheepish smile and clicked the light off once more. It had been awhile since she'd spent a night in the woods. She had forgotten all its sounds.

Katy brushed a few strands of dark red hair back from her face and adjusted the knot in the white handkerchief that kept it all back. The cloth was saturated with her sweat. The air was warm for September, yet the smell of autumn rode on the breeze. It was that eeriest time of year when the world hung between seasons.

She strained her eyes to see the peaks of the Catskills over the clove rim. There was little to detect but a few giant shadows against the darkness of the night. She could hear them, though, the mountains, whispering with ancient muffled voices—murmurings and mutterings, like old men in their sleep.

The wild blew over her face again, lending an added chill to the mist on her cheeks. How different it all seemed here, she thought to herself. Once you got away from the resorts and the social clubs and the hotels, the Catskills still had secret hidden places like this one, dark corners and cloves, valleys full of mystery where few people, or no one at all, had ever set foot.

She'd spent too much time these last few years behind the desk at the Dowdsville Library. The mountains still murmured to her at night when the wind blew through the open window by her bed, but she had tuned out their voices. Why had she stopped coming to the mountains? Why had it taken trouble to bring her back?

The moon's reflection danced on the rippling surface of the pool, teasing her. The moon knew the answers, as it knew every secret in her heart. She glanced toward the waterfall again, her eyes narrowing as she attempted to see into the small cave that she knew was there behind it.

What if it's all a lie? she wondered. *What if he really is dead?* A tempest rose up inside her at the thought. If he was dead, then she would laugh and dance on his grave. Or maybe she would lie down quietly and die, too.

Katy swallowed, and her right hand tightened around the flashlight even as her left hand felt for the small medallion around her neck, seeking its outline through the thin windbreaker and white cotton pullover she wore. All afternoon and evening she had waited here, watching the trees and the stream, the peaks, listening to the waterfall and the wind as darkness settled and the moon crept into the sky, feeling the medallion under her garments, always through the layers of cloth, dreading to take it out.

Night had fallen several hours ago, though, and the full moon was where it should be. She had hesitated for a while, telling herself her legs were tired and needed rest. She hadn't hiked in ages. But her legs were strong and fine. There was no real reason to delay. Her mouth felt dry, though she had just drunk from the pool. Her heart beat faster as she slipped the chain over her head and held the medallion up.

It drew the moonlight like an arcane magnet, shimmering and gleaming as the breeze brushed it and set it swinging back and forth like a pendulum. It was no more than a flat, silver cartouche, about the size of a dog tag or a razor blade, smooth and polished on one side, covered with tiny glyphs on the other. She had wasted hours in the library puzzling over that strange writing, finding nothing at all remotely similar.

The wind ripped through the clove with renewed vigor, pushing her toward the waterfall. She clutched the chain tightly in one fist and licked her lips. She was ready. There was no point in further delay. Either it was all a lie and she was the biggest fool in Dowdsville . . . or it wasn't.

Please, she prayed silently as she cast a glance toward the moon. A pale gray wisp of cloud streamed across it. *Don't let it be a lie.*

She adjusted her backpack once more and thumbed on the flashlight. It was the medallion she held before her, though, as if it were a lantern to light the way. The flashlight's beam bounced off the water, and the mist above the pool sparkled. The slate shelf extended all the way back to the wall, but it turned slick underfoot and slanted at a subtle angle. There was no way she was going to stay dry. Fortunately, the fall wasn't wide. With a swift, lithe movement, she stepped through the silver curtain.

She gasped as icy water sluiced over her, and nearly fell backward into the pool as her hiking boots slipped on wet stone. The cave floor behind the fall had a steep upward slope she hadn't been prepared for, yet somehow she caught her balance and clambered up. She was drenched to the bone. The flashlight hadn't fared well, either. Apparently the batteries had gotten wet. No matter how she shook it, the beam refused to come on. She flung it down in disgust. So much for waterproof guarantees.

Shivering and hugging herself, Katy faced back toward the entrance. The moon shone like a pale milky ball through the cascade of water, its light weakened and diffused. Yet there was another light somewhere in the cave, a shallow, emerald glow. Slowly, she held up the medallion, the source of that glow, and knew then, in that moment, that everything she'd been told was true.

Her heart beat faster than ever, but there was no turning back now. The crash of the waterfall filled the cave, its sound greatly magnified in the narrow rocky confines. "I'm ready for this!" she shouted, as much to convince herself as for any other reason. She held the medallion up again by the end of its chain. Rolling the links between a thumb and forefinger, she set it to spinning, as she'd been told. Around and around the cartouche whirled, flashing like an impossible prism, casting spears of light.

As if in answer, out of the darkness at the far end of the cave, a spark of green fire flared to sudden life, pulsing, growing, burning brighter and brighter, losing its emerald color until it filled the air with an aching white radiance.

That light shot toward Katy Dowd like a tongue of dazzling flame. With a long scream, she flung up an arm to protect her eyes as she tried desperately to flatten against the wall; but there was no wall. She felt herself falling. Every nerve in her body shrieked, individually on fire, as she tumbled over and over in a pure white space where stars and planets and galaxies hung like black dots.

Then her feet were on solid ground again. With one hand still flung protectively across her eyes, she reached out and touched the cool stone of the cave wall.

Something was different. The wall was dry. And the air smelled, not of water, but of dust.

Slowly, Katy Dowd lowered her arm and opened her eyes. It was not far to the cave opening. Nor was there a curtain of water to weaken the resplendent sunset beyond. She wet her lips again, her eyes widening with wonder even as she trembled with fear. It was not yet night in this new world to which she had come.

On her belt hung a small black box, attached by a clip. One hand stole toward it and rested there briefly. The silver medallion in her other hand hung suspended from its chain, absolutely still. She glanced toward the rear of the cave. Nothing there but stone.

A short, breathless sigh slipped between her lips. She eased the chain over her head again and dropped it down the front of her cotton pullover. Streamers of iodine and violet colored the small patch of sky she could see outside the cave. It was warm, warm as a midsummer evening. Dripping water, she moved toward the mouth and hesitated there. Then she stepped beyond.

Katy felt a tiny laugh gurgle up and repressed it, pressing her fingers to her lips. It was like a fairy tale. She hadn't really believed before. But it was all true! Was the meadow that sprawled before her really greener than any green she had ever known? The red and yellow flowers that dotted it poured a rich, honey scent into the air. The trees in the forest beyond waltzed to an unheard breeze as an orange ball of fire sank below the highest branches.

"Palenoc." She spoke the name of this world with quiet, awful reverence, as she had been taught, breaking it down into its appropriate syllables. "Pale knock." The bare sound of it made her tremble.

Once more, she adjusted her backpack. After a full day's hiking, the straps had left her shoulders sore and raw. It was easy to dismiss the discomfort, though, faced with this adventure. She gave it barely a thought as she left the cave and began her journey in this strange Never-neverland.

She didn't get far. The barest rush of wind in her ears and a fleeting shadow alerted her too late. Something smashed her to the ground. She hit hard, eating grass, tiny stars exploding in her head. Her backpack, though, had taken the brunt of the blow's impact.

Katy raised up uncertainly on her hands and knees. The shadow fell over her again before she could regain her breath. Desperately, she kicked backward with all her strength, hoping to strike a shin or a knee-cap, and made a solid connection. A sharp cry of surprise was her reward, and the shadow fell away from her.

She rose swiftly, shrugging free of her backpack, casting it aside as her attacker found his feet and came at her again. He was huge. Dark eyes burned with anger beneath his bushy black brows. A thick beard covered most of his face, but there was no hiding the toothy scowl he showed her as he charged, and no avoiding the reach of those massive arms. They encircled her, crushed the breath from her lungs, and lifted her from the ground.

The earthy, unwashed smell of the man crept up her nostrils as she screamed and ripped the black box from her belt. Her thumb found the trigger. A blue-white spark leaped between the pair of small metal studs at one end of the box, eliciting a harsh crackle. Without hesitation, she slammed the studs into her attacker's ribs.

The bearded man's eyes snapped wide with pain and surprise, and his grip weakened. But he didn't fall or let her go. Again, she jammed the box against his body, this time striking one of the arms that held her. He shrieked, and suddenly Katy was free, but rather than backing away, she stepped in quickly again and struck once more with her stun gun.

With the third touch, the man collapsed like a marionette whose strings had been severed. Three touches. One hundred-and-twenty-thousand volts each time, and it had taken three! She pressed the trigger and watched the blue arc leap between the studs. A sharp crack and a powerful strobe accompanied it. The gun worked fine. She noted his garments. Loose-fitting leather, mostly, dark tunic and britches and boots.

That wouldn't have stopped the stun gun, though. He was just that big.

Something struck the sleeve of her windbreaker, lodging in the cuff above the hand that held the gun. A needle-thin dart. Katy glanced up. The cave was part of a towering cliff. Above the mouth was a ledge. Farther back on that lip of rock, she spied the roof of some cabin, but directly above her another man stood with some kind of pipe to his lips.

"Wait!" she cried, raising a hand even as she saw his cheeks puff. She ran back into the cave before the second dart took flight, clutching her gun, leaving behind her pack. Momentarily safe, she ripped the first dart free and cast it aside. Morbidly, she wondered what kind of poison tipped it. "Goddamn it, stop!" she shouted from the cave shadows, her voice going shrill. "I'm a friend! You understand? Friend!"

A long silence. Katy clung to the rocky wall near the cave mouth, crouching in the shadows. Out on the lawn, her first attacker gave a low groan and began to stir. He tried to roll over, but couldn't quite manage it, still disoriented by the heavy jolts of electricity.

A smaller man appeared suddenly at his side, moving swiftly, clutching another blowpipe as he gazed toward the cave. He touched his comrade briefly on the shoulder and shouted something meant for her. Katy spoke French and Spanish, besides good old American English, but she had no idea in the world what the small man was saying. She slipped a little farther back into the cave as he loaded another dart into his pipe and stole cautiously forward.

He spoke again, but she didn't answer. What was the point? As long as he held that weapon, all she would do was give herself away. She touched the medallion under her clothes and thought about using it to get out of here. She had come to Palenoc for a purpose, though, and she wasn't ready to retreat.

The short man reached the cave mouth. Framed against the sunset colors, he made a black, ominous silhouette. The outline of the pipe hovered near his mouth, ready for use. Again, he called. Katy hunkered deeper into the shadows, biting her lip as she tried to figure what to do.

Slowly, she drew the medallion out again, slipped it from around her neck, and gathered it in her fist. With a little motion, she tossed it onto the cave floor a few feet away. It made a small clatter as it landed on the stone. The short man heard and turned toward it. He took a step inside and stopped, eyes straining toward the sound. He called out again in that strange language. Unmoving, Katy held her breath.

The larger man outside had managed to get to his hands and knees, though he couldn't quite stand yet. He shouted something, and his shorter companion glanced back to offer a curt response. Then, more boldly, he crept into the cave, blowpipe at the ready. When he spied the medallion on the floor, he gave a little gasp, letting the pipe slide away from his lips as he bent down to retrieve it.

Katy sprang out of the shadows, pressing the trigger on her stun gun. A sharp white light strobed between the studs, just inches from the short man's face. With her other hand, she snatched the pipe. He gave a cry and flung himself away, tripped on his own heel, and sprawled on the floor. He rolled up on one elbow, rubbing his eyes, as he called to his comrade with a voice full of fear.

"Hey, I'm not going to hurt you," Katy said, standing over him. Plainly he didn't understand her. He blinked furiously to clear his vision as she knelt down beside him. "Look," she said with a calm she didn't feel. "You can have this back." She laid the pipe down near his hand without mentioning that it no longer contained the dart. On the ground beside him lay the medallion. He'd dropped it when he fell. She picked it up one-handed and slipped it over her head.

The short man's eyes widened suddenly, and the fear seemed to leave his face. His gaze fixed on the silver cartouche, and he muttered something in a low tone of wonderment.

"You recognize this?" Katy asked, touching the ornament delicately.

Outside, the larger man was trying desperately to stand. His angry shouts nearly drowned out Katy's soft-spoken question. His shorter partner barked an order, and for a moment there was silence. Katy rose and made a deliberate show of returning the stun gun to her belt. She held up both hands and forced a smile.

The short man paused, obviously studying her, then thrust his blowpipe into his own belt. A noise and a moan drew their attention back outside. His comrade lay flat on his face, spewing a torrent of curses.

"He'll be a little disoriented for about fifteen or twenty minutes," she explained as she walked to the cave mouth and peered out. It occurred to her to wonder if there were more than two of them, and she glanced hastily around before stepping away from the shelter of the cave.

The short man touched her arm and urged her to accompany him as he went to his partner's side. He spoke excitedly, repeatedly pointing to the medallion. The big man's eyes finally focused. He squinted, then reached out with a fingertip to touch the shiny object. He looked at her with a long, hard glare, his anger still not completely abated. He mumbled something to his friend, then he turned to her again and said something.

His speech was as incomprehensible to Katy as ever, except for one word: *Podlowsky.*

"Yes!" she said, leaning forward eagerly as she grasped the medallion in her fist. "Podlowsky!"

Both men stared at her. A rush of words poured from them. Over and over she heard that one name, but she could make no more of what they were saying. "Robert gave me this!" she cried, showing them the medallion again. "Robert Podlowsky. He's in trouble. You understand? I've got to find his brother, Eric! Eric Podlowsky!"

"Eric Podlowsky!" the larger man answered suddenly, nodding his head. He gripped her arm, but there was no menace in it this time. "Eric Podlowsky!" He said something to his friend, but the short man was no longer beside them. Katy looked around and saw him racing back toward the cliff and up a narrow set of steps that someone had carved into the rocky face. He disappeared over the ledge. A wooden door slammed.

The large man's grip tightened on her arm, then he released her. "Jago," he said, thumping his chest. He pointed to the ledge. "Trevin."

Katy seized his hand and pumped it. "Pleased to meet you, Jake," she answered. She pointed to herself. "Katy Dowd."

"Paradane!" Jago said, indicating the cave.

Katy remembered that word from Robert's wild stories. Only they weren't really stories, after all, and *Paradane* was this world's name for Earth. "That's right," she answered thoughtfully, "Katy Dowd from Paradane, Dowdsville, USA."

Jago glanced impatiently toward the ledge and shouted to his friend. Katy took the opportunity to study him. Black hair, long and tied back with a leather string. Coal black eyes. Black beard. There was a hard, weathered look to his face, and she considered for a moment that she would like the chance to paint him sometime.

The thought startled her. It had been more than a year since she'd last bothered to pick up a brush or touch a canvas.

Trevin came running back down the stone steps. He stopped breathlessly beside them, clutching a leather-wrapped bundle under one arm. His eyes were brown as chocolate, but he had the same thick black hair as his partner.

Jago held out a hand and demanded the bundle as he scrambled around on his knees and sat back on his heels. The effects of the stun had apparently worn off. Trevin knelt down by him as he cast the leather wrapping aside to expose a small wooden box. Jago threw back the hinged lid and lifted out a narrow wand of intricately carven gold. On one end a large red stone was mounted. Katy recognized it from her researches in the Dowdsville Library. Carnelian.

"It's beautiful," she whispered. But a chill shivered slowly up her spine. Robert had told her stories.

Jago gripped the wand in both hands and jammed the blunt end into the grassy ground with sufficient force to embed it. At the moment it came into contact with the earth, the carnelian began to glow with a red fire. Jago closed his eyes and, humming, leaned over it. The scarlet light shone up into his face to eerie effect. Trevin moved closer to Katy, who became suddenly aware that the sun was nearly down and darkness was closing in.

"What's he doing?" Katy whispered. But Trevin gave a stern shake of his head and laid a finger against her lips. She shut up after that. When the glow ebbed and Jago leaned back, she was almost relieved, considering the things Robert had told her, that nothing more dramatic had transpired.

But then, she wondered. Trevin got up and fixed his gaze on the western sky. Jago hurriedly pulled the wand out of the earth, used his tunic to wipe the dirt from it, and put it back in the box. Carefully, he re-wrapped it with the piece of leather and tucked it under one arm. She had no idea what he said to her, but his tone sounded urgent. He, too, turned his attention to the west.

A dull scarlet glow, not unlike the glow of the car-nelian, was all that remained of the sun's light. The sun had long since fallen below the horizon. Jago touched her arm again and pointed. Out of the heart of that glow came a black-winged shape.

Her own heart quickened, and she clutched Rob-ert's medallion in a fist. The shape crossed the border from the light into darkness, but it was no longer black. The wings burned with a deep red fire as they rose and fell. Even from a distance she knew it was huge. Huge and splendid and frightening. Now she could make out the long reach of its neck and the proud undulation of its lashing tail. And as it came on, sweeping out of the sky straight for them, she thought of running back into the cave—the gateway, Robert called it—for the safety of her familiar little home in the Catskills.

Yet, if she did that, Robert Podlowsky would be convicted for certain.

The dragon gyred high above them, then circled lower and lower, the glow of its wings lighting up the meadow, the treetops, the face of the cliff as it sank down. The creature arched its neck and gave a warn-ing cry, a high-pitched trumpeting like nothing Katy had ever heard. Jago called to Trevin and gave a tug on Katy's arm, and together they moved back toward the cave to give the beast the full expanse of the field to make its landing. The dragon suddenly fanned the air with its wings, and for a moment it seemed to hover. Then the wings stilled, and it settled with strange grace to the ground. Immense talons flexed in the earth as the wings folded tightly against a sleek, scaled form.

A long neck stretched out over the grass. Two men climbed down from a saddle, the first turning to help the second, who was obviously older. Jago hailed them with a wave, and the two came toward them.

One was very tall and powerfully built. Like a weight lifter, she thought, in her own world. He wore a somber, concerned expression as he regarded Katy. The old man was something else, though. His face lit up as he approached her. His eyes actually twinkled. While his friend wore practical garments of thin leather, he himself was dressed in more colorful robes that stirred with the slightest breeze or movement.

"Welcome to Palenoc, Katy Dowd," the old man said pleasantly. There was the faintest trace of a Spanish accent to his English. He made a gesture toward his muscular companion. "This is Valis," he told her by way of introduction. "My name is Roderigo Diez."

She nodded a bit breathlessly, grateful to find someone who could understand her. "Robert told me all about you," she answered, extending her hand.

The old Spaniard smiled. "Then he may have told you," he replied, "that on Palenoc we greet each other this way." He raised both her hands to shoulder height and pressed his palms to hers. "So tell me, how is our young Brother of the Dragon?"

"He's in jail," she answered.

Chapter Three

BARS. Rows of cold metal bars. A beam of moonlight squeezed through the narrow, barred window. It palely illuminated the edge of the porcelain stool, a corner of the tiny sink. Four bunks. Four thin mattresses. Four rough army blankets. No pillows. The floor, appropriately, dull gray cement. Styrofoam cup on the sink. Dog-eared paperback pressed open on the bottom left bunk.

A black roach crawled across the moonlit floor, drawing Robert's attention. He stopped the mental inventory. He already knew intimately every last thing there was to know about his cell. The roach, however, that was new. That was a diversion. He watched as it made its halting way across the moonbeam until it vanished once more in the darkness.

Well, he told himself when the roach was gone, *that probably killed a whole ten minutes.*

He leaned against the only solid wall. Spine stiff, arms at his sides, fingertips barely drumming against the hard, cool surface. Lightly, he banged his head backward three times. The window above was almost too high for him. He turned toward it and raised on tiptoe. It was little more than a slash, a yard long and maybe six inches wide. A man could never have slipped through it. Still, it was barred and sealed with wire-mesh glass.

He could barely see the moon shining down on the dark rooftops of sleepy Dowdsville. The treetops glimmered with its powdery light. Leaves trembled at the touch of some random breeze. Branches shivered.

Robert wet his lips. There was an eerie quality to it that made him think of his friend Scott Silver. He'd come back from Palenoc, hoping to solve the mystery posed by his friend's murder. He'd failed, though. All he'd found were more mysteries, more questions. More than ever, Robert believed the answers lay in Palenoc. He pressed his face to the bars and gazed out through the glass, wondering if he would ever get back to that other world.

It was the last night of the full moon. He strained his gaze upward again. It floated high in the night, sinking ever so slowly toward the west, dragging his hopes with it. He touched his throat, unconsciously seeking the medallion that was no longer there. Fighting despair, he turned away from the window.

Bars. Rows of bars. Sink. Stool. Bunks. If only he could read, but ten o'clock had brought "Lights Out." The damn little asshole deputy had smirked as he'd thrown the switch. A fellow prisoner might even have helped pass the time. But there was no one else.

Scott, he thought. He missed his friend.

His mouth drew into a taut line as he unbuttoned the thin blue shirt they'd given him to wear and tossed it on the bunk. Seven days, he thought to himself. He moved to the middle of his cell and began the first movements of Heian kata. *Peaceful Mind,* its name meant. He pushed his fist slowly through space, moving like water, flowing with fluid grace from one end of the cell to the other. *Let go of thought,* he told himself as he moved. *Let go of concern.*

Instead, he found himself growing tense. *I can smash that lock.* The thought flickered through his awareness like slender lightning, and there was no doubt in it. He stood perfectly still, the kata abandoned, poised, balanced on his right leg as he aimed down the length of his left and over the edge of his heel straight at the mechanism.

But he dared not try to escape. *Patience,* he counseled himself. It was hard to be patient, though, caged like an animal. He frowned as he forced himself to relax. He looked at each of the bunks. Which one tonight? There was plenty of room at the inn. Finally, he slumped down on the lower mattress beside the book he'd tossed there earlier and let go a sigh.

It was too dark to read, but the pale moonlight illumined the garish foil-embossed cover with its lurid illustration of some spectral creature crouching over a helpless girl. *A Pale Knock,* the title read, by Robert Polo. His pen name, a shortened version of Podlowsky. It was his last published book, written almost a year before he and his brother had made their astonishing discovery. He doubted, though, that the similarity between his title and the name of that strange world into which they'd stumbled was mere coincidence. In the month since his return to Earth, he'd read and reread his own words, seeking answers and again finding only more questions.

Frustrated, he flung the book across the cell. The pages fluttered noisily. It hit the bars, bounced between them, and fell with a thump in the corridor out of reach.

Out of reach. His mind locked into that thought. He sprang up from the bunk, paced to the window again, rose on his tiptoes. Beyond the rooftops and the trees, the mountains loomed. Starlight and moonlight dusted the dark Catskill peaks. He could almost hear the wind blowing down from those peaks, feel it cool on his face. His fingernails made a soft scraping as he reached between the bars and drew them down the inside of the window glass.

He longed to breathe fresh air again. The Dowdsville jail reeked of Lysol and Spic and Span. The mountains hunched out there like giants, crouched and peering down, waiting impatiently for him, and the breezes called him to hurry. He slammed his fists against the bars.

It was all just out of reach.

Robert's heart hammered in his chest. His mouth went dry. There at that window in the moonlight, staring out at a world he couldn't touch, for the first time he faced the reality of his situation. He tried unsuccessfully to fight back a tremor of fear.

He might be convicted of his brother's murder. The evidence was all circumstantial, but it was all stacked against him. He'd already been arraigned, bound over for trial, imprisoned, and denied bail. All in the space of seven days. Things could move fast in a sleepy, lazy town like Dowdsville. Give the locals a whiff of scandal, and they woke up fast enough.

The headline in the *Dowdsville Mirror* had been juicy. "LOCAL AUTHOR CHARGED IN BROTHER'S MURDER." Robert frowned at that. He hadn't been a *local* for nearly eight years, not since leaving for college.

More importantly, though, Eric wasn't dead. But Robert couldn't tell anyone that.

He groped self-consciously for the medallion around his neck and remembered once again he didn't have it anymore. He had dared to tell one person. Had Katy believed him? he wondered. She hadn't come to see him for days. He had pressed the medallion—it had taken considerable convincing to get Sheriff Patterson to let him keep it—into her hands in the jail's visiting room as he spilled the whole story privately to her.

He recalled the look on her face. He was completely mad in her mind. Yet he'd gambled on the love Katy felt for Eric and given her the only thing that could get him back to Palenoc. For years, since they were all children growing up together, Katy had loved his brother. That love would make her hope just enough that an impossible story might be true. The medallion was the key. He was sure she'd use it.

The only question that remained was had she used it in time? He gazed at the moon, his legs beginning to cramp as he strained to see out the window. It was the last night of the full moon. Soon, the gate between the worlds would close. Another month would have to pass before they opened again.

He sank down, leaned against the wall, stared around the bleak cell. Cup, sink, stool. Bars, bunks, blankets. Robert made his mental inventory again as he felt another prick of despair. What would he do in here for a month?

Stretched out on the bunk once more, he folded his hands under his head and turned glazed eyes up toward the bottom of the upper bunk. Without any fore-thought, he brought his feet up sharply, angrily, and kicked at the springs. Mattress, blanket, and sheets flew into the air. The mattress landed with a *whump* in the center of the cell. Sheets and blanket fluttered down, ghostlike.

"My, my, in a mood tonight, ain't we?"

Robert didn't bother to look around. He hadn't heard the corridor door open. The lights, too, were still off, and that worried him, though he determined not to let it show.

"Fuck off, Zelinsky," he said in a flat voice. He despised the diminutive Dowdsville deputy. At five feet four, Zelinsky had always been the most obnox-ious person in Dowdsville's elementary and high school. They'd been classmates together. Eight years had passed, and God still hadn't seen fit to give him any more height.

Well, Zelinsky had a badge on his chest now. He obviously thought it made him a bigger man.

The deputy struck the bars with his nightstick. "Pick that mess up in there, Podlowsky," he ordered, trying to force his voice an octave lower than Robert knew it naturally was. "Or maybe I should call you, *Mister Polo*?" He tapped the bars with the stick again. "Make that bunk up neat as it was before your little tantrum."

Robert didn't move, though he was suddenly aware of how close his head was to the bars. A faint half smile turned up the corners of his lips. "Come in and make me, Eddie." A chilling moment of quiet, then came the very faint squeak of shoe leather. Robert listened with all his senses. Zelinsky stood right over him now. Only the bars separated them.

He felt as much as saw the nightstick as it came down. He moved his head ever so slightly. The weapon slammed into the mattress. Before Zelinsky could pull it back, Robert caught the weapon and jerked it from the deputy's grasp. With an almost serene satisfaction, he sprang up, thrust the stick halfway between a pair of bars, as if it was a fulcrum, and smashed his elbow against it. A loud *crack!* rifled through the corridor. Two pieces clattered and rolled on the cement floor.

Lying back down again, he folded his hands under his head. "You try that again, Eddie," he said in quiet tones, "and I'll fold you in half and feed you your own feet."

A snap opened. Metal scraped against leather. Eddie cocked the hammer on his revolver. "Think you're pretty tough shit with all that martial arts crap, don't you, hotshot."

Robert rolled over on his side and lifted up on one arm. Zelinsky was little more than a shadow in the black corridor. The faint moonlight from the cell window didn't touch him, but it glinted on the short barrel of a .38 revolver.

"I want to thank you for paying me this visit, Eddie," Robert sneered. "I was feeling a little sorry for myself while I was lying here alone. Now I can feel sorry for you, instead."

Zelinsky shuffled nervously in the corridor. "You got a smart mouth, Podlowsky," he hissed. "I could blow you away and claim you tried to break the stick over my head."

Robert gave a disgusted sigh, unwilling to let up on his old high school acquaintance. Zelinsky was the best entertainment he'd had all night. Infinitely better company than the *other* roach on the floor. "You're the only cop in town," he muttered, "who can demonstrate a correlation between the caliber of his pistol and his IQ."

Zelinsky pointed the gun toward the ceiling as he eased the hammer back down. Grunting, he holstered the weapon. "Well, maybe I'm not very smart, but then I'm out here, and you're in there." He bent down and picked up the battered copy of *A Pale Knock* from where it lay near his foot. He turned it a bit toward the moonlight. "Your books aren't even very good."

Robert sat up and folded his legs on the bunk. Then he hugged himself and faked a very exaggerated shiver. "Please, deputy," he deadpanned. "Your putdowns are killing me. I can't take this verbal abuse."

Zelinsky put on an ugly smile. "Your ass, pretty boy," he said with a sneer. "They get you up in state pen, you'll take a lot more than verbal abuse. And no fancy lawyer's gonna save you from that."

Certainly not the public defender who'd represented him at his arraignment, Robert admitted privately. "You know, Eddie," he replied with a tilt of his head, "I look at you, and I think to myself that it's a shame you'll probably die a natural death."

The corridor lights flipped on. Robert covered his eyes, wincing at the sudden brightness from the bare two hundred watt bulb just outside his cell. Zelinsky whirled around, startled. A gruff voice called from the other side of the doorway. "You got no business back here, Eddie. Get your ass back out front! *Now!*"

Dan Patterson, Dowdsville's sheriff, glared at his red-faced deputy as the little man retreated, then he came toward the cell door. In his hand he clutched a ring of keys. He stopped as he prepared to insert a key into the lock and pushed half of a broken nightstick with his toe. "I'm not even gonna ask about that," he muttered as he turned the mechanism and swung the door open. "Get out here, Bobby. Seems there's been a puzzlin' development in your case."

Patterson had been the sheriff as long as Robert could remember. Like a lot of other townspeople, he'd always called Robert by his nickname. It had a nice familiar sound to it now. Nevertheless, Robert rose cautiously, slipped on his blue prison shirt, and stepped into the corridor where he expected to be handcuffed. Patterson just turned around and beckoned for him to follow.

Something indeed was up. The deputy on duty at the front desk stared at him, then averted his gaze and became suddenly busy with a stack of file folders. Patterson pushed back the door to the visiting room and ushered Robert through. "You got to be the luckiest boy alive, Bobby," Patterson commented as he moved aside and motioned for Robert to enter. "Him turnin' up unexpected like this."

Katy Dowd sprang up from a chair. "Robert!" she said in a barely controlled voice. She came around the room's only table, hugged him, and pressed the silver medallion into his hand. "It was all true," she whispered as she quickly kissed his cheek. "I didn't believe you at first, but it was all true!"

He embraced Katy with all his strength, laughing with relief. He released her long enough to slip the silver chain around his neck and drop the medallion down the front of his shirt. He was never more glad to see anyone in his life, except maybe the tall figure behind her. Eric was still dressed in his black *sekour-nen* leathers. "Hi ya, big brother! Am I glad to see you."

"You okay, Bobby?" Eric asked, his eyes narrowing to slits as he glanced first at Dan Patterson, and then behind the sheriff at Eddie Zelinsky, who'd crept in behind them. "Anybody hurt you?"

Robert only rolled his eyes and hugged Katy again, pressing his nose into her neck until she gave an uncharacteristic giggle. He pushed her back to arm's length and looked at her with surprise. Katherine Dowd, the great-granddaughter of the town's founder, did *not* giggle.

"Get a grip, girl!" he murmured, grinning himself.

She passed a hand over her face and put on her best serious expression.

Eric pointed a finger at Sheriff Patterson. "You've got nothing to hold my brother on now," he pointed out. "So get his clothes and anything else that belongs to him. We're getting out of here."

Robert let go of Katy and turned toward his brother. "What's the matter, big brother?" he quipped as he grabbed twin handfuls of his unbuttoned shirt. "You don't like me in jailhouse blue?"

Patterson leaned a shoulder against the wall and rubbed a hand over his chin. "Now just slow down there, Eric," he said calmly. "Eddie'll bring Bobby's stuff right up." Zelinsky disappeared through the doorway like a shot. "There's a few questions I got about this whole business, though. Like where you been for more'n a month?" He held up a hand and ticked off fingers. "You ain't been seen. Didn't call in at your work. We know you didn't touch so much as a penny in your bank account even." He looked at Eric with an odd leer. "An' why're you dressed like some kind of New York City weirdo?"

Robert raised three fingers of his own, then four, then two as he turned to his brother. "And why, after all these years in Dowdsville, does he still talk like a Missouri hick?" He scratched his head in his best Oliver Hardy fashion.

Eric glared at the sheriff. "Dan, I came here to get my brother. That's all. I don't have to answer any damn questions. If you give us any shit or try to stop us, I'm sure my brother's going to sue you and Dowdsville for every dime and brick this damn town's got."

Katy brushed a stray lock of red hair back with one hand. "Eric knows everything that's gone on, Dan," she said sternly. "About the whole kangaroo court and everything. I told him."

Eddie Zelinsky appeared in the doorway with a wire basket. It contained Robert's clothes. He set it gently on an old wooden conference table in the center of the room. Under his arm, he carried a manilla envelope. Opening the bronze clasp, he upended it beside the basket. Robert's wrist watch and wallet slid out.

Katy shot a hand into the basket and lifted out a

pair of pale blue briefs. "Oooh, baby!" she said with a hand to her heart. Robert snatched them away.

"You can change in the men's room right around the corner," Patterson said, inclining his head toward the door.

Robert slipped on his watch, then picked up the basket and his wallet and left the conference room. The officer at the desk was talking quietly into the phone. He found the men's room only a few paces away. In no time he was out of his prison clothes and into Levi's, a black cotton pullover, and nearly new Reebok high-tops. Wadding his jailhouse blues into a ball, he thrust them into the basket and carried it back to the conference room.

"All I want to know," Patterson was saying stubbornly, "is where you been, Eric. That's not too much to ask, now, is it? I'm gonna have to file some kind of report on this."

Eric shook his head stubbornly and turned his back to the sheriff. "You ready, Bobby?" he called. "There's not much time left."

Robert tossed the basket carelessly on the conference table. "Can we make it?" he asked. The fingers of his right hand felt for the medallion under his shirt as he glanced at the watch on his left wrist.

Eric frowned. "It'll be close."

Suddenly voices were shouting in the outer office. Through the conference room's open door, Robert caught a fleeting glimpse of the desk officer leaping up from his seat. White papers fluttered about the outer room, as if someone had swept them off the officer's desk with an angry gesture. Eddie Zelinsky made a dash for the door, but Dan Patterson caught his arm and jerked him back. Then Patterson turned and calmly blocked the conference room door with one arm.

Another man appeared suddenly in the doorway nose to nose with the sheriff. He was a good-looking man of slightly more than middle age, still strong and tall, and his eyes were a familiar shade of green that had faded only a little with the years. His face, though, was wild and furious, and his fists were clenched as he tried to thrust his way into the room.

"Michael . . ." Sheriff Patterson started in a quietly controlled voice.

Robert caught his breath as his father knocked Patterson's obstructing arm out of his way. Michael Podlowsky stepped into the room. It was plain someone had awakened him. He'd gotten dressed hurriedly. His shirttail wasn't quite tucked in, and his thick gray hair was mashed in back where his head had rested on the pillow. Robert guessed that Sheriff Patterson had sent a deputy for him.

Michael Podlowsky glared about the room. Then his narrowed eyes snapped wide when he sighted Eric. "Thank God!" he muttered, his fists slowly unclenching.

Another figure appeared in the doorway. Marian Podlowsky was a small woman aging faster than her husband. She was slightly stooped through the shoulders and seemed to move with difficulty. She started into the room, then stopped at the threshold and stayed by Patterson's side, a beaming but nervous little willow of a woman.

"Thank God!" her husband said again. He held out his arms to embrace Eric. "Marian, he's alive!"

No one was prepared for Eric's reaction. His brother's face colored with rage. He knocked his father's hands away and shoved him roughly against the wall. "Keep your damn hands off me!" Eric shouted. He raised a fist and took a step toward Michael Podlowsky.

Katy moved quickly, putting herself physically between son and father. "Eric!" she said, planting a hand on his chest. "Don't. It's not worth it!"

Eric pointed an accusing finger at his father. "You had him arrested, you son of a bitch! You brought the charges on Bobby!"

Robert eased Katy out of the way and took her place between his brother and father. "Let it go, big brother," he urged in a tightly controlled voice. "It doesn't matter."

"The hell it doesn't!" Eric screamed. He glared at his mother in the doorway. "Why didn't you stop him, Mom?" he demanded. "Why don't you ever stand up to him? It wasn't right, but you just stood by, didn't you? Just like you're doing now!"

Marian Podlowsky bit her lip. Tears streamed suddenly over her cheeks as, wordlessly, she looked down at her shoes.

Michael Podlowsky pulled himself erect, his back to the wall, and tried to summon a semblance of pride as he smoothed his hair. "What were we to supposed to think?" he said in an almost plaintive voice. "You left on a weekend hiking trip in the mountains and disappeared." The older Podlowsky jerked a thumb toward Robert. "Then he came back a month later without you."

"We went crazy with worry, Eric," Marian Podlowsky said, speaking for the first time.

Patterson nodded from the doorway. Eddie Zelinsky and two more deputies hovered just behind him. "We had teams searchin' the trails for days," he agreed. "Never found hide nor trace of either of you boys."

"He refused to tell us where you were," Michael Podlowsky continued, without even a glance toward his youngest son. His voice rose as he became angry again. "He wouldn't tell us where *he'd* been, either! He wouldn't tell us anything!"

Eric's face darkened again. "So you just naturally thought he'd cut my throat and rolled me under some log." He backed off a pace and dealt the table leg a kick. The wire basket Robert had placed there went flying across the room and landed with a noisy crash.

Eric spun back around and faced his father. "You make me sick!" he shouted. "And I'm sick of the way you treat Bobby. He may forgive you for this, Dad, but I won't. I swear I never will!"

Marian Podlowsky's small, pleading voice was barely audible over the shouting. "Eric, don't say that to your father. Please!"

Robert stood paralyzed in the center of the room as Katy clung to his arm. He felt he should say something to stop the fighting. Yet, he couldn't think of any words. The animosity between him and his father ran deeper than even Eric knew. Now, it was tearing his whole family apart, and all he seemed able to do was stand by and watch.

"Eric," he managed at last, "we've got an appointment to keep."

Sheriff Patterson tried to assert himself again. "Now, why don't we all just settle down a little. Nobody's got any appointments, and nobody's goin' anywhere."

Eric drew himself to his full six-foot-two, broadshouldered height. "I told you, Dan," he said resolutely. "You've got nothing to hold Bobby for. You let us go, or there's going to be hell to pay."

Robert forced a little smile. "False arrest," he reminded. "But, I'm willing to forget all about this if you are."

Sheriff Patterson rubbed his chin. "Well, I really

don't have a reason to hold any of you," he admitted. "Eric looks alive enough to me."

"Son ..." Michael Podlowsky said, touching Eric's arm.

Eric shrugged him off violently. "Sons, goddamn it! Robert's your son, too. Yet you won't even tell him you're sorry." Eric backed up a pace, held up both his hands, and let go a slow breath. "Just keep away from me, Dad. Don't touch me. Don't even talk to me."

Robert stood less than two feet from his father. Michael Podlowsky turned toward him and glared. There was nothing in those eyes but hatred, hard and unyielding. His father just stood there, back to the wall, hands at his side, unwilling to reach out to him as he had to Eric.

It was no more than Robert expected. He slid past his father and went to his mother, put his arms around her, and patted the back of her head. Her hair, once the same bright blond as his own, was streaked with gray. He hadn't noticed before how rapidly she was aging. "I love you, Mom," he whispered. There was a finality in his voice that chilled him even as he said the words.

"I bought your last book," she whispered back. Her fingers clenched in his shirtsleeve as she clung to him. "I put it on the television with all your others between the bookends you gave me. Everybody sees them when they come visit."

He kissed her cheek, tasting the salt of her tears, then moved past her into the outer office. Katy Dowd came behind him.

"You've lost your job at the post office!" Michael Podlowsky shouted suddenly. "What are you going to do for money?"

Eric bent over his mother and wrapped her in his

big arms. "Fuck the post office," he answered without looking back at his father. He took his mother's face between his hands and gave her a quick kiss on the lips. "Don't worry, Mom. We'll be gone for a while, but we'll be fine."

Her lower lip trembled ever so slightly, and she bit down on it. Then she glanced past Eric. "Is Katy going with you?" she asked.

Katy spoke up before Eric could answer. "You bet I am, Mrs. Podlowsky."

Marian Podlowsky nodded then as she pushed Eric away. "Well, I won't worry so much if she's with you," she said as she reached out and squeezed Katy's hand. "You children have been together as long as I can remember."

Katy smiled and gave her a hug, too.

Michael Podlowsky stepped out of the conference room, making a visible effort to summon his dignity. Eric had humiliated him in front of Sheriff Patterson and all of Dowdsville's deputies. His face was bloodless. He couldn't seem to find anything to do with his hands.

Robert almost felt sorry for him. "Not much time," he reminded his brother.

Eddie Zelinsky suddenly stepped up with a pen in hand. He held out the battered copy of *A Pale Knock* that Robert had been reading in his cell. "I really love this horror stuff," he confessed. "If you're gonna leave this behind, would you mind autographing it?"

Robert stared at his old schoolmate in cool contempt. Then he took pen and book and wrote on the title page, *To Eddie: an asshole in high school, an utter asshole now*. He affixed his name with a flourish, closed the cover, and handed it back. "Best regards," he said with a wink.

Eric shoved open the outer door with more force

than was necessary. The heavy glass rattled in the metal frame as it struck the outside wall and started to swing shut again. He caught it and held it open.

"Bye, Mom," Robert called. He stared at his father, who hadn't made any further effort to move from his spot just outside the conference room. "Bye, Dad," he said quietly.

Katy gave Marian Podlowsky a final embrace. "Will you tell the library board members something for me?" she asked politely. When the older women nodded, Katy said, "I quit."

The three of them hurried out the door. Katy's jeep waited in the shadow of the old Dowdsville courthouse, which housed the jail. Katy turned the key and gunned the engine, put it in gear, and floored the accelerator, leaving a smear of rubber on the parking lot pavement as they pulled out.

Eric stared straight ahead, grim-faced in the front passenger's seat, gripping the roll bar with one hand so tightly his knuckles turned white.

In the backseat, Robert twisted to watch the police station's door. "I'll bet you anything Zelinsky tries to follow us."

Katy held the pedal all the way to the floorboard. "He's welcome to try," she muttered. The jeep flew down Dowdsville's Main Street past the library and the historical museum. The wind blew in their faces, cold and invigorating. Past the school and the gas stations they went, past the fast-food burger joints, past parked cars and darkened homes where citizens slept in peaceful, small-town bliss. In no time they reached the edge of town.

The Catskill Mountains loomed. "There's the reservoir," Robert said half to himself as a large lake glimmered off to their right. "We've got a good thirty-mile drive. It'll be a long hard hike on those trails in the dark. We'll have to ditch your jeep, too."

Katy nodded without speaking.

Eric took his harmonica out from its special pocket on his belt. He didn't play it, but tapped it nervously on his thigh.

The moon sank slowly toward the black rim of the world, like a cosmic clock ticking the desperate seconds. In its light, the shadow of the vehicle and its three occupants stretched far, far up the road.

Chapter Four

THANADOR, Palenoc's moon, floated just above the western horizon. No longer quite full, the mares and mountains still showed plainly upon its milky surface, creating its own otherworldly version of the Man-in-the-moon.

Mianur, the planet's pale blue ring, cut a swath across the zenith of night. Its timorous glow stretched from north to south, an unbroken bracelet upon which stars hung like jewels. Slowly, slowly it followed Thanador westward.

A tenuous gray cloud streamed ghostlike across the heavens. A wind was coming up.

Katy Dowd gave a small sigh as she brushed back a strand of hair that fluttered over her eyes. "I can't get used to it," she whispered as she gazed up at Mianur and Thanador. "All my life I've dreamed of a place like this. But books were as close as I ever expected to come to finding it." She ran a finger over the sleeve of her bleached *sekournen* leathers. "I can't believe how I entombed myself in that library."

Eric leaned on the waist-high wall that encircled the rooftop of Sheren-Chad. Far below the soaring tower sprawled the city of Rasoul, capital of Guran. Here and there, watch fires sparkled on some of the roofs. Along a few of the major streets, small glass globes of *sekoy-melin* shone, suspended from posts. Otherwise the dark outlines of houses, shops, and buildings spread farther and farther outward and up into the distant eastern hills.

"Look!" Katy murmured suddenly, pointing.

In the distance a matched pair of dragons swept inland from the Great Lake. The undersides of their wings burned with a golden, bioluminescent fire. "*Sekournen*," Eric explained. "Dragonriders returning from patrol."

"I haven't seen that color before," Katy replied, wide-eyed as she followed the dragons' flight toward the black hills. "Where are they going?"

"The Valley of Beasts," Eric answered. "Sometimes a *sekournen* on important business will land right here." He ran his hand along a particularly deep scar in the thick stone wall, the mark left by a huge talon. "Most often, though, a rider leaves his *sekoye* in the valley. It's"—he hesitated thoughtfully—"an unusual place."

"I hope I can see it someday," Katy said. The pair of dragons disappeared beyond the hills. "That gold was beautiful."

He nodded. Doe's mount, Sunrunner, gave a gold to make the sun itself envious. But Doe and Evander were far away in Wystoweem by now, and Katy had yet to meet them. She'd seen Alanna's mount, Mirrormist, whose wings gave a pale amber light, and Valis's Brightstar, who gave a red glow to rival a ruby's charm. Along with Roderigo Diez, Valis and Alanna had been waiting outside the cave with Jago and Trevin to fly them to Rasoul upon their return.

Katy had met Shadowfire, too, his own dragon. Eric had carried her in his arms upon his *sekoye's* neck, her breathing deep against him, her hands closed tight on his wrists as the wind whipped by them, filling his nostrils with the smell of her hair. She'd shown no fear at all of Shadowfire or flying. She'd even sang a little when she knew the tunes that he played on his harmonica.

Eric gently closed his eyes and touched the small silver instrument in the pocket of his belt. He could feel Shadowfire stirring like a faint strand of music in the recesses of his mind. It was ever with him now, that soft music. As long as he or Shadowfire lived, he would hear it. He opened his eyes again and gazed toward the hills, envisioning an opalescent fire soaring out of the night. But the music in his head was muted, and he knew that in the Valley of Beasts, Shadowfire was at rest.

He still couldn't quite believe he had been lucky enough to bond with one of the great *sekoye*. He leaned his elbows on the wall and pressed his palms together under his chin as he stared outward. The wind whispered in his ears. The sweet clean smell of the Great Lake hung in the air like a perfume. He felt completely at ease for the first time in years.

Katy's hand settled softly on his shoulder. "I've never felt this kind of peace in you before," she said quietly.

He wondered how to respond to that. On Paradane, he and Katy had been sometime-lovers. Paradane. He didn't even think of it as Earth anymore.

"Right now," he said solemnly, "we're smack in the middle of a war that's lasted more than a thousand years." He turned and took her hand in his, then drew her close against him. "There are forces and powers at work you don't understand yet. But you're right, Katy, I've never known the kind of peace I've found here."

Eric felt the slight tremor that ran through her, but she said no more. He wrapped her tightly in his arms, and together they gazed toward Thanador. Eventually, he lifted her chin with a finger, turned her lips up to his own, and kissed her.

"I'm glad you're here," he whispered. "I want to share this world with you."

The wind whipped her hair across her face again. Katy gave a toss of her head as she bit her lip. Her eyes seemed on the verge of misting over for an instant, then her expression hardened. She seemed to go cold in Eric's arms, and he felt all her mental walls dropping quietly into place.

"What does that mean, Eric?" she said in a voice thick with old emotion.

He swallowed as he met her unflinching gaze, realizing he had hurt her. "I don't know," he admitted. "Maybe it's time I tried to figure out what I want."

She freed herself from his embrace and looked beyond Sheren-Chad's wall. The wind made streamers of her hair. "Yeah," she said distantly, hugging herself. "Maybe it's time."

Eric stood there with his arms empty, unable to think of anything to say.

Metal gears creaked, interrupting his confusion. He looked toward the sound. Sheren-Chad's roof was a wide, circular expanse. In the very center, a huge iron tripod rose. Atop it sat a great glass globe containing radiant *sekoy-melin*—a luciferase-like chemical milked from the dragons' wings—that gave off light. Directly beneath the tripod was the door and stairway that led down inside the tower.

The door swung upward slowly on a concealed mechanism, and Roderigo Diez emerged. He hailed them with a quiet wave. *"Namue rana sekoye!"* he said pleasantly.

"Namue shi hami rana sekoye," Eric responded with a grin and a nod toward Katy.

Katy's eyes narrowed suspiciously. "You're talking

about me again," she accused. The hurt was gone from her voice. She regarded the two of them, playful once more.

The little Spaniard pushed his hands into his sleeves and made a slight bow. His old eyes twinkled. "Forgive me, Katy Dowd," he said in his oddly accented English. "I've been here a long time, but I haven't quite forgotten all the languages of Paradane. *Namue rana sekoye* is how we call Eric and Robert here. It means Brothers of the Dragon."

"And I corrected him," Eric interrupted, reaching out for her hand again, glad when she didn't resist. "*Namue shi hami rana sekoye*—Brothers and Sisters of the Dragon. You, me, and Robert. But also Alanna and Valis, Evander and Doe ... anyone who fights with us against the Heart of Darkness."

Katy gave him a questioning look, but Roderigo Diez caught her other hand and pressed it between his two palms. "Don't worry," he told her, rushing on. "Shortly you will speak the Guran language as well as Eric and Robert do. That is what I came to tell you." His bald head bobbed up and down as he glanced at Eric. "Phlogis is ready."

"What are we waiting for, then?" Eric said. He pulled Katy toward the door.

"You sure know how to show a girl a good time," Katy remarked as she let herself be led. Then she added, "This just better be a good time."

Roderigo Diez paused with one foot on the top stair. "You've seen a lot of strange things, Katy Dowd," he said gently, "and there are more to come. Just remember, no harm can come to you while you're within these walls, and we will both be at your side."

Katy raised one eyebrow and squeezed Eric's hand. "Was that supposed to put me at ease?" she asked.

They followed Diez down the narrow stone staircase. At the bottom of the steps, the old Spaniard touched the lever that closed the door to the rooftop. He then turned, touched Katy's shoulder, and waved his right arm to direct her attention to the chamber in which they stood. More than a dozen fist-sized globes of *sekoy-melin,* mounted in brackets on the walls, provided illumination. Broad, rectangular tables stood at equal intervals around the circular room. Upon the tables, neatly arranged, were rows of basins and pitchers. Around the walls, lockers and shelves were placed, containing towels and piles of the soft leather garments the dragonriders wore.

"This is the lavatorium," Diez explained. "Some of the riders land their *sekoye* on the roof and enter the Sheren this way. They wash and clean themselves here and take fresh clothing if they need it."

"Eric brought me here for a bath after our flight from the gate," Katy said, brushing a hand down the front of her tunic. The cream-colored leather matched the leather trousers she wore. Her boots were a shade darker. "He gave me these clothes, too. This is the softest stuff I've ever felt."

"It's the molted skin of young, growing *sekoye,*" Diez said as he led the way across the chamber, through a door on the opposite side, and down yet another flight of stairs.

They emerged in a wide hallway. Heavy tapestries hung from the walls. The embroidery on them told stories of Guran's history and of the history of the Domains of Light. A small globe of *melin,* perched on a narrow iron tripod, cast a yellowish light on a pair of huge wooden doors. The dark wood of those doors was painted with strange wheel-like patterns and symbols.

"Bobby says they resemble the hex signs found on

the barns and homes of the Pennsylvania Dutch," Eric whispered to her.

Katy shrugged even as she frowned. "He's the horror writer, so I guess he'd know such things." She gave Eric a look from the corner of her eye. "Why are you whispering?"

"A librarian should ask," he said. "This is Phlogis's sanctum."

Before he could knock, one of the two large doors abruptly opened and swung outward. Robert poked his head around. "Welcome to Language 101," he said. Then his voice dropped. In a surprisingly good Boris Karloff accent, he added, "Come in." He hunched one shoulder, crooked a finger, and gestured for them to enter.

"It's a set from an old Fu Manchu movie," Katy muttered as she passed through the doors and swept her gaze around the chamber.

The only illumination came from two big cauldrons on the west side of the room. Twin spears of dark red radiance lanced up from their bowels and bled a peculiar light over everything. A haze of smoke wafted through the room as well. Here and there, eddies of vapor curled and fluttered in unfelt drafts.

The center of the room was marked with a wide circle, the border of which was formed of gold that had been melted and poured in a track. The stone floor within the circle was painted with a pattern far more elaborate than those on the outer doors. Set at various points within the pattern, gems and crystals of astonishing size shimmered and glimmered.

Eric paid little attention to the gems, though. He looked to a place *above* the circle, a place in midair where shadow held sway and strands of darkness radiated into the unseeable upper reaches of the sanctum, a place where even the arcane light of the cauldrons feared to go. His heartbeat quickened, and he felt himself tensing. No matter how many times he came to this room, he could never prepare himself to meet the creature called Phlogis. He could not see him yet. But he could feel him, stirring there like a spider at the heart of a horrible black web.

"Eric, tell me what's going on," Katy demanded. Her voice rose sharply as she stared into that dark place. She took a deep breath and blew it out. She crept right up to the edge of the golden circle and stopped. When she spoke again, her voice was under control. "I feel something," she said curiously. She pointed straight at Phlogis. "Coming from there."

"Stay calm, Kat," Robert told her as he left his place at the door to stand beside Eric. "The anger you feel isn't yours."

Katy turned toward him and raised an eyebrow. "I'm not angry," she answered. "Why did you say that?"

Eric, Robert, and Diez all exchanged glances. Eric was acutely aware of the knot of tension in his own shoulders, and his fists were clenched at his sides. In Phlogis's presence it was always like this. "What *do* you feel, then?" he asked.

Katy tilted her head thoughtfully and stared once more into the darkness. Eric still couldn't actually *see* Phlogis in his web, yet he felt sure that Katy somehow could. "It's like a wave," she said, "or a constant breeze inside my head. Kind of warm, but not threatening."

Diez's eyes narrowed as he moved to one side of the circle, the better to observe her. "That is a most unusual reaction, *señorita*."

"Not threatening?" Robert muttered. He shouted toward the web. "You're slipping Phlogis. You must be getting old."

A vague form stirred at the center of the darkness. There was the hint of an arm, a turn of a head. *I am five hundred years, Robert Podlowsky.*

Robert gave a small gasp and grabbed his head. Eric clutched his temple at the same time. Even Diez winced and took an involuntary step away from the golden boundary. Phlogis's mental touch possessed a saw-edge.

Katy looked at them in surprise, then turned back toward Phlogis. "Hello," she said calmly. She touched her temple. "I'm hearing you in my head, aren't I?"

"It doesn't hurt her, big brother," Robert whispered incredulously.

Eric remembered the first time Phlogis spoke to him. He'd felt like a knife was being pushed slowly through his brain. It wasn't much different now, though he'd grown more accustomed to the experience. Why didn't it bother Katy? And why didn't she feel the wave of psychic anger that permeated the sanctum?

"Can you hear me?" Katy called when Phlogis didn't answer her question. She started to step across the circle. Her toes touched the edge of the pattern painted within.

"Please, *señorita*!" Roderigo Diez caught her arm and pulled her back. "You must never violate the circle!"

Katy retreated a step, but she appealed again to the being in the dark web. "Why have you brought me here?" she asked reasonably.

Robert put a hand to his throat, miming self-strangulation with his tongue hanging out, his head bobbing from side to side. "To pluck out your eyes with red-hot tweezers, singe your toes with pokers, drive spikes under your nails, and make you read Kant until your brain runs out your ear," he told her. He took her hand and drew her over to the pair of red-glowing cauldrons.

"How can I read Kant if they pluck out my eyes?" Katy responded sarcastically.

Robert squinted at her as if through one monocled eye as he walked away from her to stand beside his brother. "Ve haf our vays."

Pain stabbed through Eric's head again. *She is most unusual, Eric Podlowsky,* Phlogis said. *She does not fear me, nor does she feel my anger.*

Eric bit his lip and pressed fingers to his temple, realizing that Phlogis was speaking only to him. He replied silently, allowing Phlogis to drink his thoughts. *Katy's strong, stronger than anyone I know. There's no one else from Paradane I would have trusted enough to bring here. I don't understand, though. It's almost as if she's immune to you.*

The vague shape that was Phlogis answered with a hint of bemusement. *Am I a disease? But yes, I sense her strength, and there is more about her that intrigues me. Yet I have little time to spend here, Eric. Our enemy is moving in the night, and a strange new force stirs the ether. It commends my attention.*

"Whatever it is we're here to do," Katy said suddenly, almost as if she had somehow overheard Phlogis, "let's do it and get it over with."

"That's my Kat," Robert muttered approvingly.

Phlogis sent his voice throughout the chamber. *It is already begun, Katherine Dowd.* A hand of smoke and shadow pointed toward the cauldrons. Between the twin lances of light, another shadow began to form, but quickly the darkness fell from it like old skin. A boy floated there, perhaps fourteen years of age, naked, balanced in the air between the beams, dark hair flowing about his shoulders, eyes laughing.

Eric's heart lurched as he recognized the boy. "Danyel!" he shouted, lunging forward. Roderigo Diez shot out a hand to stop him. Robert also caught him from behind.

Katy turned a confused look from Eric to the young figure that hovered spectrally above the cauldrons. He was not quite tangible. The light shone through him, and the wall, too, could be seen right through his skin. She took a step back, then stopped, one hand to her mouth as if to stifle a cry.

Danyel smiled and extended a small hand toward her. Katy hesitated. Tentatively, she reached out to accept it. Fingertips touched. Without warning, Danyel's form melted and changed. No more than a shimmer of light, he flowed around her, enveloping her. Katy flung back her head and closed her eyes. A sigh, almost of pleasure, escaped her parted lips. For a long moment she stood absolutely still, her expression relaxed, as she bathed in the glow.

Eric had not forgotten the moment when he stood in that same place, when a creature named Sumeek stepped out of the cauldrons' light and entered him. Possession, Diez had called it, though it was nothing like the possession his brother wrote about in some of his horror books.

While he kept his eyes on Katy, he leaned over and touched his brother's arm. "We haven't had time to talk," he whispered. "What did you learn about your friend, Scott?"

"Later," Robert said curtly. His gaze was not on Katy, but on Phlogis, and he wore a calculating look. Eric started to object, then realized he was interrupting a private conversation between his brother and their shadowy host.

The light withdrew from Katy and became Danyel once more. Katy opened her eyes and a smile of understanding lit up her face. "Now is the time for all good men and women to come to the aid of their country," she said flawlessly in the language of Guran. "He touched my brain somehow and taught me his speech!"

"Welcome to Palenoc, Katherine Dowd," Phlogis said in a sonorous voice from within his circle. Rarely did he waste his power to manifest real speech.

Roderigo Diez nodded approvingly. "Now you are truly *Hami rana sekoye,*" he added.

Above the cauldrons, Danyel put on a wistful grin. Silently, he fixed Eric with a pale, lingering gaze. One hand made the slightest of waves as he faded slowly away, becoming a vapor that wafted into nothingness.

A tear seeped down Eric's cheek. For a moment, Katy was forgotten. He moved past her, clutched at both the cauldrons as if for support and stared up into the empty space where Danyel had appeared. The boy had been a little brother to him, a *sekournen* in his own right, and a young partner to Alanna and Valis. He had given his life, though, in this very chamber to save Phlogis and destroy an evil necromancer named Keris Chaterit.

"I'm taking care of Shadowfire," Eric whispered through a tight throat, hoping Danyel could somehow hear. The boy had been Shadowfire's original rider. The great *sekoye* had nearly died from loneliness at the breaking of that bond.

"He knows," Phlogis said. His words sounded almost soothing, despite the ever-present anger than tinged them. "Danyel wanted to help in this way."

"I still don't understand everything," Katy said, scratching her red head in puzzlement. "You speak as if Danyel was dead."

Barely visible within the circle, Phlogis nodded. "He *is* dead, Katherine" came the answer. "So am I."

* * *

Eric tried hard to fall asleep. Though he had slept most of the day away after the long flight from the Gate to Rasoul, he still felt tired. He'd spent the entire evening after the events in Phlogis's sanctum explaining things to Katy, answering her questions, and it had left him exhausted.

The Sheren was quiet as a tomb. He opened his eyes long enough to glance around his darkened room. He should have left a lamp burning, but he'd extinguished it earlier. He turned on his right side. He turned on his back. Folding his hands under his head, he gazed through the unshuttered window on the far side of his small chamber. Gray bands of clouds rolled across the stars, but the wind was too high. It made no sound that he could hear.

Tomorrow, he would resume his journey to Wystoweem to rejoin Evander and Doe. Councillor Salyt had sent a message to Phlogis requesting his presence. The old woman refused to leave Sheren Shago without him as part of her escort. Eric wished that he knew something of the nature of her mission, but not even Phlogis would tell him more. The specifics awaited him in Wystoweem, a nation that bordered the Dark Lands. That alone was enough to make him restless.

He turned over on his stomach, punched his pillow a few times until it made a crumpled wad around which he wrapped his arms. With a sigh, he laid down his head and closed his eyes. A soundless breeze played over his body as he stretched nude upon the sheets. "Sleep," he muttered to himself. It was almost a pleading. "Sleep."

His parents' faces swirled up dreamlike as his breathing slowed. He remembered pushing his father at the Dowdsville jail. He'd never done such a thing before, had never considered raising a hand to either of his parents. Yet he'd never admitted the anger he felt toward his father. He didn't want to deal with such emotions now, though; he pushed the faces away. "Sleep," he murmured.

Robert stared up at him from the darkness behind his closed lids, and his lips curled in a weary smile. It felt good to have his little brother back. He'd missed him. But Bobby had returned to Paradane seeking answers to questions about the death of his friend, Scott Silver, whose ghost had led them to this fantastic world.

There hadn't been time to ask what, if anything, his brother had learned. *Time to share your secrets, Bobby,* Eric thought drowsily. *I know some of them, but not all.* He punched his pillow without opening his eyes and adjusted his position. "Soon," he promised himself, whispering into the pillowcase. There was a clipping he'd found in his brother's wallet shortly after coming to Palenoc. Something about Scott's murder.

He shifted his legs until one foot hung off the side of the bed. Robert's face faded. For a time there was only the darkness and a kind of slow, unending tumble past all awareness.

The parade of faces resumed with a pair of burning eyes and a half-seen visage. Phlogis was an old and dangerous creature in this world where ghosts were real. A *dando,* a murdered soul, he sought revenge on his killer in the only way possible: by guiding the war against the ruler of the Dark Lands, Shandal Karg. He alone, in his time, had stood against her with his sorcery when she turned her greedy eyes on his nation, and she had struck him down. Now, though dead, he ran the closest thing this world had to a secret service.

Phlogis melted away.

Katy regarded him from the sea of his repose. Her red hair stirred about her face, and her blue eyes flashed with a crystalline fire. Lips that he knew so well parted ever so slightly.

Eric loved her. Or maybe he only loved the idea of loving her. He'd never made up his mind. Katy had always been there by his side, close when he needed her, ever since they were kids. The fact both attracted and repelled him. Maybe he didn't love her at all. Maybe she was just comfortable. Why hadn't either of them ever really left Dowdsville the way Robert had?

She held out her arms and waved to him. Her body gleamed, clothed only in a soft, nebulous light. Saying nothing, she kissed him. Her hands were cool on his face as she drew him down, and he responded to her touch, feeling stirrings that only confused him. She sighed into his ear, ran her nails down his back, and kissed him again. Her knee pressed between his legs.

Then quietly, Katy began to laugh. It was a high, tinkling sound, musical, like the breaking of delicate glass. Eric listened to her with a budding unease. Katy's laugh was not like that at all. He tried to free himself, to back away and look at her, but she clung to him with surprising strength and shook her head, sweeping her hair teasingly across his face, all the while laughing until he caught her head between his hands and forced her to hold still.

The gleam in her eyes was too hard, and it was not a fire that filled them, but the glitter of ice! The red strands of her hair darkened as he held her, turned black as the night, and began to lash wildly at his face. Screaming, he tried to turn away, but not before he saw sprouting among those locks a twisted ebony horn!

Eric sat bolt upright in bed, horribly aroused, shivering and drenched with sweat. His pillow lay on the floor. The sound of laughter still rang out of his dream, and he could still see that face as he had in so many other nightmares.

"Shandal Karg!" The name exploded from him like a curse. *The Heart of Darkness.* She ruled the Dark Lands, and in his first hour on Palenoc, he had earned her enmity by accidentally discovering a thousand years old secret—how her precious creatures, the *chimorgs,* once thought to be nearly immortal, could be killed with their own horns. Now she wanted to punish him for that deed.

A cold dread seized him. He had never had a premonition before, but Shandal Karg had just appeared to him in Katy's form. She knew about Katy! He leaped from bed and ran from his room. The hall beyond his door was dimly lit, not with precious *sekoymelin,* but with cresset oil lamps. Naked, he raced through the corridors to find Katy's room.

"Katy!" he cried, throwing his weight against the wooden door. It didn't budge. His terror growing, he called her name again. A second time the door held as he slammed his shoulder against it. "Katy!"

Another door swung open halfway up the corridor. Roderigo Diez thrust his bald head out. "What's wrong?" he called, clutching a thin robe about his body.

Eric didn't answer. He backed up a step. With an iron fury, he kicked the door. The force of his *ki* shout did nothing to muffle the splintering of the wooden framework. The door smashed backward and twisted off the upper hinge.

Katy lay upon her narrow bed, heaving and gasping, still apparently deep asleep, unable to awaken. Over her hovered a black amorphous shape with eyes that shone with a cold malevolence. A semblance of a hand reached down to cover Katy's mouth and nose. It began to suffocate her!

Eric swung a fist at the creature, encountering nothing save a numbing cold as his hand passed through it. It had no substance! Nevertheless, he threw a kick. "Katy!" he shouted desperately, "wake up! Fight back!"

Roderigo Diez brushed him aside. In one hand he held a leather pouch. With a sweeping motion he flung it, scattering its contents on the air. Dried brown leaves fluttered over and through the vaguely human shape, settled about the room and on Katy's sheeted form.

Those icy eyes turned briefly toward the old Spaniard as if to mock him, and the grip tightened on Katy's face.

"The cremat leaves have no effect!" Diez shouted in dismay.

The leaves of the cremat tree could drive off any ghostly presence. Eric had seen them work before. There was no time to ponder it. Maybe the monster wasn't a ghost. He had no doubt at all, though, that Shandal Karg had sent it. The Heart of Darkness was jealous and wanted him for herself.

Eric grabbed Katy's hand and tried to pull her from the bed. Maybe he could drag her from the creature's grasp. Yet, even as he tried, it reached out with another hand and caught his face.

A cold like nothing Eric had ever experienced forced him to leap away. A cough wracked him, and he gasped for air. His lungs felt frozen. Diez tried to pull him back, but Eric shrugged him off. Katy's chest rose and fell in violent jerks. One hand clenched in the sheets, as if she were somehow struggling to wake up. How much longer could she last?

Eric seized up a chair from the small writing table near the door and flung it with all his might. It passed completely through the monster, shattering into pieces against the opposite wall with a noise like brittle thunder.

A psychic shriek ripped through the room. Eric reeled, staggering back against the small table, toppling it as he fell sideways. Roderigo Diez crumpled to the floor, clutching his head. On the bed Katy screamed, too, and gasped for air.

The black shape fled for the open window near the bed. It dissolved before reaching it, turning into a vapor, a noxious odor, then nothing.

Diez rose to his knees. "It smells like a rotted corpse!" he said disgustedly as he adjusted his sleeping robe.

Eric extricated himself from the wreckage of the table and rushed to Katy's side. She struggled up on one elbow, pale as frost on a windowpane in winter, coughing and rubbing her throat. Snagging Eric's hand, she pulled herself into a sitting position.

"What the hell *was* that thing?" Eric demanded as Roderigo Diez bent over the bedside.

"I don't know," the old Spaniard said. "It was like nothing I've experienced before, and I've been here a lot longer than you." He reached out and touched a spot on Katy's face with a fingertip. She pushed his hand away.

"Let him look at you," Eric told her sternly. "He's a doctor."

"A doctor?" Katy managed.

Roderigo Diez nodded as he touched her face again. "We all earn our way around here somehow, *bonita mia.*"

Eric bit his lip and walked around the foot of the bed to the place where the thing had disappeared. Diez was right about the smell of rotted flesh. The odor still hung in the air. He went to the window and stared out, seeing nothing but the darkened rooftops of sleeping Rasoul. When he turned back, though, something caught his eye.

Among the fragments of the broken chair, lay a dirty bone.

Chapter Five

WHEN his friends were all in bed, Robert crept silently back in the sanctum. The upper levels of the Sheren were all but empty in the hours before dawn. He encountered no one. A few small cresset lamps lit the corridors, creating wavering puddles of light separated by stretches of darkness.

Robert slipped inside the sanctum. The cauldrons gave a smaller glow than before, and shadows ruled the chamber. He paid them little attention as he turned toward the circle. He bit his lip. The golden boundary possessed its own dim glow. He had never seen that before. Each of the gems and crystals within, no matter how small, also shimmered with barely perceptible light. The painted pattern of which they were part, indeed the floor itself within the circle, was gone.

It was as if he were looking down through a hole in the floor into a star field that went on forever, on and on into infinity, and the stars were bits of rose and red and green and yellow, white crystal and diamond, turquoise and sapphire.

He backed away from the golden edge, feeling an unaccustomed vertigo. He climbed cliffs and mountains. Heights didn't bother him. This, though, was something beyond his experience. Still, he swallowed and stole forward once again and peered past the boundary.

You will not fall, Robert Podlowsky. Phlogis's voice rasped across his brain. *There is nothing there but the floor.*

Robert brushed a hand gingerly across his forehead. "Polo," he corrected with a frown. There was nothing to do but endure the discomfort inside his head. Phlogis could manifest a voice only with difficulty. He gazed up into the blackness above the circle. A pair of red eyes gleamed, fixed on him.

There were many kinds of ghosts on Palenoc. *Dandos* such as Phlogis were among the most feared. When someone committed murder, the victim's ghost always sought vengeance. That spirit, focused totally on one task, was called a *dando*. Once avenged, the placated spirit rested.

But if the ghost could not avenge itself, it became an *ankou,* a creature of unfocused anger, malevolent, a danger to all.

For five hundred years, Phlogis had striven to avenge himself on the Heart of Darkness. He was close, though, close to crossing whatever line separated the *dando* from the *ankou.* His anger radiated throughout the chamber like raw heat. Only the circle and the gems within it, pattern magic of his own design, allowed him to retain a semblance of sanity.

The being before him was the prime guardian of all the Domains of Light, the last loose alliance that stood against the Dark Lands and Shandal Karg. Robert didn't waste time with pleasantries, but got straight to the point.

"When I was here before," he spoke grimly, "you said there was a spot of darkness in me. It made you suspicious. You didn't trust me."

Phlogis interrupted. *That has changed, Namue rana Sekoye.*

Robert raised a surprised eyebrow. "It's not there anymore?"

A part of the shadows coalesced around those eyes. A thin, old man, no more than a silhouette, sat cross-legged among the softly glowing gems and crystals, seeming to hover in a lotus position in the center of the strange star field. Phlogis folded his hands in his lap and regarded Robert.

The darkness is still inside you, he answered without hesitation. *I trust you despite it.*

"I want you to try to penetrate it," Robert said quickly. "You tried before. Try harder this time."

Phlogis fixed him with that red-eyed gaze. *You know that I can see your thoughts, Robert. I know that you have murdered a man.*

Robert bristled. "Executed," he answered stonily. "The punk gunned down my friend, Scott Silver, and ran away. I hunted him down and found him. Then, yes, I killed him with my bare hands." He didn't mention the bastard had pulled another gun once Robert had cornered him in an alley, alone and separated from his gang. He didn't even pretend to himself it had been self-defense. He had stalked the punk for nights, picked his moment, then confronted him, all with the intention of avenging his friend.

"Except . . ." Robert swallowed and glanced away. He had requested this meeting. Now, he didn't know what to say, how to explain his feelings to this five-hundred-year-old ghost of a wizard. When he resumed, he couldn't keep the confusion from his voice. "Except I don't think Scott is dead. I think he's here. In Palenoc. Maybe in the Dark Lands."

Phlogis made a half-remembered imitation of a sigh. His shoulders drew up, and he tilted his head sympathetically. *Your friend died in your arms on the sidewalk outside the club where the attack occurred. I see the thought and the image in your mind with painful clarity. I taste your grief.*

Robert paced across the room toward the cauldrons, turned back toward the circle and lifted his head stubbornly. "I have the memory of that," he snapped. "But I have no proof that any of it ever happened!" He threw up his hands and bit his lip, trying to organize his thoughts. "Phlogis, on Paradane the authorities have made a religion of keeping records. I checked everything! No death certificate, no police report. The county coroner had never heard of Scott Silver. The bar owner has no recollection of any shooting. Not one of New York's newspapers carried an obituary mentioning Scott's name!"

The clipping you carry in your wallet, Phlogis responded evenly.

Robert reached into the left hip pocket of his Levi's. He had not yet given himself completely over to the leather fashions of the dragonriders. From his wallet he extracted the clipping he had carried for months. That, too, Phlogis had seen in his mind. He read:

MAN SHOT TO DEATH OUTSIDE BAR

A twenty-five-year-old man was attacked and shot to death as he exited a popular West Village bar at Seventh Avenue and Grove Street about 10:20 p.m. last night.

The man, who has not been identified pending notification of family, had just left The Monster, a popular bar, when witnesses say a gang of five youths, approaching from the opposite direction, attacked him without apparent provocation. Two witnesses reported that when the victim attempted to fight back, one of the youths drew a pistol and fired three shots. The youths then fled.

The victim was taken by ambulance to St. Vincent's Hospital where he was pronounced dead on arrival of gunshot wounds to the chest.

Robert crumpled the clipping and shoved it back into the wallet. "It doesn't mention Scott's name," he said. He thrust the wallet back into his hip pocket. "What if I just picked this up somewhere? What if it isn't really about Scott at all?"

A vapor swirled around Phlogis and wafted away into the upper reaches. For a moment, silence dominated the room. Phlogis touched one of the nearest crystals with a long finger before he looked again at Robert. *Perhaps you want to* believe *your friend is alive,"* he said gently.

Robert stared at the creature inside the circle. Phlogis's tone caught him completely by surprise. He could still feel the *dando's* rage, and their communication still hurt his brain. He held a secret dread of Phlogis, which was no longer secret, he realized a split second after the thought took form. It had not occurred to him that Phlogis might yet be capable of compassion.

"There's more," Robert said finally. "Scott and I took a trip together. We toured the Orient, visiting the great temples and martial arts centers, studying and refining our techniques." A wan smile turned up the corners of his mouth as he remembered his friend. "Scott's almost as good a karateka as Eric and I. Anyway, when the trip was over I talked him into moving from Florida to New York. He took an apartment near mine."

Phlogis raised a hand to interrupt him. *I see these things in your thoughts,* he reminded.

Robert threw his hands up again and paced to the edge of the circle once more. "Why not?" he said. "The memories are crystal clear in my head, Phlogis. And yet ..." He bit his lip and rubbed the palms of his hands nervously together. He'd tried to reason all this out before coming here. Sometimes, he thought it almost made sense. Other times, he thought he was going crazy.

"Phlogis," he finally said, "while Scott and I were in China, the last stop on our tour, we made a pilgrimage to Hangzhou City in the Zhejian Province. Not far from there is a mountain called Hengshan."

The creature in the circle nodded. *You love mountains. You are a skilled climber.*

Robert ignored the interruption. His mind raced as he tried to make sense of his memories. "It's considered a holy mountain by the locals," he continued. "Very high up, there's a Buddhist monastery called the Suspended Temple. It's built on the side of the mountain and seemingly hangs straight out into air."

You and Scott Silver spent the night there, Phlogis said, reading his thoughts again.

Robert sucked hard on his upper lip and curled one hand into a fist. "We left the next morning," he said. "Halfway down the trail, I fell and broke my leg. Scott carried me the rest of the way down. I remember it as if it happened yesterday." He squeezed the bridge of his nose and winced. The more he thought, the more he tried to question, the more his head hurt. And the pain had nothing to do with Phlogis's psychic voice.

"Two weeks ago I had my right leg x-rayed," he said. "It's never been broken. Scott never rented the apartment near mine. The rent on his Sarasota place is past due. He never gave notice that he was quitting at the dojo where he taught." He ran a hand through his hair and squeezed the back of his neck. "I don't think he ever left the Suspended Temple, Phlogis. I think something happened there." He paused again thoughtfully. "I think we found a gateway to Palenoc."

Phlogis failed to show surprise. *Alanna and I talked*

after you returned to Paradane, he said. *You expressed to her a disconcerting familiarity with our world.*

"I knew the name of your moon," Robert told him. "And the first time I glimpsed an image of Shandal Karg, it paralyzed me with fear. There were other things as well." He stopped his pacing at the edge of the golden circle and stared downward into that strange infinity. "The title of my last book," he said uneasily, "was *A Pale Knock.* Palenoc. Is that a coincidence?" He shook his head slowly. "I reread it three times while I was home. I think it was a message from my subconscious."

Phlogis rose slowly to his feet. If he stood on the floor or floated in that strange starry hole, Robert couldn't tell. *I cannot help you, Robert Podlowsky,* Phlogis said. *I cannot penetrate the dark veil in your mind. You must excuse me now. There is mysterious activity tonight in the Gray Kingdoms and a phenomenon unknown to me. I must learn what I can before sunrise compels me to rest.*

Robert knew that not all of his host's information came from living sources. On Palenoc, the dead told tales. He frowned to himself, aware that he was taking too much of Phlogis's time. "Wait," he asked anyway. "What is the Dream Stream, and how do I get there?"

For a brief instant, surprise totally replaced the rage that Phlogis generated. *How do you know of the Dream Stream?*

Robert closed his eyes and spoke in a somber voice:

> "Sing woe, remember,
> And pity us our plight;
> The Dead dwell in the Dark Lands
> And the Kingdoms of Night."

"That's a fragment of a poem that closes the first chapter of *A Pale Knock,*" he said, opening his eyes again. "In my book, it's a ghost that speaks those words. But here, in this world, the Dark Lands and the Kingdoms of Night are real. They exist." He closed his eyes again and recited a verse from another part of his book.

> "I sail a tide
> That is not what it seems;
> The soul is a ship
> That rides the Dream Stream."

Robert forced a self-conscious smile. "All the ghosts in my book speak in poetry," he said. "But if the Dark Lands and the Kingdoms of Night exist in Palenoc," he said, "then I ask you again. What is the Dream Stream? I think there's a chance that Scott is waiting for me there."

Phlogis bent down and plucked two of the starlike gems that shone at his feet and closed his fists around them. When he opened his hands a moment later, small balls of diamond-colored light levitated from his palms into the air. One drifted toward the great wooden doors and through them. The other floated slowly between the pair of cauldrons and through the wall. Robert knew there was a panel there. In fact, there were several panels throughout the sanctum that led to other parts of the Sheren.

The Dream Stream, Phlogis said somberly, *is what your world calls the Astral Plane. It is a place frought with danger, yet I know how desperately you seek your friend and will not discourage you. If you get into trouble, though, you must allow me to draw you back.*

"Agreed," Robert said.

The sanctum's main doors opened, and a sleepy-eyed Alanna walked in. She wore nothing more than a thin white robe that was belted with a cord. Her bare feet made soft sounds as she strode across the stone floor to Robert's side.

He touched her hand, noting how the red light shone on her raven hair. Her fingers curled into his and interlaced. There had been little time to talk since his return, but he had so much to say to her. He had missed Alanna in his time away from Guran.

"Hello, *Kaesha*," he whispered, using a local endearment. "I trust you've been practicing?" His martial art techniques fascinated her, and he had spent some time teaching her the basics. She was a superb student.

Alanna nodded. "Eric took over my training in your absence."

"He's probably ruined you," Robert said with a mock frown.

A soft grinding of gears and a brief, cool draft caused them both to turn. A section of wall just beyond the cauldrons slid closed again, and Maris, Alanna's sister, walked toward them. The soft white hem of her nightdress swept the floor behind her. She moved with tiny, delicate steps.

"Welcome back, Robert," she said gently. She offered her hand. Robert raised it to his lips and kissed it.

"It's Councillor Maris now, I understand," he said. Her eyes were the same dark brown as Alanna's, her hair the same shining black. She wore it loose, though, while her sister bound hers at the nape of her neck. They might have been twins. Robert knew, though, that Maris was two years younger.

"You're in your nightclothes, sister," Alanna said suddenly, "but you don't look as if you've slept."

Maris shook her head and looked suddenly worried. "There are disturbing reports from the Gray Kingdoms," she said. "The entire Council is awake. Two riders returned tonight with news that Sybo has fallen."

"To Markmor?" Alanna's eyes narrowed. She glanced at Robert, then Maris. "Eric and I were in Sybo a few days ago. We found a village burning, everyone dead. . . ."

"Not Markmor," Maris interrupted.

All indications are, Phlogis said, breaking in, *that the invaders came from Chol-Hecate. I told you we had little time, Robert. If you still wish to search for your friend in the Dream Stream, we must do it now.*

That was the Phlogis Robert knew: blunt to the point of rudeness. He didn't mind, though. If Sybo had fallen to Shandal Karg, both Maris and Phlogis had important war matters demanding their attention. Yet they were here with him. "What do I do?" he asked.

Phlogis moved inside his circle, chose a point of starlight, and raised his palm above it. It rose into the air, hovered near his fingertips for a moment, then sailed toward Robert. He plucked it from the air and held it up to admire its milky translucence.

That is tourmalated quartz, his host explained. *Lie down, Robert, and hold it tightly to your chest.*

Robert did as Phlogis told him. Alanna knelt down at his feet. Maris positioned herself at his head. Her fingers touched his temples and lingered there, cool and warm at the same time. "Relax," she whispered, smiling.

The stone floor pressed against his spine, but he did his best to get comfortable as he clutched the bit of quartz over his heart with both hands. He drew a deep breath and let it out, aware of Maris's gentle touch on his head. Alanna's hands likewise rested lightly on his ankles.

The women are your anchors, Phlogis said. *The*

quartz is your gateway into the Dream Stream. Feel its shape in your hands and against your heart. Picture its light in your mind. Phlogis paused. *Imagine your soul separating from your body, Robert Polo,* he continued. *Imagine separating and rising up. You can look down at Maris and Alanna. Look down at your own body.*

Robert felt weightless. He could no longer feel the floor against his spine, nor the touches of his friends. Only the crystal gripped against his heart, that he could still feel. No, not gripped. He looked at his empty hands, how they gleamed with a strange, silvery light. Then he looked at his chest. Where his heart should have been was the piece of quartz. It pulsed with a steady rhythm like a living organ, pumping light instead of blood.

There came a fleeting moment of panic, then calm. He gazed down at his real body lying on the floor and thought how silly he looked with such a serious expression on his face. Maris still rubbed his temples, and Alanna still held his ankles as she bent over him with a look of concern.

Robert.

He jumped, startled by the clarity and power of the voice inside his head. It no longer hurt him! He turned toward Phlogis. The *dando* had never appeared to him as more than a shadowy form inside a circle full of shadows. Now, Phlogis glowed with a controlled white light, like one of his jewels.

It's beautiful, is it not? his host said.

Fantastic, Robert answered with his thoughts. He had no voice now, no true voice. He raised his arms and stretched, reveling in his own splendidness.

It is very hard for some to find their dream form, Phlogis said. *You achieved it with surprising ease.*

Robert looked slowly about the chamber. His vision seemed too sharp. Colors looked brighter. The golden boundary of Phlogis's circle burned like molten fire. The gems and crystals within, through which Phlogis worked his magic, shimmered like miniature suns. *Is this it, then?* he asked. *Is this the Dream Stream?*

No came the answer. *For that, you must use your imagination again. Imagine the crystal that is part of you now. Imagine it before you, shining and huge. Imagine that it is a doorway, and that it is swinging open. Imagination is everything in the Dream Stream, Robert. Now go through the door. Go through . . .*

He didn't hesitate. The crystal loomed before him, floating in the air, swinging open. Beyond lay a sky full of stars, and nothing more that he could see. Robert stared, filled with wonder, and walked to the threshold. *How will I find Scott?* he called back.

Call him with your heart, Phlogis answered. *If he's there, your desire will guide you.*

Robert stepped up onto the threshold of his door and peered beyond. It was like looking into Phlogis's circle. Stars as far as he could see in all directions. It was like staring into the depths of space. There was no experience of vertigo, however, only anticipation and excitement. With Scott's name on his lips, he spread his arms and leaped, swan-like, from one world into the next.

The doorway disappeared behind him, and the stars swept past. The beauty of it burned into his brain until he was almost dizzy with exhilaration. The crystal in his chest pulsed with excited bursts of light. He threw back his head and laughed.

Scott! he cried. He imagined his thoughts were a beacon, and he sent them probing into the darkness ahead. *Scott, I'm coming for you!*

In the far distance, a pale blue arc of light formed. Beyond hung a fat but waning moon. Mianur, he realized, and Thanador. He looked down. The black silhouette of the land raced underneath. Oceans made of treetops rippled and tossed in the wind. Streams and lakes gleamed with silver flashes as he passed over them. Now Thanador floated straight before him, and Mianur was just over his shoulders. West, then. If direction meant anything in the Dream Stream, he was flying west.

Scott! he called again. He would crisscross this entire world if he had to, calling and calling until he got an answer or gave up hope. If his friend was here, nothing would stop Robert from finding him.

Then a soft laughter touched his mind. It came from the stars, from the land, from the very air around him. He felt it on his silvery skin like a chill breeze.

He knew the laughter of Shandal Karg. *I'm not afraid of you!* he screamed, but panic welled up in him. He tried to fight it down. He was no longer flying. He floated in the air, seeking in all directions for his tormentor, afraid to move. Where was she?

Scott! Her voice was soft and mocking as she drew the name into two syllables, then three. The Heart of Darkness let go another low, musical laugh. *Poor Bobby! Sweet little Bobby! Where is your lover, little Bobby?* The stars and the land and the air all laughed.

Shut up! Robert shrieked, his fear turning to anger as she mocked him. *You bitch!*

Silence. The temperature dropped until even his dream form began to shiver. *Did you think you were alone in the Dream Stream, little Bobby? Or that Scott would be waiting for you here?* That hateful laughter came again, rolling over him like waves.

Robert's hands curled into fists, but he forced himself to be calm. She had power to crush him with a thought. But if this was his time to die, he wouldn't grovel to her. In any case, he was tired of talking to the air. *You're never been shy before, babycakes,* he said, turning her own mocking tone against her. *Why don't you show your ugly face so I can spit in your eye?*

Her voice became softer. *Guard your heart, my little puppet,* she whispered in his ear. *There are many things in the Dream Stream that would like to eat it.*

A shrill screech raked suddenly across his mind. From the corner of his eye, he spied a shape. Barely in time, he threw himself aside. Talons stripped flesh from his shoulder. No, not flesh. He didn't have any flesh here. Nor was there any blood. Pain, though, that he felt. He clutched the wound, cursing, and searched the sky for his attacker.

A crystal eagle gyred high above him, then folded its light-faceted wings and dived at him again. Again, he heard its shriek deep in his mind. Its tiny eyes gleamed. Those talons reached for his heart.

Robert lifted his head, measuring its speed, gauging its descent. With no more than a snarl of annoyance, he brought the knife-edge of his left hand up, then down. The eagle exploded in a shower of glittering shards. He blinked long enough to protect his eyes.

Two more shrieks alerted him. From left and right a pair of eagles plummeted. Moonlight glimmered on razor-sharp feathers, on claws like daggers. Robert dodged the first one. A split second later, he swung his left fist in a wide arc and struck the second eagle. It exploded in a burst of light. He waited for the third and remaining bird to make its dive. Pressing both palms together, moving them downward in a tense line from the top of his head to just over his heart, he prepared himself.

An impossible wind whistled around the eagle as it screamed toward him. Twice, Robert had scored with his left hand. At the last instant, the eagle appeared to anticipate him. It opened one wing and swerved, as if expecting him to sidestep to the right in order to use the same left-hand technique. Those claws reached to rip out his heart.

Instead, Robert dropped to one knee and smashed his right fist straight upward into the eagle's shining underbelly. It shattered in a rainbow of prismatic color.

This is not even a challenge, Robert said with a sneer as he mentally dusted himself off. There was still no visible sign of Shandal Karg, but she was there. He could feel her.

Poor little Bobby. Her voice brushed against his brain as if it were a gentle hand petting a prized cat. *You still don't understand.* She laughed. *All the better to draw out the entertainment.* The stars gave a sigh, and the land and air echoed it. *However, you are not the only game I play this night. Let me leave you with this.*

Darkness filled his vision. Palenoc vanished. He felt himself flying again, rocketing through a void, drawn by a will not his own. Then, out of the darkness something gleamed, a blackness darker than the void itself. A strange five-towered castle rose up suddenly before him, its walls made of black glass or volcanic rock. It loomed, huge, floating in the nothingness. Unable to stop himself, he raced straight for it. Human instincts made him throw up his hands, made him cry out at the expected fatal impact. But he passed unharmed through those walls, then through more walls, down through floors and floors, deeper and deeper . . .

Suddenly his uncontrolled flight ended. He found himself in a chamber whose walls gleamed like the castle's outer walls, totally smooth, glass-like in appearance, without decoration or feature or blemish. In the center of the chamber, on a small dais, stood a coffin seemingly of white stone. Robert approached it cautiously. It was not stone at all, he discovered when he touched it, but ice. Carefully, he lifted the lid.

The blond hair on the pillow was like his own, but curly where his was straight. The open eyes were blue and staring. A rime of frost lay upon the lips. *Scott,* Robert whispered in despair. He reached inside the coffin and touched the hands that were folded formally upon a still chest.

Robert frowned. Scott's hands were not stiff, as he'd expected. The fingers were soft and flexible. He bent over the side of the coffin and placed his own hand over Scott's heart. There was a beat!

Laughter filled the chamber. Her laughter. *Now go home, my little puppet,* said the Heart of Darkness. *Your other playmates are calling you.*

No! he cried. He seized one of Scott's arms and tried to pull him out of the coffin.

They're calling you, Sweet Bobby. Can't you hear your friends? Home again, home again, ally in free.

He didn't hear anything but her mockery. But he felt something, someone tugging at his head, hands at his ankles pulling him. Alanna and Maris, he realized. They were trying to draw him back. *Let go!* he screamed. *Not when I'm so close!*

But there was no resisting. He swept backward out of the chamber, through the walls of the strange floating castle and through the void of the Dream Stream. Even Shandal Karg's cruel laughter dimmed and faded in the distance. The doorway of tourmaline quartz shone suddenly like a star. Blinding light engulfed him.

Eyes of flesh and blood snapped open. Maris leaned over him, her hands hot on either side of his face. He pushed her away roughly as he sat up. Alanna tried to take his hand, but he shrugged her off.

"Why?" he demanded, rising to his feet. He felt the small piece of quartz still clutched in his fist. In a rage, he flung it across the circle at Phlogis. "Why did you bring me back? Damn you! I almost had him! I might have gotten him back!"

An unexpected slap set his ears to ringing. He reeled back a step, stunned.

"Don't you ever push me!" Alanna said. Her eyes blazed with anger. "Or my sister. Never again, you selfish bastard!"

Wide-eyed, Robert stared at her, then at Maris. He vaguely recalled pushing Maris, but the councillor was still kneeling on the floor holding her cheek, gazing at him in shock and surprise. Had he hit her? He didn't remember that, but it was plain he had.

"I'm sorry," he mumbled stupidly, crossing to her side.

"You're hurt," Maris said, pointing to his left shoulder. The eagle's talons had done nothing to his dream form, but his flesh was bleeding from a trio of scratches. "And your friend Katy was attacked only a few moments ago."

Phlogis's thought-voice rasped disapprovingly. *We thought it best to bring you back. You say you found Scott Silver?*

"I found Shandal Karg," Robert said. He felt like a fool. Alanna glared at him as she wrapped an arm protectively around her sister's shoulders, and Phlogis's impatience was an almost tangible force. "She showed me a vision. Or took me to a place. I'm not sure which."

"That's the elusive nature of the Dream Stream," Maris said as she rubbed her cheek.

Robert nodded. "But he was alive."

The sanctum doors flung suddenly back, and Eric strode into the room. His face was angry and desperate. Katy Dowd and Roderigo Diez came right behind him, and a few moments later, the entire Council of Guran followed.

Chapter Six

SHEREN Shago stood high on a hilltop. A soaring stone tower, its look and construction made it identical to Sheren-Chad. An immense blue sky stretched impressively above it as far as the eye could see, finally breaking in the west against the sharp, cloud-capped peaks of a distant mountain range.

In the valley below lay Capreet, Wystoweem's capital. It was a small city, compared to Rasoul. The Baradanis River, no more than a wide stream, really, ran right through the middle of it, but tiny fishing boats moved up and down between its gracefully flowing banks.

It was an idyllic illusion. The people were small and thin. Men, women, and children turned out to line the main street to watch the Brothers of the Dragon go by.

Katy studied them as she walked at Eric's side. An old man leaned in a doorway. His ribs showed plainly through his shirtless body. A girl-child clung to her mother's tattered skirts. Her little eyes gleamed with hopeful interest, but looked too wide, unnaturally protruded.

"They look half-starved," Katy whispered to Eric.

"Wystoweem is on the front line of the war," he said grimly.

Katy ran a hand through her hair. She'd bound it

back after Alanna's fashion, but a few wisps still stuck to her brow and cheeks. It was hot and humid, and after three days of travel she ached down to her toes. She flicked a bead of sweat from her chin and glanced back at Robert, who was following with Alanna at his side. The citizens of Capreet seemed to take a special interest in him that had nothing to do with his jeans and Reeboks. Their gazes sought him out, but as he passed, many subtly averted their eyes and fell silent.

Katy noticed Robert's discomfort. "These people seem to hold you in some reverence," she said quietly.

"You have a knack for choosing your words," Robert said with a tone of annoyance. "There's a legend here that says The Son of the Morning always has blond hair and green eyes."

Katy raised an eyebrow. "They think you're their savior?"

"It's no legend," Valis interrupted. The huge, dark-haired dragonrider glanced from side to side as they walked up the street. In one hand he carried a staff made from a red-colored wood Katy had never seen before. Eric called it war-willow.

Alanna took Robert's hand and squeezed it. "Even if he's not the Shae'aluth," she said, "when people see him, it gives them hope that the true Son of the Morning may come soon."

Robert didn't say anything. The expression on his face, though, was enough for Katy to realize how uncomfortable he felt with that idea. His mood had changed in the last few days. There was a distant gleam in his eyes that she couldn't understand, as if he was constantly watching for something to suddenly appear on the horizon.

Evander and Doe led the way across an arched footbridge to the other side of the Baradanis. The two had met them on the outskirts of town in a meadow where Shadowfire, Mirrormist, and Brightstar had been left, and Eric had made introductions. Both seemed younger than Eric had led her to expect—no more than late teens—but she liked them immediately.

There were fewer houses and shops on the north side of the river, and fewer people staring. As they began to climb the hill to Sheren Shago, Katy noticed how brown and lifeless the grass on either side of the road appeared. In fact, the grass everywhere seemed withered. The few trees also had a sinister and twisted look. She felt the sun on her neck and guessed that drought was the cause. But then she glanced back. If there was drought in Wystoweem, would the river be so full between its banks?

A wall surrounded the Sheren, but the gates stood open. Just before the gates, on either side of the road, a pair of exquisitely sculpted marble dragons, each twice the height of a man, stood guard on stone pedestals. Each block of stone that formed the gate's vast archway was likewise carved with a dragon's stern visage, and each pair of chiseled eyes was focused upon the roadway to give the impression that the creatures were keeping watch.

The stone, however, was weathered and pitted with black rot, and here and there a thin dark moss grew in the cracks. The huge timbers that made the gate doors were worn and discolored, and the massive hinges were rusted.

An oppressive sense of age hung over Sheren Shago. Katy shivered as they passed through the gate and entered a small courtyard. Low outbuildings stood on either side of them, but she gave them no attention. Her gaze climbed the ponderous tower they were approaching.

"Do they have dragonriders here, too?" Katy whispered, leaning closer to Eric.

"Only a few," he answered, turning his head up to scan the sky. "Salyt has probably sent them to patrol the south."

"No other Domain ally shares a border with three Dark Land nations," Valis explained. "Pyre, Dargra, and Chol-Hecate all lie just below Wystoweem on the map."

Their small company stopped before a pair of fantastic doors. They were not unlike the doors to Phlogis's sanctum in faraway Rasoul. The painted hex signs even appeared similar. But these doors were far larger, and Katy wondered just who or what the hell they had been designed to accommodate. "A cheap attempt to impress the rubes," she decided, mumbling to herself as she shook her head. The doors were for show, not for practical use.

Almost as if to prove her theory, Evander took a slender green crystal from a pouch at his belt. Katy blinked, at first thinking it the largest emerald she had ever imagined, but its color was much too pale. She tapped Eric's shoulder. He was the geologist.

"Fluorite," he answered. "I think. Not all their minerals have Earth equivalents."

Evander grinned as he held the small wand up for Katy to see. "We call it," he paused dramatically, then pressed it against the painted wood of the door, "a key."

A tiny hole formed where the crystal touched the door and swiftly irised open to form an entrance. Katy realized she'd just seen a bit of sorcery. "Oh, my stars and garters," she murmured, pressing a hand to her mouth. A large round piece of the door had simply vanished. Eric ushered her through.

The first level of Sheren Shago looked like a dimly lit warehouse. Huge vessels, similar to Greek *pithos* jars, stood around like grim sentinels. Wooden barrels were stacked everywhere. Vast bolts of cloth lay in careless piles. A number of wagons and carts sat with their beds full of strange and unidentifiable things.

A pair of great stone staircases curled up from either side of the entrance. A sputtering light on the left one drew Katy's attention. A small girl, no more than nine or ten, was descending with delicate grace, the folds of a lovely white dress trailing behind her. In her right hand, she carried a smoking pitch torch.

The little girl stopped on the third step, which left her at eye level with the adults. Her gaze fixed on Robert for a moment, and her tiny eyebrows arched with amazement. She lifted the torch a bit higher, the better to illuminate him. Then she swallowed. "Welcome to Sheren Shago," she said in a sweetly nervous voice. "My mother said I could guide you to the council chambers, but we're supposed to hurry because everyone is waiting."

"This is Weena," Evander said, grinning, as he started up the stairs behind the little girl. He and Doe were familiar with the Sheren, having been there for some days. "Salyt's daughter."

Katy sneezed as the smoke from the pitch torch tickled her nose.

Weena stopped at once and looked down apologetically. "I'm sorry," she offered holding the torch higher so the smoke wouldn't be so bothersome. "We have little *melin* to spare these days. Our dragons are so few."

Evander took the torch from her. "Perhaps it would be better if I carried it, little butterfly," he said gently. He lifted it higher, and the smoke passed above their heads.

"I'm not a butterfly," Weena shot back with a childish frown. "Butterflies don't live very long."

The words shocked Katy. She started to say something, then stopped. That was war, she reminded herself, and war did strange things to kids. What must a thousand-year war have done to the children of Palenoc?

Weena quickened the pace. Level after level, they rose, climbing stairs until Katy's thighs turned to lead, and still they climbed. Occasional torches and lamps provided the only light. In a narrow passage between flights of steps, they passed an old man with an armload of scrolls and books, who stopped in his tracks, pressed himself against the wall, and watched Robert go by. Moments later they encountered a gaunt young woman descending toward them. The pitcher she carried slipped from her hand and shattered. Water splattered the front of her dress, her bare feet, and cascaded down the steps.

With a barely audible sigh, Robert separated himself from the group, and mounted the few steps to where the woman stood wide-eyed and apparently paralyzed. He bent slowly down and picked up a couple of the larger fragments of the vessel, then placed them in the woman's hands, smiling at her. She returned a frightened imitation of a smile, then fled back up the way she had come.

Robert turned back to his friends, shrugged, and rolled his eyes.

Weena shook her little head in disgust. "Katrina is so immature," she commented. "She probably thought you were the Son of the Morning."

"You don't think he is?" Katy said, amused by the disapproving look on Weena's face and the tone in her small voice.

"Of course not," Weena snapped indignantly. "I'm a child, but I'm not stupid. I don't believe in fairy tales." She led the way up the steps again, lifting the hem of her dress to avoid the mess of Katrina's broken pitcher.

Finally they left the stairway and turned into a wide corridor. The cresset lamps burned a finer oil that gave better light. The smoke that hung in the air had a pleasant cinnamon scent. Weena led the way straight to a pair of doors at the corridor's end. Seizing a large wooden ring with both hands, she pulled one open. Evander opened the other. "After you, little ladybug," he said.

"I'm not a bug," Weena responded with a lift of her nose. "Bugs are icky."

Katy allowed an inward smile at what was obviously a game between Evander and Weena as she followed them through the doors. The chamber beyond was not unlike Phlogis's sanctum. It was far better lit, however. Open crenelations let in both sunlight and fresh air, and gave view of the outside world. The entire floor was one huge elaborately painted hex sign. Twelve chairs stood in a semicircle facing the entrance. Seven women and five men, all of varying ages, regarded them.

A severe-looking woman near the center rose from her chair and strode to the middle of the room. Her hair was pulled back into a tight knot behind her head. Her high-necked dress pinched her in too many places. "Welcome to Sheren Shago," she said. "I regret your lateness, but Phlogis assures me it was unavoidable, and I suppose I must believe him."

Katy glanced upward, noting how the domed shape of the ceiling made even a whisper audible. Then she returned her attention to Councillor Salyt. Unless she was mistaken, that dress was raw silk. So, in fact, was Weena's. And the way the light shimmered on the other councillors' garments, they were also clad in silk.

Katy frowned, remembering the tattered rags on Capreet's citizens.

Alanna and Valis approached Salyt. Alanna raised her hands, palms outward and touched them to the councillor's in the Palenoc equivalent of a handshake. Valis did the same.

"We came as quickly as we could," Alanna assured her, undaunted by the woman's status. "Sybo has fallen to the Heart of Darkness."

"You get right to business," Salyt said, eyeing Alanna critically. "I like that. The news is worse, I'm afraid. While you've been traveling, Vakris has also fallen in the same mysterious manner." She approached Eric and offered him her palms. "I asked Phlogis for your help," she said to him, "when I learned how you defeated Keris Chaterit and returned the Terreborne nation to the Domains of Light."

"We were lucky," Eric said, touching her palms.

She turned away from him to Katy. "I don't believe in luck," she said bluntly. Her eyes bore rudely into Katy's. She paused before offering her palms, did so peremptorily, then moved on to Robert.

Bitch, Katy decided, employing Robert's favorite word. That was definitely silk she was wearing while her people went hungry and wore rags. Nor had she said a word of thanks or acknowledgment to Weena. The nerve, sending a child that small down so many stairs. She made up her mind to dislike this woman.

One hand on her chin, Salyt studied Robert as if he were a piece of sculpture. He stood for it, wearing a bored expression, studying her back. When she leaned closer to peer at his green eyes, he leaned closer to peer into her brown ones. It was a subtle bit mockery, and Katy almost giggled. Robert must have reached the same conclusion she had.

Finally, the councillor held up her palms. "You are not the Shae'aluth," she announced firmly.

Robert completed the gesture, brushing his hands over hers. "I admire an astute woman," he said without flinching.

Alanna interrupted with a little more volume than necessary under the belled ceiling, and Katy gave an inward smile. Alanna had learned to read Robert well. She knew when he was on the verge of causing trouble, and had acted to avert it. Katy had already decided she liked Alanna.

"What are the reports from Vakris?" Alanna said, returning to business. "After the fall of Sybo, every council in the Domains must have sent spies to the Gray Kingdoms."

Salyt turned toward Eric, seemingly ignoring Alanna as she answered. "There was barely time to get spies in place," she replied. "Sybo's capital fell three days ago. Some of the villages and towns continue to resist, but there's no hope they can hold out. Vakris fell last night, apparently in a single evening."

A willowy young councillor leaned forward on the arm of his chair, but he didn't rise. "A few stories tell of black clouds sweeping over cities and villages."

Another councillor, older and heavier, slammed his fist on the arm of his chair and leaped up. "Stories?" he shouted. "You call them stories? People are being murdered! Deaths are in the thousands!" He sat down again, white-faced, and wiped a hand over his brow.

"Thank you, Devin-*kaesha*," said yet another councillor, an old woman whose hair hung across her face in wisps. She spoke with a weary voice. "Nothing enlivens the conversation like a body count." The remaining members of Wystoweem's council smiled patiently. Most seemed content to let Salyt dominate the show, a role she was obviously used to playing.

Valis leaned on his staff. "What proof do you have that these attacks are coming out of Chol-Hecate?"

Salyt lifted her head. Valis stood more than a foot taller than she, yet she looked him in the eyes. "You can draw a line through the ravaged villages from Chol-Hecate's border straight to Sybo's capital."

Devin waved a hand from his chair. "There've been stories for some time that Kajin Lure was developing a new weapon—a new magic—for the Heart of Darkness to use against the Domains, but we ignored them. The Gray Kingdoms are just a testing ground, I tell you! Soon this weapon will be turned on us!"

Eric turned to Valis. "Who is Kajin Lure?"

Before Valis could answer, Salyt supplied the information. "Chol-Hecate's governor, and a sorcerer to rival Keris Chaterit, or even Phlogis in his living days." She paused long enough to cast a baleful look at Devin. "And we didn't ignore the stories. We simply couldn't find any proof of them." She waved a hand as if to dismiss him. "There are always stories about new weapons and new magics."

"Oh," Robert said with one raised eyebrow. "You fucked up."

Again Alanna broke in to prevent harsh words. "We've traveled a long way," she said, turning to appeal to the rest of the councillors. "I'm quite thirsty, as are my comrades."

Salyt pressed her hands together and hung her head briefly. "Forgive me," she said. "I've been rude and impatient. Weena will find someone to bring refreshments. There's little wine, I'm afraid, and not much in the larders. But I'm sure we can manage some beer and fresh bread before supper." She glanced back at her fellow councillors and added, "On this occasion."

Eric held up one hand. "No beer for me, thanks. Water would be fine."

Weena gathered double handfuls of her dress and skipped out of the room. As she went past Evander, he murmured, "Be careful, little grasshopper."

"I'm not hopping," she said as the dark tresses of her hair flew up and down, "I'm skipping. And I don't spit that black stuff."

Evander reached out and took Doe's hand. The two men grinned and watched the little girl until she pulled the door closed behind her.

Eric paced into the center of the room, taking a place near Valis and Alanna. "You asked Phlogis to send us here days before Sybo fell, Councillor," he pointed out. "Something about a mission. Does that connect with what's happening now?"

Salyt nodded. "It's even more urgent now than before," she said. "The Gray Kingdoms haven't been Kajin Lure's only targets. Wystoweem has suffered his attacks for years. We've managed to defend ourselves, but finally we're prepared to launch our own attack."

"I hope your armies are in better shape than your townspeople below," Katy said, speaking for the first time.

"Armies?" Salyt put on a condescending smile. "Oh yes. You have a Paradane concept of warfare, Katherine Dowd. I suppose you might consider my border guards and my few *sekournen* an army. But they play only a small part in this strategy."

"And these outsiders should play no part at all!" A black-bearded councillor rose from his seat. Like Salyt, he wore silk, and the light glimmered on every fold of his garments. He stood as tall as Eric and looked as heavily muscled as Valis. With an angry stride, he moved to the center of the chamber. He glowered at the stern-faced councilwoman. "We've always taken care of ourselves, Salyt," he said in a booming voice. "We don't need help now. My *sekour-nen* can do what needs to be done."

Salyt looked at him as if he were a disobedient child. "Don't be a fool, Shubal," she answered. "You and your riders have a part to play, and you'll learn what that is soon enough."

"I don't like this secrecy!" he shot back, half turning to include the rest of the council in his argument. "You've told us precious little about this plan of yours. It's bad enough that you involve Guran, but now you insult us by involving these *shaloh*." He sneered as he looked directly from Katy to Robert to Eric.

The gray-haired councilwoman who had spoken earlier to Devin spoke up again. "I'm not insulted," she said lightly. "The one who looks like the Shae'aluth has nice legs."

"Sit down, Shubal," Salyt said, her voice low and impatient. "You will play your part."

Shubal didn't sit. He strode toward Robert and stopped before him. "You're a fraud, *shaloh*," he said with a heavy sneer. "You wear the Shae'aluth's face, but you are not him. Maybe someone should scar it a little so people will know the difference."

"I wouldn't do that if I were you," Katy muttered as Shubal thumped a finger on Robert's chest. She glanced at Salyt. The councilwoman had dominated the proceedings until this moment. Now she seemed to hang back as if she was content to let this scene play itself out. In fact, Katy realized with a start, Salyt was *interested* in seeing it played out. She was watching Robert intently.

"One of my *sekournen* warriors is worth all three of these *shaloh*," Shubal grumbled. He thumped Robert a second time. "Right, *shaloh*?"

Robert forced a tight smile and spoke past Shubal

to his brother. "Why do the dummies always pick on me?" he asked with a sardonic tilt of his head.

"Karma?" Eric answered with a shrug.

Katy felt for the stun gun in the small holster on her belt. Shubal stood nearly half a foot taller than Robert and weighed at least fifty pounds more.

"Don't call me shallow," Robert warned, still forcing a strained smile as he looked straight back into Shubal's eyes. "I'm educated, well traveled, and I know a hawk from a handsaw."

Shubal's eyes narrowed to slits. "You mock me, *shaloh*. No one mocks me!" He swung a fist.

Robert merely leaned aside and let the blow pass harmlessly by his ear. "It's an ego thing, uh?" he said to Shubal as he hooked his thumbs nonchalantly in his pockets. The look in his eyes, though, was anything but relaxed. Katy knew that look.

Shubal's fist paused in the air. "Salyt says you have a fancy fighting technique, *shaloh*," he hissed. "I think you're just a *shaloh*."

Katy couldn't just stand by and watch. Half the Wystoweem councillors were on their feet, creeping closer for a better view. "What the hell is this?" she shouted. "You people invited us here!"

Robert's smile wavered and vanished. "I won't use anything fancy," he said evenly. He held out his hands and beckoned Shubal to come on.

Shubal approached with the stealth of a practiced fighter. Without warning, his left fist shot out. Robert shook his head and put on a look of boredom as he caught the bigger man's fist, stepped aside, and gave it a sharp twist. Shubal cartwheeled through the air and hit the floor hard. Robert turned to his brother and lifted his arms in an apologetic shrug. "I lied," he said.

But the councilman was not out of it yet. Unfazed,

he found his feet. Before Robert could turn around again, Shubal caught him in a bear hug.

"Oh, please!" Robert muttered in disgust. He locked his right arm over Shubal's elbow, trapping it, then slid his right foot to the outside of Shubal's ankle. When he dropped his weight, the councilman went flying again. The force of his groan as he hit the stone floor filled the chamber.

For a moment there was silence. Shubal lay on his back, staring at the dome. Slowly, he got up again, reeling like a drunken man. It was only an act to get closer to Valis. With a sudden growl he seized the dragonrider's war-willow staff and ran at Robert.

Katy had had enough. As Shubal moved, so did she, straight for Salyt. In an instant, she slipped one arm around the councilwoman's throat. In the next, she ripped the stun gun free and pressed the metal studs to Salyt's temple. Her finger hovered over the trigger.

"Stop right there, you overgrown son of a bitch!" Katy shouted. She tightened her grip on Salyt's throat until the woman made a wincing noise.

A collective sigh of disbelief went up from the council members. Shubal stopped in his tracks.

Katy had their attention. "The testosterone stinks in here!"

Devin walked sheepishly forward. "Please don't hurt Salyt," he begged. "We wished only to observe the fighting skills we've heard so much about. Shubal is the commander of our *sekournen,* and one of our greatest warriors. We asked him to test you."

Katy's cheeks reddened with anger. "You knew about this?" she said incredulously in Salyt's ear. "You set it up?"

Salyt nodded as best she could.

"Don't worry, Kat," Robert said. "I knew what was happening. It's happened before. It's the nature of this world that sometimes you have to prove yourself to strangers. In some places, it's even a ritual." He inclined his head toward Shubal, unable to resist the barb, "They usually field better competition."

Katy muttered a low curse and let Salyt go, giving her the slightest push to express the contempt she felt.

"Back off, Shubal," Salyt said, looking very embarrassed as she rubbed her throat. The black-bearded councilman looked as if he wanted to continue.

"Nice choke hold," Eric murmured approvingly as he went to Katy's side. "You know your stun gun wouldn't have done much damage there."

"I know it," Katy scowled. "But they don't."

Valis took his staff back from Shubal, who returned to his chair and slumped into it. Alanna, Evander, and Doe went to Robert.

"I told you this was unnecessary," Evander said to Salyt with a voice full of bitterness and betrayal. "Phlogis told you it was unnecessary."

Alanna looked at him with surprise. "You knew about this?"

He glared at Salyt. "She assured me it wouldn't happen."

Devin rubbed his hands together nervously. "Don't blame Councillor Salyt," he said. "We all requested this demonstration. There's too much at stake, and we wished to have some knowledge of your abilities." He swallowed as his gaze lingered on Robert. "And if you can all fight like this, we are most impressed."

Salyt turned and pointed to Katy's hip. "I'd like to know more about that weapon," she said.

Katy couldn't believe the woman's nerve. She put one hand on the stun gun's butt and pushed it deeper into the holster. "Get fucked, bitch."

Eric clucked his tongue. "Remember, you're a librarian."

"My Kat has sharp claws," Robert said. He turned to Salyt, "I assume we pass?"

Salyt gave him an imperious look. "Had there been any real doubt," she told him coolly, "I wouldn't have bothered to call you here."

Valis leaned on his staff. "Then you're ready to tell us more about this plan of yours, Councillor?"

A shake of her head was her answer. "You'll know each phase as it unfolds. The Heart of Darkness has eyes and ears everywhere, and Kajin Lure has his own spies. You may know this much now." She paused and looked straight at Shubal. "In two days, the Domains of Lights will attack Chol-Hecate from the north and northeast. A small number of forces from the Gray Kingdoms will try to push into Sybo and Vakris. You, Shubal, will lead our *sekournen*, along with our border guards, on a physical assault against our enemy's northwest border."

Shubal rose to his feet, his eagerness masking the pain of the beating Robert had given him. "Then it's all-out war?" he exclaimed.

Salyt smiled maternally. "Don't be a fool," she said. A grim note slipped into her voice. "It's all a diversion. Long before then, these Brothers and Sisters of the Dragon will be deep into Chol-Hecate." She let go a sigh and drew herself stiffly erect. "And I will be with them."

The council chamber doors suddenly pushed open. Weena bounced in with half a dozen silk-clad women behind her, each bearing trays and pitchers. "Refreshments!" she called brightly. "Water and beer and bread and"—she held up a hand full of round, brown things—"cookies!"

Katy forced a smile, but inside she felt the simmering of a slowly building rage. Palenoc had seemed to her like a fairy tale a few days ago. But the fairy tale was turning ugly. Eric hadn't lifted a hand to help Robert, nor had any of his so-called Brothers of the Dragon. Even Robert, with his unreadable moods, seemed to accept all this violence with total complacency.

Eric touched her arm. "You okay, Katy-did?"

She looked at him for a long moment, reading the concern on his face, remembering how well he could read her, too. "Fine," she said, then looked quickly away.

But she watched him from the corner of her eye when he was no longer looking, and wondered. What had this world made him? What had it made Robert? What would it make her?

Chapter Seven

ERIC sat in the tall grass with his legs folded. The strains of "God Bless the Child," rose from the harmonica at his lips. Shadowfire lay curled on the ground, the tip of his huge gray nose mere feet from his rider, his diamond-colored eyes wide and unblinking, as if the music had entranced him.

Farther away, Mirrormist and Brightstar lazily fanned their wings. In the morning light, the membranes had lost their brilliant luciferase color and taken on a uniform milky translucence. Even without the fire in their wings, Eric had no trouble telling them apart. They were all his friends by now, even Sunrunner and Heartsong who glided overhead, cavorting side by side.

The tune came to an end. Eric held the final note, wavering it, letting it fade slowly. Shadowfire lifted his great head and laid it down again just a foot closer to his rider. Eric felt his *sekoye* deep in his mind. It was a kind of purring that expressed pleasure. His was a discriminating dragon who knew good music. He liked the blues.

Shadowfire lifted his head again. Eric heard a footstep in the dry grass and put down his harmonica.

"I knew I'd find you here." Valis put aside his warwillow staff and squatted down beside Eric.

"I got up early," Eric confessed. "I wanted to spend a little time with Shadowfire before we left."

Valis leaned forward and patted the dragon's snout. The beasts would not be coming with them on this journey. They would be too visible to agents and observers on the ground, and Salyt wanted to get as far into Chol-Hecate as possible in total secrecy. Eric frowned. He didn't like the idea of leaving Shadowfire behind even though he understood the councillor's reasoning.

"He's like a giant house cat curled up at your feet," Valis said as he sat back again. He gestured far afield where Brightstar expanded his wings to their full span, lifted his head, and gave a grand yawn. "My Brightstar," he continued with some amusement, "is far too vain for this kind of fawning."

"Can you hear him?" Eric asked suddenly as he tapped his temple. "In here, right now?"

Valis gave him a bemused look. "Of course," he answered. "He's scolding me in three octaves for petting your Shadowfire when I haven't even gone over to say hello to him, yet."

Eric nodded appreciatively. "It's incredible," he said. "It's like I'm never without him, even when we're out of each other's sight. Like I'm never truly alone because he's always here"—he touched his head again—"inside me." His lips drew into a taut line as he tapped the harmonica against his palm to clear it of saliva.

"You've got an awfully thoughtful look," Valis said after a few moments.

Eric chewed his lower lip before speaking. "You hear Brightstar, and I hear Shadowfire," he finally said. "I was wondering what it's like for Alanna. She hears them all."

Valis regarded him with an understanding gaze. "I

wonder what it's like for Robert," he said pointedly. "He doesn't hear any."

Eric drew a breath and let it out. "I'm sorry," he apologized with an embarrassed grin. "I *was* feeling a little bit jealous." He pulled up a handful of brown grass and scattered it with a toss over Shadowfire's nose. The dragon turned an eye toward him, but gave no other reaction. "I've already got so much more than other men."

Valis gave him an even stranger look and shifted his position to observe Eric better. "My friend, you've got more on your mind than dragons. You have the look and tone of a man with woman trouble."

Eric reacted with surprise. Was he that obvious? "I've been asking myself if I was right to let Katy come along," he said. "In fact, ever since that thing attacked her in her sleep, I've been wondering if I should have let her stay in Palenoc at all."

Valis's fingers burrowed into the grass at his side and pulled out a small twig. Without looking up, he broke off a miniscule piece and tossed it to the wind. "You speak as if the choice was yours," he said at last.

Eric looked defensive. "Well, maybe she chose to stay, but I picked the people who came on this mission."

Valis broke off another piece of twig. With a flip of his wrist, he flung it upward. The breeze swept it away. "Did you?" He broke off a third piece and flung it. "Perhaps the Or-dhamu made that choice long before you made it."

Eric frowned and looked away. He plucked a blade of grass and began tearing it in thin strips, which he tossed after the pieces of Valis's stick as he thought about his friend's words. He'd learned a bit of Palenoc's dominant religion, though he didn't pretend to understand it well. They believed in no god, as such.

The Or-dhamu was Universal Responsibility, the highest point toward which all souls evolved, a cosmic oneness that maintained the workings and the balance of all things. The Son of the Morning was the ultimate expression of the Or-dhamu on earth. The Heart of Darkness was its antithesis.

"You're telling me she's here because she was fated to be here," Eric said at last.

Valis cast the last remaining piece of his stick and brushed his hands. "Fate?" he said doubtfully. He shrugged. "Katy's here, not because she has to be, but because Or-dhamu gave her courage and will to *want* to be. No one, not even you, *Namue rana sekoye,* can tell her to go or stay."

Eric put on an amused grin and wiped his hands on his trousers. "I hear that," he answered wryly. "Nobody can tell Katy-did anything."

Valis stood up and offered his hand to Eric. "That won't stop you from worrying about her, though, will it?"

Eric got to his feet and clapped the big dragonrider on the shoulder. "What can I say? I love her."

Valis fixed Eric with a dark-eyed gaze. "Tell her," he said seriously.

Eric's grin widened as he shook his head. "It's easy to say it to you," he shot back. "Saying it to her is another matter, entirely."

But Valis didn't grin. "I loved a woman once," he said. "Her name was Byrlen. She was just a plain-faced village girl, a blacksmith's daughter, but she was kind and good. No child went hungry in that village if she had food. If another woman was sick, Byrlen would go and care for the family." A distant look crept into Valis's eyes. His head moved ever so slightly up and down as he remembered. "I didn't see her often. I was a young and eager *sekournen* then, and my duties took me many places. Still, I loved her with all my heart."

Eric waited, but Valis said no more. "Well," he said. "What happened?"

Valis took a deep breath and drew himself to his full height. "She perished in the death camps," he said finally, "when Chule fell to the Kingdoms of Night. I was on the other side of the continent in Pylanthim. All of Sinnagar separated us. When I heard, I leaped on Brightstar and flew home as fast as he could carry us, and all I could think of was that I'd never told her how I felt."

A chill passed through Eric, and his own memories took over. He thought of Danyel. The boy had lived in Chule, but had escaped in the chaos of its fall and made his way to Guran to join the ranks of the *sekournen*. His parents, though, had died in Keris Chaterit's death camps, where captives were allowed to slowly starve to death. It was one of the few *safe* forms of murder of Palenoc. He, himself, had seen the misery and cruelty of such a camp in Terreborne. That one, at least, he had helped to destroy.

"Here come our comrades," Valis said suddenly.

Eric blinked. "My God!" he cried, putting his memories away as he followed the direction of his friend's gaze. "What are those things?"

Four huge white worms undulated across the field from the direction of the Baradanis River. Hundreds of feathery legs rippled under their massive, ugly bodies, and sapphire-colored eyes as big as basketballs gleamed on heads that brushed the ground as the creatures moved.

Three of the worms carried humans. Robert and Alanna rode together on a peculiar kind of saddle that seemed stapled to the monster's body. Robert handled a pair of slender rods. As he tapped his creature on the right side of its head, it made a subtle course adjustment. Katy and Doe rode another of the worms, and Councillor Salyt and Evander also shared a saddle. The fourth beast was led by Devin and Shubal. A number of the other councillors, plus a few of the townspeople followed after, but they stayed well back.

"We're supposed to ride those things?" Eric muttered in disbelief.

"*Chelit* make good, reliable mounts," Valis said. "Our *sekoye* would be too easily spotted in the air by our enemies."

The *chelit* stopped, and his friends slid to the ground, leaving only Salyt remaining in her saddle. The councillor had traded her silk dress for *sekournen* leathers. More practical for traveling. Over her shoulders, she also wore a small backpack. Her hair, however, was twisted in the same stern knot and pierced with an ornamental jeweled spike that seemed very out of keeping with the rest of her outfit. Eric nodded a greeting to her, and she returned it wordlessly.

"Send the *sekoye* aloft," Alanna said as she came forward. "They'll find their own resting places away from the city while they await our return."

"Or our summons," Valis added with a sidewise glance at Eric. Then, without hesitating, he turned and sang a low-pitched note. His rich bass voice soared out over the field. In one flowing breath, he pushed it higher up the scale. Brightstar stopped fanning his wings and looked suddenly alert. Once more the dragon opened those splendid pinions, only this time it took to the sky and sailed rapidly toward a small cloud bank in the east.

Before Valis's note had faded, Alanna began to sing. Her soprano made a perfect counterpoint, continuing where the big dragonrider's song had ended, clear as perfect crystal. Farther down the valley, Mirrormist raised his head and gave a trumpeting answer. A moment later, he rose into the bright blue sky and turned northward.

Evander and Doe sang out in unison, one tenor voice overlaying the other, interweaving in a dazzling harmony as they gazed upward and waved to Sunrunner and Heartsong. The pair of dragons gyred higher and higher overhead until they became small specks and finally vanished.

"Then we're ready?" Councillor Salyt said with barely controlled impatience. She made a show of adjusting the straps of her pack.

Eric turned his back to her and took out his harmonica. He had a passable singing voice, but it was the music that flowed from his small silver instrument that Shadowfire responded to best. The dragon lifted his head at the sight of the instrument, stretched his neck, and laid down again right at Eric's feet. Eric brushed his fingertips affectionately along that great snout as he raised the harmonica to his mouth with the other.

He blew a short, mournful riff and quavered the last note. The connection he shared with the dragon shivered like a plucked string. Slowly, Shadowfire backed away, creeping, dragging his belly over the grass, his glittering eyes fixed on his rider.

Eric blew another riff, a basic *G-C-D* chord progression, then settled into a slow version of "Farewell to Tarwaithe." Shadowfire's tail lashed languidly back and forth. He spread his wings, fanned them once. At last, the dragon sprang into the sky.

The wind from Shadowfire's wings whipped Eric's hair and fluttered the loose sleeves of his leather shirt. The harmonica went back into the small pocket on his belt. Eric watched his *sekoye* flying eastward with increasing speed until the creature was lost in the blinding glare of the sun.

"Now we're ready," he said to Salyt. He went to Shubal and took the pair of rods the councilman held. "Teach me how to ride this monster," he said.

But Valis took the rods from him. "Leave the driving to me," he advised. "At least for now. It's simple enough, though. You want the *chelit* to turn, touch him on the side that corresponds to the direction you wish to go. To slow down, stroke them on both sides at the same time. To speed up, whack them on the center of the head."

"Whack them?" Eric said, raising an eyebrow.

Evander called down to him, having already re-mounted. He sat before Salyt with the rods in his hands, her arms lightly around his waist. "*Chelit* are not intelligent like the *sekoye*," he said. "Nor do they have much feeling. You can see the saddles are pinned to their sides. These creatures don't feel pain."

"You *shaloh* are going to get yourselves killed," Shubal said as he stepped away. "And Salyt with you."

For the first time, Eric noticed the dark bruise that colored one side of Shubal's head where it had struck the floor. "You know, I'm sure I'm just an ignorant *shaloh*," he conceded, "but just what the heck does *shaloh* mean?" Whatever it was, it wasn't in the Guran language, which was spoken throughout most of the Domains. It had to be a word from an old Wystoweem tongue, he guessed.

"It means *newborn*," Devin piped up with an embarrassed look.

"Newborn with a shitty ass," Shubal corrected with a challenging sneer.

The *chelit* was nearly twenty feet long and stood as high as a horse. Valis swung up into the saddle and held a hand down toward Eric. "Well, just remember," Eric said as he settled himself behind his friend, "it was my *baby* brother that gave you that shiner."

"I'm a pacifist," Robert said, faking a bored yawn. He was in the passenger end of the saddle now, and Alanna held the rods. "He must have tripped on something. His own feet, maybe."

Shubal merely scowled and marched off. Devin lingered long enough to bid Salyt a safe journey. He, at least, had the courtesy to look worried about her. She gave him a tolerant smile and reached down to touch her palm to his upraised hand. "If anything should happen to me," she said, quietly conspiratorial, "try not to let that man dominate the council." Devin managed a weak grin before she dismissed him.

Doe hadn't said a word through the whole proceeding, but that was like him. The boy was as quiet as the ghosts he talked to. Eric glanced behind him toward Katy. She'd tied a white strip of cloth around her head to keep her hair out of her eyes, and she wore the backpack that she'd brought with her from Paradane.

"Well, Katy-did," he said lightly, "there's still time to send you home."

Katy gave him a long, lingering look, and he wondered for a moment if she'd taken it as an insult. Just as he was about to offer an apology, she leaned back and slapped the *chelit* on its pale hide. The worm didn't stir. "Hi ho Silver," she said impatiently. "Let's get this show on the road."

"Amen," Robert agreed.

"Amen," Doe echoed, causing all gazes to briefly turn his way.

They started southward, rising up out of the valley carved by the Baradanis River to the edge of a vast, rolling plain. Evander and Salyt led the way through brown grass that stood as tall as a man. Here and there, twisted shrubs and scrawny, malnourished trees grew in lonely isolation. The mountains in the far west made a long cloud-capped wall that stretched as far as the eye could see.

No one spoke. The only sounds were the rasping rustle the worms made as they dragged their great bulks through the dry vegetation, and the random startled cries and desperate wing beating of pheasant-like birds they occasionally flushed from the grass.

And the wind. The wind whispered over the prairie. Sometimes it was a soft whistle, sometimes a sibilant sigh that set the moisture-starved grasses to an almost musical whisking. The wind bent the grasses flat sometimes. Sometimes it caressed the blades more gently, causing the land to ripple and roll like a strange brown sea.

High sun found them at a small river. Little water flowed between the low banks, only a trickle in the middle of a wide, muddy bed. The worms crossed cautiously, leaving deep scars in the dark mud. For a short distance on the other side of the river, the grass grew as tall and thick as before and with the same dead color. Soon, though, it began to thin, or grow only in clumps. Not long after that, the land changed again.

Eric peered ahead at the baked earth. It was no longer brown like the mud by the stream, but bleached a strange, sickly shade like the color of dried flesh. He had never seen such a sight before, and he wondered if the hot sun alone was responsible. No blade of grass challenged that harsh environment, and the few trees that poked up out of the cracked, hard soil were leafless dead things. It was a vision of hell, and it repulsed him. Even his worm paused at the edge of this peculiar desert and sniffed before it followed the others forward.

For a while the sun beat down mercilessly. Sweat ran in rivulets on Eric's neck and chest and back until his shirt was saturated. Robert took his off, and Alanna quickly followed suit. Her bare, tanned breasts flashed in the sunlight. Katy only lifted an eyebrow, then rolled her own shirt up as high as her modesty allowed, exposing her flat midriff. The rest merely suffered.

However, when the sun was just past zenith, a cooler wind blew up from the south. The southern horizon turned gray, then dark gray. A bank of clouds crept slowly toward them. When the wind blew again, it brought with it the smell of rain.

"This land could use a good soaking," Katy said as she watched the sky.

"It won't help," Salyt answered curtly. She fell silent again.

Eric scanned the countryside. There was no hope of shelter; if it rained, they'd be drenched. He leaned in the saddle and looked down at the *chelit's* ridiculously tiny legs. If worst came to worst, he and his companions might huddle up against the sides of the beasts and try to wait out the storm.

The sky grew increasingly dark. A jagged bolt of lightning tore open the clouds with such thunderous ferocity, Eric nearly jumped from the saddle. The world flashed stark white. For moments following that blast, afterimages danced across his blurred vision. Valis reached back to steady him.

"Christ!" he muttered, realizing that while they were mounted, they made tall, tempting targets for the lightning to strike. The sudden wail of the wind nearly drowned his voice. "We should get off and walk!" he cried.

"No!" Salyt shouted back as she clung to Evander. "We push on!" She slapped Evander's shoulder with the flat of her hand as if he was no more than a beast himself. "Go!" she ordered. "Go on!"

For an instant the sky became a red lacework, and the air crackled. In the distance to their right, a tree exploded. Flames shot up the splintered trunk. Salyt ignored it and stabbed an insistent finger over Evander's shoulder as she pointed the way.

"Hold tight, my friend," Valis called back. He tapped the *chelit's* head with the rods, and the worm responded by increasing the pace.

For the better part of an hour, Eric estimated, the lightning flashed and the wind tore at the land. Great veils of dust and topsoil swirled upward, stinging their eyes and choking them. Katy and Alanna used the strips of cloth they wore around their heads to cover their mouths and noses. The rest managed as best they could.

Although the smell of rain hung in the air like a thick, tantalizing perfume, not a drop of moisture fell. The clouds rolled overhead at a frantic pace, full of lightning and thunder, but they offered no relief to the thirsty countryside. Eric, who had first dreaded the idea of rain, found himself praying for it for Wystoweem's sake. But the clouds raced on, and the wind laughed at him.

It ended almost as suddenly as it had begun. The lightning stopped. The wind subsided into a softly teasing breeze. The dust settled. The darker clouds rolled on northward, leaving an oppressive steel gray sky. The sun, no more than a fuzzy yellow ball, seemed to sink through it as if it was an ooze.

At Alanna's suggestion, they dismounted and stretched themselves. Eric took a sip from a canteen that Doe offered him. His mouth was full of dust; his clothes and body were covered with it. When he slapped his sleeves, a small brown cloud formed around him. "Welcome to the dust bowl days," he grumbled to nobody in particular.

Alanna gave him a curious look as she tied her headband back in place. "Dust bowl days?" she asked.

Eric frowned as he brushed the dust from his hair, fanning both hands rapidly through his thick brown locks. "An unpleasant time in Paradane's history."

She tilted her head as she brushed dust from her own clothes. "Even without Shandal Karg, your world seems to have a lot of unpleasantness," she commented.

Robert gave her a nudge as he tipped a canteen to his lips. "We don't need Dark Lords," he told her. "We have politicians."

Salyt showed the first hint that she had any sense of humor at all as she climbed back into the saddle of her *chelit*. "We have those, too," she reminded him.

Evander gave a wink, saying as he climbed up after her, "Palenoc is doubly cursed."

Katy's backpack rested on the ground at her feet, and she bent over it. "I'm starved," she said. "Anybody else?" She pulled out a handful of Snickers bars and offered them around.

Robert wagged a finger. "Do you realize how far you are from a dentist?" he demanded. Nevertheless, he was the first to take one. He peeled back the wrapper, broke the bar in half and offered the other part to Alanna. "I don't suppose you have a Coke in there?"

Katy shook her head as she passed another bar to Valis, who proceeded to share his with Doe. "Be grateful for this small taste of civilization," she told him.

Alanna's eyes lit up as she chewed her first bite. "You said there was no magic in your world, Robert!"

Salyt looked on curiously, though she made no effort to dismount. Evander, too, looked interested. Eric took yet another bar and tossed it up to him. Following the others' examples, he gave the councillor half.

"We'll share this one," Katy said, holding up another as he turned around. "There's two more left after this, and they're both mine."

Eric licked chocolate from his fingers and transferred his piece to the other hand. The bars were already half-melted, but that didn't matter to anyone. He smiled at Katy-did's possessiveness as he sucked his and felt the gooey candy slide down his throat. "I still remember your recipe for trail mix," he said before his mouth closed on a second bite.

Katy nodded and sputtered bits of peanuts. "M&M's, peanut M&M's, and Hershey's kisses," she affirmed.

"Hey!" Robert protested. "That was *my* recipe!"

"You stole it from me," Katy insisted stubbornly.

Salyt interrupted them. "This is disgusting." She held up ten chocolate-covered fingers and looked around as if for a napkin or something to wipe them on. With a small shrug, she followed Katy's example, thrust a digit into her mouth, and sucked it clean. A reserved smile turned up the corners of her mouth as she added, "But also very gratifying."

They resumed their southward journey with a lighter spirit. Without planning it, without even quite realizing it, Katy had brought them all a little closer together. Eric had seen it happen before; it was a talent of hers. In playground fights when they were kids, in arguments between Robert and the family, at Dowdsville town council meetings, Katy was always the one who somehow united the disparate parties.

He bit his lip as he regarded her. The worm upon which she and Doe rode kept pace right beside his and Valis's beast, and he could watch her from the corner of his eye without her noticing. Even dirty, he found her beautiful. It wasn't the delicate, porcelain beauty of cover-girl models. Rather, it was a rugged, proud handsomeness. A strange word, he thought, to describe a woman, but it fit Katy. He remembered how it had felt to hold her, remembered the strength in her body, its suppleness and her soft places.

He'd hurt her. He knew that. And not just once, but numerous times. He didn't want to do that again, yet he didn't seem to know what to say to her, what to do. Every time he drew her close, something inside also pulled away.

Abruptly he noticed that Katy was watching him, too. He looked quickly in the opposite direction and tried not to wonder what she was thinking.

On the far horizon, a long dark wall of trees stretched from east to west. The four *chelit* kept an unwavering pace, and it was soon plain they were heading for a vast forest.

The grass began to grow again. It had the same brown, unhealthy look, but at least it held the topsoil down when the wind blew.

As they rode closer, the trees towered above them, seeming to support the gray sky. Eric had never seen such huge trees. They dwarfed anything on Paradane, even the great California redwoods, and the smell of wood and bark and moss and earth stole up his nostrils. The air tasted of chlorophyll.

Salyt pointed suddenly and muttered something to Evander. At a touch from his slender rod, the huge *chelit* turned eastward and followed the forest's edge. The others fell in behind, and for a while they rode single file.

"Notice anything?" Eric whispered to Valis.

Valis hesitated. Slowly he swept his gaze through the forest's shadowed recesses and up into the treetops. "No birds," he answered finally.

"No birds," Eric echoed with a growing sense of unease. "A place like this should be full of birds."

It was quite a surprise to Eric when he spied the rooftops of a tiny village nestled right at the edge of the forest. Of course, Salyt must have known it was there all along. She'd guided them to it. A string of dogs began to bark as they approached. A small pack of the mongrels rushed forward to check them out. Eric feared suddenly for the *chelit*. Their tiny legs would be vulnerable to the dogs' jaws.

But at a certain point the dogs stopped their charge and flattened out in the grass. The barking became less menacing, though no less enthusiastic. A number of children raced across the field, waving their arms, while their parents proceeded after them with greater dignity.

"We'll spend the night here," Salyt announced. She slipped her pack off and hugged it to her body, wrapping both arms around it as Evander brought their beast to a stop.

There was something in the way she held that pack that caught Eric's attention. There were other packs tied to some of the saddles. Why was she so protective of this one? He watched the subtle movement her right hand made on the coarse leather as she cradled it. It was a stroking, *petting* motion.

He felt a chill breeze. Overhead, the sky began to darken again.

Chapter Eight

ROBERT could take no more of the villagers' stares. He was grateful for the meager supper his hosts served at long wooden tables hastily set up in the open air in the center of the town's only street, but he could no longer stand the way they looked at him surreptitiously from the corners of their eyes. Even more annoying was the way they turned aside quickly when he tried to engage them in conversation and the way they murmured to each other, unaware of the sharpness of his hearing. Too many times he heard an awe-filled whisper, "Shae'aluth!"

A little girl crept up behind while he was sitting, and gently touched his blond hair. When he gave her a patient smile, she ran off as fast as her legs would carry her and hid behind her mother's skirts. His hair, his eyes unsettled these people. They, in turn, unsettled him.

A silence fell over the festive gathering when he suddenly pushed back from the table and stood up. For a moment, it occurred to him that the villagers expected him to say something, but he rejected that notion. Instead, he leaned toward Eric on his right and said, "I'm calling it a day." He nodded to the rest and left them.

It was a small town without even a name. There were perhaps twenty buildings all told, and maybe eighty residents, counting men, women, and children. It had no inn, and no house big enough to hold so many guests. Alanna, Salyt, and Katy were being housed each with a local family. A large barn had been set aside for the men. The residents had brought their best blankets to make comfortable pallets in the straw.

Robert thrust his fingers into the pockets of his Levi's and headed for the barn. His brother and friends all remained at the table, and he was glad. He wanted a little time to himself.

Lightning flickered faintly overhead. The bad weather they had ridden through earlier was catching up with them. Or perhaps this was a new storm front. All afternoon and evening the sky had been a strange color. Robert glanced around before he went inside the barn. He could just make out the *chelit* huddled against each other in the field beyond the town. It was not quite dark, but night wasn't far off.

The barn had not been used for some time. In fact, Robert hadn't seen any livestock at all, other than a few chickens. The stalls had been converted into little private sleeping areas. He had other ideas, though. The loft had a door, and the breeze blew cool up there. He gathered an armload of exquisitely crafted quilts from one of the stalls and climbed the worn wooden ladder. He spread his blankets again upon the ample straw and threw open the loft door.

The wind blew upon his face, and he drew a deep breath. After a few moments, he pulled off his shirt, unlaced his Reeboks, and stretched out on his pallet. Distantly, he could hear the voices of the villagers, but he paid no attention. He folded one hand under his head as he watched another tongue of lightning lick at the clouds. His other hand worried down inside one tight-fitting pocket and extracted the bit of tourmaline quartz he had retrieved from Phlogis's sanctum.

He held it up to the fading light and turned it between his fingers, examining each facet. It wasn't really a pretty stone—rather plain, in fact—but when a random lightning bolt slashed across the heavens, the edges of the crystal came briefly alive with white fire.

He closed his fist around it and pressed it to his heart. The crystal felt warm on his bare skin, and the sound of his heartbeat seemed to rise up through it, as if amplified, louder and stronger than ever.

Robert closed his eyes and chewed his lower lip. He'd thought about this for days. Did he dare to try it on his own? "I sail a tide that is not what it seems," he whispered to himself. He listened to his own pulse and tried to slow his breathing. "The soul is a ship that sails the Dream Stream."

He repeated it again, but this time he called up an image of Scott Silver and fixed it in his mind. They might have been twins, he and Scott, they resembled each other so much. Only Scott's blond hair was curly, and his eyes were blue as the ocean. "The soul is a ship," he murmured, "that sails the Dream Stream." His hand squeezed the crystal tighter.

The wind played over his smooth chest like phantom fingers and trailed down his flat belly. It turned up the edges of his quilts and stirred the straw. Robert's awareness opened like a spring flower as he relaxed. The voices of the villagers were more audible. Somewhere a dog was barking. Though his eyes remained closed, the lightning made patterns on the insides of his lids. The bolts seemed to come more frequently now, and yet they brought no thunder. He smelled the straw, smelled the dust in the air, the dying trees.

But no door opened to him. The crystal was just a rock in his hand. Finally, he sat up and wondered if he could ever find his way into the Dream Stream without Phlogis to help him. He turned the stone over and over in his fingers, considering. It was only one failure. There would be time to try again. "Hold on, Scotty," he whispered fervently, "hold on."

After a while he pushed the crystal deep into his left front pocket and lay back down. He watched the clouds roll by through the loft door as his thoughts tumbled over and over. *A castle of black glass. Scott in an icy coffin. The Heart of Darkness.*

Boraga. The word came to him like a whimper from the deepest dungeons of his memory. He didn't know how he knew that word, but he knew, and a shiver ran down his spine. He turned over on his side, drew his knees up on his pallet, and hugged them. Nothing else came to him but that single word and the fear it brought. *Boraga.* It was the name of the black castle—Shandal Karg's fortress.

He lay there, his mind racing, until fatigue finally overtook him. He didn't sleep long, though. He woke with a start and sat up. Silence. It was the silence that had awakened him. The dinner festivities were over; the tables had been cleared from the street. He crawled to the edge of the loft and looked over the side. It was dark inside the barn, but he could just make out the dim shapes of Evander and Doe curled around each other on a pallet in the nearest stall. He hadn't heard them come in.

He crawled to the loft door, taking care to move as quietly as possible. The entire town was dark; no light shone in any of the windows. The villagers had all gone to bed. Robert wondered just how long he had slept. The sky was obscured by thick clouds, so he had no moon or stars to guage the passage of time.

He was just about to move back to his pallet and try to fall asleep again when he saw the tiny light of an oil lamp moving up the road from the far end of the village. He flattened out on the straw and watched.

Salyt. She moved with regal stiffness, carrying the small lamp in one hand, looking almost ghostlike as the amber glow reflected on her face and bleached leathers. The pack she had worn all day, she now wore slung over one shoulder. One of the village dogs padded up to her and sniffed. She paused, waited until the beast was satisfied, then continued on. The dog hung its head and followed after her heels.

Salyt paid it no more attention, though. She walked in the center of the street, looking neither left nor right. She seemed fixed upon her goal, the house directly across the street, which belonged to the barn's owners.

At the door she gave a barely audible rap and looked over her shoulders as if to see if anyone was following her or if anyone had heard. She rapped again. When the door opened, a gaunt, thin-faced man looked sleepily out. The two of them exchanged quiet words. Then the man disappeared back inside while the councillor stood at the entrance casting watchful glances.

Robert's inner alarms began to softly jangle. Rising, he picked a few pieces of straw out of the waistband of his jeans and snatched on his shirt. The loft ladder gave the barest creak as he descended. He paused long enough to see if the sound had disturbed Evander and Doe, but the pair didn't stir. Cautiously he stole past the next stall. Eric lay curled on his side among a pile of quilts. Valis slept in the stall closest to the door.

He wondered if he should wake them, then decided against it. In utter silence he eased back the door just wide enough to slip out, and flattened against the outer wall in the shadows.

Salyt stood waiting outside the half-open door of

the house across the street, lamp in hand. Impatiently she fingered the strap of her pack. The dog still sniffed around at her feet, but abruptly it lost interest in her and looked straight at Robert. Its tail lifted a bit, and it trotted toward him.

Robert remained absolutely still, giving the animal no excuse to bark. It sniffed his ankles, his knees and back, tried to put its head in his crotch. At that he drew the linc and pushed it away, but he gave it a scratch between the ears. It sat down next to him, tongue hanging.

Across the street, Katy appeared in the door. She was dressed in a sleeping gown the owner's wife must have provided for her, and she stared at Salyt in confusion. There was a whispered conversation, but Robert could hear none of it. He began to consider his chances of sneaking nearer without being seen. Then Katy spun about and went back inside. Salyt remained waiting, her gaze sweeping around, and Robert decided to stay where he was a little longer.

A few moments later Katy reappeared, dressed in her *sekournen* leathers, her hair tied back. The whispered exchange between the two women was sharp enough for Robert to hear its tone, if not the specific words. Katy wasn't happy. Still, the two of them started up the street side by side with Salyt's lamp to show the way.

Robert followed, hugging the shadows.

At the end of the street, the forest loomed like a huge black wall. The high treetops swayed menacingly. The breeze rustled the dry leaves that clung to the gnarled and twisted branches, filling the night with a raspy susurrus. The street did not end at the forest's edge, but pushed a little way into it. Still, it was black as pitch in there. Salyt put a finger to her lips, warning

Katy to silence. Then, shielding her pitiful little light with one cupped hand, she walked into that darkness.

Robert heard a small whine right behind him and looked back. The dog had followed him. It pleaded with big, moist eyes and wouldn't go any farther. "Sorry boy," he murmured, giving his new friend another pat between the ears. Then he rushed on. If he lost view of that small lamplight, he would lose the women. He didn't intend to let that happen. He was much too curious to know what the hell was going on.

The road soon turned into no more than a beaten path. It surprised him when Salyt and Katy abruptly turned off it and pushed into the forest, itself. The lamplight winked and wavered, eclipsed by trees and foliage. Robert had to quicken his pace to keep it in sight, a task made more difficult by his need to move soundlessly.

Without any warning, the light disappeared. Robert cursed under his breath. He listened, hoping Katy or Salyt might speak, but no voice touched his ears.

He felt uncomfortably alone. Holding his breath, he crept forward, never taking his eyes from the place where he'd last seen the flame. A low branch swatted his face. He stumbled over an unnoticed root.

He found himself under a low overhang. A black, dry moss hung from the jutting stones above. Katy and Salyt couldn't have climbed it in the dark, not even with the lamp. He sniffed. A faint whiff of Salyt's oil lingered in the air. This was the spot then where the light had winked out, but where the hell had they gone?

He moved back and forth before the overhang. It wasn't all that deep, but he hesitated to explore beneath it in the dark. Visions of snakes and spiders and worse came to him. He stared both ways, hoping for a glimpse of the lamp. Perhaps the women had simply turned and gone a different direction. He saw nothing, though, and the smell of burned oil said they had been *here*.

Muttering another curse, he picked up a stick and jabbed it back under the overhang. The tip scraped against a stony wall. He took a step to the left and jabbed again. The stick encountered nothing. Robert bit his lip. Then he swung the stick from left to right, fanning it before him. Twice it struck stone. There was an opening under there. A cave.

How do I get myself into these things, he sighed nervously. Now he knew why it was so easy to smell the smoke and oil from the lamp. The fumes were trapped in that narrow opening. Inwardly he cringed. Still, he stared inside, feeling the wall on one side with his right hand, holding his left straight out before him, moving his feet slowly so as not to trip.

"It's safe to speak now."

Salyt's voice. The words echoed back to him from far ahead.

"This circle is a seal," the councillor continued. "Neither the Heart of Darkness, nor any of her minions, can hear us while we stand within it."

Robert moved a little quicker. The cave floor was a fine, dusty pounce, and his Reeboks made little sound at all. His curiosity grew stronger than ever.

Katy's voice whispered out of the darkness. "That's what that elaborate circle in Phlogis's sanctum is for?" she asked. There was a thin edge to her voice, as if she were afraid, but trying boldly not to let it show. "And in your council chamber? Robert called it a hex sign."

Robert hesitated at the sound of his name, then continued on. A soft amber glow reflected on the dull stone ahead. The cave made a subtle curve. Pressing himself to the wall, he approached it.

"They are seals," Salyt repeated sternly. "The designs deflect any magical attack. We can't even be detected while we stand here."

Wanna bet? Robert thought as he crept still closer. The cave ended in a roughly circular chamber. The walls were almost smooth, leading him to realize he wasn't in a natural cave at all, but a construct that had actually been carved into the hillside. Two small candle stubs placed on the ground on either side of the chamber added to the lamp's light.

The floor of the chamber was painted in the same elaborate manner as the council room in Sheren Shago. The seal might ward off magic, he thought to himself, but it didn't prevent somebody from just creeping up and listening.

Katy seemed impatient. There was nothing to sit on, so she paced around the chamber. The uplighting from the candles and lamp on the floor gave her face a skeletal look, but set her red tresses to shimmering. "So why was it so all-fired important to drag me out here in the middle of the night?"

Salyt knelt down in the center of the circle, unslung the pack from her shoulder, and placed it between her knees. "Because I must ask your help, *hami*," she said.

Katy raised one eyebrow and put her hands on her hips. "*You* need *my* help?" she said sarcastically. "Lady, I don't even like you."

Robert half grinned. His Kat wasn't one to mince words. His gaze went to Salyt's pack, though. What did the councillor have in there that was so precious to her?

"I don't ask you to like me!" Salyt snapped with surprising venom. "Only that you love Palenoc. Or if that's not enough, that you love your man, who loves this world enough to risk his life for it!"

Katy's hands clenched at her sides. "What I feel for Eric is none of your fucking business!"

Great, Robert thought. *I sneak all this way through the darkness, risking lions and tigers and bears, oh my, and for what? A catfight.*

Salyt, ever the politician, held up her hands and spread her fingers. "Let's start again," she suggested more calmly. "Whether I like you or not is irrelevant." Katy bristled, but Salyt went on. "The fact is, I trust you, Katherine Dowd. *Hami rana sekoye.*" She inclined her head ever so slightly and fixed Katy with her gaze.

Katy stared back, eyes gleaming and hard as marbles. Then, with a sigh, she relented. Folding her legs, she sat lotus style on the floor facing Salyt.

"You aren't aware of it," the councillor went on, "but you have a power within you. Phlogis noticed it. And since the moment we first met, I've been testing you."

"Power?" Katy said doubtfully. "What are you talking about?"

Salyt waved a hand. "We don't understand it yet," she admitted. "Phlogis is a *dando,* a vengeful spirit. The wave of psychic anger he projects touches everyone who comes into his presence. Yet, he said it failed to affect you." She reached into the neck of her shirt and pulled out a blue stone, which hung on a chain. In the candlelight it shone like sapphire. "I've tried several times with the aid of this to see into your thoughts."

"Telepathy?" Katy leaned forward to peer at the gem.

The councilwoman shrugged. "After a fashion." She put the stone back inside her shirt and adjusted her collar. "I only achieved the barest success at first. That's since turned to total failure."

Katy leaned back, bracing her hands on the floor. She frowned. "How can a crystal let you read my mind?"

"All our magic is worked through crystals," Salyt said. "Stones have power." She leaned forward and pointed a finger at Katy. "But not over you." She sucked in her lower lip, searching for the right words. She thumped her fist on the floor. "This circle is for my sake," she continued. "I doubt even the Heart of Darkness herself can look inside you."

Katy shook her head stubbornly. "She managed to see me well enough to send that *thing* to kill me in my sleep."

"That was days ago," Salyt reminded her. "This power was a small, weak thing then. But it's growing stronger within you. You're turning invisible, Katherine Dowd. We can see you with our eyes, but not with any magical senses."

Katy got up and paced to the back of the chamber, her arms folded across her chest. "This is way over my head," she said wearing a troubled expression. "Is this power something I can use to help further this mission?"

A smile lit up Salyt's face. "I can see that Phlogis was right to send you along. You are truly a Sister of the Dragon." She opened the pack in front of her and put one hand inside. "If anything happens to me," she said, "you, Katherine Dowd, are best suited to take my place. Listen."

Robert listened too, fascinated, as he eased himself down into a sitting position in the shadows just outside the chamber. The animosity between Kat and the councillor had dissolved. Salyt was a teacher now, and Katy an eager pupil. Katy stopped her pacing again and crouched down before Salyt, the pack between them. Robert leaned his head back against the stone wall and learned secrets not meant for his ears.

"There is a plain at the very center of Chol-Hecate," Salyt told Katy. "It is the Plain of Nazrit, which in the Hecate language means, *spider.*"

"The Spider Plain," Katy repeated, nodding.

"It is an ancient and sacred place," Salyt went on. "A monument to evil . . . only this monument is made of immense scars and scratchings cut deep into the ground. These scratchings, seen from the cliffs on either side of Nazrit, form the image of a giant spider. The image is at the center of the plain, which is at the center of Chol-Hecate."

Katy nodded again as she clasped her hands together. "I'm with you so far."

So am I, Robert thought to himself. He felt a vague sense of guilt for spying on his friends, but he didn't like the way the councillor had cloaked this whole expedition in secrecy. He was nobody's good soldier. He wanted to know what was going on.

"We're going to plant something in the heart of that spider," Salyt said grimly. "This."

A bloodred ruby came out of the pack. It was the size of a softball, and the candlelight danced dizzyingly on its perfect facets. Spears of red fire shot about the chamber until Salyt's hand became still.

Robert's breath caught in his throat. He'd never seen such a stone. The air itself seemed to tingle with a strange electricity. Salyt had spoken of power before. He could feel the *power* of this fabulous gem like a wave breaking on his skin. He shifted onto his hands and knees and crawled as close as he dared without being seen, his gaze riveted on the ruby.

There was a small black spot in its center.

Katy's eyes were wide saucers. Tentatively she reached out her hands, and Salyt placed the ruby on her palms. Katy lifted it until it was mere inches from her face.

"A wasp!" she cried suddenly. "There's a wasp at the center of it!"

"Yes," Salyt said. "A wasp to sting the spider." She laid one hand on Katy's wrist and squeezed. "If anything happens to me, Katherine, my task falls to you. Bury this talisman in the spider's heart. When that's done, neither the Gray Kingdoms nor the Domains of Light will have any more to fear from Chol-Hecate."

"What does it do?" Katy whispered.

Salyt shook her head and took the ruby back. Carefully she returned it to the pack and closed it up. "You know enough, *hami*," she said. "Just remember, wars on our planet are not fought like the wars on Paradane."

Robert crawled back into the deeper shadows as Salyt leaned over and blew out one of the candles. It was plain the conference was over. The image of the jewel still burned in his mind as he rose to his feet. The light dimmed again as the other candle was extinguished.

"Speak no more of this," he heard Salyt caution. "Once we leave the circle, it would not be safe. Shandal Karg and her puppet, Kajin Lure, have eyes and ears everywhere."

The remaining lamplight flickered and shifted and started to come his way. Robert figured it was time to get out. He could either beat them back to the village, or hide in the woods and follow them back. He felt along the wall with one hand as he made his way toward the mouth of the cave.

A sudden blast rocked the stone under his touch. At first, he thought someone had dynamited the hill, but an instant later the world beyond the entrance flashed white. The brilliance stabbed at his eyes, eliciting an audible groan of shock and surprise. He threw up a hand to protect his vision. The air stank of ozone.

Forgetting stealth, he raced to the opening and peered out. The storm that had threatened all day had arrived at last. Rain poured down in torrents. The trees shivered and shook under the onslaught. A crackling filled the sky, causing him to jump. Jagged lightning tore across the blackness. Again, thunder rocked the hillside.

He heard the women scrambling up behind him and wondered if he'd been seen. That last lightning burst would have silhouetted him perfectly if they'd been looking. He glanced back to see the glow of the lamp reflecting on the stone walls. Maybe they hadn't seen him after all.

The rain soaked him instantly as he moved away from the cave and hid in the trees. The thickest branches were no shelter at all. Solid sheets of water fell, stripping the half-dead leaves from their limbs. The wind whipped through the forest, bending the skeletal frames of the trees, cracking them. The night was full of the sounds of crashing.

Katy and Salyt poked their heads out of the cave entrance. Robert hoped they would stay there to wait out the storm. In the cave they were safe from the lightning or from falling trees. But the women had other ideas. "This way!" Salyt called, slinging her precious pack over her shoulder. She took Katy's unresisting hand in her own. They dashed out into the tempest. The little lamp was instantly extinguished by wind or water. With a curse, Salyt flung it down.

He didn't worry about moving quietly now. The crackling lightning, the thunder, the ravaging wind and rain all hid any sound he might make. The women plunged into the forest, headed for the road back to the village, and he raced after them, playing the role of protector now, following to ensure they made it safely.

Salyt was sure of her direction. They arrived straight back at the narrow road, which was now a ribbon of black mud. Robert emerged about ten yards farther up. The pair was still not aware of him. "There hasn't been a rain like this in five years!" he heard the councillor cry excitedly to Katy. She turned her face up to it, laughing.

Lightning shattered the sky. For an instant the night shimmered like a million falling splinters of black glass.

Then Robert screamed. A familiar form stood revealed not five feet away in the heart of that momentary whiteness. Blond curls whipped in the wind. Eyes impossibly blue in a pale face fixed him with an imploring look. Naked, muscled flesh glowed with an eerie luminescence.

He stared at his friend, Scott Silver.

And then the world went black again. Robert blinked, and Scott was gone.

The women whirled, startled to discover they weren't alone. Katy recognized him at once. She ran back up the road, and Salyt came fast on her heels. "Robert!" she shouted. Rivulets of water ran down her face. Streams made waterfalls on her nose and chin. Her hair hung in wild ropes. "What are you doing out here!"

"Scott!" he shouted back. He realized he was trembling, filled with a sudden, inexplicable fear. "I just saw Scott!"

"A trick of the lightning!" Salyt said doubtfully. Nevertheless, she spun about, her gaze searching the nearest shadows.

"No, it was Scott!" Robert insisted. He caught his breath suddenly, feeling as if a giant hand was squeezing his chest. "Something's wrong!" he cried. "He's appeared like this before to me and Eric both! Always when there's trouble!" He hesitated, staring ahead past Katy and Salyt, hoping another lightning burst would bring Scott back again. Thunder rattled the trees, and the wind drove wild leaves with stinging force. But his friend did not return. "Let's get back to the village!" Robert insisted.

They hadn't gone five steps when they heard the screaming. The rain muffled the sounds only a little. They froze in their tracks, turned stricken looks on each other. All three began to run.

A pair of huge shapes lurched out of the trees and stood by the roadside staring at them with hungry, luminous eyes. Water gleamed in the creatures' thick, sodden fur.

"Magoths!" Salyt shouted as they ran around the beasts. "They shouldn't be this far north!"

The monsters merely watched as the humans raced past them. Robert dared to lift his gaze. Two more of the shaggy apelike *magoths* moved through the trees above the road. There were probably more.

But something else moved up there, too. He couldn't make out what it was. Something blacker than the night, something that flowed with a swift and terrible grace, unhindered by the storm. He had a fleeting image of a huge leech before it swooped straight at them. He tried to shout a warning. At the same time, he grabbed Katy and flung her to the ground.

Salyt gave a high-pitched shriek. Robert rolled over, soaked with mud and filth as something folded around the councillor. It was like a black cloak with some eldritch life of its own. It covered her from head to toe, constricting around her, suffocating her, bearing her down.

"It's the same thing that attacked me!" Katy cried, terror filling her voice. She cringed, started to crawl toward the bushes that grew by the roadside. Then something changed inside her. The fear on her face turned to rage. "Let her go, goddamn you!" she screamed. She seized up a broken branch, scrambled to her feet, and ran at the creature. Before Robert could stop her, she raised her makeshift club and swung it. Salyt screamed again as the blow landed across her back.

"Stop it!" Robert shouted as he grabbed the branch out of Katy's hands and flung it away. She stared at him, stunned. "You're hitting Salyt!" He bent over the councillor's struggling form and plunged his hands into the black misty substance that covered her, giving a sharp intake of breath at the cold that threatened to freeze his skin. He could feel her body inside the creature. Revulsion seized him, but he fought it down. There wasn't time for that kind of emotion. The creature ignored him, totally intent upon murdering Salyt. He could feel its malevolence.

"Find the bone!" he screamed at himself as he swept his hands through the chilling vapor. "Eric said there'd be a bone!"

Those words were for his own encouragement, but Katy heard and shoved her hands in alongside his. It was like looking for something underwater with your eyes closed. Now the creature noticed them, not with eyes or any sensory organs Robert could determine, but he felt that malevolence turn his way, felt it rasp like sandpaper in his mind. Salyt was near death. The creature exerted itself. It squeezed her, and Robert heard the councillor's weakening gasp, knowing it would turn on him next.

Then Katy gave a shout of triumph and ripped a black bone from the creature's heart. A streamer of mist, like a spray of blood, came away with it. A psychic scream cut across Robert's mind, sending him reeling backward. The creature convulsed and reared up, freeing Salyt's upper body. Then it leaped into the air and dissolved into nothingness.

Katy knelt down by the councillor's side. Salyt batted her eyes weakly and tried to sit up. "She's alive," Katy said needlessly.

"We'd better get her on her feet," Robert said. The magoths on the road were shambling closer, drawn by the thought of fresh meat. He couldn't see the ones in the trees, but he was sure they were drawing nearer as well.

"I'm all right," Salyt managed. She caught Robert's hand and let him help her up. Her face was ashen, even in the darkness, and her touch felt like ice. "The village!" The words came out in a harsh rasp, as if she'd been strangled, but she caught his arm and propelled him into motion. "The village!"

The village was in chaos. Leeches flitted through the air, attacking fleeing citizens. Bodies littered the street. A man hung half out of the front window of his home. A woman lay dead on the stoop of her doorway. Dogs howled and leaped as high as their hind legs would carry them, snapping their jaws at the unholy things that menaced their masters. Despite the heavy rain, a shop burned at the far end of the street.

Eric, Valis, and Alanna fought for their lives just outside the barn where the men had slept. Valis's staff made a blur in his hands. Eric swung a rake. Alanna gripped a wide board in both her hands. The leech creatures darted at them. Valis struck and cut with his staff. A black bone went spinning through the air.

The sky flashed white. The violent light stabbed Robert's eyes, but he looked around desperately for something to use for a weapon. He didn't need it. As if the lightning was a signal, the leeches abandoned the village.

Robert let go a sigh of relief and hugged Katy to him, his gaze still trained overhead. In that brief moment when the world had been bright as daylight, he had seen a horror. Thousands of black amorphous shapes streaming like an evil river through the night, all heading northward. Only a handful had descended upon the village, only a few from a vast and terrifying vanguard.

Salyt had seen them, too. "Capreet," she whispered through terse and trembling lips. "Weena."

Eric ran over to join them. Blood ran from a cut over his eyebrow. He wiped it away with his palm as Katy sprang out of Robert's embrace and into his brother's. "You're hurt!" she exclaimed.

"My fault," Alanna said grimly. "Things were a bit tense. I got a little wild swinging this board."

Eric nodded and wiped his cut again. "She has a nasty backhand," he admitted. He regarded Robert with an exhausted look. "Where were you, Bobby?"

"Walking in the woods," Robert said. It was half the truth anyway. He glanced at Salyt's pack, still on her shoulder. Then he remembered, "I saw Scott!"

Alanna whirled about suddenly. "Where's Evander and Doe?"

Everyone turned toward the barn. The doors were partially open, but it was dark inside and silent. Robert started forward. Alanna quickly fell in at his side. The others came behind.

They found Doe in his stall kneeling on the straw bedding, clutching a large femur-like bone to his chest. Evander lay before him, partially wrapped in the soft quilts. His empty eyes, wide as china plates, stared upward at the rafters.

"Oh, my God," Katy muttered. She curled into Eric's shoulder and hid her face.

Alanna flung herself down beside Doe and put her arms around him. They were *sekournen* together; they served the same Sheren. That made them far more than friends. They were *namue shi hami*. Brother and sister.

But Doe barely acknowledged her presence. He sat unmoving, the fingers of one hand intertwined with Evander's. Though he shed not a single tear, his grief was a palpable force, and no one could urge him from the spot. Finally, the others slipped out, all but Alanna, who would not leave him alone.

Robert wiped the rain from his face as he stared up and down the street. The fire down the way had spread to the next house. Despite the storm, he had little doubt it would consume the whole town. He tried to count the bodies he saw and his throat went dry. Could it be that no one else was alive? Or had some of the villagers escaped into the fields or the woods?

"We should gather all the dead," he said suddenly, "and burn them."

Eric touched his shoulder and turned him slightly. "Why, little brother? You know something?"

Robert frowned. His eyes stung, and blinking didn't seem to help. Maybe it was the smoke. But the wind was carrying the smoke the other way. He wiped at his eyes. He couldn't be crying. He never cried. He glanced at the woman dead on her stoop and averted his gaze. He thought of Evander, beautiful Evander. Doe's twin.

"It's Australian magic," he told his brother, as if it was the simplest, most obvious explanation in the world. "I researched it for a book once. The aborigines call it *the killing bone.*"

Eric gave him a queer look, but Salyt pressed closer.

"You know what these creatures are? They are from Paradane?"

"Of course not!" Robert snapped, barely in control of himself. He put his mind to work. It was the best way to master his emotions. "But it must be the same theory. With a piece of human bone, you can conjure up the spirit of the person it belonged to, then bend and twist that spirit and send it out to do murder. The spirit is called a sending. That's got to be what we're up against!"

Valis made a face as he leaned on his staff. "How would Shandal Karg have learned this bit of Earth-magic?"

Robert kicked a spray of mud into the air. "I don't have all the answers, damn it! I'm just telling you what we're facing. She can raise as large an army as she needs just by raiding the cemeteries." He gestured up and down the street. "At least if we burn these bodies, she'll never be able to use them."

Salyt shielded her eyes from the rain as she stared southward. "Maybe it's Kajin Lure doing the raising," she said. "This must be the *new magic* we've heard rumors of."

Eric turned his gaze up toward the sky again. It was empty now. The enemy had passed on. "Well, we certainly know what the reports of black clouds were about."

Salyt nodded. "The Gray Kingdoms were just the testing grounds, but as they fell, so will Wystoweem fall. Your sendings will reach Capreet before morning."

"They're not *my* sendings," Robert said sullenly.

Salyt didn't even hear him. Her hands clenched at her sides. She might have been speaking to herself. "I'll make Kajin Lure pay, though. I swear it."

"Shut up!" Katy said suddenly, interrupting both of

them. She pointed northward. A pale golden spark sailed from the horizon, seeming to arc toward them at incredible speed. "What is that?"

Valis spoke in a low voice. "Sunrunner," he said.

Robert spun about, ignoring the water that rilled into his eyes. "Evander's dragon ... ?" The words choked in his throat. He spun about again, the burning filling his eyes. "No," he murmured uselessly. "No!"

"What is it?" Katy demanded. "What's wrong?"

Eric pulled her into him and stroked her hair as he watched Sunrunner's advance. "You don't understand, Katy-did. The bond is broken."

In only moments, Sunrunner was above them. The dragon's screams preceded him, the terrible sound rolling over the field, shaking the forest. The light from his wings shimmered in the water that filled the street as he gyred over the village, crying for the rider who would never answer.

Suddenly Robert rushed forward and flung up his arms. "Take me!" he shouted at the dragon. "Take me!"

Alanna blocked his way suddenly and pushed him back. He hadn't seen her come out of the barn, but she must have heard Sunrunner's screams. She caught him in her arms, held him with fierce strength. "Don't, *Kaesha*!" she cried in his ear. "There's nothing you can do!"

Sunrunner climbed higher and higher above the town, shrieking with every beat of those splendid wings. Then, without warning, he turned and dove earthward. His golden glow was like a fire streaming out behind, igniting even the sheets of rain.

Valis turned away. Eric and Katy clung to each other, heads buried in each others' shoulders. Salyt stood like a statue, mesmerized. Robert locked his arms around Alanna and let go a high-pitched wail of despair.

Like a hurtling star, Sunrunner smashed himself against the earth.

For a horrified instant, no one said anything. Then Robert pushed Alanna away. "Why wouldn't Sunrunner take me?" he shouted at her, tears streaming down his face. "You must have heard him. You can hear all the dragons. Why wouldn't he take me?"

Eric could barely speak. He trembled visibly in Katy's arms, thin rain-diluted blood running down his face. "You don't understand, Bobby," he said. "It was the bond."

Robert screamed at his brother. "Shadowfire took you!"

Valis raised his staff in both hands and brought it down over his knee. The sound of it breaking was like a rifle shot. "Get Doe, and let's clear out," he said through clenched teeth. "There won't be time to burn the bodies." He pointed toward the forest.

The *magoths* shambled toward them, grunting their hunger. There would be a second feast in the village tonight.

"Where is Doe?" Alanna said in sudden alarm.

"There," Robert said, pointing past the magoths toward the village. In the street, silhouetted against the flames, Doe walked with Evander's body in his arms. When he reached a place where the fire seemed hottest, he lifted the fallen *sekournen* above his head. For a moment, he seemed to weaken under the strain and nearly fell headlong into the flames himself. But then he caught his balance.

A pause, perhaps to utter a prayer, then Doe heaved Evander into the heart of the fire. He stood there for another moment, staring into that inferno, then he ran across the field, dodging and weaving past the lumbering magoths, until he reached the *chelit* again.

"That was a stupid risk," Salyt said.

Doe refused to look at her or say anything as he mounted one of the great worms.

"He couldn't leave Evander to those beasts," Robert said bitterly. "Nor to Shandal Karg."

Chapter Nine

A flash of lightning lit up the land. In the field at the edge of town, the *chelit*, huge and pale-fleshed, were briefly illuminated. Great black eyes, unblinking, reflected the roiling sky above, but neither wind nor rain moved the creatures. Side by side, they waited as their riders raced toward them.

Katy pumped her arms as she ran, her pack banging on one shoulder. She'd retrieved it from the house across from the barn even as the *magoths* closed in. Without warning, she slipped and fell flat on her face in the wet grass. It was more than wet grass, though, that had caused her fall. Eric pulled her to her feet as she held up her hands. Her fingers were coated with a whitish slime. Her clothes were covered with it, too.

"What is this stuff?" Her face wrinkled in disgust.

"Raw silk," Valis answered roughly. "The worms produce it when they overeat, and they've had plenty of time to graze." A crashing roar sounded behind them. He cast a hurried glance back toward the village. Involuntarily, Katy followed his gaze.

The fire was spreading. The roof and near wall of a shop collapsed. Red-glowing sparks spiraled upward into the wind. Smoke and flames licked at the clouds. In the orange light, hulking shadows gnawed and chewed and fed.

Katy shuddered as she wiped her hands on her trousers, and she made a conscious effort not to think about the *magoths*. At least she knew why Wystoweem's leaders dressed so well. The ground was covered with the sticky enzyme.

"It might be silk when it dries," Robert said as he reached one of the worms and drew the riding wands from special holsters on the saddle, "but in this form, it's slicker than ..."

"Look out!" Eric cried. He launched himself at Robert, sweeping his brother to the ground as a net sailed through the air above their heads. A second net hissed out of the darkness. Valis intercepted it with his upraised staff.

Just to the right, twelve figures rose up out of the tall grass. Lightning illuminated the black armor and the strange masks they wore. For weapons, they carried nets and staves. Some held club-like batons, slender shafts of wood with weighted wooden balls at one end. At least two carried whips.

"Chols!" Salyt called. She clutched the pack containing the special ruby to her chest with both arms.

Another net whisked toward them, but draped itself over the head of one of the *chelit,* instead. The rest of the black-clad attackers rushed them, screaming. When the lightning flashed again, Katy saw the demonic faces of those hideous masks, designed to frighten.

Alanna pulled her blowpipe from her waistband, drew a dart from a special pocket on the back of her glove, and lifted it to her mouth. An instant later, the first Chol stumbled and fell. A second man folded right beside the first as Doe brought his own blowpipe into play.

Eric and Robert charged forward. A staff whistled down toward Eric's head. He brushed it aside with a sweeping block and slammed the inside edge of his hand at his foe's unprotected throat. Snatching the staff for his own use, he turned to face another attacker.

Katy looked around frantically. Three armored Chols moved swiftly to surround Robert. She cried a needless warning. He was already moving, lashing out at the closest of the three, smashing a mask with the heel of his left hand. The mask's wearer clutched at bloodied eyes, screaming, as he sank to his knees. A second man struck at Robert with a whip, its loud crack audible even over a blast of thunder, but Robert no longer in the same place. He hung, seemingly suspended in the air, caught in a flash of lightning, above the whip-man's head. His flying kick sent the second foe crashing to the ground. He landed in a catlike crouch; then, in a blur of motion, spun and executed a graceful crescent with his left leg to dispatch the third soldier.

Katy knew Robert was good, better even than Eric, but she'd never seen him move like this!

A shrill scream drew her attention. A black-clad Chol loomed over Salyt, baton raised. Katy snatched the Omega stunner from its holster on her belt. Before she could use it, however, Valis was there. The first blow of the huge *sekournen's* staff sent the baton flying. The second blow broke the Chol's knee. When the soldier fell, Valis rose over him like a vengeful, angry spirit. The end of his staff jabbed downward forcefully to crush his fallen foe's throat.

Valis barely stopped his thrust in time. For an instant, his hands trembled and his lips curled back. Katy thought he would kill the man, after all. Then, gaining a measure of control, he withdrew and turned to seek another foe.

Katy stared momentarily at the crippled man on the

ground. A fragment of bone appeared to jut through the torn fabric of his trousers. He screamed in pain through his mask, yet with Valis gone, he groped for Salyt with one feeble hand.

"Get away!" Katy shouted. She seized the councillor's arm and jerked her aside. Then she grabbed the net that hung over the head of the *chelit*. It was woven of heavy rope, and the corners were weighted with metal balls. With a clumsy grunt, she flung it over the determined Chol, who screamed again as one of the weights struck his knee. "Stay beside me!" she told Salyt, brandishing the Omega. They pressed up against the *chelit*, using its great bulk to guard their backs.

The fight ended with surprising quickness. After the first flurry of darts, Doe and Alanna entered the fray hand to hand, using the skills Eric and Robert had taught them. The Chols were poorly trained fighters, despite their weapons and armor. They seemed surprised to meet any resistance at all. Still, they fought until the last man went down.

The sounds of moaning and groaning hung over the field. Eric, Robert, Alanna, Valis, and Doe stood in a tight circle, still tensed for combat as they surveyed their work. At last, Alanna took another dart from her glove, went to those Chols who remained conscious, and made a scratch under their chins. Soon, the moaning stopped.

"Did she kill them?" Katy whispered fearfully to Salyt.

The councilwoman shook her head. "I told you, Katherine. Warfare is different on Palenoc. If you kill someone, you make a ghost, and that ghost may come after you." She pointed toward the nearest Chol under the net. "That's why they wear those masks. They think if they kill inadvertently, the ghost won't recognize them."

"You don't sound as if it works that way," Katy said as she holstered the unused stunner.

Valis had overheard as he approached them. He handed his staff to Katy, then unslung a small leather canteen from the saddle of his *chelit.* "It's an old superstition among some of the nations of the Kingdoms of Night, fostered by the leaders to give their soldiers a false courage in the field of battle. But recently the practice has spread to the Dark Land armies as well." He took a quick drink and capped his canteen again. "No, it doesn't work. A ghost knows its killer." He took his staff back from her.

"Looks like a scouting party," Eric said as he came to Katy's side. He gave her a once-over look, as if to reassure himself she was all right. Then he glanced back toward the village. The flames were high now. Smoke poured off into the east. There wouldn't be much of anything left in another hour. "They were probably sent to observe the attack."

Alanna nodded. "Somebody will be expecting their report," she pointed out.

Robert twirled a Chol baton between his fingers. Katy noticed a splotch of blood on one of his white Reeboks. "Which means we should clear out fast," he said, "before another patrol comes looking for them." He drew back and threw the baton as far as he could. It disappeared in the darkness long before it hit the ground.

Salyt relaxed a bit as she eased into the straps of her pack and adjusted it for comfort. "I'm very impressed," she told them. "Phlogis did not overestimate your worth, *Namue shi hami rana sekoye.*" She reached out and took Katy's hand, then Eric's. "Capreet may perish tonight and all of Wystoweem fall. But with your help, we'll strike a blow to make the Heart of Darkness scream."

They mounted the four *chelit*. Katy gazed toward the burning town and the shadowy shapes that moved through its streets, and a chill seized her. "The Chols!" she cried in sudden concern. "They're drugged! What if the *magoths* find them?"

"Their blood won't be on our hands," Alanna said coldly.

"Let the *magoths* have them" came Salyt's acid response. She looked down on the broken-limbed soldier under the net and spat.

They started forward, making a wide arc around the burning town, heading toward the edge of the forest. While others watched the flames, Katy kept her eyes peeled for anyone hiding in the grass. It wasn't Chol soldiers she watched for, though. She hoped that someone from the village had escaped the destruction. Nothing moved, though, as far as she could see, except for one small dog that followed them at a distance.

They rode eastward along the forest's edge until the flames could no longer be seen. Then, acting on Salyt's advice, they pushed into the trees. Katy huddled against Doe's back and crouched as low as she could in the saddle in a useless effort to avoid the barely glimpsed limbs that snagged her hair and brushed her shoulders.

The *chelit's* huge eyes gave them an uncanny ability to see in the dark. The creatures picked their way, moving with slow probing sureness on their hundreds of legs, and with surprising silence.

The rain hardly penetrated the dense forest canopy. Droplets fell, but the leaves kept out the worst of the storm. The sounds of chittering insects rose in the night making a strange chorus. They all paused for a moment to listen.

"I thought the woods were dead," Katy whispered,

afraid to speak too loudly. "We didn't hear any insects before. And there were no birds."

"Perhaps Kajin Lure's evil has only scarred the edges of this forest and left its heart untouched," Salyt said grimly.

Katy was unsure of what the councillor meant, nor did she ask.

They resumed their journey. Deeper into the woods, fireflies winked. At least, she guessed they were fireflies. There was an eerie beauty to it all. She thought of the times when she'd camped or hiked in the Catskills, of nights spent with a tent and her guitar alone on the side of some mountain or in an isolated clove by a small trickling stream.

She missed the guitar, but suddenly everything else seemed like part of another lifetime. She tightened her grip around Doe's middle and leaned her head on his back. From the corner of her eye, she could just see Eric following behind. He scarcely guided the worm now, working the rods little, letting the *chelit* pick its way, while Valis sat watchfully in the saddle behind him.

In Dowdsville, Eric had always seemed a little bit lost to her. He'd wasted his degree in geology after attending New York University, and wasted his time, too, becoming a postman, never venturing far from the place where he'd grown up. For a while, she'd feared he would even waste his life with alcohol as he tried to forget all the hopes and dreams he'd once treasured.

She'd loved him all through those times, loved him as long as she could remember, even as a little kid when they ran and played in Dowdsville's Main Street. She loved him now, too, more than ever. He was at last the Eric he should have become, confident, determined, a natural leader. Palenoc had transformed him—awakened all his potential. She wondered if he realized it.

A small whiff of smoke caused her to look around. No, she couldn't see the flames. The town was far away now, but the random breeze that penetrated the forest depths still brought the faint odor of burning. Doe twisted around, also, and gazed in the same direction. Even in the darkness there was a haunted look in his eyes. He hadn't spoken a word since Evander's death.

The rain finally stopped. Droplets continued to seep down from the higher leaves to the lower. They made a soothing patter. Katy felt the rise and fall of Doe's breathing against her cheek. Vague traceries of lightning continued to dance across the little pieces of sky she could see through the gaps in the trees, but they were poor echoes of the brilliant flashes thrown off by the storm at its peak.

The insects sang louder. The thick canopy of foliage had kept out the worst of the storm. The ground, in fact, seemed almost dry. Without the thunder and rain for cover, the worms made a constant low rustling as they moved through the underbrush.

She lifted her head long enough to glance over Doe's shoulder. Alanna and Salyt rode together in the lead. Salyt seemed to know the way even in the dark, and sometimes she whispered half-heard instructions to the female *sekournen,* who would nod and touch her rods to the *chelit's* head.

So they made their way through the forest. Alanna and the councillor finding the course, Doe and Katy, then Eric and Valis following, finally Robert, riding alone, bringing up the rear. It wasn't the best strategic order, but they didn't expect to encounter anyone.

Fatigue teased her toward sleep, and she laid her head on Doe's back again. The movement of the *chelit,* however, was not the smooth rhythmic gait of a horse. The worm made its way in an efficient, but hesitant manner as it slipped around the trees and avoided the denser undergrowth. Each time she thought of dozing off, she would jerk alert.

Abruptly Alanna signaled for a halt. The *chelit* stopped.

"What is it?" Eric called softly.

Alanna gestured for silence as she beckoned him closer with a crooked finger. Eric, Valis, and Robert dropped from their saddles and slipped forward. Katy strained to hear. *"Magoths,"* Alanna said, pointing into the darkness.

"Headed north," Eric observed. He looked up suddenly at Alanna. "That village we found days ago in Sybo. The mysterious deaths. The *magoths* were there, too."

Alanna nodded. "You think the *magoths* can somehow follow these sendings?"

Katy slipped down from her saddle and went forward. It felt good to stretch her legs. She hadn't noticed it earlier, but her muscles were sore from the day's ride from Capreet. "There are lots of strange stories about animals and the supernatural." She gazed up into the trees. Scores of shaggy silhouettes leaped from branch to branch, all going in the same direction. "Phlogis told me dogs can sense when spirits are present," she said. "Maybe these creatures can somehow sense this new ghost."

Robert drew her close. She didn't realize until he put his arm around her that she was shivering in her rain-soaked garments. "The *magoths* must know the sendings will lead them straight to food," he said.

Alanna frowned. "That's a grisly thought, *Kaesha.*"

He forced a twisted smile. "I'm a grisly kind of guy."

"We should push on," Salyt suggested. "They don't seem to be interested in us." She wrapped her arms around herself as she watched the motion in the branches. "They're on their way to a bigger feast."

"We could be veering way off course in this darkness," Robert said.

Salyt gave him a disparaging look and opened her left fist. On her palm, a small stone glowed with a soft blue radiance. "This shows me the way," she told him. "As long as we move toward our goal, it gives off this light. If I turn a different way ..." She twisted in the saddle and extended her hand to the north. The stone's glow faded at once.

"Her has a handy dandy *homer*, honey," Robert said to Katy as he gave her a hug and released her.

"Let's ride, then, *pahdner*," Katy said, inclining her head toward the *chelit*.

"Only until we find someplace to make camp," Eric said firmly. "None of us have had much sleep. If we find a good spot, we'll hold up and wait for morning light to continue."

Salyt started to protest, then seemed to change her mind. "Your companions talk funny," she said to Eric as she gave a resigned shrug and brushed hair out of her face. She looked thoroughly miserable. The neatly arranged bun at the nape of her neck had long since come loose. Her graying hair hung in wet strands. The skin under her eyes was puffy, and her shoulders slumped. Of them all, she was probably the least physically prepared for this trip. Katy patted the councillor's knee reassuringly as she returned to her *chelit*.

Doe extended a hand to help her up. "Thank you," Katy said when she was comfortably settled behind him. He didn't answer, and Eric tapped her ankle to draw her attention.

"You doing all right up there?"

It warmed her to read the concern in his eyes. "I could use a hot bath," she confessed with a weary grin.

He sniffed, wrinkled his nose, and nodded. "You sure could."

Doe still said nothing, but he handed Katy one of the riding rods. She took a playful swing at Eric, but he was no longer there. "Coward," she called back as she returned the rod to Doe.

The company began to move again. Katy trained her eyes on the trees overhead, watchful in case any of the *magoths* should change their minds and take an interest in them. But the branches appeared empty. The creatures had passed on.

She tightened her arms around Doe and rested her chin on his shoulder. He was so quiet. Too quiet. It worried her. "Tell me about Evander," she asked, trying to engage him in conversation. "I'm sorry I didn't have a chance to know him better." He tensed, and the muscles in his neck corded. Katy wished she could see his face, but he stared rigidly ahead, and she finally gave up.

Alanna held up a hand, bringing them to an abrupt halt. Without a word to anyone, she passed one of the rods to Salyt, keeping the other for herself, and slipped to the ground. Grasping the rod as if it was a staff, she disappeared into the trees only to reappear a few moments later.

"There's an old house here," she informed them in a whisper. "Abandoned. We can stay there for the night."

"How did you spot it?" Salyt asked, leaning forward in the saddle, staring the way Alanna had gone.

"I didn't," Alanna said. "But I saw that." She paced about three steps away from her *chelit* and pointed to a square patch of ground. No trees grew there, though there were plenty of weeds. A low wall of piled rock marked a rough perimeter.

"Someone's garden," Katy murmured with renewed appreciation for the female dragonrider. In the darkness it would have been easy to pass up. "At least, it once was. You have sharp eyes."

"Bring a couple of the supply packs," Alanna said. "We'll leave the *chelit* here."

Eric was hesitant. "Will they wander off?"

Salyt shook her head. "Just lean the rods against their sides, and they'll stay perfectly still."

When the rods were placed as the councillor instructed, Doe untied two packs from the saddle of his own mount, and shouldered them wordlessly. He brought up the rear as they made their way through thick underbrush to the house.

In the dark it was hard to tell what condition the place was in. It was old and weathered, and the east and west walls seemed to lean slightly inward, as if the roof had become too heavy. Though once the house had stood in the center of a clearing, bushes and weeds now grew right up to its small stoop, and thick branches hung over it like the gnarly fingers of hands poised to crush it. On one side stood a well. Near that, an empty pen for animals.

"I wonder why the owner left?" Katy said aloud as they stood staring at their find.

"Are you kidding?" Robert scoffed as he shoved his thumbs in his jeans and surveyed the place. "I bet there's not a mall or multiplex theater for miles."

"On the other hand," Eric countered, "neighborhood crime was probably at a minimum."

"It was Kajin Lure who caused them to leave," Salyt said. There was an odd note of bitterness in her voice as she strode forward and pushed open the door. A streamer of dust cascaded from the door frame into her hair, unnoticed by her. "His sorceries have blighted our land, driven off game, withered our crops. For years we've suffered his attacks. This is just one of the results." She paused on the threshold and peered inside. "Ask yourself. Other than the *magoths,* who don't belong here, have you seen any other animals?"

Katy thought of the dogs in the village. Somehow she was sure those didn't count. "Insects," she said, listening to the chirrups that filled the night.

Salyt sneered. "Insects. We're not grub-eaters, Katherine. My people have starved."

"The birds," Eric said turning to Valis. "We noticed it earlier. There aren't any birds."

"No birds," Salyt agreed. "No deer, no bears, no rodents. This forest is empty, vacated. Except for the insects." She stepped inside, leaving the others on the stoop or in what remained of the yard. "Wish I had a light," she grumbled.

Katy unslung her backpack and unzipped a small nylon pocket on its side. "Maybe this will help," she said. She thumbed the trigger on a Bic lighter and held the flame high as she followed the councillor inside. The others came after her.

"That's my Kat," Robert said. "Ought to call you Felix. *Whenever we get into a fix, you reach into your bag of tricks.*" He sang the lines to the old cartoon show. "What else do you have in there?"

"The essentials for an outing like this," she said smugly as she shone the flame around. "Chocolate bars, a pocketknife, tampons." She gave him a wink. "The lighter was an afterthought."

Most of the furniture was intact, though covered with dust. There was a table with four chairs, a narrow bed in a corner beneath a shuttered window. The feather mattress on it was rotted. An empty cabinet for dishes stood in another corner. A plank door led into another room that might have been a bedroom. It contained no furniture at all, though.

Valis brought in an armload of logs from a moss-covered woodpile and made a second trip to gather enough kindling to get a fire going in the fireplace. In short time they had dry, warm shelter. Alanna promptly stripped off her damp shirt and claimed space on the mantel to hang it near the flames where it could dry. The orange firelight reflected on her bare flesh.

"You could get arrested for that where I come from," Katy said with a smile. She sat down in one of the chairs and started to remove her wet boots.

Alanna pulled away her headband and shook her hair free before she grinned over one shoulder. "Robert's told me about some of Paradane's peculiar attitudes."

Soon, shirts and boots and even a few pairs of trousers were hung about the room. Alanna was absolutely without modesty. Katy envied the perfectly toned body she saw before her. Oh, she was in good shape, herself, especially for a librarian. But every line and detail of Alanna's muscles showed under the taut skin.

Doe picked up the pair of supply packs and set them on the table. He opened one and set out the contents, his movements mechanical, his face emotionless. The pack contained hard biscuits, a cheese wrapped in some kind of minty broad leaves, and thin strips of dried meat. They made a quick meal on these. When it was over, they began to settle in for the night, curling up on the floor, against a wall, or wherever they could get comfortable. Alanna and Robert claimed the empty room in back. Despite the rotting mattress, Salyt took the bed.

Eric came to Katy and kissed her on the forehead.

"Get some rest," he told her. "I'm going to look around outside." He closed the door softly as he went out.

Katy looked around and let go a sigh. Salyt was already asleep, one arm folded under her head, face to the open window. A gray wisp of hair stirred lightly around her temple as a breeze teased it. At the foot of the bed, Valis sat cross-legged, his back against the wall. He, too, looked to be already asleep.

That left her alone with Doe. He stood leaning on the mantel, staring into the fire. Like Alanna, he had stripped himself naked. Katy felt herself blush as she looked at him. She'd slipped out of her boots and trousers, but put on Eric's shirt while her own dried by the fire. His was large and long enough to decently cover her, though just barely. She turned self-consciously toward the table and busied herself re-wrapping and packing away the remains of the cheese.

Doe touched her shoulder. She froze for a moment, unwilling to look at him, burningly aware of her own near-nakedness. Then she forced herself to relax. She was having a stupid reaction based on learned behaviors that had nothing to do with this world in which she found herself. Doe was not going to hurt her. Besides, Salyt and Valis were right there not ten feet away, and Robert was in the other room.

When she met his gaze, she saw the beginnings of tears glittering in the corners of his eyes, saw how he struggled to hold them back. He wasn't much more than a boy, really—nineteen, perhaps twenty. Grief was written in every strained line of his face, in the way he carried himself, the way he looked at her.

He wet his lips as he prepared to speak. "You told Robert you have a knife," he said finally. "Is that true?"

Katy bit her lip. What did he want with a knife?

"Yes," she answered uncertainly. "It's just a little pocketknife, though. Not much of a blade."

He fixed her with those moist brown eyes as he held out his hand. "I'll give it back," he promised.

Again, Katy hesitated. Then she picked up her pack from the chair where she'd put it and unzipped another pocket. She extracted a worn, single-bladed Barlowe knife and gave it to him.

"Thank you, *Hami*," he said graciously. Turning away, he opened the blade and knelt down so close to the fireplace that the flames lent his skin a burnished glow. With one hand, he loosed the thin leather strip that held his long hair back. As Katy watched, he gathered a handful, touched the sharp blade to it, and ritualistically dropped the severed locks beside the fire.

Katy felt like an intruder, so she opened the door as quietly as she could and stepped out onto the stoop. Eric leaned against a tree just a little distance away. He stared upward through a gap in the forest canopy. The sky had begun to clear, and one or two stars winked.

She went to join him, and he held out his arm to gather her in. His skin felt like velvet as she laid her head on his naked shoulder. This was the place she wanted to be most in the world. In any world. Without thinking, she turned into him and ran her fingers through the hair on his chest, kissed him on his throat. Then she put her head in the soft hollow of his shoulder again and eased one arm around his waist.

"I'm worried about Doe," she said quietly. "He's taking Evander's death hard. They were such close friends."

He lifted her chin, searched her face, then pressed her head down on his shoulder once more. "Friends?" he said in a low voice that was heavy with its own emotion. "You misunderstand." He hesitated, swallowed. "They were more than just friends." He leaned his head back against the tree. A moment later, his free hand shot out, and his fist closed. When he opened it, he showed her a firefly on his palm. It walked calmly up onto his thumb, then flew away.

"I love you, Eric," Katy whispered.

His answer was softer than a feather on her ear. "I love you, Katy-did."

She bit her lip again as she searched his face. "No fooling this time?"

He shook his head slowly as he looked up through that gap where the stars shone. "No foolin'."

She wasn't sure how long they stood there leaning against that tree, leaning on each other, and she wasn't sure exactly when the idea occurred to her. She took Eric by the hand and led him away from the house, deeper into the forest until they found a place where the ground was dry and the grass soft, a spot nestled between the exposed roots of a gigantic tree.

They lay down together, each knowing what the other wanted, each willing to give. It wasn't the first time they made love; they weren't innocent of each other. Yet Katy sensed a power and a meaning in Eric's touch that she had never experienced before.

She closed her eyes and for a moment listened to her own heartbeat, loud and strong and powerful. Then Eric was upon her, his heart beating next to hers. They were alive, and all the night was alive around them, and all of Palenoc was coming alive!

Eric's lips brushed against Katy's, and she felt her soul grow all the way down to the center of this world when he entered her.

Chapter Ten

ERIC and Katy wandered back toward the house, saying nothing, holding hands, watching the winking of the fireflies in the quiet darkness. They found Robert sitting on the stoop. He wasn't alone. Between his ankles lay a small gray dog. Robert scratched its ears and head, ran his hand down the slick length of its body, and shook its tail. He was all boyish grins.

"Look what followed us from the village," Robert said in an amused whisper.

Eric and Katy sat down beside him and joined in the petting, and the dog gave a little whine of pleasure. "You were always bringing strays home," Eric said with a soft laugh. He inclined his head toward the door. "Everyone else asleep?"

Robert nodded. "I'm surprised, though, the way this little mutt was scratching to get inside." He rumpled the dog's ears playfully.

Katy stood up and stretched, then tugged at the hem of her shirt. "Speaking of sleep," she said, "I'm going to see if my trousers are dry and then find a piece of the floor. It won't be long before morning." She bent and kissed the top of Eric's head, her hand lingering on his neck, before she turned and went inside.

Eric leaned forward, his elbows on his knees. The small silver medallion on the silver chain around his neck swung back and forth, glittering. He drew a deep breath, let it out easily. His heart felt so full.

"Anything you'd like to tell me, big brother?" Robert asked slyly.

Eric hesitated, then grinned. "I wish we never had to leave here, Bobby," he said truthfully. "But the sun's going to come up, and we'll have to get on those worms." He reached down and ran a finger over the pooch's damp nose. "Tonight, though . . ." He grinned again.

"Welcome to the circus of Dr. Lao," Robert said, putting one hand on his brother's arm and squeezing.

Eric leaned forward again. "The whole world is a circus," he recited as he peered into the forest recesses. Suddenly, the blowing of the wind was a calliope, and the fireflies inviting lights. "If you know how to look at it. The way the sun goes down when you're tired, comes up when you want to be on the move—that's real magic."

Robert scooped up the dog and settled his new friend on his lap. "Everytime you pick up a handful of dust and see, not the dust, but a mystery, a marvel there in your hand . . ." he looked at his brother, and Eric picked up the thread again.

"Every time you stop and think I'm alive, and being alive is fantastic; every time such a thing happens, you're part of the circus of Dr. Lao." Eric stood slowly up, put one foot on the stoop, and leaned over his little brother. As Katy had done to him, he bent closer and planted a kiss on the crown of Robert's head. "I hadn't thought of that in years," he confessed.

"The whole world's magic, Eric," Robert whispered, but there was a wistful note in his voice as he stroked the dog.

Eric sat down again and rubbed one of the dog's

velvet-soft ears. A thick wet tongue began to slurp at his hand. "What's wrong, Bobby?" he asked gently.

"I was just thinking of Scott," Robert admitted. "I played that movie for him just before we left for China, and he loved it as much as we did when we were kids. We joked about finding Lao's circus while we were there." He looked up suddenly, his eyes burning with intensity. "I've got to find him, Eric. I can't help thinking I should be looking for him now!"

Eric's mouth drew into a thin, taut line. His brother seemed convinced that Scott Silver was still alive, and frankly, he was beginning to wonder, too. "Bobby," he said as he continued to stroke the dog, "if you think you need to be looking for Scott more than you need to be here"—he stopped and waited for Robert to meet his gaze—"then maybe that's what you should be doing."

Robert shook his head vigorously. "No way," he said. "I'm not leaving you and Katy out here. You need me. But when this thing with Salyt is done, then nothing's going to stop me from finding him, even if I have to tear down the walls of Shandal Karg's fortress with my bare hands."

"Keep your voice down," Eric said. "No point in waking the others."

Robert fell silent. He put the dog off his lap, and it curled up between his feet again. It wasn't much of a dog. Just a plain gray pup so thin its ribs and hipbones stuck out through the thin hide. Its ears hung down on either side of its head, and its big moist eyes opened and closed with a sleepy regularity. It lifted its head a bit and laid it down again squarely across the top of his little brother's foot.

Eric thought of sleep. There was still time to stretch out on the floor beside Katy and grab a few winks. He thought of curling up next to her, slipping his arm around her waist, breathing in the sweet smell of her hair as they lay front to back, like a well-matched pair of spoons. The idea appealed to him.

Yet, if he slept he would dream, and if he dreamed *she* might be waiting for him. *Shandal Karg, the Heart of Darkness.* He dreaded sleep, never knowing when she would be there to turn his dreams into nightmares. His hands clenched into fists, but whether from anger or fear, he wasn't sure.

Abruptly, the dog lifted its head and gave a little whine. It stared straight ahead into the woods.

Before Eric could react, Robert gave a loud groan, clutched at his left temple, and sprawled sideways, unconscious. A Chol baton clattered on the stoop and slid off the edge into the grass. The dog sprang to its feet in a frenzy of barking while Eric whirled, seeking the enemy. A second baton sailed out of the darkness. The wooden ball struck him a glancing blow just above the right eye. The world exploded in a fountain of red stars, and he toppled backward, grabbing the edge of the stoop for support as he felt his knees buckle.

A dozen men in black armor rushed out of the forest. Unable to get to his feet, Eric fumbled for the baton that had struck him, but his vision wouldn't focus, nor his fingers quite obey his commands.

The Chols surged up onto the stoop as Valis, staff in hand, flung open the door. Three of them hit the big dragonrider at the same time. The door wrenched off its hinges with a violent screech of twisted metal and splintering wood as they fell back inside. Valis went down under their combined weight as Salyt's scream tore through din.

Eric struggled to get up, but a soldier kicked him in the ribs and again in the stomach. Hands seized him roughly and twisted his arms behind his back.

Someone wound thongs of raw leather around and around his wrists. His vision, at least, was beginning to clear.

The dog gave a sudden growl, lunged, and sank its teeth into the right hand of a soldier, who was binding Robert. The soldier screamed in pain, leaping up, while the determined little dog continued to cling with locked jaws to the unlucky Chol. Finally, the soldier flung him off. Another soldier threw a net, ensnaring the dog, who rolled over on its back, kicking and clawing and biting at the strands of rope. The bitten Chol, bleeding profusely from his wound, seized up a baton and began to beat the poor mutt.

Eric groaned and cursed himself for being caught off guard. A dozen soldiers were inside the house already, at least that number in the yard, and more pouring out of the shadows. Two Chols seized him under the arms and dragged him off the stoop and dumped him unceremoniously in the yard. Two more dragged Robert. His brother was bound as he was and only beginning to awaken.

An armored Chol crashed suddenly through the window over Salyt's bed. A second flew backward out the door. For an instant, Eric thought Valis must be staging his comeback. Then he heard a high-pitched *ki* shout. Through the open doorway he saw Alanna whirl Valis's staff as she knocked another Chol across the room. A soldier caught her by surprise from behind and wrapped his arms about her. Exactly as Eric had taught her, she dropped her weight and flung him over her head.

She won no respite, however. A black-masked soldier grabbed an old wooden chair and threw it. With a valiantly swift effort, Alanna tried to sweep it aside with the staff. Chair and staff splintered, and pieces of wood flew around her face, causing her to flinch.

Two Chols took advantage, hitting her hard, slamming her against the inner wall. With fists and elbows, they beat her down.

Eric raged inside as he watched Alanna fall. The Chols had taken them by surprise, and it was his fault. He hadn't thought a watch out here in the middle of nowhere would be necessary. He cursed himself again as his friends were led out of the house one by one to be cruelly bound and thrown down on the grass beside him. Salyt looked dazed. Her gray hair was a wild tangle around her face. Doe, on the other hand, had chopped off most of his hair. Short black patches stood up all over his scalp.

Behind their lacquered masks, the Chols laughed.

"What's happening, Eric?" Katy asked as she sat up and pushed hair back from her eyes with tied hands. "What are they saying?"

"I don't speak Chol," he said sullenly, glaring at his foes. He felt like a total fool. He rolled over and tried to sit up, but a soldier planted a foot on his shoulder, pushed him back down, then raised his baton and prepared to swing it at Eric's head.

"Leave him alone, you ugly son of a bitch!" Katy shouted with such vehemence that the soldier stayed his hand and glared at her. Then, he stepped toward her and lifted his weapon a menacing degree higher.

Even bound and on his back, Eric wasn't quite helpless. He piked his feet up over his head as sharply as he could, kicking the Chol in the side. It wasn't enough to hurt him, but it knocked the soldier off balance before he could strike Katy. Instantly, though, two more soldiers began to beat him, forcing him to curl into a ball to protect himself as best he could.

A shout called them off. Eric looked up to see where this sudden voice of authority had come from. His heart sank.

Out of the forest darkness strode a creature of legend. Only this legend had been twisted, degraded into something vile and evil. Its eyes burned with red fire, twin flickering pits of flame that reflected on black, scaly hide, on a mane that stood stiffly like a razor-sharp piece of metal, and on a single, slender ebon horn. The name these creatures were called on earth was far too soft and pretty. Here, they were *chimorgs*, and they were the eyes and ears of Shandal Karg.

"We've got major trouble," Robert muttered with his usual flare for understatement.

Katy strained against the rawhide strips around her wrists, her eyes widening. "My God!" she whispered.

The *chimorg* paced right up to Eric. He felt the sick intelligence behind those unholy eyes as they fastened on him, felt the animosity lurking there. This monster knew. It knew he and Robert together, on all of Palenoc, had killed one of its kind and taught the secret of *chimorg* mortality to the Domains of Light. Its hatred was a tangible force.

"My men can be such brutes," The voice was deep, silky, and spoke in impeccable Guranese.

Eric turned his gaze up to the speaker, who sat astride the *chimorg's* back. He'd never known a *chimorg* to carry a man, and that surprise alone told him this was not just another Chol soldier. The helmet upon his head was crested to resemble his mount's mane, and his mask was carved in far more demonic detail. Around his neck, he wore a gleaming torc of gold. The two end pieces, riding near the soft hollow of his throat, were clearly diamonds.

"Who the hell are you?" Eric demanded. He struggled into a kneeling position and tried to focus on the whites of the eyes and the dark pupils behind the fright mask.

The rider stiffened his spine and lifted his chin

haughtily. "I am Kajin Kasst," he announced, "Prince of Chol-Hecate."

Salyt, her hands tightly bound before her, raised her head. "Kajin Lure's baby brother," she sneered. "I doubt it would please Shandal Karg to learn you've given yourself a title."

Kajin Kasst gestured sharply to one of his soldiers. "Shut her up!" he ordered. "She dares to speak that great bitch's name for all the world to hear!"

A pair of men fell on Salyt. One grabbed her hair and yanked her head back while another produced a dirty rag from somewhere and shoved it into her mouth. Alanna launched an ineffectual kick at one, but it only earned her a return kick in the stomach. She curled up in a ball with a gasp.

"My spies informed me these woods were abandoned," Kajin Kasst said in a calmer tone. He turned his gaze upon his gathered soldiers, and they all averted their eyes. "I'll have to hang someone for providing me with faulty information." He waved a hand toward the house. "Search it," he said to the nearest of his troops. "Bring me anything of value." Two men rushed eagerly to do his bidding.

Eric's mind raced. As nearly as he could count, there were thirty soldiers besides Kajin Kasst—too many to fight even if he could get free. Maybe he could learn a few things, though.

"A Chol prince on Wystoween soil in the dead of night," he said with a calm he didn't feel. He sat back on his heel and exchanged gazes with his captor. "You didn't bring much of an invasion force."

Kajin Kasst removed his mask. He had a young face, but it was marked with cruelty. His skin was white as porcelain, and his lips curled in a twisted smirk. Beneath thin, arched brows, dark eyes gleamed.

A thick scar stretched from his left ear down along the jawline.

He gave a little laugh, exposing teeth that had been filed to tiny points. "Ah," he sighed melodramatically. "Then you missed my dear brother's pets when they flew overhead. Such a shame." He clucked his tongue as he shook his head. "By now, they've reached your capital, and my men are advancing at points all across the border." His smile widened with malice. "Wystoweem is ours."

There were more soldiers than just this group, then. The forest was probably full of them. Things looked bleaker than ever. What had happened to Shubal and his Wystoweem *sekournen*? Weren't they supposed to be distracting the Chol forces at points farther west?

A pair of men emerged unexpectedly out of the trees, and Kajin Kasst slipped gracefully down from the *chimorg* to confer with them. *Thirty-two,* Eric thought, adjusting his count. *How many more?*

The Chol prince turned abruptly and walked among his prisoners like a farmer admiring his crop. He tapped the fingers of his right hand on his lips a few times, assuming a studious look as he lingered over Alanna. His eyes glittered as he took in her nude form. Then, he looked at Eric. "I thought I'd stumbled upon a few peasants in the middle of an orgy," he said with a mocking lilt. He looked around at his men, smiled weakly, and shrugged. "In fact, I almost felt a twinge of guilt." He tapped his lips again as he moved past Eric and regarded Katy with an appreciative eye. "Instead, my men discover four *chelit* in the woods a short distance away." He bent down, gripped Katy's face, and forced her to meet his gaze. "Peasants don't ride *chelit*. So tell me, my pretty traveler, where you've traveled from?"

"Dowdsville," Katy deadpanned.

A soldier emerged from the house bearing three packs. He knelt at his lord's feet and opened the first. Eric knew from the nylon and the zippered pockets that it was Katy's. He watched as the man lifted out her Barlowe knife and passed it into Kajin Kasst's hand. He examined it briefly without discovering how to open the blade, then cast it aside.

Eric tried not to appear interested as he watched where the knife fell in the grass. He wondered, though, how he could work his way to it.

Several candy bars came out of the pack, then several packages of nine-volt batteries. Not until the soldier unzipped another pocket and lifted out Katy's Omega stunner in its holster did Eric realize what the batteries were for. The stunner caught Kajin Kasst's interest. He slid it out and examined it as best he could in the gloom, peering and squinting at it curiously.

"What is this?" he asked in obvious delight as he ran his fingers over the shiny metal studs.

Katy spoke up without hesitation. "A thingamajig," she said with a straight face, making the word sound very important. "You know—a religious object. The symbol of my God. It comforts me to hold it when I pray to Him."

Eric struggled to hide his amazement at the boldness of her lie.

A deep frown creased Kajin Kasst's face. He held the stunner out at arm's length. "I didn't think you *thin-bloods* in the Domains believed in gods."

"Some of us believe in them," Katy answered quickly. "My God died for our sins and was buried in a black box just like that. We keep a miniature of his coffin with us as a reminder."

Kajin Kasst rolled his eyes. "Well, I suppose a god who died and was buried is no threat to me. It's just like you *thin-bloods* to have thin-blooded gods." He started to toss the stunner aside as he had everything else from the pack, but Katy stopped him.

"May I have it, please?" she asked, wetting her lips. Katy's hands were bound in front of her. She lifted them now as if begging—or praying. "I'm frightened, and I wouldn't be so afraid if I could just hold it."

Eric held his breath, waiting to see just how stupid this Chol prince was. He'd tossed aside the knife without discovering how to open it. Would he give Katy the stunner? Katy's gaze flickered his way, then fixed itself on Kajin Kasst again. There was just the right amount of imploring in her face. She licked her lips again.

Kajin Kasst lifted Katy to her feet and stepped close to her. For a moment they regarded each other, then he slipped one hand up inside her shirt. Katy gasped at his touch, her expression turning defiant. Then she mastered her emotions and relaxed while he fondled her breast.

Anger surged up in Eric's heart, and he clenched his teeth together so hard he thought they would break. He fought to control himself and was thankful when Robert, on his knees with his hands bound behind his back, eased himself in front of Eric and did his best to block the view.

His brother's lips moved ever so slightly. *I'm free,* he mouthed, and he repeated it once more.

Eric had little time to rejoice. Kajin Kasst had seen the rage on his face. "Your woman has nice tits," he said to Eric, his hand still kneading and manipulating under Katy's shirt. He deliberately taunted Eric with the sight before he turned back to Katy, and smiled an evil, pointed-toothed smile.

"We don't want someone with such nice tits fearing us." Kajin Kasst pressed the stunner into her bound hands and folded his own hands over hers in an expression of excruciating sincerity. "You may keep your trinket, pretty."

"Thank you, lord!" she replied, fervently clutching the stunner. She rolled her eyes skyward and repeated, "Thank you."

Eric glanced slyly toward the knife laying in the grass. It was too far away for him to reach by any subtle means. Things were not as bleak as he had thought, though. Robert had freed his hands somehow, or at least loosened his bonds. And Katy now possessed the stunner. He looked over his shoulder at the *chimorg*. If the chance came for a break, that creature would be their greatest danger. The beast eyed him back as if it could read his mind.

He considered their situation again, counting the soldiers one more time. Thirty-two. Kajin Kasst made thirty-three. Had they come on foot, he wondered, or were there more *chimorgs* somewhere in the forest? He gazed into the trees, trying to penetrate the gloom and the darkness. The pink light of dawn colored the sky, revealing black wisps of sweeping clouds.

Kajin Kasst gave a sudden shriek, a totally unmanly sound. At his feet lay the remains of the cheese from the second pack. From the third pack, the soldier lifted a huge red gem. Kajin Kasst snatched it in both his hands and held it up to see. "Bring me light!" he shouted. "Bring me light!" Another soldier dashed into the house, only to return a few moments later with a torch hastily made from a piece of cloth and a broken chair leg. He held it high for his lord.

The light struck the facets of the gem. Beams of ruby radiance shot in all directions, seeming to ignite the leaves and branches of the overreaching trees, penetrating even the shadows of the forest. Kajin

Kasst's face lit up with its bloodred glow. His eyes shone with wonder and terror.

Eric knew instantly that this stone lay at the heart of his mission to Chol-Hecate. This was the secret Salyt had kept from them. The soldier holding the torch trembled, and his shaking caused the light to quaver and the lances of radiance to dance with a dazzling, almost hypnotic power.

He tore his gaze away, all his senses screaming. There was something about that stone, something unnatural. The *chimorg* sensed it, too. It reared up, trumpeting and shaking its mane, eyes burning with a red light that paled beside the ruby's glow. Tangled in its net, the poor dog began to howl. Kajin Kasst's soldiers shrank away with gasps of fear.

In all the confusion, Eric saw an opening. "Go, Bobby!" he hissed. "Get out of here!"

Robert was already gone. There was no sign of him at all, except for a twisted strip of rawhide lying on the ground where he had been.

Kajin Kasst gave another shriek, dropping the stone and springing back. Out of that red light swirled a shape. A hideous face took form, growing and swelling to fill the space above the clearing, its immense fanged mouth open, jaws slavering. Huge, inhuman hands curled into claws. Chol soldiers screamed, their courage broken. Suddenly, the air was full of swirling shapes, vague presences, mouths that gaped, and talons that raked air.

Eric's eyes riveted on the first creature, though, the shape that had grown out of the ruby light. For all its horror, he knew that face—Evander!

He shot a look at Doe. The young *sekournen* sat serenely on his heels, hands bound behind his back, in the midst of growing chaos. Somehow, this was his doing! Eric suddenly remembered the gift that Doe and Evander shared—the power to summon spirits. Doe had called, and Evander had come to his lover's aid.

But the other shapes, these ghosts! Why were they here?

There was no time to ponder it. Eric's hands were tied, but he could still run. "Into the trees!" he shouted to his friends. Katy, with her hands tied in front, pulled Salyt to her feet. Alanna and Valis sprang up. A soldier moved to block them. Valis knocked him aside with a head-butt, and they were gone, swallowed up in the blackness.

A blue-white flash and a sharp crackle made Eric turn.

"God be with you," Katy muttered as she swept up her backpack. She paused over Kajin Kasst's limp form, the stunner in her hand, just long enough to make the sign of the cross above him.

The *chimorg* trumpeted and reared. Eric felt the ground shake as its hooves crashed down. It fixed its fiery eyes on him and lowered the ebony spike on its brow. He had beaten such a beast once with Robert's help. With his hands tied, there was no way he could fight it now. He stared and felt the chill wind of death on his face.

Then Salyt was in front of him, facing the monster, holding the huge ruby in both her hands. Red lancets of light struck the *chimorg*. It screamed in fear and pain, pawing and stamping the earth, tearing chunks of grass and dirt. Salyt took a step toward it, holding the stone out before her, chanting words that Eric couldn't understand. With an agonized bellow, the *chimorg* spun and raced off into the night.

A soldier ran at Salyt. Eric took him down with a kick. "Run!" he ordered the councillor. Another soldier charged at him, but before he could strike with his upraised baton, a wisp of white smoke swooped into his path and ballooned suddenly into a vision of such terror that the man dropped his weapon and fell quivering to the ground.

Eric looked swiftly around, making sure all his people had gone. No! Doe still remained seated on the ground, scores of shapes whirling and swirling about him as if he were the eye in a supernatural storm. Doe's hands were untied—Eric didn't question how—and he held them up as if to embrace one of the spectral forms. But if Evander was still among those swirling wisps, he was indistinguishable from the other ghosts.

Eric ran to Doe, jumping over Kajin Kasst's prone figure, and flung himself down on his knees before his friend. "Snap out of it, Doe!" he shouted. "Evander's dead. Let him go!" The ghosts flew faster and faster around them, weaving and spiraling through the air, no longer as interested in the terror-stricken soldiers. And in some part of his mind, Eric could hear the voices of the dead, angry mutterings and murmurings, all calling to Doe, urging him to join them.

Eric leaped to his feet. "Doe!" he screamed. "Wake up! I need you, kid." He threw himself back on his knees when his words failed to have an effect. He put his face right against Doe's as he pleaded with his young comrade. "Alanna and Valis need you, Doe. Palenoc needs you more than Evander needs you now. Let him go!"

Finally, a light came into Doe's eyes. He focused on Eric for a moment, then shook his head as if to clear it. He stared upward at the ghosts and uttered Evander's name. Then he shook his head again and cast a wild, disoriented look around. His gaze settled on Eric's face.

"We've got to get out of here!" Doe said, in control of himself at last.

"An idea whose time has come," Eric agreed. He didn't know what had put Doe into such a trance. He'd watched both Doe and Evander speak to spirits before, but such a thing had never happened. He knew so little about any of the gifts his *sekournen* friends possessed.

They dashed into the woods, Eric running awkwardly with his hands bound behind him. He watched fearfully for a pair of red, flaming eyes and the too-late glimpse of a deadly horn, but there was no sign of the *chimorg*.

Nor, unfortunately, was there any sign of the rest of his friends.

"Stop! Stop!" he panted when he thought they were far enough from the house and Kajin Kasst's soldiers. They were atop a low-forested rise, looking back the way they had come. He turned his back and let Doe unbind his hands. The rawhide had been painfully tight. He flexed his fingers, trying to work some feeling into them.

"What happened back there?" he asked when he had his breath back. "I've never seen you blank out like that."

Doe hesitated. "I almost joined them," he admitted. "I summoned Evander, but those others heard my call, too. The *ankous*—angry, malevolent spirits without focus or purpose. They tempted me to join Evander in death, and I was caught for a moment between this world and the next." He looked at Eric with an intense expression. "Evander held me back from them," he said, "and so did you, Eric. Evander and I were strong when we were together. We were always there to hold each other back and to mute the voices of the *ankous*." He hung his head. "It will be riskier now, alone, for me to speak to the dead."

Eric squeezed his friend's hand, moved by the sadness in his voice. "I wish you'd get it into your head," he insisted, "you're not alone."

Doe looked sheepish and ran a hand across his shorn hair. "We'd better try to find the others," he said with a nod toward the sky. "It's getting toward dawn."

Eric looked toward the pink light, just visible through the trees. Suddenly, he had a sick feeling in the pit of his stomach. He'd noticed it earlier, that light, and the streamers of dark clouds. His mouth went dry. "Even on Palenoc," he managed quietly, "the sun comes up in the east." He pointed over his shoulder. "East is that way."

"Then what . . . ?" Doe turned in alarm toward the dawn. It wasn't pink at all, but a pale shade of orange and red reflected on the dark of night.

Eric sniffed the air. Dark streamers of clouds, indeed. He didn't smell smoke yet, but it wouldn't be long. He thought of the burning village they'd left behind. Even with the rain, the forest was dry as tinder. It probably hadn't taken much, maybe a single spark borne on the wind.

He heard sound off to the right and spun, heart racing. A huge shadow moved out of the trees and became Valis.

The big *sekournen* didn't waste time with reunion greetings. "Do you see it?" he said, staring toward the sky.

Eric nodded as he regarded his two companions. Doe was buck naked. He and Valis had only their trousers. The others were in no better shape wherever they were. Well, Robert was. For once in his life, Bobby had kept his clothes on.

"We can't just wander around out here," he said abruptly. "Let's go."

No explanation was needed. Doe and Valis knew where he meant. Back to the house. Back to their clothes, their supplies, their mounts. Back to the only things that could get them out of this cursed land alive. Hopefully, back to their friends.

Eric cast another glance toward the forest fire and shuddered.

Chapter Eleven

THE *chimorg* charged out of the trees. Warned barely in time by the unnatural glow of the beast's eyes, Robert hurled himself aside. A lashing, serpentine tail struck him across the ribs with stunning force as he went down. The monster spun about with an angry snort, black hooves gouging deep wounds in the earth. Heart pounding, Robert sprang up and ran. Limbs and branches slapped at his face. He crashed through the brush, dodged around thick trunks, fell, picked himself up, and ran.

The *chimorg* lunged after him. Its hot breath bellowed in his ears. Its great spike thrust at his back. Robert jumped desperately aside and ran in a new direction, but a tree loomed up unexpectedly out of the darkness, and he ran straight into it. Stars exploded in his head as he bounced off the black boll and fell flat on the ground. Dazed and breathless, he scrambled up into half crouch, putting his back to the same tree while he tried to clear his senses.

The ground shook under his feet. His eyes snapped wide. He dodged, then started to run again as the beast's horn sent a shower of bark and splinters into the air.

Suddenly, the ground took a steep rise. He raced up the side of a long knoll, blessing the tread on his Reeboks and his physical conditioning. Halfway up, the treacherous soil loosened under his steps. A cascade of dirt slithered down. With a cry, he slipped forward. Fingers dug for purchase, but he slid anyway, taking part of the hillside with him.

The *chimorg* trumpeted with anticipated victory as Robert struggled to stop his descent. Lowering its horn, the beast lunged up the rise to meet him, its hooves finding surer purchase in the loose earth. It reared above Robert, and those hooves crashed down inches from his ribs. Near panic, Robert stopped trying to end his slide. Instead he flung himself down the hill, tumbling head over heels, rolling wildly away from the *chimorg*. The monster screamed in disappointment and whirled to charge downhill after him, but this time the soil proved treacherous even to its hooves. In turning, it slipped, stumbled, and rolled down after him.

Sore in a dozen places, Robert found his feet, leaped up, and started to run.

Straight into an unseen tree branch. Something sharp and jagged ripped his head right above the hairline. The impact knocked him off his feet. A scarlet haze filled his vision. "Get up!" he hissed to himself through the blinding pain. "Get up!"

Too late.

The *chimorg* trumpeted again as it reared over him, raking the air with its hooves. Robert made a last desperate effort to roll away as those hooves slammed down, and found his back pressed against the roots of yet another tree. He stared up at his death.

The *chimorg* lowered its horn, and he gazed into the coldly flickering pools of flame that served this monster for eyes. They locked on him, those eyes. A great, hideous head bent closer, gleaming not with hair or hide, but with scales like those on a snake's skin. He could feel the heat of its huge body, smell the stench of its oily sweat. Its horrible breathing rumbled in his ears.

The deadly tip of that spike hovered over his heart. *This is it,* Robert thought to himself.

But death didn't come. The *chimorg* snorted, lifted its head, and took a step back. Its gaze lingered on him a moment longer, its powerful form tense and quivering. Then the beast turned, trotted off into the trees, and disappeared in the shadowy darkness.

Robert stared into the deep gloom, awash in his disbelief. It was a trick. The creature wouldn't just leave him. It was there somewhere, hidden, waiting for him to stand up so it could chase him again. It was toying with him, wearing him down before it killed him. Cat and mouse. That had to be it. He listened for the smallest sound, watched for those burning eyes.

Why? Why would it spare his life?

A warm trickle of blood ran down over his scalp and toward his right eye. He put up a hand to staunch it, feeling the dirt and grit on his palm and in his hair, in the wound. With a groan, he lumbered to his feet.

Tag. The thought played over and over again in his mind as he leaned for support against the tree trunk to catch his breath and regain his senses. *Tag, you're it.*

Something important had just happened, but he couldn't make any sense of it.

The cut on his head burned like hell as he probed it with his fingers. It felt like a crevasse in that delicate skin. He gingerly traced the outline of the goose egg rising around it. His neck and spine ached from the impact with the branch, but he moved a few shaky steps away from the tree and stared around.

He had to find his brother and the others. But which way was the house? If the knoll was right in front of him, then it had to be back that way. Or did it? He hadn't run in a straight line. How far had he gone with the *chimorg* in pursuit?

A sense of dread shivered through him as he realized he was lost. The woods seemed darker, more menacing than ever. He tried to retrace his course, but nothing looked familiar. A narrow ravine suddenly blocked his path. He was sure he hadn't crossed that. He worked his way down one side and up the other, disturbing a cloud of midges or gnats at the bottom. They swarmed angrily around his face until he reached the top again, then they left him alone.

With no clear idea where he was going, he paused to rest against a stout tree. His hair was matted with crusty blood, but at least the wound had scabbed. A dull drum continued to throb inside his skull, and his neck wanted to stiffen. He turned his head experimentally from side to side. It hurt, but he figured he'd live.

He wondered about his brother again, and his friends. He'd seen Valis and Alanna escape into the woods before the *chimorg,* fleeing from Salyt's weird ruby, came crashing through his hiding place. The beast had nearly trampled him before it realized he was there.

Where were the others now? In the woods someplace, like him, separately or together. *Eric,* he thought miserably. *I've let you down.*

He gazed upward into the branches above his head. There was only a small chance that he could see anything if he climbed it, but that was better than no chance at all. The lowest limb was about nine feet above the ground. He leaped, caught it, and muscled himself up. The rough bark abraded the skin on his palms. He didn't care. What was one more pain? Higher and higher he climbed, picking his way carefully in the dark, testing limbs before putting his full weight on them. The leaves were too thick to give him a view of the ground, and the shadows were too deep. He was about to climb down again when he looked to his left through a gap in the branches.

A wall of fire towered like the judgment of God. The entire horizon burned. He edged out as far as he dared among the limbs and stared with a numb horror. The flames were miles away yet, but there was no comfort in that. A blaze that size would rip through this dry forest.

He fought down a surge of panic. His brother was out there. Katy and Alanna, too, somewhere. If he could wait until morning, he'd stand a better chance of finding them in the daylight. But that fire wasn't going to give him time. There was too much wind to fan it.

Was this why the *chimorg* let him live? Had it smelled the fire or its smoke?

He bit his lip as he stared toward those soaring flames. That still didn't make sense. It could have finished him and had plenty of time to make its own escape. *Chimorgs* weren't natural animals. They were creations, monsters made and bred by Shandal Karg. They didn't tire. It could have killed him and just run away from the deadly blaze, run all night if it had to.

He climbed down as quickly as he could and jumped to the ground. If the fire had spread from the burning village, which seemed likely, then the flames were in the northwest. If he traveled *this* way, he should at least be heading in the proper direction toward the house. He wondered if he dared to call out. One of his friends might hear him. On the other hand, maybe Kajin Kasst and his soldiers would hear. Better to keep quiet.

Trees, darkness, shadow—nothing even resembled a path. He pushed through thickets, crossed a dry creek bed, and stopped. From the ground, he couldn't see the wall of fire. Without it, he realized, he couldn't be sure he was still going in the right direction. "Shit!" he said aloud.

He forced himself to be calm. He wasn't going to find his brother this way. The forest was too large, the night just too dark. Nor was Eric going to find him. Eric had the whole company and the mission to think about. If he'd gotten everybody free, he'd be trying to put some distance between them and Kajin Kasst's soldiers. By now, Eric was certainly aware of the fire, too.

But what if they hadn't escaped? He drew in a breath and blew it out with a slow, hissing sound. Then they were either dead, or Kajin Kasst was marching them off as prisoners with his men. The threat of the fire guaranteed that in almost any case his brother wouldn't be standing still waiting for him to show up.

He could almost hear Eric telling the others, *Don't worry, Bobby can take care of himself.*

What then should he do? Chol-Hecate had been their destination. It made sense to keep to that plan. This forest sat on the border. Once he got through to the other side, maybe he'd have some chance of picking them up again. It seemed the only solution.

A stray wind bore the first hint of smoke. He climbed another tree for a look at the fire. From the upper branches, the view was startling. An entire section of the sky glowed with an angry red color. Sheets of flame tongued hungrily at the clouds. It was close enough now that he could almost measure its spread from tree to tree. It advanced in an ever-widening line, like arms reaching out, threatening to encircle everything.

He jumped to the ground again, ripping the right knee of his Levi's as he landed in a crouch. Frowning, he fingered the flap of denim, then put it out of his mind. It was a trivial matter in the face of other concerns. He wasn't a praying man, but he uttered a short prayer for his brother and his friends and wished them luck. Then, putting the fire over his left shoulder, he started in the direction he judged to be south.

He pushed through the forest with a grim determination, periodically climbing a tree to note the fire's advance. No matter how fast his own progress, each time the blaze seemed closer. Each time a breeze blew, it brought the smell of smoke. The insects stopped their chirruping, as if they sensed the danger. The fireflies disappeared.

He thanked his luck when he stumbled over an old stump. Some rainwater from the storm had collected in it, and he wet his lips. It had a brackish taste, but he wasn't squeamish. He cupped his hands and drank. It was cool and eased his thirst, and he laved a handful over his face before continuing on.

The cut and the surrounding bump on his scalp still stung when he touched them, but at least his headache was abating.

Without any warning the air turned sharply cold. He gasped, and his breath came out in a steamy cloud. He stopped in his tracks, heart pounding as he hugged himself. Abruptly, the cold was gone, and the air was warm again. Then just as abruptly, he felt cold once more.

He knew the reason now.

A *chill.*

Cautiously, he walked forward. "Hello," he said in a soft voice. He didn't have Evander's or Doe's power to speak with spirits, but he hoped this one might somehow understand. His gaze darted from side to side. There was nothing to see, of course. *Chills* had no form. They manifested only as spots of intense cold.

The air turned warm again.

Robert remembered what little he knew of the ghosts of Palenoc. A *chill* was a kind of ghost that had evolved far beyond the forms of *dandos* and *ankous*. A *chill* was a very old soul whose anger had long since ebbed away, but who had still never found peace or the path to Or-dhamu.

Despite all his talks with Phlogis and Alanna, he still didn't understand the elaborate metamorphoses of this world's ghosts. He knew, though, that *chills* and other spirits often haunted the woods and forests of this world.

"It's okay," he said gently. Unlike other kinds of ghosts, *chills* were nothing to fear. "I don't mind. Take a little of my warmth."

For a moment, nothing happened, but then he felt the cold settle around him. With the softest feathery touch, it embraced him, moving over his body. There was almost a sensuality in it. In some deep part of him, he sensed this ancient creature's loneliness, heard the dim and fading echo of its grief, like a whisper of the wind through autumn leaves.

When it ended, he gave a small sigh. Then to his surprise, another presence brushed against him, causing him to shiver. He braced himself as he nodded and spoke to the newcomer. "Yes," he agreed. "I've enough warmth for you, too."

He held out his arms and gave himself to this new *chill*. How could he not? These were the sad souls, the old souls, phantoms who had gotten lost on the path to heaven, just as he was lost in these woods. All they wanted was to touch him, to share the heat of his body for a brief moment.

A tiny moan escaped his lips. Loneliness—

isolation—despair. Grief wrapped around his heart like a pair of delicate hands. Impressions strobed through him, vague shadows of emotions not his own. A barest memory of a memory of anger.

It was not one *chill* that touched him, nor two, but many. One after another, two and three at a time, they reached out for him. His breath made white streamers, and he felt as if his blood was freezing. Still he gave his warmth. Sorrow—melancholy—woe.

Hope. For just an instant, he gave them that. Tiny, nova-bright flares in the ashes of their minds faded to sparks and died again. But for an instant, the warmth and light, the joy, lingered.

Finally, he could bear it no more. "Please," he managed through numbed and trembling lips. The one word was enough. The phantoms departed like scattering birds on invisible wings, leaving him alone.

Alone. The thought filled him with a strange fear. It took a moment to realize it was only an echo of the loneliness of the *chills*. He found himself on his knees without quite remembering how he got there. He picked himself up and brushed himself off, still shivering.

The wind rustled the upper branches of the trees, bringing a stronger smell of smoke, reminding him to keep moving. He couldn't help but wonder, though. If he died on Palenoc what would become of his soul? Would he undergo the same terrible evolution? Could his spirit—the spirit of an Earthman—hope to find the peace of Or-dhamu?

He looked around, trying to get his bearings. All his life, he'd loved the forests of the Catskills, loved to wander through them, yes, even by night sometimes when he camped. But on Earth, there were familiar stars to guide him. He didn't know the stars and constellations of Palenoc. Nor could he gauge direction by the moon, Thanador, or the ring, Mianur. Those were hidden by the thick clouds.

It was a frightening thing, to be lost.

He took a few steps, staring into the pitch darkness, trying to discern the way of least resistance. A low branch slapped at his face, and he batted it aside. The world had become a tangle of vines and bushes and thickets. He cast a glance in the direction of the fire, wondering if he would ever get out.

Something cold brushed the back of his right hand. He jumped, but it was just another *chill* seeking his warmth. He wanted to give it, but he didn't dare waste any more time. The odor of smoke was too strong. "I'm sorry," he murmured as he sought a way around the tangle.

The *chill* touched the back of his head. Robert shivered, and every hair on the nape of his neck stood straight up. "Stop that!" he snapped. "You don't understand. I'm in trouble out here."

But the *chill* rubbed insistently against his neck again.

Robert stopped, aware that something was different in that touch. This phantom wasn't trying to share his warmth. Its touch was too specific, just a brush on the neck, on his hand, and no more.

"What do you want?" he asked suspiciously.

The only answer was the briefest touch on the tip of his nose. Robert didn't understand. He frowned and sniffed the air. The fire was getting closer. An icy touch on his nose again. Then, a dozen touches on his neck, his shoulders, and his back.

Like hands, he realized with a start. It wasn't a single *chill.* Those he had shared his warmth with were still here, still with him. *Pushing me.*

"You want me to follow you?" he whispered.

All the touches withdrew. Then, a spot of cold settled on his nose again. "That way?" he said doubtfully, staring straight ahead. The tangle was on his left now. Did these spirits know a way around it? If he went the way they seemed to be urging him, it would be on a course perpendicular to the fire, not away from it.

"All right," he said nervously, rubbing a hand briskly over the end of his nose to warm it. He started forward with his invisible guides. Off to his right, the little piece of sky he could see through the trees glowed with a dull orange light. He gritted his teeth and moved faster.

It was still tough going, but he encountered no more obstacles. He clambered down the bank of another dry streambed and up the other side, over a hill and down into a wooded valley. If he deviated from the course, a cold finger touched his nose.

He could no longer see the glow in the sky, nor was the smell of smoke as strong.

Abruptly, the trees parted, and he found himself on the side of an old road. It wasn't much of a road, just a wide, worn path, but it ran straight south. Robert barely restrained his joy. Biting his lip to keep from shouting, he jumped up and down and beat his fists on his thighs. "Thank you!" he whispered excitedly. "Thank you, thank you, thank you!" He flung out his arms. "Have some warmth, guys!"

But the *chills* had slipped away. Somehow they had known he was lost, and in exchange for his warmth, they had brought him to this road. He felt suddenly lonely again, and this time it was not an echo from his spirit friends, but his own emotion.

An image of Sunrunner diving headlong into the earth, screaming in grief, caused him to squeeze his eyes shut. He'd screamed, too, begging the dragon to accept him in Evander's place as Shadowfire had accepted Eric. It was hard to admit, but he envied his brother. Eric had found his place somehow in this world. Not just Shadowfire, but Palenoc itself had accepted him.

Robert didn't feel that same acceptance. The world seemed instead to watch him, measure him, and withhold its judgment. Eric was *part* of Palenoc now. Robert only felt *apart* from it. *Look at me,* he thought glumly, *still in jeans and Reeboks.*

But for a moment he had reached out to these *chills.* They, at least, seemed to accept him. He had touched one of Palenoc's many mysteries, something fantastic, and for the first time it hadn't tried to bite him.

He swallowed, then bid the spirits a silent good-bye as he stepped out onto the path.

Something jabbered in the trees overhead, and the unexpected sound sent him diving behind a bush. His heart skipped a beat as he peered upward. A pair of *magoths* swung through the high branches with impressive speed and disappeared. Running from the fire, Robert figured. Doubtless, there would soon be more.

He began to jog up the trail, watching the trees to the left and the right, every sense alert. He felt the fire like a hand at his back even though he couldn't see the flames. He was certain, though, that he could stay ahead of them. Thoughts of Eric and Katy and the others crept up on him as he settled into a comfortable rhythm.

Alanna. He'd never met a woman like her. So much confusion filled him when he thought about her, and more when he held her in his arms. There was so much that she needed to know about him, and so much that he could not bring himself to tell. How could he explain that when he called an image of her into his mind, it overlapped with another—*Scott Silver*?

There was so much that he had to do, so much that he had to figure out.

After a while, he began to walk again to conserve his energy. He listened to the eerie quiet. The insects were silent, though the smoke hadn't reached here yet. Off to his left, a few isolated fireflies winked in mute harmony. It was a strange legacy for this world that it could be so beautiful and so terrible at the same time.

But then, he realized, wasn't that true of Earth?

A random breeze brushed his face, bringing an odd odor. It wasn't smoke, but something else. He stopped and sniffed, then moved forward more cautiously. A spot of fire shimmered in the dark distance on the road ahead, then another spot of fire just like the first. Yet again the breeze blew, and Robert sniffed. This time he recognized the smell—men.

Robert stepped off the road and into the brush. Crouched, he crept forward, easing himself from tree to tree.

Five low campfires burned in the middle of the road, their dull glow revealing piles of black, lacquered armor and stacks of supplies. Robert could barely make out the silhouettes of four wagons. He saw no animals, however, and guessed the Chols were their own beasts of burden.

Without making a sound, he pulled himself up into a tree and climbed as high as he dared for a better view.

The soldiers were asleep on blankets. More than fifty men, Robert estimated. Some huddled near the fires while others were stretched out in the soft weeds at either side of the road. He noted a pair of half-asleep sentries at either end of the encampment.

Supply troops for Kajin Kasst, perhaps? It seemed likely, since they were headed toward Wystoweem. His first thought was to destroy the wagons. A few brands from the campfires could help accomplish that. But what was the point?

He gazed northward. From this higher vantage, he could see the glow of the oncoming forest fire once more. He didn't need to lift a hand. Kajin Kasst would never see these supplies.

But maybe he could find a few things for himself. He climbed to the ground and, skirting the edge of the road, darted past the first pair of sentries. They leaned on a low stack of boxes and chatted in hushed tones, completely unaware of his presence.

Robert paused and scanned the camp from behind a thick boll right at the roadside. The first thing he needed was water. He looked for skins, jugs, anything that might contain liquid. From his hiding place, he spied nothing of which he could be certain.

All right, a weapon, then, he decided. Not far away, near the outstretched hand of a sleeping Chol, lay a wooden baton. That brought only a frown, which quickly turned to a smile when he spied the banner that stirred in the light breeze from a stout pole in the center of the camp. *Capture the flag,* he thought, grinning as he recalled a favorite boyhood game. It appealed to him immensely to sneak in among this stupid bunch of Chols and take their flag. He loved games, and that pole would make him a fine bo-staff.

Lying flat on his belly, he crawled cautiously out into the road. If one of the sentries glanced his way, or if a soldier woke unexpectedly, he would appear to be just another body. Silently on elbows and toes, he progressed. The road wasn't wide; he inched between a pair of sleepers. *Take a bath!* he commented wordlessly, wrinkling his nose in disgust at the pair. They must have marched all day, carrying these supplies on their backs and shoulders. They certainly smelled it. The whole camp smelled.

Someone had wedged the banner between a couple of boxes to hold it erect. He almost chuckled as he rose and snatched the pole. With a hop and skip over another pair of sleepers, he faded into the woods on the other side of the road.

What a sorry lot, Robert thought as he quietly unfastened the banner from the pole. In darkness, he couldn't see much of the pattern on the cloth, but it didn't seem to be a single symbol. Rather, it was embroidered with what appeared to be writing in a language he didn't know.

It reminded him of the small medallion he wore on a chain around his neck. It, too, was covered with writing in a language he couldn't understand. He wadded the banner up and stuffed it under his shirt as he turned back toward the road. His new staff could remain right here against this tree while he searched for water. Again, he crawled out to mingle with the sleepers.

He returned a few moments later with his prize, a flat ceramic jug, corked, and with a convenient strap. He shook it. More than half-full. He put the cork between his teeth and pulled it free. A sweet smell rose out of the bottle. It didn't contain water. Cautiously, he tipped it to his tongue, tasted some kind of mild, sweet tea, and raised an eyebrow appreciatively.

He put the strap over his shoulder and curled his fingers around his new staff. At seven feet, it was a bit too long, but he could fix that later. Water and a weapon: an acceptable haul. He patted the banner under his shirt and grinned. Let them puzzle that one out when they woke up.

He moved deeper into the woods, thinking of all

the malicious pranks he could pull on sleeping soldiers and barely alert sentries. He felt like he was cheating himself to just move on. Nevertheless, that was what he did. When he could no longer see the glow of their campfires, he stepped out onto the road again.

The trees parted long enough to let him glimpse the sky off to his left. The red glow made him catch his breath. It was not another fire, though. This time it really was the dawn. He sniffed, but didn't smell smoke yet. Maybe those Chol soldiers would wake up and resume their march, unsuspecting, straight into the inferno.

He set one end of his staff on the ground, leaned it at an angle, and brought the side of his foot forcefully against it. In the still morning, the sharp *crack!* sounded as loud as a rifle shot. He picked up the broken section and flung it far into the trees and hefted the shortened staff experimentally. It was now roughly five feet long. He rotated it between his hands, end over end, nodding approvingly.

The road took him through a range of wooded hills. At one point it crossed a stream that actually carried some water, though no more than a thin trickle. He stopped and quenched his thirst, saving the tea in his jug.

The road rose again, leading him up a high ridge. He climbed it slowly, not because he was tired, but to conserve his energy and because he felt no great reason to hurry. At the top, leaning on his staff, he turned and looked back the way he had come.

In the first rosy half-light of morning, a thin wall of dark smoke hung like a curtain over the north.

He took a sip of tea from his bottle as he thought of his brother and his comrades. He hoped they were all right. They had to be. Eric was the most reliable, competent man he knew. Eric would have found a way to get them all out safely.

He corked his bottle and, turning his back to the forest, trudged down the far side of the ridge. A vast grassy plain stretched before him. In the distance rose a line of shadowy mountains. The lengthening fingers of morning seemed to shrink from those sharp peaks.

Robert swallowed. "The road to hell," he said to himself as he descended.

Chol-Hecate.

Chapter Twelve

ERIC lay flat on his belly behind a bush, watching the scene that unfolded in the grass before the house. Kajin Kasst, his mask back in place, strode angrily before his Chol soldiers, who were kneeling before him, heads down, not daring to look upon their leader's wrath.

"You have failed Chol-Hecate!" he raged, shaking a gloved fist. "You have failed my brother, your ruler. And worst of all"—he drew back his foot and kicked the nearest soldier squarely in the ribs. With a shocked outcry, the man fell sideways—"you have failed me!"

A pair of Chols emerged from the trees on the other side of the house. Quickly, they threw themselves down upon their knees with their fellow soldiers.

"You!" Kajin Kasst shouted, causing the pair to look up. "Did you find the jewel?"

The pair exchanged nervous glances. One man whipped off his mask and spoke up in a timorous voice. "No, lord," he answered. "We chased one of the females. The warrior, I think. But she eluded us in the dark."

Eric glanced at Valis, who lay on his right behind another bush. Valis returned his glance and nodded without saying a word. The soldier could only have meant Alanna.

Kajin Kasst bent over the man, seized him by his

hair, and snapped his head back. "Incompetent fools!" he screamed. His hand made a loud *crack*! against the unfortunate soldier's cheek. "That jewel is worth more than the lot of you together! Your tiny minds can't comprehend its power!"

Another pair of soldiers stepped out of the trees not ten yards away from where Eric and Valis lay in hiding. Eric's heart beat faster. He clutched the medallion around his neck and thought of his brother, Katy, Salyt, and Alanna, all out there somewhere in the woods. He counted only twenty-four soldiers in the yard before the house. The others were probably still searching.

Doe eased from behind a tree and stretched out to Eric's left. "The *chelit* are dead," he whispered in a bitter voice. His mouth curled into a snarl. "Three of them, anyway. The bastards sharpened stakes and shoved them through the worms' eyes."

What a stupid waste, Eric thought. The Chols might have claimed the worms for their own mounts. "What about the fourth?" he asked, his mouth close to Doe's ear as he kept one eye on Kajin Kasst.

Doe shrugged. "Gone."

Kajin Kasst turned away and strode back toward the house. In the doorway, he paused and braced both his hands on the jambs. He stood there, silhouetted by the light from the fireplace. A dog snapped and barked at him. Eric strained to see the poor pooch that had followed them earlier still tangled helplessly in the net near the stoop.

"Bring the animal," the Chol prince said as he moved inside the house. Two soldiers hurried to obey. The dog growled and tried to snap at them through the heavy net until one of the soldiers produced his baton and delivered a merciless beating. The growls turned to pitiful yelps and whines.

Eric gritted his teeth, fingers digging into the soil. Doe reached over and gripped his forearm as a show of support. Valis moved his lips in soundless cursing.

The Chol soldiers grabbed the heavy rope net and carried the unfortunate dog inside. A moment later, they emerged again and knelt down in their places in the dirt. The door grated closed behind them.

A dull amber gleam from the fireplace showed under the cracks of the door and through the half-open shutters on the only visible window. The light flickered and dimmed, surged, then dimmed again. A howl rose from within the house.

The hairs on Eric's neck stood straight up. He shot a look at Valis. "What the hell's going on in there?" he demanded in a harsh whisper.

The big *sekournen* let out a slow breath and shook his head, his gaze fixed on the window where improbable shadows danced on the inner walls. "Just remember that it's only a dog," he whispered dourly. "We have ourselves and our comrades still in the woods to think about."

The dog cried again, a long high-pitched wail that dissolved into a series of choked yips, then silence. The firelight wavered again. On the narrow strip of inner wall they could see from their hiding place, shadows swirled in a dark and disturbing dance.

A low, throaty chanting came from within the house. Kajin Kasst's voice rose in passionate intensity. The words were in the Chol tongue; though neither Eric nor his friends understood them, they sent a shiver up Eric's spine.

In the yard, one of the soldiers emitted a fearful moan and covered his head. The sound spread like an infection through the Chols, and they filled the night with a pitiful keening, quaking, and trembling, but none dared to rise from his place.

"What are they afraid of?" Eric whispered nervously. He'd never seen such a reaction in men before. What power did Kajin Kasst have over them to instill this kind of fear?

"Can't you feel it, my friend?" Valis said uneasily. He rubbed his hands over his arms, which were covered with gooseflesh. His eyes gleamed. "Magic in the air, sharp as lightning, black as pitch."

Kajin Kasst's voice became a shriek. The dog howled again. But the sound of it was different. Voice and howl blended, interwove in an unholy harmony. The air turned electric; an unseen force rippled over Eric's skin like a shock. In the yard, the Chol soldiers whimpered and wailed and cowered.

Above the house, the fabric of the night quivered and shimmered like a rising wave of heat. The baying of the dog drowned out the voice of Kajin Kasst. On the wall beyond the window, the shadows whirled like crazed, orgiastic celebrants.

The howl was no longer a howl of pain. It was evil given a voice. The shimmering above the roof took on a horrible quality. The air shifted, coalesced. Canine eyes suddenly opened in the heart of that shimmering and stared hungrily down upon the Chol soldiers.

Eric choked back a scream and squeezed his eyes shut. He snapped them open again. There was nothing there above the house, and yet he saw eyes red as coals, a snout, a maw with fangs that sheened with saliva. There and not there!

"Do you see it?" he hissed, raising up on his elbows, straining forward.

Valis pushed him back down again.

"We see," Doe answered in a harsh croak.

The door to the house flung back and fell off its already twisted hinges. The black silhouette of Kajin

Kasst appeared on the threshold in a crackling corona of violet energy. Two sparks of white-hot fire blazed upon his throat.

Diamonds! Eric recalled. There were two huge diamonds on the golden torc the Chol prince wore around his neck. Through such precious stones flowed the magic of this world. But what had his magic wrought? What had he done?

The beast-thing above the house lifted its snout toward the clouds and bayed like a hound from hell. Around a throat that wasn't there burned a collar of yellow fire with twin white stars, an astral duplicate of Kajin Kasst's ornament. With another howl, the creature returned its attention to the soldiers.

A red tongue, impossibly long, shot out from that gaping maw, ensnared a man, and lifted him. The soldier screamed, flailed the air helplessly with his arms and legs. His fellow soldiers screamed, too, yet not one dared to leap up and run. The beast swallowed its victim.

"This is how I reward failure!" Kajin Kasst raged from within his violet corona. He stabbed the air with an accusing finger. "Now feed the *shriker* with your souls!"

Again, that tongue lashed out and chose a man. Its jaws opened and snapped shut, and another soldier was gone.

Kajin Kasst raised one hand and squeezed it into a fist. "Enough!" he cried. The diamonds at his throat flared like tiny novas. The deadly vision that loomed above his troops turned malevolent eyes his way. The hound licked its lips. "Go! Find the blood crystal of power and bring it to me!"

The *shriker* gave a howl that set the trees to shivering, then faded away like a dream.

Like a nightmare, Eric corrected. *One that you can't shake.*

Kajin Kasst moved out into the yard. His violet aura ebbed and disappeared. A few soldiers dared to lift their heads and turn fear-reddened eyes toward their master. They seemed like whipped dogs at his feet.

Kasst removed his mask and rubbed a hand over his sweating face. A harsh sneer of annoyance curled the corners of his mouth. "My pet has fed," he said. "Somebody remove these leftovers." He nudged with his toe one of the two masked and armored bodies that lay in the grass.

Eric pressed a hand to his mouth. "I don't understand!" he whispered incredulously. "I saw ... !"

"Their souls." Valis stared straight ahead. A muscle in his jaw twitched. The words fell from his lips like grains of bitter salt. "The creature ate their souls, and *that* is what we saw."

"But ..." Suddenly, Eric stiffened. He sniffed the air. A wisp of smoke snaked above his head. The fire! He shot a glance over his right shoulder and cursed. Deep in the woods, a gray tide flowed around the trees, over bushes and brush. It swept over Eric and his friends, into the yard.

Kajin Kasst spun about with an expression of total startlement. Even his men forgot their fear and scrambled up as the smoke oozed toward them. Without any warning, the yard brightened with an orange glow. A soldier shouted and pointed. Flames shot wildly up a single tree, turning it into a towering pinnacle of fire. A second tree caught, then a third.

Eric gazed wide-eyed at a growing wall of fire. Scorching heat burned him in a wave as he rose to his feet. Doe moved faster. Leaping out of his hiding place, the naked youth advanced on the nearest Chol, slipped an arm around the man's throat, and dragged him back into the brush without alerting any of the other soldiers. Two quick punches silenced his chosen victim.

"Evander used to say I looked good in black," he muttered as he started to strip the man's uniform off. "I hope his boots fit."

Eric turned again, one eye to the flames, one to Kajin Kasst. A look of terror and desperation flashed over the Chol prince's face. "Damn that *chimorg*!" he cried. He grabbed two of his men by their collars. "You and you! Carry me!" Obediently, the two joined hands to fashion a fireman's carry. "And if you fear the flames," Kasst added sadistically as he settled himself, "imagine what I'll do to you if you stumble!"

Kajin Kasst and his bearers vanished into the trees, and the rest of his force plunged after him. There was no order to their retreat. It was a panicked rout in the face of the fire.

When the last soldier was gone, Eric raced toward the house with Valis close on his heels. At the threshold he stopped, brought up short by the sight on the floor in the middle of the room. His gorge started to rise, and he choked it down. Valis pushed his way inside and stopped, also.

The furniture had been pushed back. The dog lay in a pool of its own blood, its throat slashed and its stomach cut open. Kajin Kasst had pulled out the intestines and arranged them in concentric circles around the corpse. Bloody symbols adorned the walls, obviously drawn with Kasst's fingers. At each of the four cardinal points around the grisly circle, four more signs were painted. In the center of the one nearest the dog's head, lay its heart. Near the tail, was its liver. Eric didn't recognize the messy chunks of meat in the other two, nor did he want to know what they were.

"My God!" he whispered. "How could anybody ... !" But a worse thought interrupted before he could finish. The howling! The howling had gone on for so long!

"Go back outside," Valis suggested. "I'll get our clothes."

Eric shook his head, trying to snap himself out of his shock. A bunch of garments lay wadded up near the fireplace. He grabbed one that looked big enough to fit him and pulled it on. Valis did the same, and they dashed back outside.

A wind blew heat and smoke into the yard, and Eric coughed. The fire was moving faster than he'd thought possible. It had seemed miles away when he'd first spotted it, but it was nearly upon them. Without their mounts, they were in serious trouble.

"A couple of shirts," he cursed. "We came back for a couple of shirts!"

"The *chelit* wouldn't have helped us, Eric," Valis replied as he stared toward the blaze. "They're too slow to outrun a fire." He gazed around in consternation. "Where's Doe?"

"Over here." Alanna stepped out of the bushes and wiped her face wearily. Her body was marred with bruises and cuts, her hair a wild tangle around her face. "Sorry, but I knocked him out. I mistook him for a Chol."

Eric's heart leaped to see another friend still in one piece. "Get her some clothes!" he snapped at Valis. He rushed forward, caught her shoulders, and gave her a quick once-over look. Most of her cuts were scrapes and scratches, the inevitable result of running bare-assed in these woods. "I can't tell you how glad I am to see you," he admitted, embracing her. Then he let her go and pushed through the bushes to where he'd last seen Doe.

The young *sekournen* lay sprawled facedown on the ground not far from a now-naked Chol. Doe hadn't stopped with the soldier's captured clothes, but donned the black lacquered armor as well. Most of it, anyway. His outstretched hand reached toward one boot.

Eric bent to examine him. He lifted one eyelid gingerly with a thumb as Alanna knelt on the ground beside him.

"I figured you'd try to sneak back here," Alanna said. "So I made my way back, too. There was no other place to reconnoiter. Anyone checked on the *chelit*?"

Rejoining them, Valis drew a thumb across his throat. "Chol efficiency," he told her. He held out a bundle of clothing. "I think these are yours."

"Thanks," Alanna said, sitting and pulling on her boots. "When I saw Doe crouched in the bushes in all that black stuff, I thought it was another Chol." She gave an apologetic shrug and reached for her shirt. "They've chased me all over these woods tonight, and I was too tired to care about fair play, so I hit him from behind. It wasn't until he fell that I realized who I'd clobbered."

Eric slapped Doe's cheeks to bring him around. His eyes fluttered open. "I'm all right," Doe said groggily as he sat up. "What happened?"

Alanna handed him the last piece of his costume. "I was overenthusiastic," she said. Then she flashed a teasing smile. "I like the haircut, by the way. You make a cute Chol."

"Compliments won't save you," he promised, forcing a weak, crooked grin as he pulled his last boot on. "I'll get even." He made a face and rubbed a hand over the back of his head.

"If we don't get out of here fast," Eric said, "the only thing you're going to get is roasted."

Not far away a burning tree, in the vanguard of the advancing flames, crashed noisily to the ground. A shower of fiery splinters and hot sparks shot into the night and rained down again, clattering on the roof, spraying into the yard. Flames swept upward through the trees behind the house.

"I think we're going to get roasted in any case," Valis said grimly.

Alanna helped Eric pull Doe to his feet. "Don't be such a pessimist," she snapped. "I'm not ready to die. Not until I find out why Robert ran out on us."

Eric bristled, stung by her accusation. "Robert wouldn't run out," he shot back. "God knows what's happened to him. Or Katy. Or Salyt. This whole mission's gone to hell!"

"You're right about that," Valis said. "Without Salyt, there's no point in going on."

"There's no way we can look for them," Alanna added. "All we can do is get out. I've taken care of that."

She turned and started off into the deep forest. The men hurried to follow her. Fire spread through the tops of some trees right above them. Smoke rolled through the air. Suddenly the ground dropped. They plunged down a steep incline, bushes scratching and slapping at their legs and thighs. At the bottom was a rocky streambed. Alanna led the way between its dry banks.

Eric thought his heart would burst as he realized he was actually leaving without Katy and his brother. What had become of them? Robert had slipped away on his own, then disappeared. The last he'd seen of Katy, she was at Salyt's side and chaos was breaking loose. His best hope was that the three of them were together. Bobby had good woodcraft skills. He could take care of them.

Still, it was hard to just run away without knowing.

He risked a glance over his shoulder as they ran along the streambed. The entire world seemed on fire. A white curtain of smoke hung above the soaring flames, reaching up to infinity, shifting and swirling on winds of unquenchable heat. He listened to the constant crackling roar, and it filled him with dread.

Abruptly a new sound rose over that, a screeching and shrieking that brought them all to a sudden stop and made them look up. On the ridge above the dry stream, the highest branches rippled with a sudden sea of motion. Huge, silhouetted shapes leaped with frantic grace from tree to tree. Other shadows lumbered along the ridge, itself, skulking with deliberate care along the ground.

"Magoths!" Alanna called. "Hundreds of them!"

"Keep going!" Eric urged. "They won't bother us. They're trying to outrun the fire, too!"

She nodded nervously, then started running again, slipping once when a rock turned underfoot. Eric caught her. "Not much farther," she told him. "I found it when the Chols were chasing me."

"Found what?" he answered, concerned about her ankle. She seemed all right, though, and in seconds they were off and running again with Valis and Doe right behind.

She didn't answer.

The streambed twisted back and forth between its banks, but it was relatively free of entangling thickets. Once, Eric figured, it must have flowed swift and deep. Now, it was only a black, stony scar in the earth, one more result of Wystoweem's drought. They made good time following it, though. Better than they could have made on the ridge.

"Here," Alanna said breathlessly. An old tree had fallen on its side across the stream. Years ago, the ground had washed away around it, allowing it to topple. The exposed root system stuck up like a modern art sculpture, illuminated by the fire glow against a haze of drifting smoke. She scrambled up the bank and offered a hand to help Eric up. Before he could accept it, though, she doubled over in a fit of coughing. "Just the smoke," she assured him as he clambered up on his own.

"Where are you leading us?" Valis asked as he came up behind Eric. Blood trickled darkly from a scratch on his cheekbone. He dabbed a finger at it, frowned, and wiped it on his sleeve.

"Up there," Alanna said, pointing.

In the darkness, he hadn't noticed how the land on the left side of the stream had risen into steep cliffs. Only a narrow expanse of flat ground and trees separated them from a high earthen wall. "Have you been up there?" Eric demanded.

Alanna pushed her hair back with one hand. Her face gleamed with sweat. "No, but we shouldn't need a path. The shear face is an illusion caused by the dark. It's steep, but climbable. I've already called our *sekoye*."

"What?" Eric exclaimed. Alanna was the only one who could call all their dragons at once. He hadn't dared hope their mounts would be close enough to get them out of this. "When?"

"Earlier tonight," Alanna admitted as she pushed away from the stream and into the trees, making straight for the cliff. "After dinner in the village. Everyone had retired, but I couldn't sleep. I was at my host's window when I saw Salyt and Katherine sneak away."

Eric batted aside a branch that slapped at his eyes.

"Sneak away? What are you talking about? Did you follow them?"

"I wasn't dressed," she said over her shoulder, "and they were gone before I could pull on clothes. They went into the forest, I think, and that made me suspicious. Why would a Wystoweem councillor lure a woman from Paradane into the woods in the middle of the night?"

"Salyt hasn't trusted us with many details," Doe grumbled. "She's been secretive right from the beginning."

Valis nodded agreement. "So you called the dragons. That's why Sunrunner reached the village so soon after ..." He paused and glanced regretfully at Doe.

"After Evander's death," the young *sekournen* finished glumly. "Sunrunner was already on the way."

Alanna pushed a thick branch out of her way and held it back for the others. "I took it on myself to summon them a bit closer, but not so close Salyt would see them from the village." The branch *whooshed* as she let go of it and moved to the lead again. "Then, when I saw that the forest was on fire, I called them again to come and get us." She cast a quick grin back toward Doe. "That was before I conked you on the head."

Eric coughed. The smoke was getting thicker. He gazed up through the trees toward the tops of the cliff again. He understood why Alanna had brought them here. The dragons would never be able to reach them under all these trees. They had to get to a high place.

She was right, too, about the illusion. It wasn't a cliff at all, but a steep, rocky ridge. The soil proved loose and treacherous underfoot, but he dug in with the toes of his boots and used his hands to steady himself. Little cascades of rock and dirt slithered down behind him, causing problems for Valis. "Spread out," he advised. "Don't come up behind each other."

At the top, he caught his breath. The entire northern horizon blazed, and an arm of fire curled around to the east. Spots of flame dotted the west and the south as well, caused, no doubt, by wind-borne sparks and ash. He had seen horrors in his short time on Palenoc, but he'd never seen anything like this.

Alanna threw back her head and began to sing. Her voice rose clear and desperate into the night as she closed her eyes. The red glow that filled the sky colored her cheeks, gleamed in her hair. Eric reached for the small harmonica in the special pocket on his belt, but Valis stayed his hand. There was no need. They could each summon their own *sekoye,* but Alanna could call them all.

The opposite side of the hill was a shallower slope, and the forest grew right up to meet them. Only at the very edge were they clear of the unwanted shelter of the trees. Eric turned to stare at the fire again, marveling at the red sky.

Then a terrible new dread filled him. "Valis," he said, clutching his friend's arm. "The blood crystal of power." He shot a gaze at Doe. "You heard him, too. Kajin Kasst. He said, *Bring me the blood crystal of power.*"

Valis and Doe both nodded. "That was his command to the *shriker,*" Valis said.

Eric's grip tightened as he drew the big *sekournen* closer. "Did he mean Salyt's ruby? Did he? Has he sent that monster after her?" *And,* he feared, *after Katy and Robert? Surely they were all together.* He recalled the look of lust and greed, of terror and wonder, all mingled on Kajin Kasst's face as he pulled the jewel out of its pack and held it up.

"Mirrormist!" Alanna cried, stopping her singing. Eric looked where she pointed. An amber light sailed out of the white smoke above the flames. Massive wings beat the vapor-filled air, and a sinuous form flew straight for them. "We can all ride out on him," she shouted. "The other *sekoye* are near, but there's no time to wait!"

She was right. The fire had already reached the streambed. As he watched, the wind carried hot sparks across it. The first small blazes flared up in territory they had crossed only minutes before.

"You go without me!" he answered. "I'll wait for Shadowfire."

"Don't be a fool!" Valis protested as Alanna began to sing again. "The fire's advancing too fast!"

Doe put a hand on Eric's shoulder. "It won't do Robert or Katherine or anyone any good to get yourself killed!" he said in a calmer voice.

Eric brushed his hand off. "I don't intend to get myself killed," he snapped. "I'll meet all of you in two days at Sheren Hiawa."

A golden glow bathed them suddenly, and a wind pressured downward from Mirrormist's mighty wings. Diamond-colored eyes regarded them, and the creature opened its great mouth to trumpet an urgent greeting. Alanna sang, and without settling to the ground, Mirrormist stretched out his long neck. His rider leaped into the saddle. "Come with us!" she shouted.

"Sheren Hiawa in two days!" Eric repeated, holding up a pair of fingers. He pushed Valis toward the edge of the hill and Mirrormist's offered neck. With obvious reluctance, he climbed up behind Alanna.

"I'll stay with you," Doe offered. "We can look for Robert and Katy and Salyt together. That's what you intend, isn't it?"

Not just that, Eric answered with silent grimness. *If anything's happened to them, I'm going to introduce Chol-Hecate to some Earth-style warfare.*

He threw his arms around Doe and embraced him. "Thanks, my friend. My *namue.* But I'll meet you in two days."

Doe hesitated, staring at him with those deep-set, dark eyes, a troubled frown on his brow. "All right, Eric," he said at last. "But remember what you told me. You're not alone."

"The talons!" Alanna called, and Doe lifted his arms. There was only room for two in the saddle. She sang a note, and Mirrormist flew away from the edge of the steep hill, banked in a high, tight circle, and dived toward Doe. Huge claws encircled him, closed, and swept him into the night. Another tight bank, then his friends sailed out of sight over the trees, heading eastward.

In the north, a red spark that could only have been Doe's Heartsong plunged through the curtain of smoke, then abruptly changed direction to pursue Mirrormist. Brightstar, Valis's dragon, chased after him.

A wracking cough seized Eric as he drew a breath of smoke. A wave of hot air rolled over him. The fire raced through the flat expanse from the streambed to the cliff. It shot up a dozen old trunks, turning trees into pillars of flame.

He drew out his harmonica and blew a riff. Then, "Call On Me," an old tune by Bobby Blue Bland, flowed out of the instrument. He poured his heart into it, letting the song take his mind off the danger as he reached out through the bond he shared with Shadowfire. He could feel his *sekoye* coming.

He stared downward. There was no sign of the streambed now, nor of the lower ridge on the other side. No *magoths*, no darkness.

There was nothing to see down there but hell.

Chapter Thirteen

THE *chelit* crashed through the forest with a speed Katy would not have thought possible. Salyt beat its head with the rods, her hands still bound together. She swung the sticks wildly, half-crazed, seeming not to care what direction the beast took so long as it was away from that sadist, Kajin Kasst. Between her thighs, she clutched the ruby in its pack.

Hundreds of scurrying legs, driven to their utmost by the councillor's desperate blows, made quite a racket in the dense undergrowth. The beast couldn't keep up such speed for long, though, and it was already slowing down. Katy cast a frantic look over her shoulder as she chewed on her rawhide bonds. In the darkness, it was impossible to see even the end of the worm they rode upon, let alone anyone who might try to follow. Half of Kajin Kasst's troops could be right behind, and she wouldn't see them.

She thought of jumping off. Salyt had promised they would stop and wait for the others, but she showed no intention of keeping that promise. Already they were a long way from the house. In the darkness, she wondered if she could find her way back. A worm this size had to leave a pretty good trail.

But follow it back to what? To Kajin Kasst? To all those horrible shapes and things flying through the air? She'd seen Robert escape into the woods. She was sure Eric had, too, but what if he hadn't? God help her, she didn't know what to do, what to think!

It was easier to let Salyt take the decision out of her hands. Eric and Robert would find her. She knew they would. All she had to do was stay alive until then, and that meant getting away from the Chols.

Her jaws ached from her efforts to chew through the rawhide, but she was rewarded when a band finally snapped. She tore the wrappings away and freed her hands. Her fingers immediately began to tingle as blood flowed back into them. She shook her hands and rubbed them briskly together.

"Let me untie you!" she called in Salyt's ear. The councillor didn't hear. Katy shook her shoulders. "Salyt?"

Salyt didn't answer. Her arms rose in unconscious rhythm as she beat the *chelit*. "Salyt!" Katy screamed again. She shook the older woman hard, then reached around and caught her arms. Salyt fought her wordlessly, entranced, or in deep shock. Katy tried to grab one of the rods. In her excitement, she wrenched too hard. Both women slid sideways out of the saddle and landed roughly in thick bushes. Riderless, the worm came to an immediate halt.

Katy gave a loud groan as she dragged herself to her feet and adjusted the straps of her backpack on her shoulders. Nearby, she heard the sound of weeping. The councillor sat against the base of a tree, knees drawn up and head in her hands.

Katy bent down beside the older woman and put an arm around her shoulders. "Hey, it's all right," she said softly. "We got away. Kasst will never find us out here." In her heart, though, she sensed that fear of Kajin Kasst was not the reason for Salyt's tears.

The councillor looked up with a forlorn expression. For an instant, she seemed like a broken toy. She put her arms around Katy's neck and drew her close, hugging her as if her life depended on not letting go. "Weena," she whispered. A heavy sob shook her, and she cried a bit before she could go on.

Katy put her arms around Salyt. "What about Weena?" she asked. A cold dread filled her as she thought of Salyt's daughter.

Salyt gave another sob, then freed herself from Katy's arms. From under her tunic came the silver chain and the sapphire stone. Even in the darkness it gave a tiny blue spark. "My child," the councillor began again. "I felt her die, Katherine. Weena is dead."

Katy gazed from Salyt to the sapphire. *Telepathy, after a fashion,* Salyt had said of its power. "When?" she asked incredulously. A memory of the little girl bouncing up the stairs of Sheren Shago stole feather-soft across her thoughts.

Salyt let the jewel fall onto her bosom as she wiped a hand over her eyes and tried to pull herself together. Her head rolled back against the tree, and she drew a deep breath. "Right after we grabbed the *chelit*," she answered faintly. Swallowing, she leaned forward and put her head in her hands again. The jewel swung on its chain between her knees. "I felt her go, Katherine. I felt it all."

Katy put her arms around the councillor again and let Salyt cry. "Was it the sendings?" she asked awkwardly.

Salyt nodded. "She was terrified." Another sob wracked her. She clutched at Katy's sleeve. "I should have been there, Katherine. I shouldn't have left her!"

"Then you'd be dead, too," Katy said bluntly as she caught Salyt's head and pressed it against her shoulder. She smoothed one hand over the councillor's tangled hair and rocked her gently. "And there'd be no one to avenge her."

Salyt looked up sharply and stared into Katy's eyes. "The ruby!" she said. "Where is it?"

"Right over there," Katy answered calmly. The pack containing the ruby lay beside the unmoving *chelit* within easy reach. She eased Salyt back down beside the tree, and started to work on the rawhide knots and the bonds on her wrists. "Let me get your hands free," she insisted.

"Only nine years old," Salyt murmured sadly. She balanced her hands and held them still while Katy worked. "Her father was a *sekournen,* you know." She paused until Katy nodded, then she closed her eyes and leaned her head back on the tree again. "He was so handsome. He never knew his daughter, though. The Black Snow got him just before Weena was born."

Katy broke a nail on the first knot and winced. "Black Snow?" she repeated. It was best to keep Salyt talking, she figured, to let her get the grief out.

Salyt opened her eyes and stared up through the branches. A tear rolled down her cheek. "Another time," she explained quietly. "Another war." A wan smile curled the corners of her mouth. "Another weapon. Chol-Hecate and Kajin Lure have a talent for inventing them. The Black Snow was a thick magic-spawned fog that flowed over the border and deep into Wystoween, freezing everything and everyone it touched, leaving behind a black snow-like residue." She looked down, watching Katy's hands labor at the knots. "I never loved another man after him, Katherine. I never took another lover. Raising Weena and governing Wystoweem, that's been my life."

The first stubborn knot came loose. Katy sighed with triumph and went immediately to the next. "You obviously found a way to beat the Black Snow. You'll find a way to beat this, too." The second knot proved easier than the first. Katy cast the rawhide strip aside as the councillor, flexing her fingers, held her hands up and looked strangely at them.

"Yes," she answered in a barely audible whisper. "I will. I promise."

The cold look in Salyt's eyes sent a chill through Katy. She rose to her feet and recovered the pack that contained the ruby. For a moment she thought of taking the stone out to admire, but then she thought better of it. She could feel the tingle of its power even through the leather pack.

"Give it to me." Salyt held out her hand, and Katy passed the pack to her. Salyt wrapped her arms around it, as if it was a child, and rocked it silently.

Katy wondered what was going through the councillor's mind in that moment. She grieved, too, for Weena, but she knew what she felt was nothing to what Salyt must be feeling. First a lover, and now a child. How much was a woman expected to give? War had always seemed so impersonal on earth, something viewed only on television that happened in some other country. Since her coming here, Evander had died, along with his dragon, Sunrunner. A village had burned, and more people had died. Now, Weena was dead, and if Weena was dead, that meant Capreet had been destroyed, too.

War was becoming very personal.

She unhooked a water flask from the *chelit's* saddle, uncorked it, and took a drink. The forest was unnaturally quiet. Even the insects were mute. She listened for any sound, but all she heard was a slight rustling of the wind through the leaves. Only a few patches of sky could be seen through the thick canopy overhead, and the clouds had a strange color.

Salyt gave no sign of moving, so slinging the strap of the water flask over one shoulder, Katy looked around for the riding rods that guided the *chelit.* She found one in a bush and the other partially under the beast. Tugging and pulling, she finally got it free. A dozen thin legs twitched in protest at her efforts, but the rest of the worm seemed oblivious.

She rubbed the inside of her left thigh to ease a cramp. Her leather trousers were still slightly damp, but she was glad that, out of modesty, she'd taken time to put her clothes back on before stretching out on the dusty floor to sleep.

Thinking of the house, she turned glum again. She felt like a traitor, running out on Eric and Robert. Walking back along the length of the worm, she stared into the darkness. The *chelit's* bulk had left an impressive scar through the undergrowth. She could probably follow it all the way back to the house—and right back into the arms of the Chols.

She thought of Eric and Robert. *I shouldn't have left them,* she told herself. She wondered if they were safe somewhere in the woods, or if they were still in the hands of Kajin Kasst. She couldn't stand not knowing.

She walked back to Salyt and leaned the rods against the tree within easy reach. "I'm going back," she said firmly. "You take the *chelit* and go on when you're ready. I'll catch up later if I can."

Salyt looked up sharply and wiped a hand at her eyes again. "Don't be a fool, Katherine," she snapped. "There's nothing you can do back there."

"I can't just leave them," she said. She turned away and went to the *chelit* where she slipped off her backpack and took out the stun gun. She wished to hell that when she'd snatched up her backpack she'd had time to recover some of the batteries Kajin Kasst had scattered all over the ground, but it was too late for wishes. Right now, she wanted it closer to hand.

Salyt jumped to her feet, leaving the ruby and its pack on the grass by the tree. "We have to think of the mission!" she insisted. "I didn't mean to cry like this!"

Katy faced her again with a patient smile. "It's okay to break down sometimes, honey. God knows, I'm close enough to a breakdown myself." She patted the older woman on the arm, then bent down and recovered the long strip of rawhide that had bound Salyt's wrists. She tied it around her waist, belting the shirt she wore, which had been Eric's. It was big and loose on her, and still bore his odor. She thrust the stunner out of sight inside the shirt and fixed the clip to the waistband of her trousers where it couldn't be seen. Then, she shouldered her pack again. "You think of the mission," she said. "I'm sorry about Weena, but I've got to think of my friends."

"But what about Kajin Kasst and his soldiers?" Salyt demanded.

"I'll take my chances."

"I need you!"

Katy shrugged helplessly. "I'm sorry." It was hard to leave Salyt alone in these woods, but this was her world, and she'd manage somehow. Eric and Robert were Katy's proper concern. She put one hand over her abdomen and paused for a moment, listening, feeling, sensing the new life within.

Now, more than ever, Eric was her proper concern.

Too late, out of the corner of her eye, she saw the rod that came whistling down at her head.

The smell of smoke brought her awake. Katy lay belly down across the front part of the *chelit's* saddle. Salyt's right hand rested lightly in the middle of her back, steadying her, as she guided the worm. An area immediately behind her right ear throbbed acutely. She didn't need to touch it to feel the welt and the broken skin on her scalp.

Without giving any warning, she slammed her elbow into Salyt's midsection with all her might. The councillor shrieked in surprise and pain as she tumbled from the saddle. Katy threw herself to the ground, snatched up the fallen rod, and spun it once with a skill that would have made Eric smile. She set the end against Salyt's throat.

"Our friendship is off, bitch!" she snarled.

Salyt's face twisted with pain, but she lifted a finger and pointed behind Katy. "I think we'd better talk later," she said.

Katy cast one leary glance over her shoulder and felt her heart lurch. The night was gone. The northern sky seethed with reds, yellows, and oranges. Through the trees she could see advancing flames. Even the nettles and leaves on the ground burned with a crackling roar. Wisps of white smoke drifted in the air. Hot ash and sparks floated on the wind.

"I've been riding away from it for an hour," Salyt informed her. "The flames are chasing us."

"An hour?" Katy said without taking her eyes from the inferno. "I've been out that long?"

Salyt got to her feet and rubbed her lower back, an expression of discomfort on her face. "It was no easy trick getting you into that saddle, let me tell you," she grumbled. "But I couldn't let you walk right back into Kajin Kasst's arms."

A hot breeze touched Katy's face. Smoke stung her eyes. "We'll discuss it later," she said, tossing the rod back.

They climbed into the saddle, and Katy wrapped her arms around the councillor's waist. Salyt drew the second rod from its holster near her right knee. With both sticks she gave the *chelit* a solid whack on the head. Hundreds of legs rippled on the forest floor, and the worm lumbered into motion.

Katy watched the flames at their back. The wind was picking up, she realized, blowing hard and driving the fire. High above the trees, red sparks swirled into the night, like crazed glowing insects caught in a tempest, each one a potential new blaze.

Salyt coughed violently as a cloud of scorching smoke flowed from between a pair of trees to engulf them. The rods banged down on the *chelit's* head. Katy doubted if the poor creature could go any faster, but its huge bulk plunged through the woods with new energy, creating a racket that filled her ears. It, too, had a sense of the fire at its back, and it ran for its life.

A puff of flame erupted in the canopy directly above them. It spread swiftly, igniting dry leaves and branches. Salyt tried to turn the worm, striking it again and again to alter its course. Burning leaves showered down around them. Katy screamed and covered her head. A fiery branch seared the back of her hand, and she clapped it to her mouth as tears of pain spilled down her cheeks.

Salyt slammed the right-side rod down upon the *chelit* with such force that it broke. Half its length went flying off into the bushes. Disgustedly, she cast the remaining piece after it while, finally getting the message, the creature turned. With new speed it slid around trees, crushing the underbrush, splintering weaker, young trees. Katy and Salyt, bending low in the saddle, used their arms to fend off limbs and low branches.

Abruptly, the worm halted of its own accord. Salyt and Katy lurched forward in the saddle, then righted themselves. The councillor cursed and struck with the rod, but the beast ignored her blow.

"Stop," Katy said. She clutched at the arm that wielded the rod and pointed straight through the trees. Ahead, a faint orange glow lit the darkness. "It knows what it's doing," she insisted. "There's fire in front of us, too."

Salyt stiffened. "We're surrounded."

Katy gave her a sharp slap on the back. "Don't say that," she snapped angrily. "Just pick another direction. Or let the worm choose one."

Salyt put the *chelit* in motion again. A fit of coughing seized Katy. Smoke hung heavily in the air. It was getting hard to breathe. She lifted the water flask and took a drink, then passed it to her companion.

"Hold it a minute," Salyt said. The councillor shoved the rod down into its holster on the saddle, then started to ease out of the straps of the backpack that contained the jewel. "Hold this, too," she said. When Katy took it, Salyt grabbed the hem of the leather tunic she wore and snatched it over her head. Under it, she wore a thin, silk chemise. "Rip it," she told Katy.

Katy understood. She slung the pack over one of her shoulders, let the flask hang by its strap and caught the delicate material in both hands. With a yank, she tore the fabric all the way down, and Salyt shrugged out of it. The councillor ripped another strip from the garment and handed it to Katy. "Wet that," she said. "Tie it over your face."

Katy did as instructed, pouring water from the flask sparingly, then tied the strip over her mouth and nose. She wet a second strip for Salyt. "Thanks," she called forward.

Salyt nodded as she slipped back into her leather

shirt. Then, once she'd tied the cloth over her face, she drew out the rod again and smacked the *chelit* until it turned the direction she wanted it to go. "Those hills," the councillor said over her shoulder. "They're our best chance."

Katy could barely make out the great black mounds, crouched like sullen toads in the distance. They seemed so far, and the flames so near. Overhead, sparks and ash flew as the wind turned malevolent. She wondered what protection could the hills offer, but without a better idea, she kept quiet. Any destination was better than sitting still.

The *chelit* slid down an incline and followed a ravine. The earth curled up on both sides of them, and for a while the flames couldn't be seen. There was no escaping the smoke, though. It stung the eyes. Katy wiped her tears away, feeling the grit and filth that clung to her skin. The burn on the back of her hand smarted.

When the worm crawled out of the ravine the hills were much nearer. Only above those rounded peaks was there any trace of blackness. The rest of the sky churned with reds and oranges as the clouds reflected back the fire's fury. A tree crashed to the ground not thirty yards behind them. Sparks and flames shot into the air. A rush of hot wind swept against Katy's back.

She felt the keen edge of panic, like a knife twisting its way into her heart. A scream bubbled up to her lips, but she choked it back. Instead, she uncorked the flask, raised the cloth that covered her face, and tossed back a drink. *First time anyone drew courage from a water bottle,* she told herself.

The hills rose before them, darkly hostile. The wind whistled up the steep slopes. The leaves shivered, and the branches rasped, and the trees bent like shamanistic monsters trying to scare them off with rattles. Salyt worked the rod, and the *chelit* dragged itself up a treacherous grade. Nervously, Katy put a hand on the stunner inside her shirt and pushed it more securely under her waistband.

Halfway up the incline, she turned and gasped.

The forest behind them was a boiling sea. Smoke swirled and curled like whitecaps on burning waves. If she got through this, she knew she would never forget that sight. She watched it until they reached the first summit and started downslope.

Her heart sank a little as she turned forward again. In the distance an arm of fire reached across the forest. Wherever she looked, islands of flame shimmered in the dark. *How long,* she thought with dismay, *before sparks and ash ride the wind into these hills, too?*

She wrapped her arms tighter about Salyt as the worm slithered downhill and into a deep valley. Darkness and gloom filled that recess, but overhead the sky glimmered red as blood. Another hill loomed on the left, and Salyt steered the *chelit* along its base. The beast seemed calmer, easier to guide, with the fire out of sight.

The side of the hill formed an earthen overhang. They followed it until the terrain dictated they turn away. Salyt uttered a soft curse and headed for the next looming hill. It looked more like an isolated cliff in the gloom. Salyt steered their mount right up to it. Stone and earth and roots and tangled vines were all Katy could see, but Salyt leaned as far out of the saddle as she dared, peering intently.

"There!" she said suddenly. She drew back the rod and threw it like a javelin at the cliff. Instead of bouncing back, it disappeared into darkness. A moment later, Katy heard its clatter.

Salyt slipped down to the ground. "This whole area is honeycombed with caves," she explained. "Once there were many springs, too, but most of them dried up after the sorcerous border wars that blighted this region." She extended a hand to help Katy dismount.

"How did you know?" Katy asked, filled with a sense of relief and amazement.

"I grew up in this part of Wystoweem," Salyt answered matter-of-factly as she moved toward the cave entrance. It was little more than a wide crack in the stone. "Not far from the town we stopped at tonight. As a child, I played in this forest." She paused at the entrance and drew a deep breath. "I wasn't sure this would still be here. Let's hope it goes back far enough."

"What about the *chelit*?" Katy said.

The councillor shook her head. "You have the water flask, already, and there are two more packs tied to the saddle. You take one, I'll take the other." She moved quickly with one eye to the smoky horizon as she untied the first pack and tossed it to Katy, who caught it, then winced at the pain it caused to her burned hand.

"What about the *chelit*?" Katy repeated stubbornly.

"We can't save it!" Salyt shouted with an anger that startled Katy. "Let's hope we can save ourselves."

Katy let go a string of curses as she followed the councillor into the hidden crevice. A stygian blackness, more complete than anything she could have imagined, swallowed them. She couldn't even see Salyt. Feeling along the wall with the palm of her injured hand, she slipped forward one cautious step at a time.

Unexpectedly, she bumped into the councillor, who seemed to be bent over, groping along the rough floor. "What are you doing?" she asked.

"Picking up the rod," Salyt said shortly. "It'll come

in handy." A moment later, a *tap-tap* sounded as Salyt proceeded forward with the rod for a probe.

Katy felt the darkness close around her like a hand crushing the breath from her lungs. The passage narrowed, and the walls pressed on her shoulders. She put a hand up. The ceiling was scant inches above her head. A small shower of dirt fell into her face and hair, causing her to sputter.

Her heart hammered. This was worse than the fire! The weight of the earth squeezed down upon her. The darkness strangled her until she couldn't draw breath. She couldn't see the entrance behind, nor Salyt ahead. She couldn't see her own hand. Her mouth went dry. No matter how she licked her lips, she couldn't wet them. Katy pressed herself rigidly up against the wall, unable to cry out, her legs unwilling to move.

Then, Salyt's voice came out of the darkness, softly singing, marked by the slightest tremble.

> *Bright was the morn and sweet the day*
> *When Renath gave his life away.*
> *It was to be his wedding day,*
> *And Starlit was to be his wife*
> *On beautiful Mianur.*
>
> *There never was a man so fair*
> *As Renath with the sun-gold hair,*
> *And many hearts he did ensnare,*
> *But Starlit was his love, his life,*
> *On beautiful Mianur.*

The sound of Salyt's song eased Katy's fear and reminded her that she wasn't alone. She slid one rubbery leg forward and then the other, fighting the paralysis that gripped her, gulped in a breath of musty air, tried to slow the hammering of her heart.

> *Starlit was a lady knight*
> *Who rode the wind in fairy-flight.*
> *She battled Darkness with her light;*
> *But for Renath she forsook the fight*
> *And dressed herself in bridal white*
> *On beautiful Mianur.*

I wish I had a flashlight, Katy thought, weakly smiling at her addition to the rhyme. She bumped her head suddenly. To her dismay, the ceiling was getting lower and lower. Still, the *tap-tap* of the wand continued. She bent forward, nearly in a crouch, and concentrated on Salyt's song.

> *In a wood by a silver glade*
> *Came these lovers, man and maid,*
> *And wedding guests to serenade*
> *On beautiful Mianur.*

> *Pledged they love to last forever,*
> *Through the ages, ending never,*
> *Bonds of faith no blade could sever*
> *On beautiful Mianur.*

> *But Darkness, Starlit's cunning foe,*
> *Begrudged this loving marriage show,*
> *Fit a crystal dart to bow,*
> *Drew back the string and let it go—*
> *A wedding gift from the world below*
> *To beautiful Mianur.*

> *As Renath swore never to part*
> *His eyes flashed, and he saw the dart*
> *Protruding from his broken heart*
> *On beautiful Mianur.*

> *Starlit cried and swept him high*
> *In her arms into the sky.*

> *"Renath!" she begged, "love cannot die*
> *On beautiful Mianur!"*
>
> *She lays him on an altar stone,*
> *Turns, without a tear or moan*
> *While the tablas beat a sullen drone,*
> *Puts on her armor all alone,*
> *Picks up the gauntlet newly thrown*
> *On beautiful Mianur.*

The song ended. Katy had been so intent on listening, she had failed to notice how the ground underfoot had turned to mud. Her steps made squishing sounds. The rod went *tap-tap* in the darkness ahead. "Sing some more," she urged. Salyt had a surprisingly nice voice, and the singing helped to ease her feelings of claustrophobia.

"There is no more," the councillor answered quietly. "That's the end of the song."

"Mianur," Katy said, hearing the song's refrain in her head. She snatched at the chance to keep a conversation going. Anything was better than silence. "I thought that was the name of the ring around your planet."

"Mianur was a world once." The whispered answer carried hints of reverence and sadness. "A beautiful world, as the song says. The people who lived there had the wild powers. They could do wonderful things."

Katy smiled to herself. "Starlit really could fly?"

The *tap-tap* paused. "So the legends tell," Salyt answered. "Only vestiges and remnants of the wild powers remain in a few of us, but the folk of Mianur were very special."

"It sounds like your version of the faerie realm," Katy said lightly.

"We have to crawl for a short distance," the councillor said.

A startled Katy realized her companion had turned around to bring her this news. She reached out and felt Salyt's face with the fingertips of her injured hand. "You look much younger in this light," she quipped, fighting new fear. How much smaller, closer, could the tunnel get?

"It's only a short distance," Salyt said. She caught Katy's hand and gave it a squeeze. "Then I'll show you a little bit of those vestiges and remnants."

Katy swallowed hard. "Just keep talking," she said. "Or singing, or whatever."

They got down on their hands and knees, then on their bellies as they splashed through mud. Katy transferred the stunner to the small of her back for safekeeping. As she did, she felt the roof of the tunnel against her head and bit her lip to keep from screaming. The pack on her back scraped against stone. She pushed the second pack ahead of her. It was impossible not to think of horrible things lurking in the darkness, tiny scuttling things that could crawl up under clothes or get in the hair.

"You can stand up, Katherine," Salyt said suddenly.

Cautiously, she rose to her feet. There was no wall on either side of her, nor could she touch any ceiling. A whisper of a breeze brushed her face, though, and to her amazement she smelled water. "Where are we?" she said. Her voice echoed.

"I promised to show you something," Salyt reminded her. "Be still and wait a moment."

How long? Katy wondered as the minutes ticked by. Her heartbeat slowed a bit, and her fear ebbed. She shifted her extra pack into her injured hand, then back to her good one. The wet mud seeped through her leather clothing and saturated her skin. She felt thoroughly fatigued and filthy.

Then, a dim amber glow suffused the space above her head. With a gentle gasp, she looked up. A lone stalactite glowed softly. No, she realized, not the entire stalactite. Just pieces of crystal embedded within it.

She glanced at Salyt by her side. The woman leaned on the rod, her pack at her feet. With eyes closed, brow furrowed, she concentrated.

The glow spread slowly across a vast chamber. Every piece of crystal in the cavern began to shine with a gentle, yellow light. In the center of this grotto was a small, still pool of water.

Katy sank to her knees and covered her mouth with both hands to keep from laughing with relief.

Chapter Fourteen

FOR two days, Robert wandered along the edge of the forest searching for some sign that his brother and friends had made it through. He nursed his small quantity of water and munched a couple handfuls of bitter-tasting berries until he vomited them up. Except for an hour or two of nausea, there were no worse effects, but with nothing to eat he was finally forced to admit the senselessness of staying.

There was still a chance they had escaped the fire and emerged from the woods at some other point. If he didn't know where they were, he knew where they were going. While he still had water left, he turned his back to the trees and headed deeper into Chol-Hecate. Somewhere ahead was a place called the Naz-rit Plain; all he had to do was find it.

The sun boiled down through a thick gray layer of clouds. It felt more like a humid summer day than early autumn. By mid-morning, he was sweating freely. Droplets of sweat rolled into his eyes, down his face, down his chest; his clothes clung damply to him. When he removed his shirt and tied the sleeves around his waist, the Chol banner fluttered to the ground. He picked it up and tied it around his head, leaving some cloth hanging to protect his neck from the sun.

A very slight breeze whispered over the grass. It

cooled him somewhat, and he sat down on the ground to rest for a few minutes. As he scanned the countryside, he felt utterly alone. Except for a couple of birds, he'd seen no game, no sign of wildlife. A few clouds seemed to hang still in the blue sky, as if afraid to move. The whole bleak land seemed to be holding its breath. He leaned back on an elbow and gazed again toward the sharp peaks in the distance. The mountains were an oppressive presence. Like a many-fingered hand, he thought, that waited, alert and watchful, to swat anything within reach that stirred.

It was better to keep moving, he decided. When he rested, he became depressed. It was too easy to think of his brother and too easy to fear that his friends hadn't escaped the fire.

He covered another few miles before stopping to wipe the stinging sweat out of his eyes again. The temperature continued to climb. He looked at his jeans. They were filthy, ruined, both knees ripped. *What the hell,* he thought, dropping his staff on the ground. With a couple of good yanks, his Levi's became shorts.

Not my usual debonair fashion statement, he admitted as he picked up his weapon.

He glanced back over his shoulder. A gauze of white smoke hung in the northern distance. The sight brought a lump to his throat. For just a moment, his emotional guard slipped. He thought of Eric and Katy and contemplated the worst. *They aren't dead,* he told himself sternly. But staring at that vast white curtain, he had to fight to put away his doubts. He turned resolutely and set his gaze on the mountains in the far south.

By late afternoon that third day after the fire, the clouds began to dissipate. The sun's full, fierce heat beat down. Robert's back and shoulders quickly reddened, and he pulled on his shirt. He gave his water flask a shake and decided to forego a drink. At the top of the next rise a lonely tree grew. Trudging up the long slope, he crawled gratefully into its shade.

Evening wasn't far off. It was as good a place as any to spend the night. He sat down with a weary sigh, leaned back, and let his gaze wander the wide, empty valley below. The tree made a hard cushion for his spine. He shifted, trying to get comfortable. *Another night without supper,* he thought morosely. *Like living at home when I was a kid.* He remembered Katy's backpack full of Snickers bars and unconsciously licked his fingers. Uncorking his bottle, he took a sip to wash down the imaginary taste of chocolate.

Watching the sunset, filled him with an unexpected queasiness. The sinking sun left streamers of pinks, yellows, and oranges across the horizon, painting an inferno on the world's western rim. At any other time, Robert would have called it spectacular. Now, it was a reminder, and more than he could bear. Clenching his fists, he got up and moved to the other side of the tree.

Darkness gathered in the east. It spread slowly like a foul oil over the fading blue sky, casting a shadow that touched first one low hilltop and then the next. A pair of birds fled from its advance and disappeared. A rising wind made a low, desolate moan.

Robert curled up on his right side and cradled his head in the crook of his arm. The leaves rustled overhead. The waving grass made a soft, teasing susserrus. He hugged the flask containing his scant supply of water protectively against his belly and listened to it all. If he stayed very still, perhaps the approaching night wouldn't notice him.

It didn't seem fair, somehow. He knew his own

world, Earth, was screwed up. He'd realized that years ago and shed any illusions about it ever getting better. But to find another world—something most people would only ever dream about—and find it in the same condition. It was more than disappointing.

"Take two Prozac," he muttered bitterly as he shut his eyes, "and call me when the depression's over."

He didn't get much of a chance to sleep. The far-away sound of voices and the creak of wagon wheels brought him to instant alertness. He grabbed his staff, pressed himself flat against the ground, and peeked cautiously around the base of the tree.

The darkness was not yet total. A vestige of twilight remained in the west, and from his vantage point atop the rise, he watched as a long double column of men marched on foot into the valley below. Six heavy wagons, two with high covered tops, rolled at the front of the ranks, drawn by slaves, who were dressed in tatters and rags and chained together in teams of ten. At various points along the columns eight well-armored officers rode on huge, oxen-like beasts. A trio of riderless *chimorgs* accompanied them at a watchful distance.

Robert estimated their number at two hundred. Two hundred men with six wagons would have food and water, both of which he needed. He made up his mind to follow this unlikely caravan. At the first opportunity, he'd take what he needed.

Then, to his pleased surprise, the wagons lumbered to a stop. The officers dismounted, calling orders, and soon the oxen-beasts were hobbled and turned loose to graze. Night closed like a tight fist over the valley as the Chols lit lanterns and set up camp. Pits were dug and a campfire built. Robert watched men move around in the darkness, catching only the gleam of a face now and then. As he took a precious sip from his flask, the wind carried a warm odor up the rise. His mouth watered at the suggestion of food. A few silhouetted shapes moved among all the others, dispensing bowls and the evening meal.

He forced himself to be patient. The *chimorgs* were his greatest danger, since they might smell him before he accomplished his goal. Reaching out, he plucked a single blade of grass, broke it, pinched it, and sniffed the pungent sap. It just might do the trick. Opening his shirt, he rubbed handfuls of grass over his chest and shoulders and belly, then treated his arms and legs similarly. Next, he worked it into his hair, over his face. That left his shirt and shorts. He regretted ripping away the legs of his jeans now. The sap made his skin itch, but it would be worth it if it confused his human stink and kept the *chimorgs* off his back.

He swallowed the last of his water and set the empty flask beside the tree. With his staff in hand, he started down into the valley in a low crouch, relying on the dark and the taller grass for concealment.

A pair of red eyes brought him to an instant halt. A *chimorg* moved around one of the wagons and stared up the hill in his direction, its tail lashing lazily back and forth. After a few moments, it lowered its head and began to graze.

Three wagons down, a pair of soldiers stepped away from the camp, unlaced their trousers, and took a leak. The muted sound of their voices rolled up the hill. A quiet bit of laughter followed.

Robert's hunger had gotten the better of him. It was a mistake to move this soon, he realized. The camp was too active. He sat down where he was, placed his staff on the ground, wrapped his arms around his knees, and tried to be patient. When the Chols were asleep, then his time would come.

If only he could ignore the smell and the thought of food.

Thanador, a thinning crescent, crept slowly up in the east. Several times larger than the moon of his home world, it poured a pale lumination upon the valley, banishing old shadows, casting new ones. The oxen-beasts eventually huddled together, folded their legs, and settled themselves in the grass. The grazing *chimorg* drifted around the wagons, across the field, and up the far incline. There was no sign of the other two *chimorgs*.

The campfires began to burn lower; the lanterns were extinguished. The clank of a kettle, a cough, a wooden creak, all random sounds drifted up to Robert. Only a few men stirred below. Two pairs of guards paced back and forth with little apparent enthusiasm for their jobs, and a few others sat around one of the fires, passing some kind of pipe and sipping from a common flask. The rest curled up on the bare ground and gave themselves to sleep.

If they had circled the wagons, it might have made Robert's task easier, but the Chols obviously felt they had nothing to fear inside their own borders. Picking up his staff, he stole down the hillside, every sense alert. Twenty yards away from the wagons, he stretched out on his belly and crawled forward. Off to his left, one of the oxen watched him with huge, moist eyes, but made no sound.

Off to his right, a group of four men lay asleep around the dying embers of their fire. Officers, he guessed, judging by the way they had chosen a spot separate from the rest of the men. He started toward them, snaking his way through the grass, then froze.

Another cough.

Robert peered cautiously around. The sound of a piece of cloth snapping in the wind drew his attention to the second wagon from the end. It was one of the covered ones. A small stepladder hung from its bed at the rear. A shirtless figure, barely visible, stood in the opening between the parted canvas flaps, hands on his hips, as he surveyed the Palenoc sky. Another officer, Robert figured, probably the commander if he had his own mobile home. He waited unmoving until the man went back inside and pulled together the flaps.

None of the four Chols stirred as he approached their small isolated camp. They'd dug a pit in the ground and made a small retaining wall with the dirt to contain their fire. The flames were nearly out. A black pot hung on a metal tripod over the embers, and Robert eyed it hungrily. He shot another look around, then taking a risk, he rose to his feet, tiptoed between a pair of sleepers, and stuck in his finger.

The pot contained some kind of cereal, oatmeal-like in consistency, and he made a disgusted face. He hated oatmeal. Now, Malt-O Meal he could handle, especially if it was covered with chocolate chips. Nevertheless, he scooped a fingerful into his mouth and swallowed. Not great, but not bad. He scooped several fingers full and looked around. No bowls or spoons in sight. He touched the chain that suspended the pot from the tripod, thinking he might just steal the whole thing, but the metal was too hot. *Might as well make a mess of it, then,* he decided. But first, he glanced around for a water flask, and found two just like the one he'd carried for the past three days. He eased the straps around his neck, and slipped them inside his shirt so they wouldn't bang together. Then, he shoved his hand down into the pot and filled it with as much of the warm, sticky cereal as he could hold. As quickly and silently as he could, he fled into a patch of higher grass and sat down to eat.

He glanced up at Thanador, at the dazzling stars, at the first edge of blue Mianur as the ring rose above the hills. Smugly satisfied with himself, he licked and chewed and swallowed his meager dinner. It was not a bad night, as Palenoc nights went. Not bad at all.

"You fool!"

Robert froze with two fingers in his mouth as the last of the cereal slid down his throat. His gaze darted toward the covered wagon where he'd first seen the shirtless shadow. The wagon rocked unexpectedly. An awkward cry and a crash. A figure flew backward through the flaps and landed gracelessly on the ground in a tangle of robes.

The shirtless figure loomed in the opening between the flaps again, one foot on the top step of the ladder. He clutched a cloth to the left side of his face as he shouted at the object of his rage. "Incompetent!" His voice boomed, shattering the stillness. "I should have your hands cut off!"

The fallen man struggled to his knees, but dared to rise no farther. Still, he gathered his robes about him and tried to assume a semblance of dignity as he rubbed at the small of his back with one hand. In a pinched voice, he answered, "My lord, if you'd just allow a little light so I could see . . . !"

"See what?" the shadow on the wagon screamed. He hurled the wadded cloth at the kneeling man. "My face? I'll pluck out your eyes first!"

The robed man cowered, folding his hands to his chest. "But, lord," he pleaded, "I can't heal what I can't see!"

A handful of stones glittered in the air, flung by the shadow. They scattered around the healer. "Get out of my sight, sniveler!" the shadow ordered. "And take your pebbles with you. When we get to Noh-Ferien, I'll find real physicians."

The healer scrambled in the grass for his gems while the shadow went back inside the wagon. The entire camp was awake, and two soldiers ran to help the physician to his feet. Robert flattened out, afraid to move, his hand still sticky from his hasty meal. Hesitantly watchful, he licked at his palm, found a little bit of grain yet between his fingers, and sucked it down. Waste not, want not.

He stared toward the wagon again, contemplating the shadow's identity. Same voice, same arrogant attitude. Kajin Kasst had escaped from the forest fire, probably at a more eastern point where he must have commandeered this caravan.

But something else just as startling caught his attention. Some of the men in the camp, alarmed by the disturbance, were on their feet. Firelight gleamed redly on the heavy collars and chains around their necks, on the manacles that encircled their wrists. Robert crawled closer for a better look.

Only a handful of the men in the camp were Chol soldiers. The rest were captives, not slaves as he'd first thought, all chained together with stout chains. From the top of the rise, he'd been too far away to see clearly. Their tattered garments were the remains of *sekournen*-like garments. Many wore haircuts that tapered to points at the nape of the neck, a fashion among the Domains' *Kur-Zorin*—the common soldiery.

Robert clenched a fist and bit his lip at the same time. According to Salyt's master plan, Domain troops and dragonriders were to have attacked Chol-Hecate's borders. These men were prisoners taken in the battle. He studied them as best he could as they began to settle down again. He didn't know the nations of the Domain alliance as well as Eric. His brother had become the true expert on Palenoc. But there, sewn to a sleeve, was a ragged dragon emblem from Guran, and there an insignia like a compass rose from Virashai, and there the double star of Imansirit.

He knew too well what fate awaited these men. He'd seen for himself the death camps of Terreborne where prisoners were slowly starved to death. That was the way of the Dark Lands. Either that, or they would be taken to Noh-Ferien, Chol-Hecate's capital, paraded through the streets and sold as slaves, human spoils of war.

Over at the small camp to his right, one of the officers, awakened by his prince's outburst, discovered his water flask was missing. He jabbered at his three comrades in the Chol language. Robert didn't need to understand. To his left, one of the oxen gave a snort and a soft *moo* and batted its great eyes.

Not tonight, babe, Robert thought with a frown. *Paul Bunyon feels a headache coming on.* He clutched his staff and crawled away from the camp. When he dared get to his feet, he slouched his way up the rise.

The same lonely tree waved to him in the wind. "Honey, I'm home!" he intoned in a whisper as he sat wearily down and folded his legs into a lotus position.

That's right, Polo, he told himself ruefully, *crack wise. Play the funny man to hide the fact that you've got a serious decision to make.* He stared down into the valley, almost resenting the presences below. Without thinking, he slipped his left hand into his jeans' pocket and drew out the piece of tourmaline quartz. He held it between his fingers and the ball of his thumb.

"Scott," he murmured, as if his friend was sitting right there beside him. "How do we get caught up in these things?" He turned the quartz. It caught the moonlight and shone like a small soft star on his palm. "I wanted to look for you," he continued, moving his lips soundlessly. "But I had to help Eric and Kat. Now I want to look for Eric and Kat." He stared down at the camp again. "But I have to stay here and help these guys. Trouble is, I don't know what to do. Guess I'm going to sit here and think about it awhile. If you want to suddenly pop in, in your ghostlike way, and make a suggestion, now would be a really good time."

He pulled out the water flasks from inside his shirt and set them on the ground before him. The empty flask was right where he'd left it at the base of the tree. He reached for it and put it next to the other two. "Looks like a three-kegger night, Scotty," he said to the quartz. "Wanna drink?" He picked up one of the bottles, pulled out the cork with his teeth, and spit it out. "Phooey, real man's style." He put the flask to his lips and drained it with rapid gulps. Small rivulets ran from the corners of his mouth, down his chin and neck into his collar. Then he poured a quantity over his head and wiped his face with the back of his sleeve. "Yessir, real man's style."

Thanador began its long downward slide. Mianur arched across the middle of the sky like a surreal, monochrome rainbow. Robert closed his fist around the bit of quartz as he watched the stars slip across the heavens. "I've missed you, Scotty. Missed talking to you, you know? You never used to be such a quiet guy. Maybe you've been taking life a little too seriously."

The wind blew. The leaves rustled. The tree swayed and creaked ever so gently. Below, the last campfires winked out. Robert reached for the third water flask. There was no reason to save it. Shortly, he would either have all the water in the camp below—or he wouldn't need water ever again.

"*Borracho,*" he muttered as he spat out the second cork and raised the bottle. He'd never really consumed alcohol back on Earth. But tonight, he wished: *"Muy borracho."*

As the sun came up, Robert untied the cloth from around his head and shook his blond hair free. By now, he sported a close blond beard as well. All his misgivings and meditations were behind him. Many thoughts had passed through his mind during the night, and some had fallen into place.

He removed his shirt of dragonskin leather. He was not a *sekournen*. He would never be a *sekournen*. That was Eric's role in this world. There was another part for Robert, though he didn't yet see clearly what it was. He folded the shirt with ritual care and laid it on the ground beside the three empty water flasks. Once more, he took the piece of quartz from his pocket, looked at it, and thought of Scott before he put it away. Finally, grasping his staff, he started downhill.

The camp was just beginning to stir. A black-clad Chol saw him coming and shouted to a companion. Robert lifted his head and fixed the pair with his gaze. He kept a calm and even pace as he descended. Another soldier, an officer perhaps, shouldered the two men aside and drew a baton from his belt. Robert turned his gaze on the officer, caught his eyes, held them. The captives came awake. He heard the shaking of their chains.

A squad of armored men rushed up behind the officer, weapons drawn. Robert didn't slacken or increase his pace. A muttering went up through the camp. As if picking up on the tension, one of the hobbled oxen began to bellow.

The officer gave a command in the Chol tongue and wagged a finger. Two soldiers ran to meet him, raising their batons with menacing intent. Robert only looked at them, each in turn. They slowed, then stopped in their tracks. Robert gently touched the nearest one on the shoulder, and the man hung his head. The baton fell from a limp grasp to the ground.

The officer gasped and took an involuntary step backward as Robert approached. Fear widened the man's eyes, but he was not, apparently, a man accustomed to fear. Perhaps conscious of his status before his subordinates, he swung his baton and brought it whistling down.

Robert's hand shot out, caught the weapon, and snatched it away. A stunned look flashed across the officer's face. Robert kept his own expression impassive. He dropped the baton at the officer's feet and passed on, leaving the man to stare.

He heard it then, the muttering and muffled exclamations that he knew would come. First, in the Chol language, as they saw his hair and his green eyes. He didn't understand what they said, but one singsong, musical word passed over and over among them.

Then, from the Domain warriors, a more familiar word, uttered, not with fear, but with awe and hope. "Shae'aluth! Shae'aluth!"

The Son of the Morning.

The Chols parted to let him pass as he strode into the center of the camp. Pausing there, he looked down into the dark, upturned eyes of a young Imansirit soldier that reminded him of Danyel and Evander, a boy too young for war. But then, everybody was too young for war.

An enraged shout marked the beginning of the confrontation he knew had to come. All night he had meditated on this moment, stripping away fear, anger, all thoughts of revenge. Calmly, he turned.

Kajin Kasst held his elaborate mask in place with one hand. Behind it, his eyes glimmered with anger as they fixed on Robert. The mask was all the armor he wore. A soft violet rope draped over his naked shoulders. It swirled about his legs as he grabbed one of his officers by the arm and propelled him at Robert.

The officer barely kept from falling on his face, but he caught his balance and affected something of an attack posture. Trembling visibly, he raised his baton. Robert fixed him with a green-eyed gaze and slowly shook his head. The Chol shot a look at his prince, then lowered his weapon and slunk away.

Kasst shrieked in outrage.

The robed physician sprang suddenly forward, perhaps hoping to redeem himself in his lord's eyes for his effrontery of the previous night. He opened his hand and began to chant. On his palm rested a cut diamond the size of a robin's egg. Sunlight struck its facets. The air around the stone shimmered and sparkled.

Robert's vision filled with that sparkling. Something tickled across his mind. Sleep suddenly seemed like such a wonderful idea. *Magic,* he told himself. The thought was a mental slap. Resisting the sluggishness that tried to seize him, he stepped forward. With serpentine quickness, he snatched the gem from the surprised physician's hand. The poor man tripped on his own feet as he tried to jump away. His robes splayed around him on the ground like dark, broken wings. He stared in panic at Robert, making no effort to get up, though his lord cursed and berated him.

Robert tossed the diamond aside and pointed his staff at Kajin Kasst. The Chol prince fell abruptly silent and glowered at him. The hand that held the mask, though, betrayed his true emotion and shook with fear.

In a low, controlled voice, Robert said, "Let these people go."

Kajin Kasst seized a baton from the nearest soldier.

"You are not *Na-kaya Amun!*" he answered scornfully in the language of Guran. Only the last part was Chol. It didn't need translating. "Your weak-kneed Son of the Morning will never return. The Queen of Darkness is too strong!"

Robert paced slowly toward him. "Look at my hair," he said. "Look at my eyes. You know who I am, Kajin Kasst. I *have* returned."

The mask slipped ever so slightly. Kajin Kasst caught himself and lifted it back into place. He brandished the baton and backed a step as Robert walked toward him. "There's something familiar about you," he admitted. His shouting could not disguise the fear and doubt in his voice. He drew himself erect as he looked to his soldiers for support. "But you are not *Na-kaya Amun!*"

Robert stopped. *"Na-kaya Amun,"* he repeated. The name rolled on his tongue. A collective shiver went through the Chols as he spoke it. All that Alanna and Phlogis had told him, the remembered legends, the stories, came back to him. "In the Dark Lands," he recited, "he will arise and draw breath once more, bringing Fire and Light to banish the Shadow." He pointed with his staff once more. "You have seen the Fire."

Kajin Kasst stumbled back as if struck a blow. "No!" he screamed. With animalistic rage, he flung the baton. "It can't be!"

Robert caught the weapon in midair, held it for a moment, then opened his fingers and let it fall into the dust. He started forward again with a serene calm. "In the hour of his coming, Shandal Karg and all her minions shall drink the cup of Fear and eat of their own Despair."

Shocked gasps went up from the Chol soldiers. "You speak her name!" Kajin Kasst cried in disbelief.

He raised an arm as if to ward off a lightning strike. "You dare!"

"That and more," Robert affirmed. He took another step forward. The physician scrambled on hands and knees to get out of the way, spilling gems from a loose pocket. On Robert's right, a soldier sank to his knees and abased himself, muttering plaintively into the dirt.

Then, a wild trumpeting sounded on the far rim of the valley. All eyes shot toward it. A moan went up from the captives as three *chimorgs* raced down the hillside straight for the camp.

"Now you'll pay for your blasphemy!" Kasst shouted, finding a measure of courage again. He shook one fist, careful to keep his mask in place. "And if her beasts leave anything of you at all, I'll hang a piece of your flesh on every bush from here to Noh-Ferien!"

Robert's gaze lingered on the Chol leader for just a moment. The *chimorgs* bellowed another challenge as they raced over the ground. "They only herald the end of your world," he said to Kajin Kasst.

He turned with such suddenness that three soldiers stumbled backward and fell in a heap. He grinned. Then, staff in hand, he leaped over them and ran to meet the *chimorgs*. He wanted open space for this battle, and plenty of room to fight. This wasn't the forest. There would be no running away this time. A cry went up behind him. It might have been the Domain warriors shouting encouragement. Maybe it was the Chols cheering the *chimorgs*.

The sun gleamed on the slick black scales of the monsters as they charged. Robert stopped and brought his staff into a defensive posture. His heart hammered against his ribs. Gone was the calm with which he faced the Chols. Adrenaline surged in his veins.

The earth shook with the thunder of hooves. Robert cast his staff aside. No weapon would serve him now. On impulse, he thrust a hand into one denim pocket and drew out the piece of quartz. He didn't believe in luck, but maybe it would bring him some. He closed his fingers around it. Then, drawing a deep breath, he pressed his fists together, centering himself, focusing his energy.

The first *chimorg* lowered its horn. *Not yet,* Robert told himself. He leaped aside, arching in a nimble dive-roll that brought him to his feet again. The second beast barely missed him. He flung himself backward, taking a brush from its powerful shoulder that knocked him flat.

The third beast reared above him. Its hooves crashed down inches from his head. Robert rolled aside, scrambled to his feet, and ran around the deadly creature. It spun, tearing divits from the ground, to chase him. Without warning, Robert turned, too, stopped and braced himself. The *chimorg* gave a startled bellow, stumbled, and lunged past him.

He felt a shaking in the earth and shot a look over his shoulder. Side by side, the other two charged. Robert brought his fists up and drew another deep breath, looking straight into their eyes. It was like gazing into the pits of hell. *Not yet,* he reminded himself. He pressed his lips together with grim determination as he drew his focus tighter.

The *chimorgs* parted, passing on either side. For a brief moment he felt himself sandwiched between them, bounced from one to the other. The heat of their sweating flesh scorched him, their smell filled his nostrils.

A black horn flashed above him. Hooves slashed the air over his head. A shoulder knocked him down, and he picked himself up. Again and again, the monsters charged. Robert stood his ground, held his focus. *Now,* he told himself. *Now!*

All three *chimorgs* circled him, bellowing, shaking their unnatural manes, lashing serpentine tails. One lowered its horn and charged. Robert's shout exploded from him as he struck with the stiffened edge of his left hand. All his carefully pent rage suddenly found release in a single blow.

The shattering of the *chimorg's* horn sounded like a crack of thunder. The beast screamed. Its front legs folded under it and it pitched forward, twisting its neck, tumbling.

Robert lifted the horn from the grass and raised it triumphantly above his head. "You won't hurt me!" he cried savagely to the fallen *chimorg.* It scrambled up clumsily, shrieking with shock and pain, shaking its massive head. "She won't let you, will she?" He grasped the horn in both hands, point outward, ready to stab.

This was the secret he and his brother had discovered and given to the Domains. The *chimorgs* were the creatures of Shandal Karg, created and bred by her. They roamed about the countryside as her eyes and ears, carrying her messages, doing her will. Nothing could kill them. Nothing, except a dragon's talons—or the horn of a *chimorg.*

"Come on!" he challenged, narrowly eyeing the beasts.

The hornless *chimorg* fled across the valley. The remaining pair snorted and pawed the ground, glaring with hatred and impotent menace. One of the beasts trumpeted suddenly and charged him. Robert raised the captured horn, determined to ram it into the *chimorg's* breast with all his might, but the monster swerved away at the last moment and chased after his hornless companion. The third *chimorg* followed.

A loud cheer went up from the Domain warriors as he turned and walked back to the camp. The far side of the valley was dotted with black-clad figures as most of the Chol soldiers fled in terror.

Screaming curses, Kajin Kasst waded among the chained captives, swinging a baton left and right to vent his anger and frustration. Blood sprayed. A pair of Domain warriors rose up, despite their chains, and tried to drag the Chol down, but he beat them back with numbing blows.

Uttering a curse of his own, Robert raced back to the camp.

Kasst saw him and leaped away, his violet robe swirling about his legs. It was not fear that drove him this time. Behind his mask, eyes blazed with madness. He raised the baton, daring Robert to come nearer. "You are not *Na-kaya Amun!*" he raged, obsessed with that name.

Robert knelt down and thrust the *chimorg* horn point first into the earth. "It was dark in the forest, wasn't it?" he said, rising. "Too dark to tell the color of my hair, too dark to see my eyes. You were far more interested in other things. A woman's breasts. A ruby jewel."

Kajin Kasst's eyes went wide, then narrowed to slits. Slowly, he lowered the mask he had so carefully held in place with one hand. The right side of his face was a massive red blister that extended from his chin and the corner of his mouth right up to the ear. The eyebrow was singed away. He was lucky to have the eye at all.

The mask fell to the ground. Kajin Kasst grasped his weapon in both hands. "The house in the woods. You were the quiet one!" he hissed in sudden recognition. His lips curled back in a snarl. "The fire may have spared your life, *thin-blood*! You won't escape me!"

Robert allowed a halfhearted smile. "If anything's thin around here, it's your threats," Robert said. "Thin as the wind."

Kajin Kasst shrieked and ran at him with the upraised baton. Robert moved lithely aside and brought his leg up in a roundhouse kick. A wet snap. Kasst stumbled to his knees, a shocked look on his tortured face as he clutched his ribs.

The captives cheered wildly.

Kasst glared and let go a catlike howl, raking the air with fingers curled like claws. Then he struggled up and charged again.

Robert dropped low and swept his opponent's legs. Kajin Kasst's feet flew up in the air, and he landed hard on his back and neck, screaming in pain, dropping his weapon. The gasping Chol prince reached out for the baton, which was mere inches from his grasp. Robert brought his heel down sharply. Bones crunched. Kasst screamed again, and rolled away, hugging a ruined hand.

"Get up," Robert invited. With a toe, he nudged the baton closer to Kasst.

"You are not *Na-kaya Amun*!" came the madman's shrill cry as he got his feet under him and crouched like an animal. He shook his good fist defiantly.

"It doesn't matter," Robert answered flatly. "I'm still the end of your world."

Kajin Kasst screamed furiously and reached for the baton. The move was a clumsy feint. Instead, he flung himself bodily at Robert, his arms open wide, teeth bared. Robert caught an arm, twisted, feeling tissue and tendon snap. Kasst spun through the air in a violet tangle and hit the earth with jarring force.

The Domain warriors rattled their chains and sent

another cheer into the air. They heaped insults and jeers on the broken Chol. Kajin Kasst turned on his side and defiantly spat at them.

Robert pulled the *chimorg* horn from the ground and walked toward his enemy. The captives fell suddenly silent. Kasst rolled to his back and glared as Robert stood over him. The point of the horn hovered over Kasst's right eye until he turned his head aside.

"What happened to my brother and my friends?" Robert asked grimly.

A malignant glee lit up the Chol's burned face. "Dead," he answered. He looked up again, ignoring the horn's threat. His mouth formed a cruel smile. "The fire got them. I watched the flesh melt from their bones."

Robert stiffened. "You're lying," he said. But he heard the fear and doubt in his own voice. "They got away."

The blister on Kasst's face oozed blood and infection. Slowly, the Chol raised a hand, dabbed at it with a finger, and brought the finger to his lips. He sucked the tip. "They were bound like pigs for roasting." He spoke with a disconcerting calm, savoring each word as he met Robert's gaze. "You would know that I'm telling the truth if you hadn't run away."

Darkness enfolded Robert, not cold, but warm and comforting, insulating him from pain, dulling the grief, dulling thought. He closed his eyes. Behind his lids he saw the shape of the darkness, the void, and it was his shape. The darkness was part of him. *Inside him.*

He leaned on the horn, felt the soft resistance, the sudden give, heard the sharp sigh of escaping life, and for a moment he was transported in a flash of memory to a dark, garbage-strewn alley in New York's Greenwich Village. This wasn't the first time he'd taken a man apart bone by bone, and not the first time he'd killed for revenge. For a moment he was horrified by the parallel.

Opening his eyes, he looked down on Kajin Kasst and withdrew the horn. Blood bubbled up from the hole in his throat, but the Chol was already dead. Robert bent and wiped the horn clean with a handful of violet cloth.

"Now take your revenge, you bastard," he whispered. "If you can."

Chapter Fifteen

"EACH crystal has its own unique vibrational frequency," Salyt explained as she moved among the stalactites and stalagmites. With a gentle hand, she stroked each one and let its light fade out until the only illumination came from the embedded clusters and fragments of calcite in the cavern walls. It was barely enough to see by.

"With time, I could teach you to hear them," Salyt continued. "You could learn to manipulate their energies."

Katy was only half listening. She stood naked, waist deep in the pool, laving water over her body. Her red hair hung in ropes about her shoulders and streamed rivulets over her full breasts. Droplets fell from her upraised hand, from her nipples, and struck the black surface like shattering pearls.

Her other hand rested on her belly. It was still a matter of quiet amazement how she knew she was pregnant. She'd heard of women who claimed such awareness from the very moment of conception, but she'd always written such statements off as motherly exaggeration.

She considered telling Salyt, but bit her lip. It didn't seem right to tell someone else before she told Eric. Where was he? she wondered. Was he even alive? In unguarded moments, she still had visions of the fire, devouring, destroying.

She glanced at the back of her hand. The burn was completely healed. Salyt had passed a piece of crystal over the wound and hummed some little melody. Oddly, Katy had felt a vibration on her skin, and when the song was done her pain was reduced. After a couple such treatments, there was no mark at all and no discomfort.

The councilwoman sat down at the edge of the pool and took her gray hair into her hands and drew it over one shoulder. Out of its bun, it was long and straight and fine as silk. Her fingers moved with skillful dexterity as she plaited it into a single braid.

The dim light glimmered on the sapphire Salyt wore on a thin silver chain about her neck. It rested in the cleavage of her pale, blue-veined breasts and was the only thing the older woman wore. They'd washed the filth and the ash out of their clothes in the pool and spread everything to dry on the rocks, but neither woman had bothered to dress again.

Katy climbed out of the pool and stood dripping on the opposite side from her companion. She wrung out her hair and tossed it back. Then, with her hands, she squeezed as much water as she could off her arms and legs. The air was still and warm. It wouldn't take her long to dry.

Salyt took her place in the pool. The councillor bathed in a characteristically businesslike manner, submerging herself, briskly scrubbing her skin, then getting out. The sapphire swung wildly, sparkling with blue fire, as she hauled herself onto the edge again and stood up.

When both women were reasonably dry, they moved to the eastern side of the cave. A natural limestone shelf on that side had become their living and sleeping area. Salyt kneeled down and reached for two of the packs, leaving the third, which contained the ruby jewel, where it rested. There was still half a round of cheese left in the first one, as well as a couple of flasks of water. With the pool below providing drink, they had decided to leave the flasks untouched. From the second, she took a handmade wooden box containing biscuits. It was half-empty. In the same pack were some dried leather strips that the councillor swore was meat. Katy, however, had her doubts.

Katy sat down on the corner of a thin blanket that had come in one of the packs, watching as the food was spread out. Then, she broke one of the biscuits in half and set the other half back in the box. A few crumbles of hard cheese and one of the meat strips made the rest of her meal. She crawled back against the wall and nibbled slowly, making it last. Salyt took even less, the other half of her biscuit and a piece of cheese.

"You should eat more than that," Katy urged.

"Who are you to talk?" Salyt replied in a mildly scolding tone. "I'm just not very hungry."

There was no point in arguing. In fact, Katy was famished, and she was sure Salyt felt the same. It had become almost a ritual, though, to set everything out and take almost nothing. No telling how long their meager supplies would have to last. Neither had said anything about rationing, but they were both realists in their own ways. She chewed a tiny bite of biscuit and considered putting the dried strip of meat back for later. Guiltily, she changed her mind. *I'm eating for two,* she reminded herself.

Her meal quickly finished, Salyt leaned back against the wall. One fist squeezed around the sapphire as she closed her eyes. "Nothing," she muttered in quiet awe.

She looked at Katy and held the gem toward her on its chain. "You simply are not there."

"I'm right here," Katy snapped testily. She eyed the sapphire, a glimmer of an idea taking shape in her mind.

"I see you with my eyes," Salyt answered patiently. "I can reach over and touch you." She did so, poking Katy's bicep with a fingertip. She dangled the sapphire again. "But I can't read you with this. To my inner senses, you're completely invisible." She leaned back against the wall, held the sapphire up, and set it to spinning by twirling the chain between her thumb and forefinger. "It's a mystery to me, Katherine. I've never experienced anything quite like it."

"Why don't you try to use that to find Eric?" she suggested, giving voice to her idea.

Salyt looked askance. "I have tried," she confessed in a bare whisper.

A cold hand clutched at Katy's heart. Unable to speak, she set the remains of her biscuit back in the box and wiped her fingers on her thighs. "Are you telling me he's dead?" she finally asked.

Salyt hesitated before answering. "He may just be too far away. My gifts are limited." Her tone, however, didn't offer much hope.

"You read Weena's ..." Katy thrust her knuckles into her mouth, stopping herself. But she saw the change that came over Salyt's face. The councillor hung her head for just an instant, let go a sigh, then began rewrapping and repacking their supplies.

"Weena was my daughter," she explained as she busied herself. "A mother can sense her child, no matter what."

Katy placed a hand on her belly. "I suppose you've tried Robert, too?"

A nod was answer enough. Salyt pushed the two

food packs back against the wall beside the third pack before she turned to Katy again.

"I'm afraid I'm quite tired, Katherine," she said apologetically. "Can you handle the darkness if I let the crystals go?"

Katy swallowed. It took an effort of will on Salyt's part to keep the calcite glowing. Each time the councillor fell asleep, the light died completely, leaving them in the impenetrable blackness. "No problem," she answered unconvincingly. "I think I'm getting used to it."

"You don't lie very well," Salyt said with a sympathetic grin.

Katy drew a deep breath and forced a grin of her own. "And you're a bitch for pointing it out." Then, the grin faded as she glanced up toward the cavern's roof. "It's not the dark I'm afraid of anyway. It's—" She groped for the right words, wondering how to explain claustrophobia.

"The closeness," Salyt supplied. "The fear of being buried alive."

Katy didn't answer. She stretched out on her side on the thin blanket and hugged her backpack, which served as her pillow. Glancing nervously around the cavern for a final time before the light died, she closed her eyes. A few moments later, Salyt curled up behind her and slipped an arm around her waist. "It's dark now," she whispered. Katy bit her lip and nodded.

They lay like that, huddled together, sharing a blanket on a hard stone floor, with only each others' touch to anchor them in a blackness that seemed deeper than infinity.

Katy's eyes shot open. Every hair on her neck stood straight up. A chill shivered down her spine. "It's back," she said to her companion as she stared into the dark.

Salyt's hand tightened on her arm. "I hear it," she answered.

The sound came again, a distant baying, a howl from the outside world that penetrated right to the bowels of the earth. It sounded like a dog in absolute torment. Yet there was an angry edge to it. A hunter's edge.

One by one the calcite crystals in the walls ignited and began to glow. Then the stalagmites and stalactites, one by one, until every spar and fragment burned with a nervous white fire. Salyt got up, slipped down from the shelf, and crept across the cavern floor to the narrow opening on the far side. Katy quickly followed. Crouching down on either side of it, they listened as the howl echoed down through the outer tunnel.

"Five times," Katy muttered. "What kind of dog comes back to the same place over and over?"

Salyt stuck her head and shoulders into the small opening. "It's not a dog," she answered grimly as she withdrew and sat back on her heels. The worry was plain on her face. The fingers of her right hand played with the sapphire pendant between her breasts. "It's a *shriker*. The soul of a ritually sacrificed animal. Such creatures can be sent out to do a sorcerer's bidding."

Katy stood up. "You're telling me this is a ghost?" She slapped one palm against the wall and frowned in consternation. "The ghost of some dog?"

"It's a perversion," Salyt answered sharply. She rose and paced away from the opening. "In the Domains of Light we work our magic by manipulating the natural energies in gems and crystals." She stopped beside a stalagmite, examined it briefly, and moved on to another as she continued speaking. "But the Dark Land sorcerers practice more foul arts. Death itself is a source of energy to them. Anything that dies is a well of power."

Katy watched, hugging herself, as Salyt examined still another stalagmite. The baying of the *shriker* grated at her nerves. She tried to ignore the awful sound by listening carefully to her companion. "You really hate them, don't you?" she said as she moved down by the pool.

Salyt reached up to finger a low-hanging, milky white spar. It glowed with a bright crystalline fire. Without looking at Katy, she answered, "They are abominations." The words hissed from her. She made no effort to hide her contempt and animosity. "Every Dark Land sorcerer. They've sold their souls into slavery to the Heart of Darkness, herself. Do you think she rules their wills? Most of them come willingly, seeking power in exchange for service and loyalty to her. Kajin Lure is the worst." Standing on tiptoe, she seized the stalactite in both hands and jerked. A loud crack followed, and a piece about two feet long came free. She held up her prize.

"You have cause to hate Kajin Lure," Katy responded with a faint trepidation, doubting her right to say such a thing. Nevertheless, she said it. "But don't let it cloud your judgment. Your worst enemy is Shandal Karg."

The *shriker* gave a bone-chilling howl that reverberated down the narrow tunnel into the cavern.

"Hush, Katherine!" Salyt snapped. She pressed a finger to her lips, eyes narrowed with warning. "It's not wise to speak that name aloud."

"Well, why doesn't it just come in and get us!" Katy shouted in sudden frustration. She felt totally helpless, trapped, and afraid. She didn't like feeling any of those things.

Salyt grabbed her clothes from the various places where she'd spread them to dry. With those draped over one arm, carrying her needle of stone in her other hand, she climbed up onto the shelf where they slept and ate. With deliberate speed, she dressed. Then she sat down on the rim of the shelf, dangling her legs over the side, and picked up the broken stalactite.

It glowed in her hands. The tip of Salyt's tongue protruded ever so slightly, and an expression of total concentration settled over her face as she scraped a section of the spar against the shelf's edge, using exactly the same motion Katy might have used to sharpen a knife.

Katy gathered her clothes, too, and pulled them on. The leather felt stiff against her skin, but free of grit and ash and mud. She stepped into her boots, then climbed up onto the shelf, and bent over Salyt.

Stone rasped on stone as Salyt worked the splinter. "You should get some sleep, Katherine. We'll have to leave here at the first light of dawn."

Katy snorted as the shriker gave another howl. "Sleep?" she commented with a glance toward the tunnel. "Fat chance. Anyway, how will you know when it's morning? For that matter, how can you be sure that it's night?"

"The *shriker*," Salyt answered simply, pausing long enough to wipe a hand across her brow. She was already sweating from her labor. "It's a ghost, and except in very rare circumstances, ghosts only walk at night. When it shuts up, it'll be morning."

Katy thought back. The beast had awakened them on at least five occasions. She clapped a hand to her mouth. "We've been down here five nights?"

"Time passes when you're having fun," Salyt answered without missing a stroke.

Katy sat down on the blanket. "You're beginning to sound like Robert," she said weakly. She leaned back against the wall and drew her knees up. "By the way, why *doesn't* it come down here to get us?"

Scrape, scrape, scrape. Salyt paused long enough to draw a deep breath. "A ghost won't go underground," she answered in professorial tones. "A ghost won't follow you across water. Throw water on a ghost to drive it away, or cremat leaves, if you have them. Listen to dogs—" She stopped suddenly, turned around and grinned. It was always an odd sight to see Salyt grin. She did it so rarely. "Well, not *that* dog." She pointed toward the tunnel and chuckled. "But dogs can detect the presence of ghosts before we can. That's why so many households keep them."

Katy rubbed at the growing knot of tension in the back of her neck. "So much to learn," she muttered. "So much I need to know."

"And little time to learn it, Katherine," Salyt said as she returned to work. "Believe me, I'm not unsympathetic to your plight." She paused again and looked thoughtfully up at the ceiling. "Nothing has worked out the way I intended. I'm not the strategist I thought I was."

Katy moved up to the shelf edge and threw her legs over the side, too. She watched Salyt's hands, the expressions that flickered over the older woman's face. She envied the sense of purpose she saw there. "We have a saying on my world . . ." she started.

Scrape, scrape, scrape. Salyt put her muscles into it now. A fine gray powder sifted into the air with every downward stroke. "Something about the best laid plans of mice and men, if I remember correctly," Salyt interrupted.

Genuine surprise flashed through Katy. "How did you know that?"

"Roderigo Diez," the councillor answered. "We've shared a few meals and conversations, though it's been some years since I last saw him."

Katy drummed her heels against the stone as she listened to the howls that echoed down the tunnel. It was difficult to imagine that it was night outside. Down here, time had no meaning, and her sense of its passage seemed to have deserted her. *Five nights.* She touched her belly and tried not to think about Eric.

"Salyt," she said suddenly, "there used to be a lot more traffic between our worlds, didn't there?"

The councillor nodded. "A long time ago, the gates between Palenoc and Paradane were more stable."

Katy pursed her lips, experiencing a strangely satisfying moment of peace as a warm understanding swept over her. The *sekoye* of Palenoc probably gave rise to the earthly tales of dragons, just as the *chimorgs,* over time and with a little revisionism and embellishment, lay behind the legends of unicorns. Palenoc, itself, probably lay at the heart of all the stories of Faerie, Never-neverland, the Twilight Realms.

She thought of Stonehenge, then the mysterious mounds of North America, as well as all the great oracular temples. Did those ancient structures once mark the locations of the gates between the worlds? Almost every culture down through time told tales of sacred places or mystical Places of Power, yet such tales and places were now mostly the stuff of myth and folklore.

"What happened?" she asked aloud.

"The Destruction of Mianur," Salyt said matter-of-factly without looking up. "The gates opened only when all three moons, yours and ours, were in their full phases. Not a very common occurrence, but a predictable one. Then, Mianur exploded. Terrible upheavals shook Palenoc. Our oceans and the land itself changed shape. Thanador shifted in its orbit. Most of the gates collapsed, never to be reopened. Only a very few remained stable, but their locations were generally lost or forgotten.

"Not all the gates were lost, though. A few are still known to us. However, something had changed. Some cosmic balance had been disturbed. The children of Paradane could traverse the gateways, but we could not. Some said it was our punishment for failing to save that most beautiful of moons."

Katy leaned back on her hands and gazed upward as she remembered the song Salyt had taught her. "Did people really live on Mianur?" she asked.

Scrape, scrape, scrape. Salyt nodded again as stone dust formed a small cloud around her. "Yes, and on Thanador, too."

The illumination in the cavern began to slip a bit as Salyt diverted her concentration to her task. Katy no longer felt quite the same fear of the dark, however. She studied the shadows, the fantastic limestone formations. There was a strange, stark beauty in the rocks and crystals. Her mind filled with thoughts of life on Palenoc's moons. She felt herself unfolding like a flower. With each new wonder, each added bit of knowledge, another petal unfurled.

Outside, the *shriker* howled a fearsome note. Salyt paused and glanced toward the tunnel opening, her eyes narrowed as if she could almost see the creature in the upper world. With the sapphire around her neck, maybe she could. After a moment, she returned to work, scraping the calcite crystal on the harder stone shelf, wearing away the excess deposits of limestone and dripstone, small buds and impurities.

Katy drew a deep breath, feeling pleased with herself. Even the moments of terror were learning experiences. *So much to discover,* she thought again, *so much to know.* She placed a hand on her belly, sensing somehow all the minute changes taking place inside her body. With or without Eric, she would go on. Let this world do its worst. She had a new reason to survive.

Salyt rose abruptly, walked down to the pool, knelt and dipped the crystal into the water. Gentle, carbonaceous bubbles broke the surface around her hand as the last traces of limestone and tufa dissolved. When she lifted it into the air, a crystal wand gleamed.

"It's not perfect," the councillor announced with a critical frown. "Without tools, I can't do better."

Katy hurried down to join her and touched the wand cautiously, running one hand down a portion of its length. An odd tingling danced over her fingertips, and she gasped in pleased surprise.

"You do feel its vibration!" Salyt whispered, as surprised and pleased as Katy felt. She reached out and laid a hand on Katy's shoulder, her gaze softening. "You're a special woman, Katherine of Paradane. I wish we'd met sooner. I'm sure I would have called you *friend.*"

Katy took Salyt's hand and pressed it between her own hands. "Why not call me your friend now?" she answered sincerely.

Salyt's expression clouded over. She pulled free, turned away, and climbed back up onto the limestone shelf. "If I was your friend, I'd do my best to get you out of here and head for safety." She set the wand down carefully by the pack that contained the ruby jewel. "But we're going on to Nazrit Plain." She gathered the blanket from the floor and began to fold it.

Katy regarded her without flinching. "I knew that," she said evenly. She climbed up on the shelf, took the blanket from Salyt, and bent down beside their supply packs. Shoving the blanket into one, she upended the other, which contained their food. "I think we can get most of this into my backpack," she continued as she went to work. "Then we'll have one less thing to carry."

Salyt watched Katy make the transfer and pull the nylon zippers closed. "Knowing the danger, you'll still come along?" The hint of astonishment in her voice was almost amusing.

Katy shouldered her backpack and stood up. "I'm damn well not wandering around this crazy world by myself," she answered. She grabbed the second pack, which contained their blankets. That left only the pack with the ruby for Salyt. "Besides, like you said—you need me."

The councillor scratched her head, her expression caught somewhere between a smile and a frown. "Thank you, Katherine. I have no way to sufficiently express my gratitude." She looked down suddenly.

Katy tapped her booted foot on the limestone and adjusted the pack on her shoulder. "You were about to suggest we wait in the outer cave for sunrise in order to get the earliest start."

Salyt glanced up again, her eyes wide. One hand closed around the sapphire on its chain. "Are you reading me, Katherine?" she asked uneasily.

"Like a book," Katy assured her with mock solemnity.

The councillor didn't seem to take it as a joke. She watched Katy from the corner of her eye as she picked up the pack containing the ruby, then the wand. Katy grinned to herself.

At the tunnel opening, they paused. Salyt allowed the illumination in the cavern to die. With only the calcite wand providing light, they knelt and faced each other. "I'm afraid we're going to get muddy again," Salyt said.

A long, mournful howl echoed down the tunnel.

Katy reached out, caught the sapphire swinging on the silver chain around her companion's neck, and dropped it down the front of Salyt's shirt for safekeeping. "If mud is the worst we have to face today," she quipped, "little Katy will be a happy girl."

Salyt squeezed into the tiny opening and began to crawl toward the outside world. Katy swallowed hard, glanced back into the cavern darkness, then followed. Pushing her packs before her, she inched forward on her elbows. Her heart thundered against her ribs. She wasn't afraid, she told herself, but the space was still tight and close and cramped. At least, this time, Salyt's wand lit the way.

The air in the outer cave was markedly different. The lingering odor of ash and smoke was overpowering, but there was something else, too, another more nauseous smell. "The *chelit,*" Katy said, covering her mouth and nose. Its cooked and rotting carcass had to be close by. She crept closer to the cave entrance, hoping for a look outside, but Salyt pulled her back.

The *shriker* gave a piercing howl, sounding as if it was right outside the cave. Goose bumps rose on Katy's arms. "You won't need to remind me twice," she whispered to the councillor as they huddled together in the gloom.

Still, a part of her wondered what a shriker looked like. She glanced at the pack with the ruby jewel. "You drove away Kajin Kasst's unicorn with that," she said. "Can't it protect us from this thing?"

Salyt shook her head. "The *chimorg* was alive," she answered. "The *shriker* is a ghost. We'll wait until morning, then make our run."

About an hour before sunrise, the howling stopped. At the first hint of dawn, the women ventured out.

In the half-light, the devastation seemed almost surreal. It brought a sickening sensation to Katy's gut. Charred spurs of trees jutted from blackened hillsides. Wisps of smoke still curled upward from smouldering timbers. Thin gray ash hung in the air like an omnipresent cloud. The morning light, shining down through all those layers, diffused and diffracted. The sun rose, redder than blood.

Twenty feet from the cave entrance they found all that remained of the *chelit*. Katy averted her eyes and hurried past, trying not to breathe in the potent stench. Nor did she want to think about the gentleness of the creature that had brought them this far. She felt vaguely traitorous for not doing something to save it.

Salyt paused. Thrusting a pair of fingers deep into the side of her boot, she extracted the blue direction-finding gem. With the marble-sized stone on her palm, she turned until it gave off a soft azure light. "This way," she announced, returning it to her boot and starting off.

There was little to impede their way, no underbrush, no thickets. Katy kept a sharp eye out nonetheless. The slightest breeze might push over any of the standing trunks. She didn't intend to be under one if it fell.

Ash and dust formed tiny hurricanes under every footfall. It was as if a gray snow had fallen overnight, covering everything. She reached out once and touched a scorched limb. It crumbled to powder.

Katy tried not to think. It was enough to move, to set and keep a pace that would take them out of this vision of damnation as fast and as soon as possible. Despite such resolve, thoughts of Eric and Robert troubled her. How could they have survived such devastation? What of Alanna and Valis and Doe? As far as she could see in any direction, not a tree, not a blade of grass, remained untouched.

Her heart sinking, she attacked the next hill, out-distancing Salyt as she climbed the steep, uneven slope. The remains of a single, limbless tree crowned the summit. Heat still radiated from the smoking boll. Standing in its shadow, she gazed outward. Miles and miles of destruction, and in the eastern distance, hints that the fire had not yet burned itself completely out.

Even Salyt caught her breath at the sight as she achieved the summit. Katy hastily wiped at her eyes. "I've seen photos of Hiroshima and Nagasaki that looked a lot like this," she said.

The councillor gave her a puzzled look. "Photos?"

Katy started down the hill without explaining, choked by too many emotions. The cavern was better than this. Down there, she could have at least imag-ined that Eric had had a chance of escaping the flames. It was hard to maintain that hope as she walked.

"High sun," Salyt called a short time later. "I could use a drink, Katherine."

Snapped out of her reverie, Katy glanced up at the sky. They had covered a good distance without a break, and she had hardly noticed. She brought out one of the flasks and handed it over.

"You're not very communicative," Salyt com-mented as she removed the cork.

"What's to say?" she said with a shrug and a half-hearted smile. "I feel like I'm living in one of Robert's novels." She accepted the flask as Salyt passed it back, took a drink, herself, and replaced the cork.

Salyt's expression softened. "I told you once, you're not a very good liar. It's Eric you're thinking about."

Katy returned the flask to her pack and drew a deep breath. She faced south, ready to resume the journey.

Yet, she hesitated. "I keep thinking of your song about Starlit," she answered truthfully.

> *"She lays him on an altar stone,*
> *Turns, without a tear or moan*
> *While the tablas beat a sullen drone,*
> *Puts on her armor all alone,*
> *Picks up the gauntlet newly thrown ..."*

She ended the recitation and fixed her companion with a gaze. "Only I don't have an altar stone, and I don't have him." She swallowed hard and hugged herself as she spun away again. "I'm scared, Salyt," she confessed. "Scared like I've never been."

The councillor came up behind and placed both hands on Katy's shoulders. On the verge of speaking, she suddenly shook her head, adjusted her pack, and moved on. Katy watched the older woman's back. *She's lost her daughter, her husband, her nation,* she thought, striving to put aside her own sadness, *and still she goes on.* Wetting her lips, Katy resumed the journey, too.

Midafternoon brought a pleasant surprise: the first sight of greenery. The wind had apparently turned the fire in another direction at this point. The trees and leaves were withered from heat, but they were not burned. In shade, they paused again to eat a biscuit and drink more water.

The forest turned lush and thick once more as they left the devastation behind. Sunshine streamed down through the branches as a gentle breeze bearing the sweet odors of moss and bark rustled the leaves. It was like awaking from a nightmare, except there was still only the two of them without their comrades.

As the sun perched on the horizon, they emerged from the woods. A vast, grassy plain extended southward to a soaring wall of jagged purple mountains whose shadowed peaks strained to pierce the black veil of clouds that floated over them. Unexplainably, Katy shivered.

"Lurun Bar" came Salyt's subdued whisper. "The Mountains of Torment. The city of Noh-Ferien is nestled in the foothills, but we won't go that far."

Those words brought a sense of vague relief. "Nazrit Plain is closer?"

The councillor nodded and cast a glance back the way they had come. "But still a long way. There's some light left. Let's not waste it."

Even after darkness settled over the world, they continued on with Salyt's direction-finding stone to guide them. Finally, though, weariness took its toll. There were no trees, no shelter of any kind. Just waving grass as high as their knees.

"At least we can make soft beds," Katy said as she set her packs aside and began ripping up handfuls of grass. She cleared a roughly square patch, using the blades to form a mattress over which she spread their single blanket. "Now this is heaven," she sighed, stretching out on her back.

Stars dotted the sky. The bright edge of Thanador floated up over the eastern rim of the world. Katy thought briefly of younger days when, with Eric, she would lie on blankets out by the Ashokan Reservoir and look up at the constellations. He knew them all by name. She never really cared; it was enough for her just to be with him.

"Come lie down," she said, patting a spot on the blanket.

Salyt seemed tense. The sun's setting had brought a change in her mood. Without speaking, she put her pack down, but she remained on her feet, watchful, clutching the crystal wand to her heart.

Katy sat up, concerned. "Why are you so uneasy?"

A dog howled in the distance, a long and lonely sound. Katy's heart skipped a beat. "It's back again, isn't it?" She stared across the plain back the way they had come. There was nothing to see but the gentle roll of the land and the waving grass and the dark cloak of night.

Salyt clutched the wand as if it were a dagger. In her hand, it began to glow softly. "Remember, *hami*," she murmured. "No matter what happens to me, take the ruby to Nazrit Plain and bury it in the spider's heart."

A cool wind blew a red strand of hair across Katy's eyes. She pushed it back nervously as she stood up. "Let's just get out of here," she said. "I didn't know it could follow us."

Salyt shook her head and stood her ground. "Nothing's more important than the ruby," she said stubbornly. "It's the only hope for Wystoweem and all the Gray Kingdoms that have already fallen. Maybe for the Domains of Light." She lifted the sapphire from under her shirt and slipped the silver chain over her head. "I want you to take this," she said, pressing the talisman into Katy's hands. "In time, you may learn to use it."

Katy stared at the sapphire on her palm, then flung it down on the blanket. She grabbed the councillor by the shoulders and spun her around. "Stop talking like that!" she snapped in sudden anger. "Now pick up your pack and let's get going. We'll outrun the son of a bitch if we have to!"

The *shriker* howled again, still far away, yet closer. It was not such a lonely sound this time, but something more aggressive, more purposeful. The sound of the hunter.

Thanador continued to rise, its light washing over

the plain. Salyt's shadow stretched upon the ground like a thin and emaciated thing. "You don't understand, Katherine, *hami*," she stated with a calm that frightened Katy. "I'm too tired to go on. I'm not as young as you. I have to make a stand here. Now."

Katy stepped back with sudden realization, nearly tripping on one of the packs. She kicked it, venting the hurt and sense of betrayal she felt. "You planned this all along," she screamed. "Goddamn you for not telling me. That's what the wand is for." Her bitter laughter nearly drowned the *shriker's* next howl. "I thought it was a fancy flashlight to get us through the tunnel. It's a weapon, isn't it? You intend to fight this thing."

"From moonrise until dawn, night after night, that beast will pursue us," Salyt explained. "It can change size or shape within certain limitations—even take a tangible form." Her words took on a new urgency. "It has one reason for existence: to carry out its master's command." She turned and gazed out across the plain again as the *shriker's* baying achieved a new frenzy. Her voice dropped a note. "Kajin Kasst must have recognized me, or maybe he understood the nature of the talisman we carry. Either way, he's trying to stop me. He's a known practitioner of the magic that makes such monsters."

The wind rose. The *shriker* howled excitedly as Thanador's crescent cleared the horizon.

Katy struggled to put aside her anger. "Can we fight it?" she demanded. "Don't lie; you're not very good at it, either."

An uncertain frown danced over Salyt's face. "If I can find its heart with this," she said, holding up the wand, "there's a chance. It depends on the quality of the crystal and the alignment of its cleavage points. I didn't have tools to work with."

The *shriker's* bay sounded much closer, much louder. The wind blew Katy's hair in her face again. "You should have told me, Councillor," she said, glaring. "I had a right to know."

Salyt turned a little away. "It wants *me*," she said defensively. "It can't even sense you. It's not a natural ghost; it's a creation of magic. You're invisible to it."

"That doesn't matter," Katy said. Her anger ebbed away, replaced with a grim resolve. "*Hami*. That means *sister* or *sisters*. We'll fight this sucker—" Her breath caught in her throat.

A huge black hound with eyes that burned like red hellfire stood in the grass only a few feet away. Around its neck was a gold collar, and a pair of diamond-like gems shimmered on its throat. It growled menacingly as it bared fangs that dripped saliva. Its pointed ears suddenly flattened back.

"Look out!" Katy cried, knocking Salyt aside as the beast sprang at them. They fell in a heap as the *shriker* sailed above their heads and landed on the blanket. Its jaws closed on one of the packs.

"No!" Salyt screamed, disentangling herself from Katy. Grasping the wand, she jumped on the creature's back and stabbed wildly. Unharmed, the *shriker* hurled her off, but somehow she got one hand on the pack. As she went flying, the top ripped open.

The ruby tumbled free, glowing with a bloodred light that lit up the grass surrounding it. An angry buzzing filled the air, as if thousands of wasps had suddenly been disturbed in their nest.

Jaws snapping, the *shriker* lunged for it. Salyt moved faster. With a desperate shriek, she threw herself over the jewel like a mother protecting her babe. Teeth closed on the back of her neck, and she screamed.

Katy screamed, too, and dived for her backpack.

She found one of the water flasks. Jerking out the cork, she flung the contents over the monster.

The *shriker* let go of Salyt, threw back its head, and howled, this time in rage and anguish. Its fur began to smoulder. In less than a moment it faded away, leaving only its cry to echo out over the night.

Katy rushed to help Salyt and felt a new kind of panic well up in her chest. Blood poured from savage bites on the councillor's neck and scalp, and ran in rivulets down her shoulders into her shirt, into her gray braid. Heavy dark splotches stained the grass where she lay.

"Don't move," Katy whispered in her ear. She bit her lip, trying to think what to do.

"It was after the ruby," Salyt sighed as she tried to raise up on one elbow. "It didn't want me. It wanted *this*." She pulled the radiant jewel out from under her body and held it up. It seemed bigger than before, larger than her hand. Its glow turned her face a deep, sickly scarlet, made her blood look like flowing black ichor.

Katy stared at the wasp inside. She had thought it dead before, sealed somehow in the jewel's facets like a fly trapped in amber. Now, though it remained suspended in the gem's center, its wings vibrated furiously, and it shook its stinger.

"Take it, quickly!" Salyt insisted, pressing the ruby into Katy's blood-covered hands. "Hold it close, *hami*! Hold it tight!"

"Fuck the ruby," Katy answered through clenched teeth. She tossed it toward the other packs and slipped an arm around Salyt, determined to get her onto the blanket. "We've got to do something for your wounds."

Salyt's eyes were starting to glaze. "You don't understand," she cried weakly as she let Katy move her.

"You didn't destroy it; you only drove it off. It'll come back."

"What happened to the goddamned wand?" Katy demanded as she eased her friend onto the blanket. They were both drenched in blood now. Tears burned her eyes. What to do? What to do?

Salyt smiled a faint apology. "I told you it was imperfect," she said. She raised it ever so slightly, her fingers locked tightly around the slender rod.

A vicious snarl.

Katy whirled around on her knees to stare at the *shriker*, not ten feet away. "Give it to me!" she cried, snatching the wand from Salyt's grip, determined to fight the monster to her last breath.

"The ruby," Salyt's voice was only a whisper as she pointed with a quivering finger. "Pick up the ruby!"

Katy moved in the same instant as the *shriker*, snatching the gem virtually from its mouth. It spun about, and for a heart-stopping moment, she thought her life was done. The beast growled, then sniffed the earth. Its ears relaxed. It walked a few paces off and sniffed again and gave a tiny, pathetic whine that Katy thought she vaguely recognized.

The beast faded away again, melted into nothingness.

"It can't sense you." Salyt's words sounded small and far off. "You're invisible to magic. While you hold the ruby, it's invisible, too."

Katy crawled back beside the councillor and drew the sign of the cross with her fingertips lightly over her friend's brow. She managed to stop her tears. It wouldn't do to cry anymore. Not for a while, anyway. Putting the ruby between them, she stretched out on her side and slipped an arm around Salyt.

"Nazrit Plain." It might have been the breeze murmuring for all the power behind the words.

"I promise" came the whispered answer.

Salyt's life slipped quietly through Katy's fingers. For a long while she lay there, clinging to her friend, to the ruby, to the useless crystal wand. When Thanador reached high moon and Mianur hung low in the east, she wrapped the councillor in the blanket, and dug a grave with her own hands.

The ruby, quiescent, rested in a pack on her back while she worked. When it was all done, then it was safe to cry again.

Chapter Sixteen

DEEP in the bowels of Sheren Hiawa, the oil lamps burned almost continuously. People hurried through the subterranean passages with frantic urgency, darting in and out of chambers whose doorways were covered only with curtains or crude hides. The air was hot and reeked of dust and sweat and chemical fumes.

Eric descended the narrow stone steps from the upper levels. Dark circles ringed his eyes, and a scowl seemed permanently etched on his face. He'd eaten and slept little the past few days, and shaved and bathed irregularly. There had been too much to do to worry about such luxuries.

Doe hurried along beside him, bearing a small round globe of *sekoy-melin* to light their way through the busy corridors. His lips were set in a thin, taut line.

Just ahead, a heavy curtain flung suddenly back, and Valis poked his head out through the doorway. "I was just coming to find you," he said. He stepped out and held the curtain open. He was shirtless, and his hair hung in wet ropes. "Come see what we've got."

The chemical odor was overpowering, the heat stifling. Eric made a disgusted face as he stared around the huge chamber. It was a primitive laboratory with tables and beakers, basins, clay pots, mortars, and pestles of various sizes, strange jars containing stranger liquids. Shelves of old books lined one wall, and charts hung upon another. Eric wondered how anyone could read them. The fires that burned in braziers stationed in each corner filled the room with shadows and smoke.

This was Sheren Hiawa's pharmacy, where its scientists and herbalists researched and manufactured the paralytic poisons used for their dart weapons. Five nearly naked old men clustered around a shallow iron cauldron that perched on three clawed legs close to the floor. Their thin bodies shimmered with sweat in the ruddy glow.

One of the old men looked up, wiped his hands on a leather apron, and waved them over. Eric struggled to remember his name. *Heron.* The other four executed smooth bows. One of them held a glass vial clutched to his chest. Heron beamed with a mischievous glee. "I think we have what you want, Eric Podlowsky." He rubbed his palms together. "It's a common oil, but we've put it through a little refinement."

The man holding the vial upended it over the cauldron while Heron picked up a slender straw from the nearest table and thrust it into one of the braziers. It came away with a small blue flame at one end. "Stand back," he ordered as he approached the cauldron again. His assistants obeyed. With a flip of his wrist, he tossed the straw into the iron vessel. A flash of blue fire *whooshed* into the air, then settled down again until the oil burned away. A smoky residue curled upward, smelling like cinnamon.

"By tomorrow we can have all you need," Heron said, grinning. He was obviously a man who enjoyed his work.

"Double your staff," Eric instructed gruffly. "Triple it. I want as much as you can produce by midnight."

Valis bent over the cauldron and watched the fire flicker out, leaving only a deep scorch on the vessel's metal interior. "We don't know how much time we have," he told Heron. "Imansirit is surely Kajin Lure's next target."

Heron threw back his head and cackled. "We'll fry his egg for him," he cried. He gestured to two of his assistants. "Pavit, Jol! Wake up anyone who doesn't have a job to do and get their asses down here!" He laughed again as he went to a barrel, picked up the ladle that hung on its lip, and dipped it. He turned back to Eric and winked. "We'll fry his egg, all right," he said. "And roast his chicken, too!"

Valis held the curtain back again as Eric and Doe departed. "I'm afraid Heron doesn't fly on both wings," he muttered as Eric went past and into the corridor.

Eric didn't care about Heron's mental state so long as the job got done. "I'll be with Shubal," he told Valis. "As soon as you can, bring another sample of Heron's compound there."

"He calls it Hiawa Fire," Valis informed him with a hint of amusement, "and he's guarding the formula like a kid guards his candy."

Eric paused in mid-step and turned back to his old comrade. "You seem in an awfully good mood," he observed.

Valis shrugged. "Let others be sullen," he answered with a pointed look at Eric. "We're doing something I've dreamed about."

"Spitting in the Eye of Darkness?" Doe replied, and the two exchanged quick grins.

Eric put a hand on the shoulders of both his friends. "Let's hope your dream doesn't turn into a nightmare," he said. Then he started down the corridor with Doe and the *melin* light hurrying after.

A young woman stopped him before he got far. Her arms were full of folded nets, and she obviously strained under the weight of her burden. Nevertheless, she hailed him, her dark eyes flashing with an eager, worshipful look he found disconcerting. "See, *Eric Namue Rana Sekoye*?" she said proudly. "Every woman and child in the Sheren is helping." She bobbed her nose toward the pile of nets. "It's good work, is it not?"

Eric lifted a corner of the top net and examined it. It was made with a much finer, tighter weave than the nets the Chols used. It was also much lighter. He grabbed a section in his fists and gave a yank, testing its strength, and nodded with satisfaction. "It's exactly what I wanted," he told her. "Take them straight to the roof. You'll find *Alanna Hami Rana Sekoye* waiting to receive them."

"This is a great day for Sheren Hiawa," the woman sang as she hurried down the passage. "A great day!"

Eric watched her go. "Am I doing the right thing, Doe?" he asked.

Doe inclined his head. "You are *Namue rana Sekoye*," he answered with barely concealed impatience. "Eric of the Green Eyes. A Son of Paradane who rides the great dragon, Shadowfire." He waved the globe of *melin* under Eric's eyes, then lifted it as high as he could reach. "Look around, my brother. Nobody here doubts you. Stop doubting yourself."

Eric stepped out of the way as a pair of men hurried by with buckets of water and sand. "That still doesn't answer my question," he muttered.

Doe frowned and shrugged. "Because it's a question that will be answered only through hindsight, once the deed is done." He gestured toward a fork in the corridor. "Now I believe Shubal is waiting down this way."

Shubal spied them from the far side of a redly glowing chamber as Doe held back the entranceway curtain. Small kilns and clay furnaces blazed throughout the room, built up from the floor like stalagmites in a cave. Shirtless workers moved about. The chamber was stiflingly hot; smoke and steam hung in the air. The hissing of fire and water and sand made a constant cacophony.

"Over here!" Shubal called. His broad, muscled chest glistened, and he'd tied a rag around his head to keep the sweat out of his eyes. His skin was reddened from the heat, and his dark beard showed several singed places.

Eric started toward him, but halted abruptly to watch as a workman raised a long tube and blew a gleaming bubble of new, fragile glass. The workman's look, however, suggested that Eric was only in the way, so he hurried past.

Shubal raised his palms and touched them to Eric's, the traditional Domain greeting, but then he clapped him on the back as well. Shubal had lost more than half the men under his command when Kajin Lure's first wave of sendings crossed the border from Chol-Hecate to Wystoweem. With no other safe place to go, he had brought the remnant of his forces here to the nearest Sheren.

"It's too hot in here," Shubal said. "Come into the next room." He led the way into an adjoining chamber and helped himself to a ladle of water from a barrel near the doorway. He poured it over his head, letting the excess spill on the stone floor, then took a drink. "Look at these," he continued, beckoning them toward a long wooden table. "Beautiful, aren't they!"

Laid out in neat rows on the table were scores of arrows, all made of hollow glass. A silent workman pressed glue and fletchings into the still warm shafts, ignoring Eric's presence as he concentrated on his task through squinting eyes. Right beside him, a second worker wrapped and tied soft, guazelike fabric near the point ends. He, too, spared them neither word nor glance. His fingers flew as he worked.

Eric glanced around at the half-dozen candles that lit the chamber. "Get some better light down here before these men go blind," he instructed Doe. The young *sekournen* set the globe of *sekoy-melin* down between the pair of workmen. It brightened the immediate table space considerably, but Doe excused himself to fetch more such globes.

The shafts were better than he had dared to hope. He lifted an arrow and sighted down the narrow tube, finding it straight and true. There was no point, only a rounded end, just as he had instructed. Nor was there a nock, yet, to fit the arrow to a string. That would come later. "How many?" he asked. "Have the nocks been carved?"

Shubal flung open a cask on the next table that contained a cache of wooden nocks. He plunged a hand in and let them sift through his fingers. "The entire sheren has been working without pause," he said. He picked up a candle that stood beside the cask and carried it across the room. A score of leather quivers hung on pegs, each full of unfinished arrows. He bent lower with the tiny flame. Hundreds more of the delicate tubes leaned against the wall. Then, he went to the farthest end of the chamber where the shadows predominated. "Tell me again what you call these," he asked, taking a slender wooden rod from a rack where dozens of similar rods stood.

"It's a bow," Eric answered, going to Shubal's side. A thin length of gut was wrapped around the grip. Unwinding it, he showed his new ally how to bend and string the weapon. He found it interesting that in the course of its long war, Palenoc had never developed the bow. It was completely new to them. On the other hand, he reminded himself, the aborigines of his own world had never developed it, either; nor had the Incas, despite the advanced level of their culture, ever developed something so simple as the wheel. He put the bow into Shubal's hands and explained how to hold it.

A familiar cackling laugh sounded from the outer room. An instant later, Heron flung back the curtain and joined them. In his hand he held a flask of pale amber liquid. Valis came right behind him. "He wants a test," the big *sekournen* explained apologetically.

"So do I," Eric answered. He gazed around the chamber. "These walls are rock. Clear everything away from that wall. And get a couple of those sand buckets in here."

Shubal and Valis went to the opposite end of the room and dragged a heavy worktable away from it. Eric tried to take the flask from Heron. "No!" the old man cried excitedly. "I'll do it." He picked up one of the hollow shafts. With a steady hand, squinting through one rheumy eye, he poured the amber liquid into the tube. When it was half-full, he passed the shaft to Eric. "That should be enough," he said with a wink. "Don't want to burn the place down, do we?"

Eric took a nock from the cask, dipped the open end carefully into the fletcher's glue pot, and fit it in place on the arrow, sealing Heron's compound inside. He held the nock tightly for a moment, letting the glue set.

Word had apparently spread through the outer chamber that something interesting was about to happen. Workers crowded into the doorway to watch, their eager faces gleaming. A pair of sand buckets were passed in to Shubal and Valis, then a second pair, just in case.

Eric drew a deep breath as he considered the size of the chamber. "This won't work," he announced suddenly. The room was too small, too cramped, the chances of an accident too great. "Out into the corridor. Bring that table. A candle, too."

The throng of workers parted to let him pass. Bow in one hand, his precious arrow in the other, he strode among the kilns and furnaces and out into the passageway beyond. With the help of other workers who had put down their glassblowing rods, Shubal and Valis turned the heavy table on its side, lifted it into the air, and followed. There was some difficulty getting it through the doorway, but they managed. In short order, it was standing on its end, like a barricade, in the middle of the corridor. Valis cleared everyone out of the way.

Eric checked the nock to make sure the glue had set firmly enough. From a distance of about twenty paces, he put the arrow to the string. Beside him, Heron brought the candle's flame into contact with the gauze wrapping. Eric bent the bow, drawing the shaft back until the burning cloth nearly scorched his bare hand. It took no strength to anchor the nock at his chin. He'd designed a purposefully weak bow from war-willow, a light and flexible wood. A stronger pull would cause too much buck and shatter a glass shaft in mid-flight.

He let go of the string. The arrow flashed through tne air, glittering in the light of the corridor's lamps, and smashed against the table. Heron's oil splashed on the wood, and the burning gauze ignited it with dramatic effect.

"Sand!" Valis shouted, grabbing one of the buckets himself and flinging it to smother the flames. In no time, the fire was put out.

"Now, that's what I call a successful test!" Heron

shrieked excitedly, clapping his hands. "Hiawa Fire!" he called to the assembled workers. "I made it! My discovery! Hiawa Fire!"

Eric stared at the blackened scorch in the center of the table, at the fragments of glass that lay scattered about the floor. "Back to work, everyone," he ordered quietly. "There's plenty yet to do."

Shubal marched to his side and took the bow from his hand. "What a weapon!" He lifted it up, his gaze transfixed on it, as if it were a holy relic and he'd just discovered religion. "We can change the course of the war with this!"

Eric's mouth set in a grim line. "Take charge down here, Shubal," he said. "See that the arrows are prepared as soon as possible and have everything transported to the roof. We leave for Noh-Ferien two hours before dawn." He waved a hand toward the table blocking the passage. "Somebody move that out of the way."

A cheer went up from the workers, and they turned to complete their tasks. Shubal clapped Eric's shoulder enthusiastically and hurried after Heron. After their first meeting in Capreet, it felt odd to have Shubal as such a willing ally.

"War makes strange bedfellows," Valis said as he rubbed one hand over his chin. It was not Shubal he was watching, though, but Eric, and his expression mirrored his concern. "You should get some rest while you have the chance."

Eric drew a deep breath and let it out. It was a sensible suggestion. He hadn't slept more than a few hours since he came to Sheren Hiawa four days ago. There had been too much to do, too many plans to make.

"Four hours," he agreed reluctantly. "No more, Valis. You'll wake me?"

When his friend nodded, Eric headed for his room eleven levels above. The staircase seemed to wind upward forever. Men and women passed him, rushing up and down. He studied their faces. Not one of them showed any fear or worry about the impending battle.

Reaching his room, he closed the door behind and leaned wearily against it, allowing his shoulders to slump, hanging his head. For a while, he stood there like that, unmoving, trying not to think about anything, until a cool breeze blew in through the unshuttered window near the top of his bed. It brushed his stubbled cheek, bringing a soft scent of autumn nights.

Alone finally, where no one else could see him, a pair of tears squeezed from the corners of his eyes and purled down his face as he thought of Katy-did. With thumb and forefinger he pinched the bridge of his nose, then wiped the tears away. If only it were so simple to wipe away the pain that stabbed his heart. He felt hollow without Katy, like a shell with no soul.

For two days he'd flown on Shadowfire over the flames and through the smoke, searching for some sign of Katy or Robert or Salyt. All he'd seen were a few of Kajin Kasst's soldiers, and he couldn't save them, either. The flames devoured everything, every tree, every blade of grass. Finally, they devoured his hopes.

His chest heaved in a dry, silent sob, but he refused to allow any more tears. Crossing the room, he sat down on the side of his bed and ran his palm over the exquisite, handmade quilt that covered his mattress. The needle stitches were fine and delicate, the workmanship executed with special care. Someone with a special talent had labored days and nights, weeks probably, to make it.

He couldn't bring his Katy-did back, nor could he bring back Bobby. But so help him, if it was possible, he intended to stop Kajin Lure and Kajin Kasst from spreading their brand of misery any further.

Without undressing, he lay down on the bed and cradled his head in the crook of an elbow. It was so long since he'd slept. All he had to do was give in to his fatigue and shut his eyes. He wondered, would she come? Was she waiting in his dreams, nested like a spider in her web of darkness, to taunt and tease him as she had so many other nights in so many other dreams?

He hoped so. He was ready for her at last. For no particular reason, he remembered a line from his brother's last book:

> *Now lay me down and close my eyes;*
> *To Darkness' Heart my soul will fly.*

He hadn't noticed before when first he read those words how like a prayer they sounded. Had Bobby intended that? His brother had never been much for prayer, nor had he. Eric repeated the lines again, listening to the sound of each word, feeling its shape in his mouth. It didn't seem complete somehow, though he was sure Bobby had written no more. Once again he whispered those verses, but this time he added a couplet of his own:

> *If I should die before I wake,*
> *Cut out that heart, for vengeance' sake.*

* * *

Alanna leaned on the wall at the edge of the roof and sang to the scores of *sekoye* that swept through the black skies above Sheren Hiawa. There was nothing sweet about her voice. She sang with a raw, bitter edge that communicated straight to the dragons. They answered her with angry cries, displaying aggression in swift, precipitous flights, strafing the tower, gyring the tight arcs. The air filled with the thunder of their wings.

"She grieves for your brother," Doe said to Eric. He adjusted the blowpipe in his belt as he regarded her from a distance.

"That's not grief," Valis replied as he set down a pair of quivers. The exposed glass shafts glimmered with the myriad colors the dragons' wings gave off. "It's something much harder and far more dangerous."

"Dangerous to Kajin Lure," Eric said. He wanted to go to Alanna, to hold her and comfort her, but there was too much to do. He gazed around the rooftop. It was almost identical to Sheren Chad in Guran, except there was no tripod and no huge globe of *sekoy-melin* to provide light. He had no trouble seeing, though. Thanador shone brightly above, and Mianur volunteered its own pale radiance.

All of Sheren Hiawa's *sekournen* stood gathered to one side. Shubal was there, too, with the surviving Wystoweem *sekournen* under his command. Every man and woman had dressed in white leather, even down to their boots, and purified themselves with oil from crushed *cremat* leaves. Their expressions were grim, and yet the fire of anticipation burned in their eyes.

Piles of nets, stacks of bows and quivers full of arrows were ranged about the rooftop. In addition, there were two fat cauldrons full of red-hot coals. A thin white smoke curled upward from each and wafted into the night.

The members of Imansirit's Council filed up from the stairs and onto the roof. They, too, had dressed themselves in robes and cloaks of white cloth for the occasion. The rest of the Sheren's members emerged behind them, seeking one last chance to say good-bye to friends and family, or merely to watch.

Jonathay, the council's eldest member, approached Eric with his hands folded inside his sleeves. The wind whipped his gray hair about his face and set the hems of his garments flapping, yet he moved with an air of perfect, unshakable dignity. He held up his palms and offered them to Eric, who pressed his own to them.

"Our hopes fly with you, *Eric Namue Rana Sekoye*," he said. "With Wystoweem fallen, there can be no doubt that Kajin Lure will direct his next wave of sendings against Imansirit. Our fates are in your hands." He paused and let his gaze linger on Doe. A wistful frown flickered over his face. "This one is so young for such a battle."

Doe interrupted, lifting his head proudly. "I'm a man," he answered. His words were not rude, only self-affirming.

"He is *Doe Namue Rana Sekoye*," Valis informed the councillor. "Rider of Heartsong, and worthy of your respect."

Jonathay inclined his head toward Doe. "You have that, young man. I meant no disrespect." He turned back to Eric, and his hands disappeared once more into his sleeves. "Will you take lives in this battle, Son of Paradane? You know the way of our world. A ghost will seek its vengeance."

Eric's mouth drew into a taut line. "I know," he answered truthfully. It was his greatest concern that he might be leading his *sekournen* into a strange kind of suicide mission. "We'll place our arrows as carefully as we can. Most of Noh-Ferien will flee. But lives may be lost." He gazed past Jonathay to the assembled *sekournen* in their white leathers. "Every rider here knows the risk."

Valis stepped to one side and gazed skyward as his

own dragon, Brightstar, strafed the rooftop. The wind of his *sekoye's* passage swept the black ropes of his hair straight back. A stack of bows fell, and someone hurried to right them.

"The game has changed, Jonathay," Valis said, turning back to face the councillor. "So it always changes in the days before the coming of the Shae'aluth. Kajin Lure has found a new way to safely kill, and with his sendings he has already razed Sybo, Vakris, and Wystoweem. Can't you feel it, old man? These are the Last Hours before the Dawn."

Jonathay nodded, his face set in a grim expression. "Yes," came his reverently whispered answer. "The Last Hours of Darkness when she and her servants are never more desperate and never more cunning." He reached out with both hands and caught Eric's and Valis's arms in firm grips. "Be careful, my sons. Fly with Taedra, the mother-dragon, and with Or-dhamu in your hearts." He departed then to rejoin the rest of Sheren Hiawa's councillors as they moved among their *sekournen* offering blessings.

Valis bent closer to Eric. "Did you dream of her in your sleep?" he asked.

Eric wasn't startled by the question. He'd discussed his dreams often with Valis. He shook his head.

"Good," the taller man answered gruffly. "Perhaps something else diverts her attention."

It was time to depart. Eric felt for his harmonica in its special pocket on his belt and scanned the sky. Shadowfire glided far above, apart from the other *sekoye*, the opalescent fire in his wings shifting and shimmering. Thoughts of his brother stole into his mind as he watched Shadowfire. He'd secretly hoped that one day Bobby would find a dragon to call his own, and they would ride the winds together, fly across this world called Palenoc.

It wasn't to be. He had lost Bobby and Katy-did both, lost them to fire and to the Heart of Darkness.

But today, it would be Kajin Lure who lost.

He picked up one of the quivers Valis had set down and put it over his shoulder. The crowded rooftop fell silent. All eyes turned expectantly his way. He gave orders, and one by one the remaining *sekournen* of Imansirit, Wystoweem, and Guran filed by the piles of nets, chose one, and draped it over their shoulders. Past the stacks of bows and the quivers of arrows they went, arming themselves with the new weapons.

Eric went to Alanna at the edge of the roof. Only she could sing to all the dragons and summon them in readiness for this moment, but it was time for her to rest. Her voice was raw.

He touched her shoulders. "Enough," he said, turning her around. "Let each rider call his own *sekoye*."

Her eyes were red and swollen, her face tracked with dried tears. For an instant, looking at this woman who loved his brother, Eric's careful guard slipped, and he felt his own heart breaking. For days he'd avoided Alanna, fearing just this moment. Looking up at him, she bit her lip. Then, wordlessly, they slipped into each others' arms.

"I want to shoot the first arrow," she said, stepping back. Her eyes were suddenly hard as glittering stones, and her hands curled into fists. "I want to watch the fire take Noh-Ferien as it took Robert."

"Choose your weapons," he told her quietly, "and call Mirrormist. You'll fly by my right side."

One by one each *sekournen* summoned his dragon. One by one the great beasts folded their wings and perched on the wall, talons scrabbling noisily on the thick stone, and stretching forth their necks to receive their riders. Heron, heavily gloved, followed each one with a small shovel full of glowing coals from the cauldrons. All saddles had been modified and fitted with a special covered pot just larger than a man's fist where a saddle horn might have been. Into these, Heron poured his coals and slammed each grilled lid shut.

Finally only Eric, Doe, Valis, and Alanna remained. These were his friends, his family, now. He drew them all together, touched palms with them, and exchanged embraces. "Till we meet again at *Lurun Bar*," Eric said. He watched each one depart until, finally, it was his turn.

He took out his harmonica. The light of Thanador and Mianur gleamed on the scroll work carved into its silver body. In the southwestern distance, his *sekournen* flew slowly, waiting for him. Shadowfire circled overhead, impatient to be called. Eric put the instrument to his lips and wondered what to play. He glanced down at his own white leathers and faintly grinned.

Oh when the saints go marching in, he played, *when the saints go marching in.*

Chapter Seventeen

THE dragons swept out of the skies above *Lurun Bar,* skimming those shadowed peaks, and came upon Noh-Ferien from behind. On Mirrormist, Alanna surged ahead, her unbound locks lashing in the wind, her dragon's wings beating furiously. With a shaft nocked to the string of her bow, she touched the gauze-wrapped tip to her firepot.

Kajin Lure's palace stood at the heart of the city, a construction of strangely twisted towers and unbalanced minarets only a demented architect could have imagined. Its walls were black with stone rot, and huge cracks showed in the ancient facade. Still, it gleamed in the near-noon sun.

Mirrormist dipped suddenly and flew directly for the nearest tower. Alanna drew back her bow and let fly the first arrow. Her shot sped straight through an open window. A burst of flame lit up the square black opening.

Shadowfire swept low over the city. Eric leaned outward and stared into the streets below. A woman ran in panic from the shadow his dragon cast. A man overturned his cart of straw and dived beneath it. There were far fewer people and less activity than he had expected, though; Noh-Ferien was supposed to be a teeming city.

Shadowfire climbed suddenly, and they soared over

the city wall and out over a broad plain that stretched for miles. A handful of Chol troops approached the main gate in ragged formation. They looked up with thunderstruck expressions, then scattered in all directions.

With a note from his harmonica, Eric turned Shadowfire back toward the city in time to see the first wave of his *sekournen* strike. The air was black with dragon wings. A rain of fire fell on Noh-Ferien as he watched, arrows shattering on rooftops in a liquid rush of flame. Stables and barns went up like tinderboxes.

A small handful of citizens charged out of their homes and into the streets, running like frightened rats as they clutched a few pitiful belongings. Fire rapidly turned the city into a deadly maze as arrows fell and homes and shops went up. Still, Eric wondered, where were the rest of the Chols? He tucked his harmonica in its pocket as Shadowfire raced for Kajin Lure's palace. Carefully he drew out an arrow, nudged open the lid of his firepot, and touched the gauze to the hot coals. Instantly the cloth took fire. He nocked and sighted down the glass shaft. Following Alanna's example, he shot straight through an open window. The resulting orange burst of flame brought a bitter satisfaction.

Over the wall and toward the *Lurun Bar,* Shadowfire soared, and Eric took out his harmonica once more to turn the great creature for yet another pass. His companions had that advantage, that they could sing to their *sekoye* and handle their weapons at the same time, while he had to be careful with his instrument.

Without warning, a powerful wind buffeted him. Shadowfire pitched backward. Eric made a desperate grab at the rim of his saddle, nearly burning himself on the firepot, almost losing his precious harmonica. For a precipitous moment, he hung sideways in space, and the ground and the sky both tilted at frightening angles. Somehow, he managed to press his feet against his stirrups, squeeze with his knees, and right himself. Half his coals spilled out of his firepot and fell like smoking stars before he could slam the lid shut.

Shadowfire opened a great fanged mouth and bellowed. The *sekoye* pounded the air with his wings, abruptly halting his flight and hovering in position. Eric lurched forward, better prepared this time to keep his balance.

A blast of alizarin lightning tore open the clear blue sky, and the crisp odor of ozone filled the air. Someone screamed. Eric twisted in his saddle to see who it was. Shubal hung precariously by one hand, clutching a single stirrup of his dragon's saddle. His *sekoye's* wings beat the air, hovering. Then, with heart-stopping calm, Shubal let go, spread his arms, and fell. It was no grand, suicidal gesture. Doe, on Heartsong, flashed daringly beneath him and snatched Wystoweem's last councillor to safety.

Eric stared toward the towers, searching their parapets until he spied Kajin Lure. The sorcerer had at last entered the fray. The wind whipped his black robes and his waist-length black hair straight out behind him. His garments were open, exposing his naked body, and his arms were upraised. In his fists, he clutched a pair of skulls carved from some glittering black rock.

Kajin Lure smashed the skulls together. Again, a gale wind tore across the city. An instant later another bolt lanced earthward. A dragon screamed as it shook off the direct hit. Its Imansirit rider, though, was not so impervious. Already dead, he plummeted to the streets below. The dragon screamed again, a shriller cry of despair, as the bond with its rider abruptly snapped. It thrashed its wings, turned toward the nearest minaret, and smashed straight through it. The structure exploded in a shower of fragments, and the tower upon which it rested collapsed and crumbled into rubble. The riderless dragon kept right on going, driven by its grief, straight toward the horizon.

Mirrormist charged across the sky with Brightstar and Heartsong close behind. A burning hail plunged toward Kajin Lure, and fire spread like water over the parapet where he stood. Whether through his magic or his luck, the flames failed to quite reach him.

Then from the lower levels and doors of the palace, black, vaguely human shapes emerged and sprang into the air.

Sendings.

Eric had planned a daytime attack, hoping to avoid these monsters. Essentially, they were ghosts of a kind, and ghosts hated the day. Still, on rare occasions some spirits braved the pain of sunlight's touch, and no one knew exactly the extent of Lure's control over his creatures.

No matter. Eric had learned the sendings' weakness and prepared for it. He slipped his bow over his back and freed the carefully folded net tied behind him on his saddle. There was a length of lead rope and a noose to put his hand through. Without waiting to be attacked, he blew a harmonica note, sending Shadowfire in a dive toward the rising shapes. With a shoulder-popping effort, he cast his net.

It opened like a deadly flower, and the close weave sieved through a night-dark shape. A psychic cry tore at his brain as a white bone fell out of his net, tumbled end over end, and broke on the street pavings. Shadowfire carried him safely into the air again, climbing in a swift arc, as he drew his net back and readied it for another toss.

His *sekournen* fought with vengeance in their hearts. Nets whisked through the air, making easy work of the sendings, while arrows continued to rain fire on the city. Again and again, Kajin Lure slammed the onyx skulls together. Bolt after electric bolt ripped open the sky. Houses exploded, walls shattered, hurling stone and dust upward.

It was almost as if Lure was determined to destroy Noh-Ferien, and himself.

A squad of soldiers rushed out of the palace, but not with intention to fight. They ran for their lives across a marbled courtyard, as panicked as anyone in the streets. The sendings turned on them, engulfing the frightened Chols in their suffocating essences.

A Wystoweem *sekournen* drove her mount straight for Kajin Lure. Her net flashed outward against a buffeting wind to ensnare the sorcerer. A cyan bolt stabbed earthward, barely missing the rider as it blasted a crater in the marble tiles of the courtyard below. Kajin Lure dodged the net, but its rope edge caught his hand. One of the skulls went flying over the parapet.

Lure screamed, enraged, as he watched his toy fall. He shook his fist at the daring rider. As if in obedience to a silent command, a sending rushed up from the ground with incredible speed, spread its arms, and darted for the woman.

Another net flashed through the air, but not for the sending. The woman saw it and leaped clear of her saddle. For an instant she seemed to float in the blue, then her fingers caught in the weave, and she was carried away. Eric looked to see who had saved her. On Brightstar, Valis cried out as he strained to support the woman's weight on one wrist.

Defying natural laws of motion, the sending turned at an impossible angle and swept for the woman again. It was too late, though. Clinging to Doe, Shubal leaned away from Heartsong's saddle and cast another net. The creature streamed right through it, leaving a gleaming bone dangling in the weave as it melted away.

The woman's *sekoye* turned back for her, and Valis lowered her carefully into her saddle. The two exchanged comradely waves, but Eric noticed the manner in which his friend held his right hand to his chest; he'd been hurt.

Kajin Lure was no longer on the parapet. A score of arrows rained down on its tiled floor, but Eric cursed. Suddenly, it was important to him, not just to burn Noh-Ferien to the ground, but to know that Lure's evil died in its ashes. There was only one way to do that.

He blew a descending scale on his harmonica. In response, Shadowfire swooped toward the ruined courtyard before the palace. His talons scrabbled on the broken stones as he touched down and stretched out his neck. Eric leaped to the ground. The sendings were gone, defeated. Still, he folded his net over one shoulder where it would be ready if he needed it. Gripping his bow in his left hand, he started for the palace's main entrance.

Mirrormist suddenly swooped right over his head, the wind in the dragon's wake nearly flattening him. Alanna made a startling jump and rolled with catlike grace over the rough stones. The quiver on her back was empty. She'd lost her net, too, but she still clung to her bow. "What do you think you're doing?" she shouted, getting to her feet. Rage contorted her face.

"I'm going in after him," Eric answered with unruffled calm. "To make sure he's dead."

She looked shocked for a moment, then raised one eyebrow as her anger disappeared. "Oh, well, in that case," she said in more reasonable tones, "why are we standing here talking?" She cast her bow aside. "Give me that net."

Side by side, they ran past the bodies of dead Chol soldiers and toward the entrance. Massive doors of iron stood half-open. Pausing on the threshold, they exchanged looks, then slipped inside.

Eric's stomach lurched. The stench was overpowering. Low-burning braziers cast a dim glow around a vast hallway and a sweeping staircase that led to upper levels. Bodies lay everywhere, on the floor, on the stairs, some draped over the banisters. They lay in heaps, piled on each other, or singly, crumpled in corners and doorways. The palace was a slaughterhouse. Limbs had been hacked off. Flesh had been peeled away. The floor was sticky with blood.

Alanna moved further into the hallway, and Eric steeled himself to follow. Flies and gnats swarmed and buzzed. "Look at their clothes," Alanna said with a sick expression. "Rich men, poor men, ragged beggars, shopkeepers, children, women . . ."

"His own citizens," Eric murmured in disbelief as he stepped gingerly over the bloated corpse of an old man. His heel slipped suddenly in the crimson slick, and he nearly fell. To catch himself, he put one hand down in the old man's face. Revulsion gripped him, and he jerked his hand away. It was hard not to be sick. "The waves and waves of sendings he dispatched against the Gray Kingdoms and Wystoweem," he continued uneasily. "Lure needed bones to make each one, and no two bones from the same body. I assumed he was raiding cemeteries."

They opened doorways on either side of the hall, finding ballrooms that were also filled with bodies. Unlike the corpses in the hallway, these were neatly arranged in rows. "Almost as if they volunteered," Eric commented.

"They very likely did," Alanna answered coldly. "These are the Dark Lands, Eric."

They picked their way carefully up the staircase. Smoke billowed softly down from the upper levels. Even here, bodies littered the corridors, each missing an arm or a leg. Sometimes a chest was ripped open to get at a rib. Eric's boots made little squishing sounds with every step.

He reached to open the door, but Alanna stopped him. "He won't hide in a bedchamber or a library," she told him. "Find his throne room."

There was a commotion in the hallway below. Eric and Alanna hurried back to the top of the staircase to find Valis, Doe, and Shubal ascending. "Don't look," Valis ordered, giving Doe a left-handed nudge. He clutched his right hand against his chest. The wrist was hugely swollen, probably broken. "Don't stop to think about it."

Doe's face was white and bloodless as he stared at a woman on the steps at his feet. Summoning his courage, he stepped over her.

Shubal saw Eric and Alanna and called upward. "Saw you run inside," he said breathlessly. "Thought you might need more help."

Eric beckoned them on. "You have an idea where this throne room will be?" he asked Alanna.

"There could be several," she answered matter-of-factly. "One of the ballrooms downstairs probably served for public functions. But there should be a smaller chamber for affairs of state. I'd say this level or the third up."

"This place is like a maze!" Doe observed.

The smoke was growing thicker. Eric led the way

as they ran through the long corridors. The stench of death raped his senses. He couldn't comprehend the level of madness that had caused this, couldn't believe what Alanna had said about the victims' willingness to die for their ruler. He didn't want to believe it. *Find Kajin Lure.* That was all he wanted. *Find Kajin Lure.*

"Split up," he instructed suddenly. "We'll never find him this way."

With Alanna right behind, he mounted a narrow staircase, leaving Valis, Doe, and Shubal to continue the search on the second level. The corridors seemed to twist and turn endlessly. On the third level, the smoke was thicker still. It stung his eyes. He kicked open a door, as much out of frustration as from any real hope of finding Lure within, and found the room beyond filled with flames. Draperies, bedclothes, and carpets blazed. Heat and smoke billowed out into the passage. Eric covered his mouth and nose and ushered Alanna quickly past.

Suddenly footsteps rushed toward them from the opposite end of the corridor. Chol soldiers! So they hadn't all deserted the palace, after all. He ran a quick count. Eight, as near as he could tell in the smoke. Before he could move, Alanna stepped before him and threw her net, ensnaring the leading three. They went down hard, and the two right behind them tripped over their comrades. That left three on their feet. Eric shouldered Alanna aside. "My turn," he said.

"You never let me have any fun," she replied.

The first guard to charge him carried a lance, but instead of a point, it had a heavy gold ball. The Chol lunged. Eric caught the stout shaft of the weapon and jerked his foe off balance. Simultaneously, he brought his left foot up in a high side kick. The man hit the floor like a rock. Without pausing, Eric swung the lance and swept the feet of the next guard. The man landed hard on his rump, but struggled to get up. Eric kicked him in the face. The remaining guard wisely turned and ran back the way he'd come.

"Follow him!" Alanna called. One of the fallen guards rose shakily to his feet. Before he could steady himself, she slammed him against the wall, smashed her elbow under his chin, and stood back as he sank again. "He might lead us to Lure!"

But more footsteps from behind caused them both to spin about. Shubal raced around the corner. "We thought we heard trouble," he said. Doe and Valis came right behind him.

Eric didn't wait to explain. He sped after the fleeing soldier, but the dull thuds that echoed in his ears suggested that one of his friends had stopped to make sure that the netted Chols didn't cause them any more trouble for a while.

There was no sign of the escaping guard, and the smoke rolled in thick clouds as he rounded a corner. Still, he raced on, following the new passage. Then, from somewhere ahead came a pounding and shouting. Ignoring the smoke, he followed the sound and discovered his quarry before a pair of ornate brass doors, slamming a knocker down against a metal plate as he cried out in his Chol tongue.

From the elaborateness of those doors, Eric was sure he'd found Kajin Lure's throne room. The guard whirled about, wide-eyed with fear. He spread-eagled himself against the doors as if to barricade them with his body. He had no weapon, not even a baton, nothing with which to defend himself. Eric almost pitied him for his misguided loyalty. Even here, outside Kajin Lure's most private chamber, lay the hacked and butchered corpses of a dozen soldiers, whose blood made a lake upon the floor.

"Get out of the way," Eric hissed. The guard quivered, but held his ground, bracing the doors with his body. Cursing, Eric smashed his knee into the guard's groin, seized his shirt, and sent him sprawling in a long slide across the slicked tiles. A red smear marked his progress. Still, he tried to rise. With a cry, he made a hopeless lunge at Eric.

Doe emerged from the smoke-filled passage. His fist put an end to the guard's obligations.

Eric put his hands against the brass doors and pushed. No lock or bar prevented them from opening. The guard had simply not dared to enter without his lord's permission.

It wasn't a throne room at all, but a temple. Steamy incense swirled upward from a huge shallow cauldron in the center of the darkened chamber, and smoke rose from redly glowing braziers. A great rectangular block of stone made an altar at the far end of the room. Over it loomed an immense faceless statue, a hooded form vaguely feminine under carved black robes and cloaks. It had the gleam and shimmer of purest onyx.

Valis, Alanna, and Shubal charged in behind Eric and Doe, then stopped, hushed at the sight.

Kajin Lure knelt at the altar, his hands folded as he prayed in fervent tones, his own robes barely hanging from exposed shoulders. The remaining skull with which he'd called the lightning lay discarded on a step at his feet. Hearing them enter, the sorcerer climbed to his feet and turned slowly around, his back half-arched over the great block of stone. One hand closed on the hilt of a short-handled ax.

The expression he wore was a mixture of anger and defiance. Black streamers of hair swirled about a sinuously muscled body as he shrugged off his robes. The red glow of the braziers shone on pale, translucent skin, on perfect, ivory-chiseled features. There was a wild and frightening beauty to him, a darkly charismatic force.

"I will not give my life into the hands of Domain *thin-bloods!*" Lure swore savagely. His wide black eyes glittered as he picked up a cup from the altar, put it to his lips, and drained it. Trickles of red stained his chin, too thick to be wine. With a contemptuous gesture, he threw the empty cup at them. Then he whirled about, kicking his cast-off garments aside as he opened his arms and addressed the looming statue. *"Agya! Agya! Kom mi etna suni'mye shu, Agya?"*

Kajin Lure raised the ax high in salute, gripped it with both hands, and smashed the blade down against his own skull. He sprawled over the altar, his hands clutching spasmodically at the stone edges, the ax obscenely embedded in that once-beautiful face. Then he slumped to the floor.

Eric stared, unable to move, rooted to his spot as Lure's blood flowed in a thick red river down the steps from the altar to the floor. He'd been prepared to kill the madman himself and risk being haunted. He hadn't been prepared for this. He felt strangely ... *cheated.*

"I don't understand Chol," he said quietly. "What was that last bit he spoke?"

Shubal edged forward, his face a sullen mask behind which he hid his emotions as he regarded the corpse of the man who had destroyed his nation. "It was an appeal to the Heart of Darkness," he supplied grimly. "He called her *Mother,* and asked why she'd forsaken him."

Eric shivered inside and squeezed his eyes shut. He wanted to be free of this place and of the stench that pervaded it. He looked around the chamber, noting the tapestries that lined its walls, the carpets under his feet, and he slipped the arrows from the quiver on his back. He'd lost his bow in the corridor fight. He didn't need it.

Alone, he walked past Kajin Lure and around the altar until he stood before the statue. Even faceless, beneath those robes and hoods, he knew her. For too long she had filled his dreams. He smashed the glass shafts at the statue's feet, splashing Heron's amber compound. Then, with a bitter cry, he pushed over the nearest brazier. It wasn't enough to assuage his spirit. One by one, he pushed them all over as his friends looked on.

They left the temple in flames, and Kajin Lure's body to burn with it.

"Let's go home," Eric said when they were outside in the courtyard again. He gazed up at the palace. Fire burned in almost every visible window. The city burned with it. No matter which way he turned, the world seemed on fire.

"Back to Sheren Hiawa?" Valis asked.

Eric shook his head and took the harmonica from the pocket on his belt. The flames reflected on the polished silver instrument. Fire, everywhere he turned, and everywhere he turned, reminders of Katy and Robert. "Home," he whispered, barely able to speak at all. "Home to Guran."

Chapter Eighteen

KATY sat at the rocky rim of a high scarp overlooking the eastern edge of the Nazrit Plain. The blue morning had given way to a cloudy afternoon. She ran a hand idly through her hair, trying to smooth her unruly red locks back away from her face. *A comb,* she thought with small amusement, *my kingdom for a comb.*

The plain below was strangely barren. Not a blade of grass grew, not a bush or a tree. She stared at an expanse of grays and browns, of stone and dust. Only the grooved markings broke the monotony of the view. She had climbed this cliff and perched here to eat a bit of her remaining cheese while she studied them.

Up and down the length of Nazrit some of those lines ran. Ditches, actually, dug by hand and with precise care, a monumental engineering feat. Some lines were perfectly straight. Others bent at strange angles, forming geometrical patterns and symbols in their crisscrossings. Most of the markings were meaningless to her, but from her high vantage it was easy to spy the largest of those symbols.

The spider dominated the plain, and it lay among the other lines and hatchings as if they were some great, stylized web. It faced south, the direction of Noh-Ferien, while its spinnerets extended in parallel lines as far north as she could see. There was an odd, disconcerting beauty there that she found easy to appreciate.

A sacred place, Salyt had called it. It was so isolated, so forsaken. Once, when she was younger, she'd walked through an old and long-neglected cemetery just down the road from an uncle's farm. Most of the stones had been toppled, and weather had worn away most of the names. She'd felt sadly fascinated. Nazrit made her feel much the same way. It whispered to the loneliest corner of her soul.

She touched her backpack where it rested between her folded legs. The energy of the gem within tingled right through the nylon fabric. For days she'd listened as the faint buzzing of the wasp inside its facets grew stronger and more insistent. There was an eagerness and a hunger in the sound that frightened her. What, she wondered, had Salyt created?

A thing of sorcery, of that there was no doubt. A thing of vengeance.

While there was still sun left in the sky, she put away her cheese and sipped from her last flask of water. Her precious supplies were dangerously low. Everything fitted easily in her backpack. She picked it up, and retraced her steps until she found the path by which she'd ascended. It was steep, but not treacherously so.

Before she went down, she cast one more glance to the south. Against the distant peaks of *Lurun Bar*, a tenuous veil of black smoke rose to mingle with the clouds. Fire. She hated the thought of it. For the better part of the day, she'd watched it and wondered what was burning. She looked away and put the smoke out of her mind. It had nothing to do with her promise to Salyt.

The councillor's silver chain and the sapphire depending from it swung freely about Katy's neck as she worked her way down the incline. Loose dirt and pebbles made little slithering cascades. Finally she reached the plain and wiped dust and perspiration from her face. Her legs hurt, and her feet ached from days of walking.

At ground level it was much harder to identify the individual shapes and patterns carved into the plain, but she had marked in her memory exactly where the long grooves that formed the spider's spinnerets began. Pushing her hair out of her face, she started across the broad expanse.

Little clouds of soft dust rose under her footsteps, and a thin brown curtain swept the length of the plain each time the wind blew. She came upon the first ditch, a shallow trench perhaps four feet deep and four wide, clambered down one side and up the other. She paused on the opposite rim and stared back down. From the scarp, the plain had appeared barren and lifeless. Yet at the bottom of this trench, at least, there were clumps of grass and sun-browned weeds.

The next ditch was deeper than the first, but not so wide. Gripping her packs, she leaped it and peered back down into the shadowed recess. The bottom was hard gray stone, yet cracked and broken by shoots that had pushed their way upward toward the light. Even in a place like this, life struggled to survive.

"There's a lesson for us, little one," she said aloud, putting one hand to her belly. With no other company, she'd taken to talking to her unborn child. It seemed somehow natural, and reminded her that she wasn't truly alone, though she hadn't encountered another living soul since Salyt left her.

More ditches. The hum of insects drew her attention to a patch of dandelion-like weeds in a patchy carpeting of dull-colored grass. As she watched, a slender stamen unfurled like a frog's tongue, shot out, and snatched one of the insects in mid-flight. It reeled in its lunch, and the beautiful yellow petals folded up and closed around it.

Katy repressed a shiver. "There's another lesson," she whispered, patting her belly again. "Beauty hath power to lure the unsuspecting." *Funny,* she thought to herself. *That sounds like a quote, but from what?* Then, she remembered. It was from one of Robert's books.

The spinnerets were deeper than the other trenches. Standing on the rim, she gazed down, pursing her lips. Twelve feet, she estimated, deciding not to descend. She could follow them south to the spider from up here. Like the other ditches, sporadic patches of weeds and grass grew along the bottom, but now there were small trickles of water or little standing pools, as if it had stormed recently and the ditches had collected the rain. There were more of the carnivorous yellow flowers, too.

She reached down into the top of her left boot and drew out Salyt's direction-finding stone. It was no bigger than a small marble, perfectly round and smooth, but it seemed to be losing power. Placed on her palm, it glowed as she walked south along the spinneret toward the spider, but its radiance was weaker now, as if it knew somehow they were nearing the end of their journey. She closed her fist about it.

Her eye followed the edge of the scarp in the east. Above that harsh feature, the gray clouds of afternoon were giving way to encroaching night. Katy increased her pace as she gazed up at the sky and wondered if there would be any moonlight with such an overcast. There was no reason to fear the dark, though, she told herself. Even the *shriker* had ceased to follow her.

A sharp, warning hiss caused her to stop in her

tracks. A cluster of flat stones lay directly in her path, and in the narrow shadow of the largest, a small coiled creature eyed her suspiciously. Katy marveled that such a little thing could make such a noise. It looked like a snake, oily-scaled and fanged, but a spined, membranous dorsal crest ran the length of its body from just behind its head nearly to the tip of its tail. When Katy offered no threat, the strange-looking serpent seemed to relax. The crest flattened suddenly as it uncoiled and slithered beneath its rock. She set a wide course around it and resumed her trek along the spinneret's rim, but she paid greater attention to where she put her feet.

The abdomen of the great spider was a giant diamond shape. There were no curves to the markings on Nazrit Plain. The patterns were all straight lines and angles. She jumped the wide trench to stand upon the spider itself.

The nylon pack could no longer contain the angry buzzing of the wasp inside the ruby. The sudden intensity of it jangled her nerves, and the vibration of its wings seemed to penetrate right through to her spine. She snatched the pack off her shoulder and carried it by its straps at arm's length. A horrible red glow permeated the fabric, while the gem itself lay revealed within as a black silhouette, like an arcane egg inside a bloody womb.

The clouds of night surged out of the east. A little twilight seemed to pass in the span of a few heartbeats. Katy shivered as the wind brushed against her. The temperature took a noticeable drop. As she hastened up the back of the spider, the ruby's glow intensified until its radiance poured right through the pack and spilled upon the ground. Like a lantern, it lit her path.

On her palm, the small direction-finding stone

pulsed with a faint blue light of its own. Katy understood now. It would find the spider's heart for her, then its job would be done and its tiny glow would go out forever. Her own heartbeat seemed to increase to match the marble's pulsing. Her breaths came in rapid gulps. Within the backpack, the wasp screamed at her to hurry.

The blue marble flared with a sharp azure fire, then winked out to become a plain lapis stone. Katy cried out, startled, and blinked furiously to clear her vision of the bright afterimages. She regarded the dead talisman on her palm with an odd sense of loss. Unable to bring herself to dispose of something Salyt so treasured, she tucked it back into the top of her boot as she knelt down.

Here, on this spot, was the heart of the spider, the heart of Nazrit Plain, the heart of Chol-Hecate. The wind and the night echoed the insistent song of the wasp now. The harsh sound seemed to come from everywhere at once. It scraped over the land, filling the darkness with an ugly noise.

Steeling herself, Katy opened the pack and put in both hands. The nylon slipped free as she lifted out the jewel. It was huge, far larger than the first time she had held it, and it dazzled her eyes to stare within its shining facets. The ruby's glow stained the land with the shimmering color of blood.

Katy bit her lip. The air began to quiver, and the ground began to pulse at her feet. Strange feelings and sensations surged inward upon her. It was as if she was standing, not on some symbolic heart, but in the very center of an impossibly real organ. She felt the throb and beat of life all around her. She sensed the child growing in her belly, grass in the trenches, the insects and the flowers, the serpent under its stone, and so much more. Her mind filled with sparks of light, and her ears filled with the cacophony of living things.

She knew with a pure understanding it wasn't the ruby that brought her these feelings. One fist went to her throat and closed around the sapphire on its silver chain. It lit up with a cobalt glow that surged between her closed fingers and showed her knucklebones right through the skin. Powerful empathic energies channeled through the gem and flooded into her to overwhelming effect.

"Stop!" she begged, reeling under the onslaught of sensations. She sank to her knees, and without realizing it, gave a tug and broke the chain around her neck. The sapphire slipped through her fingers and fell to the ground between her knees, its light gone.

Katy gasped as her awareness contracted. Her ordeal was not over, though. She still held the ruby clutched to her body in the crook of one arm. The world buzzed with the hungry, demanding sound of the wasp, and the gem vibrated and shook like a thing trying to get free.

There was no turning back. Despite her terror, she held out the ruby with both hands and thought of all those who had died to bring about this moment: Salyt, whose life blood had seeped out between Katy's helpless fingers; Eric, her love and the father of the baby she carried; Robert, her precious, too-talented friend; Evander and glorious Sunrunner; sweet little Weena. She thought also of Alanna and Valis and Doe and of the thousands of nameless dead in Wystoweem and Sybo and Vakris.

This jewel, this powerful talisman of magic, would end the evil of Chol-Hecate. If Katy had ever doubted that a single object could do that, she doubted no longer. The waves of power rippled over her skin as she held the ruby. *Bury it,* Salyt had said. *Plant it deep.*

As if in response to her thought, the ground before her cracked, and the edges puffed up and rolled back like an obscene vaginal opening. She dropped the ruby into it. It landed with a soft, liquid squish in the center of the unnatural fissure and was sucked down. The lips of the crack folded up around it and sealed over.

Katy held her breath, expecting something to happen. Without the ruby's glow, she knelt in pitch darkness. There were no visible stars. Not even Thanador penetrated the clouds. The world was strangely silent; no wind, no whisper of a breeze blew over the plain now.

She glanced down at the sapphire between her knees. Hesitantly, she picked it up by its broken chain. Around and around it spun, its facets glimmering darkly. She bit her lip again, summoning her courage, then closed her fingers around it.

The spectral, half-transparent image of a gigantic black spider moved across Nazrit Plain. Dragging its bloated abdomen, it supported itself on four rear legs and raised up to rake the darkness with its four front legs. Chelae snapped and clacked menacingly.

Above it, a ghostly red wasp hovered, impossibly huge, wings drumming the air, stinger curled and poised to strike. A savage duel began, a graceful dance of death. Katy watched, mesmerized, as the wasp darted and plunged its deadly barb into the arachnid's body. The spider screamed silently and writhed in pain, but it was not yet finished. Again and again, the wasp darted in, scoring with its poison.

The spider rolled over. Its spindly legs curled up and shriveled, its abdomen collapsed like a wounded balloon. The wasp hovered to be sure its foe was dead. Then it plunged its stinger once more, but this time into the earth of Chol-Hecate.

Katy opened herself to the sapphire's power, no longer afraid. With a strange new vision, she saw the wasp's venom spread like a scarlet tide across Nazrit Plain and far beyond. She felt the poisoning of lakes and rivers and streams, the withering of crops and fields, heard the death gasps of entire forests. Fish died. Birds perished from the seeds they ate. Animals grazing on the grass and leaves became ill, weakened, died. It happened so quickly; she saw Chol-Hecate struggling in its last throes.

It all looked and felt familiar. With sickening knowledge, she thought of Wystoweem. It was no drought that wracked that land. Salyt had turned Kajin Lure's own magic back against him.

In Katy's mind, little sparks of light winked out as living things perished. She gazed in despair across the plain. The wasp was gone, and so was the image of the spider.

For a long time, Katy sat there, numb. Finally, she tied the ends of the broken chain into a crude knot, placed it around her neck, and got slowly to her feet. Some distant part of her said she should be horrified. She'd helped to destroy an entire ecology. All she felt, though, was empty.

She picked up her pack and began walking. The trenches were barely noticeable obstacles. She crossed them or jumped them or changed her course. Direction meant nothing to her. Dragging one foot after the other, she trudged away from Nazrit Plain.

The flat landscape began to swell and dip subtly. The dust and stone beneath her feet gave way to carpets of soft grass. Soon, the blades would turn brown and brittle, but now, they poured a gentle scent into the air as she walked. The wind's murmuring became a lullaby.

All night she walked without rest, without thought, without conscious choice of direction. Finally, at the top of a low hill, beneath a lonely tree, she dropped her pack, sank down, and leaned her back against the rough bark. The branches swayed in the breeze, and the leaves rustled invitingly. Soon, they would be dead leaves, they would fall, and the black, barren limbs would hang stark with grief.

How long, she wondered, did a land stay dead? Wystoweem had only just begun to heal. She looked up at the sky. The clouds were finally breaking apart. A few weak stars glimmered in the heavens. She hoped it was a sign of better things to come. "We're in a tough spot, baby," she muttered, putting a hand on her belly. Then, she shifted her hand and touched the sapphire around her neck. Her senses opened ever so slightly, and she smiled. "Hello in there," she whispered, awestruck.

Katy didn't understand how she could channel the crystal's empathic potentialities when Salyt had suggested in the cavern that it took training and effort. At this moment, though, she refused to question it. She tilted her head back against the tree and waited to see if Thanador and Mianur would show themselves through the cloudy veil.

A sound at the bottom of the hill startled her. She got to her feet and peered down, but it was too dark to see anything there. It came again. "Sounds like a cow, baby," Katy said quietly. Leaving her pack, she eased down the slope. A pair of huge eyes turned her way and blinked.

Katy jumped backward, stumbled, and fell on her rump. She'd damn near walked into the creature! It plodded toward her, making that *moo* sound again, dropped its head, and licked at her foot with a thick, wet tongue.

It was some sort of an ox, Katy realized as she got to her feet again. The spread of its horns was nearly as wide as she was tall; she could have lain down between the points, and probably have been perfectly comfortable on that broad skull. Most surprising, though, were the saddle and reins the monster wore. It was somebody's mount.

Tied to the saddle was a water flask that caught her eye. "Finders keepers," she announced, snatching it. Then, hanging from the saddle horn, she saw a Chol soldier's battle mask. She fingered it, slipped it free, and examined it. It fell from her hand into the grass. "Wait here," she told the ox gently. "Wait right here."

She dashed back up the hill and retrieved her pack from beneath the tree. The ox hadn't moved. "You licked my foot," she told it. "That means we're friends, right?" The ox blinked. Katy took that as agreement and reached for the reins. A moment later, she climbed into the saddle.

The ox shifted a step as she settled her weight astride its back. Something made a loud splintering crack on the ground. Leaning out of the saddle, she saw a huge hoof standing on the ruins of the lacquered mask. "Good boy," she said as she hung the water flask back over the horn and adjusted her pack on her shoulders.

She took the reins in her hands and wondered which way to go. A pair of stars, the only ones visible in the overcast sky, floated just above the horizon. She tapped the ox with her heels, as if he were a horse, and he responded. The stars were as good a destination as any other.

"I'll call you Paul Bunyon," she told the ox after they'd gone a short way. The ox answered with a long, low *mooooo*. "Me?" Katy replied. "You can call me...." She hesitated thoughtfully and looked up at the sky again. The clouds parted just long enough to give her a faint glimpse of a pale blue ring. Katy swallowed as the clouds closed once more. "You can call me Starlit."

THE world of Palenoc was once closely connected to our own Earth (or Paradane, as they called it on Palenoc), but most of the gates between worlds were destroyed in one of the magical battles between the Domains of Light and the Heart of Darkness.

Although both worlds are related, Palenoc has gone in a different direction than Earth; where we developed technology, they developed spiritual awareness. Ghosts are real, and a part of everyday life. Crystals are used to channel inner energies for healing or—more darkly—destruction. Dragons and unicorns serve the faces of good and evil, both of which are more open and clear than in our own world.

Palenoc remains connected to Earth, even if travel between them is no longer easy. If the Heart of Darkness is successful in wiping out the last strongholds of the Domains of Light, our own world will fall just as surely as Palenoc.

Magoth: The magoth was not a man, but neither was it an ape. It stood too easily erect and moved with a startling grace for a monster its size.

Katy Meets Phlogis: *She is most unusual,* Phlogis said. *She does not fear me, nor does she feel my anger.*

The Sending Attacks: Over her hovered a black shape with eyes that shone with a cold malevolence. A semblance of a hand reached down to cover Katy's mouth and nose . . .

On the Dream Stream: Moonlight glittered on razor-sharp feathers, on claws like daggers. An impossible wind whistled around the eagle as it screamed toward him.

The Fight in the Council Room: Robert caught the bigger man's fist, stepped aside, and gave it a sharp twist. Shubal cartwheeled through the air and hit the floor hard.

Chelit: "*Chelit* make good, reliable mounts," Valis said. "Our *sekoye* would be too easily spotted in the air by our enemies."

The Ruby: The air itself seemed to tingle with a strange electricity. "A wasp!" she cried suddenly. "There's a wasp in the center of it!"

The Leeches Attack: The village was in chaos. Leeches flitted through the air, attacking fleeing citizens. Eric, Valis, and Alanna fought for their lives.

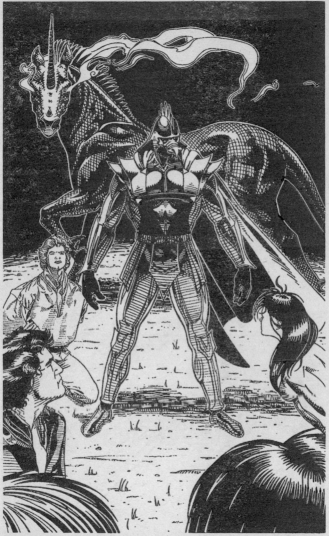

Kajin Kasst: The Chol prince turned abruptly and walked among his prisoners like a farmer admiring his crop.

The Unicorn's Charge: The *chimorg* trumpeted and reared. Eric felt the ground shake as its hooves crashed down. It fixed its fiery eyes on him and lowered the ebony spike on its brow.

The Shriker: A red tongue, impossibly long, shot out from that maw, ensnared a man and lifted him. The soldier screamed, flailing the air helplessly.

The Fire Closes In: Massive wings beat the vapor-filled air, and a sinuous form flew straight for them. As Eric watched, blazes flared up in territory they had crossed only moments before.

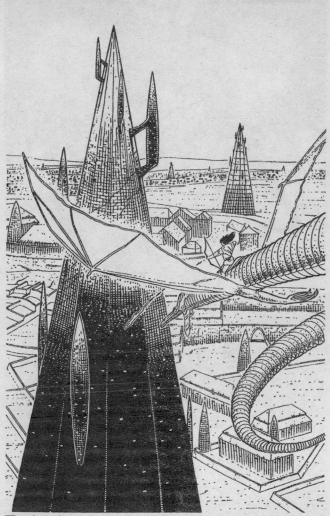

The Attack on Lurun Bar: Mirrormist dipped suddenly and flew directly for the nearest tower. Alanna drew back her bow and let fly the first arrow.

Kajin Lure: The wind whipped his black robes and his waist-length black hair straight out behind him. In his fists, he clutched a pair of skulls carved from some glittering rock.

The End of the Quest: The spider dominated the plain, and it lay among the other lines and hatchings as if they were some great, stylized web.

The brothers' adventures in
Palenoc continue in
Triumph of the Dragon,
coming soon from Roc.

The Heart of Darkness leaned forward on her onyx throne and frowned. She sat alone in her vast columned chamber. Not a shadow stirred. The blackness of night filled her abode, unrelieved by lamp or candle flame or brazier. She sighed, a vaguely troubled sound that sliced through the tomblike silence like a knife through crisp silk.

At the smallest gesture of her hand, the eastern wall vanished. Stars glittered in the black heavens, white and sharp as ice. The Heart of Darkness rose with regal grace and descended the three steps from her throne to the floor. Where the wall had been, there was now a splendid balcony. Soundlessly, she moved to the cold, marble edge and set her delicate hands upon the rail.

Her frown deepened. Beneath her palms, a long crack shivered through the stone. A piece of the railing fell away into the long, deep echoless darkness. She stared at the broken marble, not with fear, but with a feeling of strangeness and a growing unease. Unconcerned for her safety, she leaned on the rail again.

Night lay heavily over Boraga, her keep, and over the canyon on whose southern rim the great structure soared. Its five towers stretched up like slender fingers to grasp the sky and everything beyond. The smooth black stone of which they were made gleamed and glistened in the starlight and in the moonlight, in the pale illumination of the blue ring that floated across the zenith.

The Heart of Darkness regarded the blue ring, and her eyes narrowed to catlike slits. Mianur was its name, called by some *The Bridge to Paradise*. Once it had been a moon, a second moon, far more beautiful than its companion, Thanador. A taste of bitterness filled her mouth. Once, she had coveted Mianur, but its people had dared to deny her need.

The pale blue ring was all that remained of Mianur's arrogance.

Why did she think of that now? She remembered Mianur's beauty and tried to brush the memories aside. Her lush mouth curled into a sneer. She had destroyed beauty before. Tonight, though, the memories were not so easily dismissed. They seemed to possess a haunting power.

The night was too still. She craved a wind to enliven the darkness, and a wind came. It caressed the silken strands of raven hair that floated about her shoulders, rustled the folds of her satin gown, played over her face, and teased the tender globes of her exposed breasts. She touched a nipple, and it hardened in response.

Her pleasure was short-lived. Again she felt the strangeness in the air. The Heart of Darkness bit her lip and tasted her own blood. That, at least, was something to savor.

She sent her gaze out across the vast canyon, out across the deserts and shadow-haunted mountains of Srimourna, seeking the source of the strangeness. A sensation worried at her like a half-perceived irritation, a vague discomfort, and it tried to hide from her, to mask itself.

There was nothing to see, nothing to hear. Srimourna was still as death. The land was silent, perfect in its emptiness.

A door opened on the far side of her Royal Chamber. A tiny man, his legs shorter than the rest of his torso and bowed outward at the knees, waddled through the darkness bearing a wicker basket. Small silver bells jingled on his cloth slippers and on the hems of his sleeves. A tiny oil lamp lit his way around the many columns until he reached the balcony. The lamp's weak, amber light made his polished, bald head glow.

"You dare to disturb me, Gaultnimble?" The Heart of Darkness raised one eyebrow and turned a menacing expression on her fool. She did not appreciate the interruption.

"Divinity," Gaultnimble cooed, his black eyes glimmering with evil mischief as he bowed awkwardly and looked up at his dreaded mistress. "You know I love you even more than I love your sweet punishments. In my insignificant quarters in the bowels of Boraga, I sensed your mood. It sweeps through the corridors like a flood." He held up the wicker basket. "So, because I love you more than pain itself, I bring my goddess a gift for cheer."

"What have you there?" she demanded, unmoved.

Gaultnimble put on a coy look as he set his oil lamp on the balcony rail. "If Divinity doth ask it, I will tell about the basket...."

"Come fool!" she snapped, sparks of fire leaping into her stern gaze. "None of your songs or tales. You walk a narrow ledge tonight." She pointed a cold finger straight at his heart.

The little dwarf paled and tried to hide a small

shiver. He lifted the lid on the basket ever so slightly. A timorous *meow* issued from within.

"Ah, a kitten." The Heart of Darkness sighed. The anger left her face as she put her hand inside and drew the tiny, furry creature into her palm. Its eyes were barely open. A little fanged mouth gaped and emitted another pitiful, plaintive sound.

The Heart of Darkness drew the kitten to her breast and stroked its soft yellow fur until the mewls gave way to a warm, gentle purring. A small, slender tail lashed back and forth over her flesh. The sensation was almost erotic.

When the kitten was at last content, The Heart of Darkness drew a razor-sharp thumbnail down its soft belly. Tiny claws tore at her skin. The kitten cried in panic and sudden pain. The Heart of Darkness squeezed the poor animal to her breast and let its innocent blood flow over her skin, into the folds of her gown.

When it was dead, she dropped it back into the basket. "You are a considerate fool sometimes, Gaultnimble," she whispered. "That was a pleasant diversion."

"Diversion, Queen of Souls?" Gaultnimble grinned. He inclined his head toward the chamber's dark interior. "Quite a show, if I may stoop to theatrical criticism. We all enjoyed it."

The Heart of Darkness frowned again as she stared back into her Royal Chamber.

The chamber was no longer empty. The shadows stirred with shades and apparitions. Spectral forms floated in the air or wafted among the many columns. The souls of her enemies. One or two she recognized, but for the most part she no longer knew their names, if she had ever known them at all. They watched her coldly, these spirits, and she could taste their hunger, their thirst for vengeance.

She gave a little gasp. The sound was mostly surprise, but there was a note of fear in it. "How did they get in here?" she murmured in wonderment. "Into my most private sanctum? It's not possible that mere ghosts could breach my wards."

Gaultnimble waddled to the marble bannister and heaved the wicker basket with its contents over the side. He brushed his hands together noisily and wiped them on his tunic. "Some of them have been waiting at the door for generations," he reminded her with inappropriate joviality. "Perhaps, Divinity, you let the door crack a bit."

The Heart of Darkness whipped her hand across Gaultnimble's face. The fool sprawled upon the floor, then raised up on one elbow, a hand rubbing his cheek as he looked back at his mistress.

"Thank you, my Lady," he said with a twisted grin. "You so rarely play with me like that anymore." His grin turned to a pout. "Sometimes I think I am not your favorite fool."

The Heart of Darkness turned away from her fool and the staring ghosts. Let the specters glower; they were nothing to her.

Yet, that they were here at all, in her private chambers, was one more element of a night that seemed made of strangeness. Troubled, she leaned again on the marble railing. For all of Gaultnimble's impertinence, there had been something in his words.

A crack in the door.

She paled at a sudden thought. Could it be? She put her hand upon a jagged spot in the marble railing where a piece had cracked and fallen into the abyss. The kitten's blood, still warm on her fingers, made a wet, black smear on the stone.

The Heart of Darkness threw back her head and screamed, her eyes alight with dreadful understanding. The strangeness. She knew at last what it was. Her fool had put her on to it. She felt it now like a tingle in the air, like the faintest vibration in the stone beneath her touch—a barely perceptible weakening of her power.

Gaultnimble sprang to her side. "My Queen!" he said. "Why do you cry out like a pig at slaughter?"

In a black rage, the Heart of Darkness spun on her fool and beat him with her fists until he fell senseless at her feet. She continued to kick him until the worst of her anger spent itself. Then, batting at the intangible spirits that sought to block her way, she strode to her onyx throne, climbed the steps of the dais, and sat down.

Gaultnimble rolled over on his back. "Oh, Divinity!" he croaked through breathless gasps. "That was the best ever." He struggled to rise, but could get no further than his hands and knees. "We must have another bout. Just give me a few minutes and I'll be up again."

The Heart of Darkness no longer listened. With the smallest part of her power, she pushed the ghosts away from her. The gloom at the foot of her throne parted. Three crystal cauldrons appeared, gleaming with sourceless light. The water they contained was pure and perfectly still.

"Gaultnimble!" Her voice shivered through the chamber, calm once more, icy in its power. "Blood."

The fool scrambled to his feet. As fast as his dwarf's legs would carry him, he hurried to her side and thrust out his bare arm. "Open a vein, Lady!" he told her, the words hissing ecstatically through his teeth. "Open it deep!"

"Only a few droplets," she answered, raking his offered flesh with her thumbnail. A crimson line welled up on the soft underside of his arm.

Gaultnimble descended the dais steps and went to the crystal cauldrons. Their glow lit his face, masking him with eerie shadows as he extended his arm and spilled three drops of blood into each one.

The droplets struck the still water and spread, opening like small, delicate roses at the first touch of morning. Tiny ripples danced through the caldrons. In moments, the pure water turned a rosy pink.

Gaultnimble stood back, blood dripping from his arm onto the floor. Throughout the sanctum, the ghosts of his mistress's enemies dared to steal closer, drawn by a fearful curiosity to this magic-working.

The Heart of Darkness waited silently for the ripples to stop, for the water in the cauldrons to become still. There could be only one reason for even the slightest weakening of her power. *The Child.* Her bitterest foe was in the world once more. She glanced toward the open veranda. Somewhere out there, moving through her own Dark Lands, perhaps even though Srimourna, itself, He lived again.

She gazed down at her hand and curled her fingers into a fist. The wheel was turning again. This time she had almost won. The world was almost hers. Only a few nations, the cursed Domains of Light, still stood against her, and in a matter of months, they too would have fallen under her sway.

She opened her hand again and smiled darkly. Well, the game was not over yet. She still had trumps to play. She looked around for her fool. "Gaultnimble," she ordered, "send a *chimorg* to Carad Thorn in Shadark. Tell him to unleash *Cha Mak Nul.*"

The little dwarf turned toward her and cocked an eyebrow. "If I hesitate, will you beat me, Queen of Souls?" he asked.

There was no humor in her response. "If you hesitate, I will kill you quickly."

Gaultnimble frowned in displeasure as he stalked off. "Well, there would be no fun at all in that."

The Heart of Darkness returned to brooding as the moments ticked by. The cauldrons were growing still at last.

The ghosts wafted through the vast chamber like currents of wind. Their footfalls made no sound on the cold marble tiles, yet echoes seemed to cry down through the ages, echoes of the snuffing out of voices and lives, as a candle sometimes hisses when suddenly extinguished.

She allowed them to come closer, these ghosts of her enemies, as she rose from her throne and descended toward the crystal cauldrons. Let them look, she thought. Let them watch her schemes unfold. And let the despair they felt in death be ever greater for the watching.

As the specters and apparitions pressed around her, the Heart of Darkness stretched her hand over the caldrons. An image took shape in the first: a dark-haired man whose straight locks blew in the wind as he soared above the world on a great, winged *sekoye*. His green eyes flashed in the sunlight as he played upon an unfamiliar silver instrument, which he cupped in his hands and pressed to his lips.

Upon the water of the second cauldron another image began to form. The ghosts recoiled in wonderment, and the Heart of Darkness laughed at them.

"No, my old foes," she whispered teasingly. "It is not the Son of the Morning, you see."

And yet, the second image was a man with the golden hair and emerald-sharp eyes that only the *Child* should have. There was a hardness to his face that belied his youth and marked him as dangerous.

As the Heart of Darkness studied the image, it seemed almost to turn toward her, to return her gaze, and she felt a wave of hatred emanating from it that made her step back.

She bent over the third cauldron. There was no image there. The blood-pink color had faded, leaving the water crystal pure once again.

The Heart of Darkness frowned as she leaned closer. "The woman," she hissed. "Where is the woman?" She passed her hand over the cauldron, pouring her power into it, but it resisted her. The surface remained still and clear.

A strand of her own black hair slipped forward and fell into the water. The Heart of Darkness studied her reflection. She loved her own beauty, her soft ruby lips and pale cheeks, the black depths of her perfectly formed eyes, the shining strands of her hair. And most of all, she loved the smooth slender horn that sprouted upward from her brow, loved how it gleamed when it caught the light, loved its sharpness, loved how it felt cool as stone to her touch.

She drew her hair out of the water and stepped back from the third cauldron, remembering her purpose. The woman was a mystery to be solved, and any mystery right now posed a possible problem. If she were dead, the cauldron would crack and the water seep away. Yet the cauldron was intact. Katherine Dowd was not dead.

She turned back to the first and second cauldrons and regarded the two men whose images floated on the waters. How easy it was to see that they were brothers. Despite the colors of their hair, the resemblances were strong.

A little laugh rolled through the chamber, a sound full of both anticipation and nervousness. Indeed, the game was far from over. She placed one hand on the first cauldron. "Eric," she murmured. Then she touched the second. "Robert." Her whisper was sensuous and deadly, like a knife sliding over captive flesh, promising a cut, but not cutting.

"Come to me, my Brothers of the Dragon. Come to me."

And how, she wondered, could she hurry them along? So many ways, so many means, and all of them wonderfully cruel and devious. She climbed the three steps with infinite grace and sank languidly onto her throne again.

A darkly delicate smile turned up the corners of her lips. She pressed a fingernail against her right palm until a tiny crimson bud welled up. For a long moment, she stared at the droplet and wet her lips until they gleamed. Then, she pressed her palms together.

After a few moments, she opened a small space between her thumbs and peered inside. A diminutive light winked in the back chamber formed by her cupped hands. She smiled again as she felt the flutter of small wings.

"My sweet pet," she whispered as she opened her hands. The blood was gone. A lone firefly sprang away from her palm and wandered about in the darkness that filled the chamber until it found the balcony and the broad, waiting night beyond.

The Heart of Darkness laughed. She went once more to study the faces floating on the waters in her caldrons. "My pretty boys," she murmured in a tone that was both seductive and mocking. "Come play with me."

But the images melted away. Inexplicably, the water turned clear in all the cauldrons. The Heart of Darkness caught her breath. She whirled about, climbed to her throne again, and leaned one hand on the back of it as she stared at the cauldrons.

A rare sensation shivered through her. It took a full moment to identify it.

Fear.

The Heart of Darkness sat down upon the glittering onyx seat and folded her arms about herself.

Even fear was a sensation to be savored.

If you and/or a friend would like to receive the *ROC Advance*, a bimonthly newsletter featuring all the newest and hottest ROC books and authors, on a complimentary basis, please fill out this form and return it to:

ROC Books/Penguin USA
375 Hudson Street
New York, NY 10014

Your Address

Name _____

Street _____ Apt. # _____

City _____ State _____ Zip _____

Friend's Address

Name _____

Street _____ Apt. # _____

City _____ State _____ Zip _____